THE LEGEND OF THE RED SPECTER

THE LEGEND OF THE RED SPECTER

M.A. WISNIEWSKI

Tanuki Press

This book is a work of fiction. Any similarity to real people or events is a coincidence and not intended by the author.

Tanuki Press
PO Box 15212
San Francisco, CA 94115-0212
Tanukipressbiz@gmail.com

First US Trade edition: November 2018

Cover design by Justin Ritmiller www.triplemilled.com
Developmental editing by Allison Erin Wright

ISBN: 978-1-7320167-0-5

To my parents,
for always believing in me, even when I didn't.

Part 1:

Editorial Mandate

Chapter 1:

Politics

Garai sighed and tossed Joy's manuscript back at her across the desk.

"Really, Miss Fan? A political piece? Why in the world did you think the Gazette would print this? This is not what we do."

No, no, no, thought Joy, though part of her wasn't surprised. *That's not going to work. Because my savings are depleted, rent is due in two weeks, and you're the only newspaper that will still talk to me. You're going to buy something from me. You* have *to.*

"You've run political stories before, Garai," she said. "Two weeks ago, you did one on the arrest of opposition leader Stefan Huang. 'Crazy Steve in Bed with the Triads.' Remember that?"

Garai blinked, and looked thoughtful for a second.

"Ah. You're right. We did do that—but that was an exception. Extraordinary circumstances."

The editor/owner of the Dodona Gazette shook his bald, dark-skinned head. "This is, again, a problem we are having with you. You need to learn what types of stories we do here. Tales of betrayal, corruption, and organized crime are exciting. That works here.

"But this," he said, dismissively waving at her poor, rejected story. "This is nothing. Just some incendiary political rhetoric. And about the greatest leader in the history of Kallistrate? I can't print this."

"Incendiary? It's not..." Joy started to say, before stopping to think it over. "Well—okay, maybe it was a little—but that was because I knew it was for the Gazette, so I was just trying to punch it up a bit. Make it more interesting for your—"

"Ms. Fan, you are missing the point entirely," said Garai. "Excess adjectives don't make a story. A good story needs heroes and villains; struggle and strife; triumph and tragedy. A good story is about extraordinary events, but you constantly seek the mundane."

"I don't seek the mundane, Garai—I crave excitement," Joy protested. "I'm always looking for a story that will grab reader's attention, shake them up, make them care about the world. I've dreamed about that for years. What reporter hasn't?"

Garai steepled his hands and peered over his fingertips.

"Really? Then let us review one of your first assignments, where I sent you to find dragons."

Chapter 2:

Dragon Egg

"What about it?" said Joy. "I thought that was a solid bit of investigation—"

"Your investigation was the problem," said Garai. "When my readers see a headline about a dragon egg, they want to turn the page and read more excitement and mystery. Perhaps this is the last dragon remaining—the last in all the world. The first ever to be hatched outside the control of the cruel Sidhe aristocrats, and in the possession of a free citizen of Kallistrate, as well. Could a dragon hatched in the Kallistrate heartland inherit those values from a kind, simple farmer? Or, could it be that viciousness is so ingrained to the nature of dragonkind that it would turn on that loving farmer who cared for it before it was even born?"

Joy watched Garai as he ran through each bit of speculation, and couldn't help but be drawn in, just a bit.

Garai was a top-notch storyteller. Something in his eyes, and the careful intonation when he spoke commanded attention. And then his eyes fixed in on her, and she rather wished they weren't.

"These are the sorts of things my readers want to hear about," he said. "Not that the egg is from an ostrich and the farmer is a victim of a juvenile prank."

Well, Joy supposed that was disappointing. And she definitely understood being fascinated with dragons. For well over a thousand years, the Empire of Albion had ruled over the continent of Nokomis almost solely due to the power of their Dragon Knights. Dragons were huge, covered in tough scales that required heavy cannons to break, and they could spit toxic chemicals that ignited when exposed to the air, turning into a searing, sticky jelly that could melt your flesh from your bones in seconds.

4

There hadn't been an army in the world that could do a single thing to stop a Dragon Knight. There'd been no counter, no defense, nothing to do but run or die. And so the Sidhe nobles had conquered everything, and held it, until the rise of the industrial might of Kallistrate, and then everything had gone topsy-turvy in the space of just four years.

Now the dragons were all gone, either exterminated or fled to escape extermination, their great Dracariums demolished, ancient structures reduced to piles of rubble, and a good deal of the world's magic seemed to have vanished along with them.

But even before that, nearly all details about the dragons were held as closely-guarded Imperial secrets. Only Sidhe and their sworn life-bonded servants were allowed inside the massive domed structures of the Dracariums, and even the Imperial soldiers who marched alongside the Dragon Knights only got to see them while on the march.

And the mystery didn't abate when Kallistrate started massacring the great wyrms. All slain dragon carcasses had been seized by Kallistrate military intelligence and hidden away, save for one that had been stuffed and mounted as a permanent monument in the Sarpedon Museum of Natural History. Joy supposed that meant naturalists had studied it, but that information must have been classified, and at a level well above Joy's old security clearance.

So when Garai told Joy to investigate the dragon's egg, the first unanswered question she had was how people knew this was a dragon's egg when nobody outside the Sidhe Dragon Knights had ever seen one. The answer Jakob, the farmer who'd found the egg, gave her was, "Well, reckon it looks like a dragon's egg, don't it?"

Normally, that type of response would warrant a follow-up question, but at that time she'd been worn down by so much culture shock that she'd given up.

It hadn't taken her all that long to get from Dodona City to the remote farming and ranching village of Knittelfeld—four hours by train and another hour and a half by stagecoach — but she might as well have arrived on another planet. People sure stared at her like she was an alien.

That was another thing. Though Joy had been born in Kallistrate, her family's lineage traced back to Xia, the ancient empire that had ruled western Nokomis, before being conquered by the Sidhe. So Joy had all the characteristic Xia features: small nose, a pronounced almond-shape to her eyes, and straight, jet-black hair. Growing up in Gortyn, she hadn't really thought anything of it. Plenty of people there looked like her. But out in the landlocked Strata highlands of Knittelfeld, nobody did.

After the first hour of bizarre, repetitive interactions with the locals, Joy had to fight down the urge to deck herself out in a sandwich-board sign with the following inscription:

1) You don't need to welcome me to Kallistrate; I was actually born here.

2) Yes, I do speak Kallish really well. That's because I was born here.

3) Yes, I also speak Xiaish. Two dialects. Actually, I speak five languages.

4) No, Xia people don't all speak five languages. I do because I was a language major in college, and from my military training.

5) No, I'm not sad about the results of the war. My side won. I served in the Kallistrate Intelligence Bureau as a translator. BECAUSE I WAS BORN HERE.

But making a sign would be time-consuming, and she doubted the snark would be helpful in the long run, especially since she needed to interview these people. And honestly, save for a few exceptions, the villagers were really friendly. She had to remind herself how young a country Kallistrate was. It had been less than a century since Stas Lenart and Rumi Janda had unified the city-states of the Kallis coast and the feudal territories of the Strata highlands, and most of these people were barely two generations out of serfdom, if that. You could hear it in the way they spoke, a regional variant of Kallish that she hadn't heard before. It wasn't too hard to parse, but starting out she'd needed to ask folks to repeat themselves.

Still, her patience paid off, and she was able to find the egg's owner right away. Being so remote, Knittelfeld didn't have much in the way of entertainment options, so the dragon's egg was all anyone was talking about. Unfortunately, nobody had anything of substance to say about it, other than the last time they'd swung over to take a look.

Joy's big tip-off came when she talked to one resident who seemed considerably less enthused about the egg than the rest, though he refused to say it was fake. ("Well, I ain't never seen a dragon's egg before, so if Jakob says that's what he's got, well… that's his business, ain't it?") It took a bit of coaxing, but when asked if there was anyone in Knittelfeld who was inclined to be a prankster, he gave her a name: Kevin Stoecklin.

Well, that didn't surprise her. She'd already met Kevin, in fact, he'd come sniffing around almost as soon as her coach had arrived, and she'd had some difficulty getting him out of her hair. Kevin's father ran the local general store, and he was going to be a full partner in a year when he turned twenty-one.

She knew this because he'd mentioned it himself, several times, accompanied by a smirk like she should be super-impressed, while twirling an oversized jeweled pocket watch around on its gold chain. Kevin seemed to think he was some kind of big shot, going so far as to say she should be talking to him, not any of these other "dumb hicks." She also had to suppress her urge to tell him that nobody in Dodona used pocket watches any more—the society elite wore wristwatches, and had for the past decade, so if he could please quit spinning his tacky heirloom around like a complete douche, that'd be great. But she'd refrained, diplomacy and all.

Good thing, too. Because this way, she had no difficulty asking Kevin if he'd like to escort her to a nice dinner, which meant taking her to the local tavern, because that was the only restaurant in town. She'd realized this already, and had put a request with the tavern keep that when she ordered wine, he'd serve her grape juice instead. The tavern keep had been suspicious at first, but turned enthusiastic when she mentioned she was trying to get the truth out of Kevin.

Apparently the tavern keep didn't much care for Kevin.

She'd planned the dinner carefully, running the conversation in her mind, devising multiple rhetorical tricks and traps, and by the time he strutted in through the tavern doors, Joy felt like she was ready for anything. As it turned out, she needn't have bothered. She'd barely got midway through her opening salvo, noting that she wasn't sure if Jakob's egg was real or not, but that if it was fake, it was an extremely impressive one, meaning that the old farmer would have to be a very clever person—and immediately Kevin piped up, taking credit for the whole thing, going on and on about how he'd done it, how he'd gotten an infertile ostrich egg from his dad, hard-boiled and painted it up, and led poor Jakob to discover it. He was so enthusiastic, in fact, it made Joy suspicious, wondering if maybe she'd over-baited her trap, so she peppered him with detailed questions, shooting them off rapid-fire, hopefully at a faster rate than anyone could make things up.

Why'd his dad have an ostrich egg?

How did they know the egg was infertile?

How much water did he use to boil it?

How long did it take? What color was the pot? Tell her the brand name of paint he used, and the specific name the manufacturer assigned to that color.

But she didn't trip Kevin up, and he'd been able to answer every question plausibly enough. The general store served as a distribution point for even more remote towns, and someone over in Tullen had gotten into ostrich farming, because apparently that was a thing people did now. The Tullen farmer had noticed the heating element on one of the shipping crates' incubation systems had failed, and had left it at the store. Kevin had actually used two types of paint: two coats of Spring Lilac over one coat of Chrome Silver, which is what gave the egg its "magical" iridescent quality. Joy noted down all the other details to double-check later, but she was already convinced he was telling the truth.

The only question that stumped Kevin was why he'd done it. He'd just looked at her crosswise, shrugged, and said, "Why not?" Further questions got her nowhere. Didn't he have any sympathy for an old man who was one of his neighbors? Wouldn't he be horribly disappointed when he found out the truth? How would Kevin feel if someone did that to him? Didn't he have anything better to do with his time? Kevin just stared at her in baffled incomprehension, like she really was speaking Xiaish, until Joy finally gave up.

She told him that she was very sorry, but she suddenly wasn't feeling well, and would be retiring to her room. In retrospect she could see how this might've been jarring, but at that point she'd endured all the Kevin she could. Kevin didn't appreciate this, and got rather insistent and pushy about her staying.

Fortunately, Joy had thought something like this might happen, and had mentioned it to the tavern keep previously. He'd just grinned, and told her to call for Cookie if she had any trouble. Joy had barely begun to turn and raise her hand for assistance when Cookie appeared at their table and seized Kevin by the ear. It turned out that Cookie was an impressively hefty, no-nonsense woman, who served as the town butcher when she wasn't manning the tavern kitchen, and she didn't seem to like Kevin much, either, given all the various "accidents" he had as he was bulled out the door, banging himself against various tables, chairs, the support column for the roof, several times on the door frame, the porch railing outside, capped off with head-over-heels tumble over the porch railing. Luckily, the horses' watering trough broke his fall, so it all turned out okay.

The rest of the tavern regulars seemed to appreciate this rousing entertainment, so Joy decided to stay for dinner and some actual, real wine, all of which was much better than she'd expected from such a remote town. She'd planned to leave a huge tip—or at least, as huge a tip as she could manage, but the tavern keeper had grinned and refused to take her money, saying they should be paying her for the free show. Joy opted not to argue the point.

"Joy!" Garai snapped. "Are you even listening?"

"Sorry," she said. "I was just thinking about that story. Look— I guess, in hindsight, I could have made it more interesting if I'd included more of the side details about my interview with Kevin, instead of just recounting the results. I mean, I'm really not a fan of that type of journalism, where it's more about the reporter than the actual subject, but this is your paper, after all. And if—"

"Again you are missing the point," sighed Garai. "You shouldn't have bothered with that Kevin interview at all."

Joy blinked. "Not bother? But I found out the truth."

"I see," said Garai. "And did your farmer Jakob thank you for this? Was he grateful to you when you told him?"

"Uh... no," she said.

"No?" said Garai, raising his eyebrow in mock surprise. "So, how did he react? Can you tell me that?"

"He... didn't believe me," she admitted. She remembered his reaction, and she still didn't fully understand it. She'd tried to break the news as gently as possible, only to hit an impenetrable wall of truth-resistance. What was she doing believing a word that came out of that Stoeklin kid? Everybody around here knew what a liar he was. And Jakob had shrugged off all the corroborating evidence, like the purple stains on his makeshift incubator from the paint rubbing off, and refused to do anything to confirm that it was a hardboiled egg, like spinning it, or candling it. Of course it was a bit odd—it was a dragon egg, after all. You couldn't expect it to behave like a regular chicken egg, could you?

And that was that. Jakob remained resistant to all the evidence she'd collected, to the point of proud defiance. She'd left that bit out of her story, as well.

10

"Of course he didn't," said Garai. "Yet you insisted on telling him anyway. Are you trying to crush the man's dreams?"

"But that would happen anyway, even if I did nothing," Joy protested. "Jakob is expecting the egg to hatch into a baby dragon, but it's not going to. It's going to start rotting. Especially since he's keeping it warm in that incubator, and then he's going to feel awful—"

"Yes, and that was inevitable, that he would feel awful. But now, thanks to you, he will have company, for our readers feel awful as well," said Garai. "I stay in business by keeping my readers happy."

Joy winced at that. Garai had a point, but she'd thought of another problem. If the dragon egg claim had spread and been taken seriously, Jakob Ecker would never have been allowed to keep it. No way would the Kallistrate military allow such a potentially dangerous weapon as a new dragon to exist outside their control. The KIB would've descended on Knittelfeld, and either confiscated the egg or destroyed it.

So she held her tongue. Digging herself in deeper wouldn't help her sell a story to Garai. Even if her current story was a lost cause, she still had two weeks before rent came due, and that was plenty of time to write something new. She just had to figure out what Garai wanted from her. He must want something. Otherwise, why waste all this time with a lecture?

Chapter 3

The Lost Princess

"And, since we're talking about depressing things, let's review your article on the Lost Princess," Garai continued.

"All right," said Joy, trying to fake some measure of enthusiasm for a lecture she'd already endured several times in the past month, while praying her empty stomach didn't interrupt him with any embarrassing noises. She'd been hoping to treat herself to a blueberry pancake breakfast platter after selling her story, but it didn't look like that'd be happening today.

And she'd been so looking forward to it.

"I had to edit that one to the point where I was practically rewriting it," he said. "And that should not be my job. I gave you a half-dozen contacts to interview, and you came away with the worst one. Totally unusable."

"Okay, I still don't get it," said Joy. "I thought I picked the best one. I mean, most of them were pretty boring. They were just like, 'I caught a glimpse of Kiona Artaxerxes at the grocery store, or passing by on the trolley, or taking a pedicab to the train station, and that's it. Nothing else to it. At least Stanley's story had some creativity—"

"Creative?" Garai turned his face to the heavens and made a pleading gesture, as if begging the gods to lend him patience, before staring back at her. "The man was completely bonkers."

Joy figured as much, but she still didn't get why that was a problem. She thought the point of the Gazette was to print bonkers stories. Joy had thought she'd lucked out, that she'd found a way to give Garai what he obviously wanted and still face herself in the mirror the next morning. Because it wasn't like she was endorsing any part of Stanley's story. He said that Kiona had flown in through his window in the middle of the night, and she was reporting on it. That he said it happened. It was a true fact that he'd made that claim.

"Sorry, I'm still…" Joy rubbed her temples and tried to collect herself. Normally this was the point where she'd smile and nod, hope that she could still get paid for the work she'd done, so she could have a shot at making rent next month. But maybe there was some real point here she was missing. "Uh, could you explain it again, exactly what was wrong with Stanley's—"

"He said that she had wings and a tail," said Garai. "Kiona doesn't have wings or a tail. Everyone knows this. So obviously the story is false."

"Well, to be fair, the Morale Department's pamphlets have been featuring drawings of Sidhe with tails, and cloven hooves, and—"

"Ridiculous war propaganda," snapped Garai. "You should know better than to take that seriously."

Of course I don't take it seriously, Joy wanted to scream. *I'm just trying to give you what you want so I can get paid, but you're making it freaking impossible.* Joy pinched the bridge of her nose and took several long, deep breaths. What was the core point of Garai's objection, again?

"Stanley's story was obviously fake," she repeated, "because it didn't match up with what Kiona's supposed to look like. And 'everybody knows' what that is."

"Yes," he said. "You know we have the portrait. We even reprinted it with the article."

Well, of course they'd reprinted the portrait. It was one of the most well known images to come out after the war. Three years ago—well, almost exactly three years ago, since tomorrow was Liberation Day—the infamous 13th Company of Kallistrate's Steam Golem Corps broke through the last line of defenses around Albion-Xia's Terrestrial capital of Cymru and went on a rampage, burning and crushing half of the ancient city, including famed Ontonia Palace. Countless works of art, literature, and architecture were lost, much of it with thousand-plus years of history. But one recent painting had survived, though a good chunk of the upper-left corner had been burned and ripped to shreds: a family portrait of the Terrestrial Royal Family.

And it was true, none of them had wings or tails. Like all Sidhe, they looked almost identical to the regular humans who hailed from the various island chains in the northern Dagan Sea, fair-haired and light-skinned, with eyes of blue or green. The only true difference that set them apart from normal humans were their ears, which stretched out to long, thin points, extending to just below the tops of their heads.

Supposedly there were other differences as well. Sidhe lived much longer than humans, up to several hundred years, by all accounts. Their were claims about them being physically stronger, with superior reflexes, but those could've very easily been propaganda spread to keep "inferior" humans from questioning Sidhe rule. If anything, constant inbreeding within "royal" bloodlines left them prone to birth defects and other genetic ailments, if Kallistrate propaganda had any truth to it.

Certainly there was nothing about Kiona's portrait that said "superior physical specimen." Ears aside, she looked like a perfectly normal eleven-year old girl, one who was rather slim, extremely pale, and very pretty. But there was something beyond that—the way she seemed to stare straight out of the painting and at the viewer with an air of plaintive melancholy, like she was trying to send a message with her eyes, a plea for rescue.

Joy had seen art stores selling prints of that image—not the whole family portrait, just the part with Kiona. Cropping the image like that was pretty easy, since Kiona sat apart from her sisters on the other side of her parents, neither of whom had their hands or arms around her. So isolating the Lost Princess for her own portrait was simplicity itself.

"Okay," said Joy. "But remember—that portrait was done six years ago. Sidhe are supposed to mature at the same rate as humans, so by now she—"

"—Would still not have wings or a tail!" said Garai. "Nobody wants to read that. And nobody wants to read dark, depressing allegations about their national heroes committing massacres. Honestly, if I'd printed your article as you gave it to me, we would have a mob outside our offices the next day—with torches and pitchforks! Is that what you want?"

"Nobody wants a torch-bearing mob outside their office," said Joy, because that was a true statement. And, if she thought about it, maybe Garai had done her a favor. She really didn't have the evidence she needed to take down the "Bad Luck Brigade," and a weak, poorly-sourced version of the story in the Gazette could be used to discredit her if she ever got the chance to do a real version of the story in the future, for a real newspaper. But it was so hard to resist. This was one of the main reasons she'd gotten into journalism in the first place.

Joy remembered how it was early in the war, when the young nation of Kallistrate desperately needed heroes like the Bad Luck Brigade. Someone had to protect them from the wrath of the invincible Dragon Knights—a military force that had never seen a defeat for the thousand-plus years of its existence. By all accounts, dragon fire was a horrific weapon. Not only would it stick to you and burn you, it was deadly poisonous as well. If even a drop of it got on you, it would eat through your flesh and burrow into your bones, leaving the victim to suffer a slow, agonizing death as the poison did its work. And the Dragon Knights had no reservations about using their fire.

Whole towns, whole cities, even whole provinces could be scourged by the dragons as punishment. The toxic dragonfire soaked into the ground, so nothing would ever grow there again, forever.

But Kallistrate had an answer. And two months into the war, the first Steam Golem rumbled out onto the battlefield.

It was the culmination of decades of dedicated, secret research, combined with Kallistrate's industrial might: giant, steam-powered armored knights, piloted by a three-person crew, and controlled through the use of analytical engines—huge masses of intricate clockwork and electric circuits. These were the thinking machines that allowed the hulking Steam Golems to walk and fight without toppling over, and gave Kallistrate its only chance for survival.

But early on, things did not go well for the steam golems. Political tensions had come to a head before the secret Golem engineering plan was one hundred percent ready. The men and women crewing the machines were all green. There were no established tactics for steam golem warfare. Nothing like them had ever existed before. Early steam golem battles typically ended with the clumsy and awkward machines getting ripped apart by the more agile dragons, or doused in flames so the armored steel cockpits became ovens, cooking the trapped crew alive. At best, they maybe managed to maim or kill one of the great wyrms, either from the shrapnel of their exploding steam boilers, or by desperately grappling the great wyrms, holding them in place long enough for a barrage of Kallistrate artillery to kill friend and foe together.

And that was when the 13th Company, the "Bad Luck Brigade," made a name for itself. These were the misfits, chronic discipline problems—and often the only people reckless enough to strap themselves in the cockpit of a death machine. They'd been put in a unit with the unluckiest possible number, which they took as a sign that the upper brass expected them to fail. And they turned that ill omen into a perverse badge of pride.

Because the Bad Luck Brigade became the first Steam Golem unit to slay a dragon and live to tell the tale. And while part of their success had to do with the fixes and improvements made by the tacticians and engineers of the Steam Golem Corps, the rest had to be credited to their own skills and fearlessness, and their uniquely aggressive style of combat. They were the first surviving heroes of the Great War, and their photos were plastered across the newspapers and on recruitment posters, as Kallistrate forces rolled across the battlefield, liberating province after province.

16

The tipping point came when all the dragons retreated from the field, rather than fight the golems. The nature of warfare had changed completely. The Golem Corps had refined its weapons and tactics to a science, which, oddly enough, bore little resemblance to the "Bad Luck Brigade's" wild brawling.

Instead, Steam Golem Companies advanced in patient phalanxes, wielding gargantuan tower shields covered in specially-treated ceramic tiles, daring the Dragon Knights to try and break their shield wall, only to be shot with heavy golem-mounted cannons at point-blank range, or get methodically stabbed to death by the huge bayonets affixed to those cannons.

In the absence of the Dragon Knights, the war entered a new, uglier phase, for now it was Kallistrate arraying their overwhelming super-weapons against hopelessly over-matched Albion infantry and cavalry. And a new side of the "Bad Luck Brigade" began to emerge. Their enthusiasm for combat, so useful and laudable when they'd been facing monsters, turned into something much uglier when they faced regular infantry, or partisans mixed with civilian populations: a lack of restraint that veered into outright brutality.

And nothing demonstrated that more than the destruction of Ontonia Palace. This was supposed to be the culmination of the long Albion-Xia campaign. Capturing the Terrestrial royals would be a huge coup—it would potentially give Kallistrate enough leverage to force the Celestial Emperor to issue a surrender as ransom.

The raid was a disaster. By the end of the battle, most of the palace had been reduced to cinders and rubble.

And the Bad Luck Brigade had allegedly been found parading around Cymru with the Royal Family's severed heads, either spitted on pikes bolted to the decks of their golems, or strung along a steel cable hung from Sergeant Aghi's golem like a necklace. She'd heard there were photos, and that the 13th had posed for them, smiling and looking extremely pleased with themselves.

But the 13th had one head missing from their collection—Kiona's. That was the story, anyway. Joy couldn't confirm it, because the photos had been classified, if they even existed in the first place. Joy had met other people in the KIB who'd insisted, in furtive whispers, that the photos were real and that they'd seem them. Still, full proof eluded her. The official reports simply mentioned that the Royal Family had been killed in battle, and Kiona was listed as "missing." The 13th Company had been given official reprimands for disobeying orders, but their punishments were light, and they were never brought to a court-martial.

That wasn't right. But what offended her most about the story wasn't the barbarity of the 13th, but the willingness of the rest of the government to cover for them and hide the truth, if that's really what happened. How she longed for the resources to dig into that story for real.

But she'd let her mind wander. She flicked her attention back to Garai, who was still into his lecture about her story, and fortunately hadn't paused to ask her a question or anything. At least, she thought she was starting to understand what was wrong with her story. At the time she'd written it, she'd just presented the evidence for the official story: that Kiona had died in the assault, and had been counted "missing" because her corpse had likely been burned beyond recognition. Then she'd laced the story with dubious "spicy" details that she'd never have put in a regular newspaper; rumors about the 13th that she believed but couldn't prove, and unreliable witness testimony about Kiona the dragon-girl that she didn't believe but could simply repeat without endorsement.

But she had missed the point. The Gazette wasn't just about telling wild stories; it was about telling wild stories that its audience wanted to hear. They wanted to hear that the Bad Luck Brigade really were the roguish heroes they'd been made out to be in all the gushing war stories and propaganda posters, not that they were also capable of appalling acts of brutality. Even though those same propaganda posters relentlessly depicted the Sidhe as monsters, nobody wanted to believe in Princess Kiona the monster-girl. Everyone had seen her portrait, and obviously she didn't have wings or a tail. She just looked like a regular, adorable little girl who needed a hug.

Of course, they wanted to believe she was alive and that Kallistrate hadn't killed her. Because Kallistrate was good, and all of its soldiers were heroes. They were the world's light of freedom and democracy. Albion was the tyrannical empire of callous nobles. They were the commanders of monsters; dragons and huge, flying, carnivorous beetles. They commanded the brutal Caliburn Knights and the Sidhe sorcerers who summoned the giant clouds of poison gas. That was them. They were the murderers.

The people and armies of Kallistrate were different. They'd suffered, endured hardship after hardship, fought, and died to defend their homeland. Everyone had lost someone, a brother, a lover, a son or daughter, or knew someone who had. Their dearly departed would never murder a cute little girl. How dare she insinuate that.

Why not just spit on their graves, then? No, of course Kiona was still alive, somewhere: living quietly and certainly not plotting revenge or anything. Because, look at her—someone that sweet wouldn't hate good people like us. That went without saying. That's what people wanted to believe, and that was the hope that Joy's story had failed to feed.

Okay, fine. She needed to give the people what they wanted. Could she use that principle to fix her current story about Hardwicke? Joy had to fight to keep the grimace off her face. No, the hoi polloi were not going to suffer any criticism of the Great Leader, no matter how she tried to sugarcoat it. She'd definitely have to start over from scratch, though she had zero ideas for a new story. She would've asked Garai for suggestions, but he was still barreling on in full lecture mode.

Chapter 4:

Weeping Statue

"…And then there was that disaster with the weeping statue of Mithras," Garai continued. "I nearly had an entire religion coming after the Gazette. Holy men beating down the door of my office, threatening me with curses, lawsuits for harassment, defamation, and trespassing—"

"Okay, those first two are nonsense, and as for the trespassing thing…"

Joy grimaced a bit, but soldiered on. "Well… it's not like they actually had any signs that said 'Keep Out' around the back of the statue, and if I hadn't sneaked in—I mean, if I hadn't checked back there, I'd never have found that leaky pipe that was leaching through the clay and making it look like the statue was weeping tears of blood, when really—"

"And this is the whole problem with you," said Garai, throwing up his hands. "I send you out to bring back a story about miracles, and then you go out of your way to prove each and every one of those miracles to be a fake."

"But I wasn't trying to prove they were fake," Joy protested. "I was trying to confirm them. "I mean, they told me that the statue had caused a veteran's amputated leg to re-appear. That's pretty amazing, right? And you're always telling us how important interviews are. Adds that authentic, human touch to a story. You're always saying that.

"So I paid him a visit and it turns out he's still one leg short of a pair. That's not my fault. Though he did say the statue really helped him deal with the pain from his phantom limb syndrome. Not completely, but much better than before. Pretty funny how stories can get exaggerated in the retelling, huh?"

"And you couldn't have left them exaggerated, could you?" said Garai.

"Of course not," said Joy. "I mean, good story or no, we're going to look awfully silly when his neighbors read about his regrown leg, come over to visit, and find it still missing. That'd be awkward for everyone, don't you think? And—"

"And the little girl whose boils were healed by the statue? What of her?"

"Not boils, just a really bad rash," corrected Joy, before noticing Garai's irritation and rushing on. "And yes, I confirmed that it had mostly gone away, overnight after visiting the Mithras statue. So—"

"…While not failing to mention that her mother had taken her to the doctor already, and gotten medicine from him, three days before visiting the temple."

"Well, yes. I did mention that. But—well, that doesn't mean the statue did nothing, does it? I mean, you could still say—"

"Ms. Fan!"

Garai's deep voice reverberated through the cramped office, making her jump. "Do you take me for a stupid man?"

Joy opened her mouth to deny it, but Garai was already on to his next point. "None of that explains why you went around to check the back of a holy statue. How does this confirm its holiness? How would this ever serve to awe our readers? Of course, it never would."

Garai spread his hands across his desk and leaned forward, looming over her. "The issue here is that you still are not telling the type of story our readers want to hear. Tell me, what do you think that would be, for the weeping statue."

"Well… I guess they'd want to hear about the wonderful miracle of Mithras that heals people, but—"

"Then if you know that, why did you write instead the story that you did?" Garai fixed her with his gaze, making Joy squirm. He could be really intense sometimes.

"I just thought…" Joy paused to gather her thoughts. "If people believe that a statue can heal people, but it can't, that's really dangerous—"

"Dangerous?" said Garai. "How so? A woman takes her daughter to the doctor and to Mithras and she is healed. Which of these things gets the credit does not matter."

"But not everyone thinks like that!" said Joy. "There was another family, and they had a kid with this huge cyst on his forehead. And they saw the weeping statue and started yelling about how the cyst was shrinking, praise Mithras—but it didn't look like it was shrinking to me—and they were so happy, and I heard one of them say, 'Oh, thank the blessed Mithras—now we don't have to take him to a doctor,' and that really—"

"Bah," Garai waved off her concern like it was a fly buzzing around his head. "People believe what they believe. One news story will not change this."

Joy opened her mouth to protest, but stopped herself as she remembered the way Farmer Jakob, the people 'healed' by the statue, and the priests of Mithras reacted when confronted with the evidence. They'd been dismissive, indignant, or downright hostile. Those priests, especially—she'd expected holy men to be patient and kind, but they'd glared at her like she was some kind of demon. One of them had even started screaming "Blasphemer," and the like and started chanting something that sounded like an exorcism. She'd actually been frightened for her physical safety.

Garai steepled his fingers together, closed his eyes, and took a long, deep breath before continuing.

"Ms. Fan," he said. "I must confess, it is unusual for the Gazette to work with someone of your background."

"My background?"

"Your Journalism degree. From the prestigious Rouvas College of Dodona U., no less," said Garai.

Oh. That was what he meant. "Most people here don't have Journalism degrees?" she asked.

"Degrees of any kind, really," said Garai. "We value life experience here."

"Ah," she said, not trusting herself to say any more.

22

"So, when you started working for us, I will confess I had some high hopes," said Garai. "But now I am beginning to think that this hope was misplaced. It seems that you simply do not fit in here. Perhaps we should both stop wasting our time with this."

Joy heard those words and felt a surge of panic. It combined with the hollow feeling in her empty stomach to send a sick sensation of nausea in her core.

"Sir, what do you mean?" she said, trying to keep her voice level.

"I am saying that I don't believe I will be giving you more assignments," said Garai. "The time I save with proofreading and such does not make up for all the rewriting I must do to get your stories into something usable. And you don't seem to be learning."

"No, I am," protested Joy. "What about the Sindra's Wall story? I didn't put any skepticism there, right?"

"Yes, that's true," Garai admitted. "But that story was boring."

Well, of course it was boring. She'd thought it sounded boring when she'd gotten the assignment. "Sindra's Wall" was the back wall of someone's house that had a mold growth that looked a lot like common depictions of Saint Sindra. And that was it, really. There wasn't anything to investigate. It was mold on a wall and it looked like Sindra. It was like seeing faces in the clouds or in random patterns of wood grain. Either you saw it or you didn't.

"The folks at the wall thought it was exciting," said Joy. "They were really proud of it. Really enthusiastic."

Garai folded his arms and cocked an eyebrow at her. "I see. And this enthusiasm, this excitement—how did you convey that in the article you handed into me?"

Joy winced. "I... guess I didn't," she admitted.

"And this is the problem," said Garai. "However competent a writer you may be, it does not seem you have any excitement for the Gazette. And so, I think it is time for us to part ways. I wish you luck for the future, Ms. Fan."

Chapter 5:

Final Chance

"No! No, wait..." Joy protested, as a wave of dread ran through her. He wasn't going to give her another chance? She'd been sure he would. She'd thought he'd been teaching her, but she'd been wrong. He'd only been building up a justification for her termination.

This could not be happening. She'd come in hoping to sell a story and treat herself to a big pancake breakfast. But instead, not only was she not getting paid, she was getting fired. Again! No—it didn't even count as a firing. You couldn't really fire a freelancer. But this her only source of funds. How was she going to make rent? She had nothing left in savings. Two weeks was plenty of time to write a story, but not to find another paying gig. None of the other newspapers in Dodona would talk to her. They'd all deemed her unstable, crazy, and all because of... that jerk, they believed him... but not her... nobody believed her... nobody cared... nobody...

Joy tried to say something, but she felt her throat close up, felt her words come out as a garbled sob. She buried her face in her hands and slumped back in her chair. She felt the tears well up beneath her palms, despite her best efforts to tamp it down. She did not have time for this right now. She had to be strong. She had to be able to think. She needed to argue her case, had to say something. She couldn't go through this again... not again...

She felt a tap on her shoulder. Garai stood over her. He held a handkerchief in one hand and his face held a kind of embarrassed concern. She'd never seen that from him before. Something about it made things worse, and her self-control collapsed. She curled over her knees and started bawling. She retained enough presence of mind to reach out blindly for the handkerchief, which got pressed into her hand.

Eventually, she managed to regain enough control to sit back up. She blew her nose into the handkerchief. She couldn't bring herself to look at Garai again, but she had to, and fast. C'mon, deep breaths, count 'em. Breathe the good color in, breathe out the poisons, the negative emotions. She should return the handkerchief, but it had become a wadded-up damp rag of tears and mucus. This was humiliating.

"I'm sorry," she mumbled. "I think I'm a little... I haven't had breakfast yet, and I think... y'know how it is, when you're really hungry... messes with you...."

"Hungry, hmm?" said Garai, in a speculative tone. Joy hadn't heard him sound like that before. She looked up and saw he'd gone back behind his desk. Yes, that was better. The formality made things feel more normal.

"Hungry is not bad," Garai continued. "I can work with hungry. As long as it's the right kind of hungry."

"What?" said Joy, though she felt a surge of hope. This was no longer sounding like a 'you're fired' conversation.

Garai leaned back and looked her over carefully before speaking. "For a while now, Ms. Fan, I've gotten the impression that you don't really want to work here. That you simply don't care. But now I have seen that perhaps you do care, quite a bit. Am I wrong? Do you really want to work for this newspaper?"

Joy stared back, feeling drained-out and empty, as she considered the question. She needed to make rent. She needed to eat.

"I really want to work here," she said.

It didn't sound particularly convincing to Joy's own ears, but a wide, white-toothed grin split Garai's face from ear to ear.

"Yes, that's good," he said. "When I was a young boy, I and my family came to this country. We crossed the seas with only what we could carry on our backs. I remember being hungry then, my family and I. I remember how it drove me. I worked and saved, through war and turmoil, and now, many years later,

I own the Gazette. I own the most popular newspaper in Dodona. I and my family are no longer hungry. But I do not ever forget this—how it was like when I was a boy. I never forget the hunger that made me who I am. So tell me, Ms. Fan: is this the type of hunger you have? Are you hungry like I was?"

Joy stared back at Garai. She'd never heard him talk like this before.

"Oh, I'm starving," she said.

That earned her another grin from Garai. "So you say. Well, we shall see if this is true. I think that I have an assignment for you."

Joy felt her heart race. Another chance! But she didn't miss the other implication in his speech. This was going to be her very last chance.

"What's the assignment?" she said.

"Your assignment," said Garai, "is to go and get the interview of the century. You, Ms. Fan, will find and interview the Red Specter."

Chapter 6:

The Assignment

Joy stared back at Garai and tried to keep her expression neutral. Was that a joke? Should she laugh? He didn't seem like he was kidding.

"The... Red Specter," she said, trying to gather her thoughts. "That's a... that's a comic strip, right? And I think I saw it... Oh! They made a Magic Lantern show based on it, didn't they? I saw the posters downtown. You want me to interview the guy who does the Specter's voice? Or do a behind-the-scenes piece?"

Garai cocked an eyebrow at her. "Ms. Fan. Does that sound like the sort of story we would run at the Gazette? That I would assign to you? Remember what we have been discussing."

Joy heard a tone of warning in his voice. She had to be careful here.

"No, you're right," she said. "That doesn't sound like a Gazette type of story. But I'm confused. Could you explain more about what you want, please?"

Apparently that was the right answer, because now Garai was all smiles. "Very good. And it certainly is true that the Red Specter is now known mainly from the newspaper comics. But stories about the Red Specter pre-date the strip. During the Great War, there was many a soldier that saw him—bare glimpses at first—a mysterious masked figure in a trench-coat, leaving scores of dead Albion soldiers in his wake. Until the Battle of Cloudkill, and its aftermath, the Brentonsville Eviction."

"I remember that. I was still in the KIB when that happened," said Joy. It had been a huge deal at the time. There'd been whispers about the capture or annihilation of an entire squad of Albion's elite Caliburn knights, an unheard-of event. The deaths of over half of a Steam Golem Company had also been confirmed. They had to notify the families, after all. But the rest of the story remained frustratingly vague.

The official, confirmed story was this: On February 25th, the 8th Company of the Steam Golem Corps got diverted from a routine rendevous mission with allied insurgents in the riverside city of Brentonsville. For some reason, the 8th ascended to the top of the mesa known as the "Giant's Cutting" in the nearby Cloudkill mountains, where they fought a pitched battle with a squad of Caliburn Knights, which ended when Albion forces bombarded the mesa with massive amounts of Hemlock Gas.

Hemlock Gas was another nasty result of the Great War. When the Steam Golems drove the Dragon Knights from the field of battle, everyone thought that was the end of the war. Albion had lost its unbeatable superweapon, the source of all its military might, its trump card, the one tactic it could always rely on, the trick that had never failed them in over a thousand years of history. Without that, what did they have?

As it turned out, they did have other weapons—horrible weapons, that had been held as a closely-guarded secret, even from most of the Albion generals, and one of the worst of them was the Rosedeath. Actually, Joy was one of a very small number of people who knew it by that name, due to her time spent at the KIB translating intercepted Albion communications.

Everyone else called it Hemlock Gas, and that included most of the Albion military, too. Hemlock Gas was a thick, gritty pink fog that crawled across the battlefield, killing or paralyzing anything it touched. No-one knew who had started calling it Hemlock Gas, but the name had stuck, even though Kallistrate scientists insisted that there was no evidence that it actually contained any hemlock.

What it actually was, they couldn't say. But they did figure out a countermeasure—special face-masks with an attached air filter, which the 8th Company had just received, something Shiori Rosewing, the Caliburn knight leading the Albion forces at the battle, had likely not been aware of.

So the Battle of Cloudkill turned out to be a hard-fought victory for Kallistrate, and a failed suicide attack by Albion, but the battle's aftermath was what caused the biggest stir. All the Hemlock Gas that had been dropped on Giant's Cutting flowed down the mountainside and coalesced at the bottom-most point in the region: the nearby city of Brentonsville.

Incredibly, somehow the city managed to receive advance warning of the oncoming disaster, and a majority of the populace succeeded in fleeing the killer fog as it rolled over the city walls.

Considering the size of Brentonsville, with a population of over a hundred thousand souls, the fact that so many were able to get clear of the city in time had to be considered a minor miracle.

Bits of good fortune helped — the lucky appearance of a good stiff breeze at exactly the right time, combined with the gas' tendency to bleed momentum as it traveled from the foot of Giant's Cutting and crossed the flat river plain. Tales abounded of stragglers in Brentonsville running a desperate block-to-block footrace with the creeping pink fog as it inexorably engulfed the abandoned city.

Except Brentonsville hadn't been entirely abandoned. There'd been thousands of citizens too old, sick, disabled, or simply too distracted to flee in time, and they all perished in agony, with their friends, family, and neighbors stranded outside the walls, helpless to do anything but stand and watch.

But the hardships were only just beginning. Normally a cloud of Hemlock Gas would linger for a few hours before dissipating. But the thick pink fog that had conquered Brentonsville was different somehow. It hung around, roiling about like a brew in a witch's cauldron, for weeks.

The evacuees had no choice but to huddle in makeshift camps outside the city in harsh winter weather. Thousands fell ill and died, until one final freezing downpour washed the city clean, and people could finally return to their homes.

So yes, Joy remembered all of that well enough, but...

"What does the Brentonsville Eviction have to do with the Red Specter?" she said.

"The Red Specter is the one responsible for the miracle evacuation of Brentonsville," said Garai.

"What? But that's…" Joy stopped herself from saying 'ridiculous.' She had to remember where she was working. "I mean… I'd never heard that before."

Garai nodded. "This does not surprise me. You would not read the Gazette if you weren't working here. I can tell. But this is why we exist—to cover those stories that other papers are afraid to. And there are many, many citizens of Brentonsville who will tell you of that day, of how they saw the Red Specter fly down from the mountains and soar across the rooftops. And as he did, his voice rang out. It was a deep sound, and it carried to every city corner, to every man, woman, and child. And everyone who heard it felt a chill go down into their bones, a chill like the bottom of a grave. 'Death comes for this city,' it said. 'Death comes down from the mountains. Gather all who you love and flee! Flee now, or share in the cursed fate of the Red Specter!'"

"That's how it happened, huh?" said Joy.

"That is what I have heard myself, from people who were there," said Garai. "And they would swear to this, that it is no lie, on the graves of their parents."

"Okay," said Joy, not mentioning that she'd heard similar oaths from the people who'd insisted they'd seen a man's amputated leg grow back.

"Okay?" said Garai. "Is that the best you can do, Ms. Fan? This is a big story, and if that's the best you can do for enthusiasm, perhaps I should give it to someone else—"

"No, no—don't do that," said Joy, remembering that this was supposed to be her last chance. "I've got enthusiasm. I was just thinking… trying to put it all together in my head…"

"Is that so?" said Garai. "And what have you figured out?"

"Well, uh…" Joy had to think quick for something acceptable.

What was the point here? Well, there had to be a reason Garai was bringing all of this up now.

"Someone in Dodona has seen the Red Specter?" she guessed.

"Several people," corrected Garai. "We have multiple sightings. Here is the list."

He handed her a sheet of yellow lined foolscap covered with notes. It took her a second to figure out which section was the list.

There were marks going every which way. Garai was not a very organized note-taker, although he did have impeccable penmanship.

"Okay, I see five names," she said. "So I just need to interview these people, then?"

"No," said Garai. "I mean, you will of course interview them, but this is a means to an end. Your task is to take your knack for investigation and use it properly for once. You will find where the Red Specter is and convince him to give you an interview."

Joy paused and studied Garai carefully before answering. He wasn't joking. He was serious.

"That's... um. That sounds pretty..." Joy had remember that she was on thin ice here. She needed this assignment. "Does he do interviews? I mean, he sounds like kind of a shadowy figure. Has anyone ever gotten close enough to him to have a full conversation?"

"No," said Garai, beaming. "You will be the first. And the Gazette will be first to print it. An historic event in news."

"Right," said Joy, her voice sounding strangled in her own ears. Again, she had to remind herself how much she needed this job. Never mind that it was impossible. She had to do it anyway.

She looked over the notes again. "Are there addresses to go with these names? Oh, wait—I see them over here. But um—this only looks like three addresses."

"What? Show me," he said, frowning as Joy came round his desk. He stared at his own notes for a bit before flipping the paper sideways. "Right here."

"Oh, there. But that's only one more."

"Yes, that's right. Because this man doesn't have an address."

"Then how in the world am I supposed to interview..." Joy read the name by Garai's finger. "Trench?"

"Yes, Mr. Trench," said Garai. "Don't worry about him. I thought of that, so I already interviewed him myself. The notes are here."

Garai pointed to another section of the page, and Joy had to flip the paper in yet another direction to read it. And found herself disappointed by the results.

"Warehouses by docks. Shadows. Night before last," she said, reading off the only bits of the notes that seemed useful.

"Truthfully, Mr. Trench wasn't the best eyewitness," Garai admitted. "Not quite right in the head, if you ask me. I suspect he has been using Spike. It was rather hard to lock him down to anything specific. Hopefully the other people will be better."

"Haha, sure hope so," said Joy. Yes, a Spike addiction would be a great thing for the rest of the witnesses to not have. "Oh, what's this? 'Beets, Pickles, Pork Shoulder—'"

"Oh, that's my grocery list. I need that. Hold on..."

Joy waited while Garai carefully tore off about one-quarter of the foolscap and handed the rest back to her. He probably said something encouraging to her on her way out, and she probably mumbled a thank you, but she couldn't really be sure.

She felt kind of dazed and light headed. Somehow she ended up in the employee break room. Was there any food here? Because she sure as fuck wasn't getting any fucking pancakes today. She found a mostly empty bakery box with one and a half donuts still left inside. One full glazed, half powdered sugar. Of course all the good ones would be taken by now. There was still a cupful of lukewarm coffee left in the machine, made from those really bitter Southern Axum grounds Garai liked. Everyone else had to endure it with the help of cream and sugar. And the cream bottle was down to its dregs, too, since Garai refused to increase the daily delivery from the milkman. Well, whatever—as a lowly freelancer it wasn't her place to say anything. It wasn't like she was an official employee or anything.

Joy grabbed all the remaining donuts, combined the last remnants of the coffee and cream with enough sugar to make it drinkable, slumped down with her breakfast in one of the cheap, rickety chairs, and spent the next half hour trying to stave off a complete emotional meltdown.

Part 2:

Work History

Chapter 7:

Impossible Assignment

What the abyss was she supposed to do now? Final chance? She'd been given an impossible assignment. Firstly, there was no proof at all that this Red Specter was real. Some figure in a gas mask and trench coat?

That would make him a Kallistrate army infantryman or commando of some type, because only Kallistrate had gas masks during the war. The Brentonsville story was an especially huge stretch. A man flying over the rooftops? Aside from Albion's monstrous flying beetles, the only way for a person to fly was in a balloon or a dirigible. She knew there'd been attempts at heavier-than-air flight by various tinkers and dreamers, but their contraptions tended to crash after going a few feet. But never mind any of that—the big problem was that Joy had been in the KIB when the Eviction happened. Granted, she didn't have the highest clearance there, but it was hard to believe any one person could have played such a major role without it becoming common knowledge in the Bureau.

But even supposing there actually was a real Red Specter, and these five—er, four people had seen him, how in the world was she supposed to track him down? There was no guarantee that she'd be able to do it. And even if she did, there was also no guarantee that this 'Red Specter' would agree to sit down for an interview.

In fact, someone who hid his face behind a mask and managed to avoid having his existence confirmed on any official records seemed to be the type of guy who valued his privacy. In other words, someone who'd never agree to have details about their life printed in big bold type in a tabloid newspaper and spread to every street corner in Dodona and beyond.

36

The whole idea was ridiculous. There was no way, absolutely no way she could do this story. It was impossible! She was being set up to fail! This place was awful—a cheap, tawdry tabloid. She hated it. She hated that it existed. She hated that it was popular and that so many people read this garbage. And she hated most of all that she had no choice but to work here—that the Gazette was the only paper in Dodona that would still talk to her.

Chapter 8:

Hostile Work Environment

It wasn't supposed to be like this. She remembered back when she'd got her first job at the Dodona Journal, one of the oldest and most prestigious Kallish-language newspapers anywhere. That was... Lir's balls, that was only a year ago. Only a year ago, but it felt like it belonged to another lifetime. She'd been so happy.

She'd been super lucky to land a job at the Journal straight out of college. Most recent graduates would have to build their resumes working for a small-town paper before moving up to the big leagues, but she'd managed to build a nice resume based on her work for the university newspaper, her multi-language proficiency, and especially her experience working as an analyst/translator for the KIB. Her language ability was probably what put her over the top.

The first few months had mostly gone well. She had to work hard and learn fast, but she'd felt herself rise to the challenge, and it seemed to be paying off. Mr. Hartmann had been talking about an upcoming opening for a foreign correspondent in Zipang-occupied Kankul, and how she just might fit the bill. It was a plum opportunity and she couldn't wait to go to Kankul.

Especially because that would've meant not having to deal with Quintus anymore. Another junior reporter, Quintus Vogler was charming and confident—both attractive features—but she'd noticed a few times when that confidence seemed to cross a line and turn into cockiness.

She didn't like that, and it made her decision to stick to her self-imposed "don't date co-workers" rule easier when he did ask her out.

Her reservations turned out to be more than justified.

Quintus turned out to be one of those guys who couldn't take "no" for an answer. He kept pestering her for a date, practically every day. He left flowers and small gifts at her desk, which he'd refused to take back. For a while she tried to return them at his desk while he wasn't there, but that forced her to memorize his schedule, and he'd just re-gift it anyway, so she'd end up just throwing them out. After the first week of this, Quintus' gifts and comments started to take an ugly, aggressive tone. One of the gifts had been body soap with a note to "think of me while you're using it." Ew! Ew! Ewwww! It made her feel dirty, which made her want to take a shower, which reminded her of the note, to repeat on a loop in her head ad infinitum. The next gift was a set of lingerie that she wouldn't dream of wearing ever, not if Quintus had been the Prince of Sarpedon. That gift she took home, set on fire, collected the charred remains, chucked it back in the box, along with a note saying, "This stopped being cute days ago. Knock it off!!!", and hurled it on his desk at the crack of dawn the next morning. (She'd been too angry to get any sleep.)

But of course, Quintus kept at it.

Joy was at a loss. Of course, she'd dealt with this type of thing before, but never to this degree. None of her usual tactics were working. And her attempts to recruit some of her new co-workers for defense brought only haphazard success. Their jobs meant they were often in and out of the office at different times, but even that didn't fully account for how little support she was getting.

Well, when Selik said he couldn't because he was headed out, it was because of that, but he was also friends with Quintus and "didn't want to take sides." He did explain why Viveka and Khloe had been acting so weird since all of this had started: Viveka had been harboring a crush on Quintus for months and was furious with her for "stealing him away," and Khloe was Viv's best friend, so she was avoiding Joy to not offend Viv. Joy tried explaining to Viveka that she really wasn't interested in

Quintus, and that Viv was more than welcome to him, but it did no good. Viv just glared at her and accused her of "bragging," before storming off.

Joy wanted to pound her head against a wall. Was this high school? Was she still in high school? Was there a particular age at which fully grown adults quit acting like children? If so, could she go to sleep and wake up again in that magical time—so she could just focus on doing her fucking job without having to deal with all of this ridiculous drama?

And it was affecting her work. She'd noticed after the third week of this mess that almost all of her time management had become devoted to putting herself in the office when she thought Quintus would be out, and finding reasons to be out in the field when she thought he'd be in, or she could use Selik as a shield. This was ridiculous.

She was losing focus and productivity. She'd avoided going to her boss before, because she'd really wanted to handle personal matters on her own, but she had to admit she was stuck, and now it was hurting her job performance. She really needed to take this to Mr. Hartmann.

She wasn't sure what she'd been expecting from her boss, but it wasn't what she got. She'd spent a couple of hours on the previous evening mentally preparing herself for the conversation, so she'd been able to lay out the full story of what had been going on in an orderly, detailed fashion, without letting herself get too emotional during the telling. Keeping her cool was the hardest part, but she got through to the end, thinking she'd done pretty well, only to have Mr. Hartmann give her a stern look and tell her he didn't approve of inter-office romances, and certainly wasn't going to get in the middle of one.

Joy was so stunned that she didn't know how to respond. She thought she must have misheard him or something.

"I'm not..." she stuttered, "I agree with that. I think professional relationships should stay strictly professional. I said that at the beginning. But—"

"Then why are you bringing this whole mess into my office during business hours?" he said.

And it went on like that. Joy kept trying to explain the problem, that it was Quintus who refused to keep things professional. It was like she wasn't even speaking Kallish. Mr. Hartmann finally shooed her out of her office with the admonition that if she wanted to hack it as a reporter, she was going to have to learn to deal with her own personal issues herself.

Joy returned to her desk, and tried to get back to work, but she couldn't concentrate. She was so furious she was shaking. But beyond that, her editor-in-chief's behavior was so bizarre she couldn't even process it. How could he not understand this problem? Joy had lost debates before, but this was something else. He hadn't actually countered a single point she'd made; he'd just ignored them.

That was stupid people behavior, and Flynn Hartmann wasn't stupid. She'd read some of his work from his reporter days. They'd been held up as prime examples of quality investigation in her textbooks at Rouvas College. She'd dreamed of writing on that level herself, someday. So how was it possible for him to stare blankly at her from across his desk and not understand a single thing she'd said? It didn't make sense, not on any level.

So she'd had no choice but to grit her teeth and endure.

Aside from Quintus, the Journal was her dream job. This was a golden opportunity for her career, and she couldn't let some jackass spoil it for her. All she had to do was keep toughing it out for another couple of weeks until the Kankul position solidified. Then she'd be able to put a couple thousand miles between her and Quintus, and that would be the end of it.

Joy pushed on with her plan, which worked well enough until the day Quintus cornered her and shoved her into a broom closet.

Chapter 9:

Assault

At first she froze, too shocked to do anything else. Something in her brain wouldn't accept it, couldn't believe that this was actually a thing that was happening to her. She was at work. This was her co-worker. They were in an office, not an alleyway. This was absurd. No way was she really being pushed up against a stack of cleaning supplies. No way were there hands pushing her suit jacket aside and pawing at her blouse. No way. This wasn't happening.

Then something in her brain flipped over, and she was back in her KIB Supplemental Agent class, unarmed combatives portion. Defense against being grabbed. She twisted her right arm free (twist the wrist, release in the direction of the thumb) and drove the heel of her palm up into her attacker's nose. (Sink down with the knees, step in, explode up, twist hips, whole body power!) She felt a weird sensation of cartilage crumpling under her palm as Quintus cursed and clutched his nose, staggering back, but she'd already kneed him in the groin. He doubled over and things got way confused as they tangled together. Joy's body was acting before she could think, running through the steps of the combat sequence as they'd been drilled into her, over and over again. But she'd never run that drill in a such a confined space, and she couldn't get the right angle to throw the knee.

And then Quintus was clutching at her again. She remembered some bits—scratching at his face and slipping out of her suit jacket to get away, frantic fumbling with the closet door handle, and slamming the door back on Quintus' fingers as he tried to stop her from fleeing into the hallway, screaming at the top of her lungs.

Well, that was only the start of the commotion. She managed to find a group of people in the office, and some of the guys got between Quintus and her, holding him back while he screamed bloody murder, until Mr. Hartmann bellowed everyone into silence, and called both her and Quintus into his office. As soon as they sat down, they both started trying to plead their case, Joy telling the truth, and Quintus claiming she'd attacked him out of nowhere.

Mr. Hartmann wouldn't listen to either of them. He gave them a lecture on professionalism and unacceptable office behavior, and then terminated them both. Joy was beyond shock at this point. This wasn't even high school anymore. They'd gone back down to kindergarten. She'd tried to protest, vigorously, but it did no good. He wasn't listening. He told her to stop being "hysterical."

"You're a real disappointment, Flynn," Joy shot over her shoulder as she went to her desk to get her things. It took longer than she thought it would. Her hands didn't seem to be working properly. It was all she could do to shovel her books and notes and pictures into the box. Someone had given her a cardboard box. She kept her head down as she worked. It felt like everyone was staring at her, but whenever she looked back up, all eyes in the office managed to direct themselves elsewhere.

She caught a side glance of Quintus packing up his desk. He had to work with one hand, as he held a blood-soaked white handkerchief up to his nose with the other. A couple of other guys were helping him. She saw one of them nod sympathetically and pat Quintus on the back. What the hell? Yes, so sad that poor Quintus might get in trouble for attempting to rape a co-worker.

Oh. Attempted rape. That's what had just happened. That's what had just happened to her. In her office. She hadn't had a chance to think yet. Now her mind had begun working again, and it didn't help. She leaned over her desk, closed her eyes, and took several long, deep breaths. Nobody gave her a reassuring pat on the back. Nobody helped her with her things. Nobody talked to her.

She looked up as she finished to see Quintus's back heading out the door to the hallway, and felt an icy chill go through her. What if he decided to wait for her outside? Joy grabbed an official Dodona Journal-branded letter-opener from her desk, and worked it around so it was resting in her palm while she held on to the box's handle. If she needed to, she could quick-drop the box and start stabbing. That's right, she was stealing office supplies, and no-one was going to stop her.

But she didn't see Quintus on her way out, and, after walking five blocks, she let herself relax a bit, deciding that he wasn't going to come after her today after all. She didn't put the letter-opener away, though.

Chapter 10:

Recovery

She realized she was exhausted. Putting one foot in front of the other had become a major struggle, and she'd become aware of weird sharp pains all over her body, including one right on her cheekbone that throbbed with every step. Had she been punched? She didn't remember being punched. She could've banged herself against something in the broom closet, but she couldn't remember that happening, either. The full details of the assault were fuzzy in her brain—confused sensations of flailing around in the darkness.

And truthfully, she didn't think she really wanted to remember it any more clearly than that. She wanted to go home and forget this had ever happened.

Her apartment wasn't far, but it felt like it took forever to get there. She reached the foot of the stairs leading to the door of her brownstone, when a familiar voice called out, "Yoo Hoo! Joy! You're home early."

It was one of her neighbors, the Widow Jakuba, a large, matronly Kossar woman who lived in the biggest and nicest apartment in the ground floor of her building. Her husband had died some years ago, before the war began, but she kept herself busy with her hobbies, one of which was leaning out her street-side window and saying hello to people.

Joy looked up and tried to answer. Usually she'd toss off some pleasantry in Kossar, which Mrs. Jakuba loved, and Joy could get some practice in—keep the language fresh in her mind. But right then and there, she couldn't summon the energy for it. In fact, just saying anything was a struggle.

"Heavens, girl—is something wrong? You look terrible. Did something happen? Are you all right?"

Joy heard the warmth and caring that underpinned her neighbor's alarm, and it undid her. No-one else had asked her that. Not her boss, and none of her co-workers had asked her if she was okay. It wasn't asking much, just to get some basic human caring and decency. But Joy had almost forgotten it existed. She sat down on the street and began to wail.

The next thing Joy remembered was being enfolded in a big warm presence as Mrs. Jakuba was out on the street and soothing her. Joy found herself coaxed inside Mrs. Jakuba's apartment for some mothering, as she was allowed to cry herself out, and explain what happened. Joy got to learn a bunch of new Kossar swearwords to describe Quintus and her boss. She kind of liked the phrase "born from the ass" for Quintus. She'd have to remember that one.

She spent the rest of the day lounging on Mrs. Jakuba's couch while being stuffed like a goose. At first she'd said she wasn't hungry, but she changed her mind when the hot, savory plates arrived on the coffee table and the rich aroma reached her nose. She didn't bother objecting when Mrs. Jakuba insisted she stay over in the guest room. Why not? Couldn't hurt to do that just for tonight.

"And tomorrow, bright and early, we are going right to the City Guard," said Widow Jakuba.

"What?" said Joy.

"That no-good miserable bastard assaulted you, right? This is criminal, yes?" she said. "Back in the old country, a masher like him would get fifteen lashes and spend a day in the stocks, in freezing Kosstan weather, so he learns his lesson. Jails here are too nice, but still he should see the inside of one. That will teach him a thing or two."

Joy took a second to savor the mental image of Quintus shivering in cold, bare jail cell. But really, she just wanted to put this whole mess behind her and move on with her life.

"No, this bastard needs a lesson, or next time he will go after some poor girl who is not tough like you. We are going."

Joy hadn't thought about that, but Mrs. Jakuba was right. What would have happened if she hadn't taken those supplemental KIB combatives courses? The thought chilled her—made her stomach flip over, so she tried to put it out of her mind.

But the next morning, Joy and the Widow Jakuba went to the nearest City Guard station to report the assault.

If anything, the Guardsman on duty was even less helpful than her former boss'. He just sat there the whole time, as she was trying to calmly recount the events of the assault, and the events leading up to them, with this look on his face, like "why are you bothering me with this crap?" Joy was glad Mrs. Jakuba was there, to get upset and berate the Guardsman for his attitude. It spared her the effort of having to do it herself. Eventually the guard agreed to take her statement, though it was obvious he was only doing it to placate the Widow Jakuba and get rid of her.

But Joy could tell by his questions that he found the whole thing to be trivial. No, she hadn't actually been raped. She'd fought back and got away. What had she been wearing? A business jacket, blouse, and a sensible skirt—what did that have to do with... No, her blouse had been buttoned up to the top, but... About mid-thigh, no hose, what...

Because it was hot out, that's why!

It went on like that until Joy was so bored and disgusted that she just wanted it to end. The real kicker was when he noted that she seemed super calm for an assault victim. And real put-together, too. He sure wished he could get through a fight and look so nice in the mirror the next morning.

Actually, Joy did have a number of nasty bruises, and she'd been prepared to show them. But no way was she taking her clothes off for the benefit of this jackass, not when it was obvious it wouldn't make any difference anyway. The real kicker was how now her ability to appear calm was being held against her. So if she got emotional then she was hysterical, and if she didn't then she was a calculating liar. She lost either way!

She trudged out of the station with Mrs. Jakuba's arm around her, with the widow still yelling back over her shoulder about how her taxes paid the Guardsman's salary, so he'd better do his job proper.

Joy knew it was futile. At most, all they'd do is send someone to interview Quintus, and he'd point to his busted nose and whine about how she was some kind of psycho bitch who'd attacked him out of nowhere. If they even bothered to do that much. At least there was some kind of written legal record of the assault. That was something, she'd supposed. Not much, but it was all she was going to get.

Joy spent another couple of days letting Mrs. Jakuba pamper her, though after the first day the widow began to insist that Joy call her "Tishka," which meant "Auntie" in Kossar. Honestly, getting cared for like this was a real change of pace for Joy. Growing up, she'd been the eldest of seven kids, so most often she'd been expected to help her parents run the household. So unless she'd been super-sick, like can't-get-out-of-bed-without-puking levels of ill, it was her taking care of everybody else.

And the idea of lying around because she'd had a hard time and felt sad? Ridiculous — but Tishka didn't see it that way, and Joy opted to not argue with her.

But she had to get on with her life — get back on that horse. Though she found she slept better if she blocked her apartment door by propping a chair beneath the doorknob, in addition to the deadbolt and security chain, and kept her stolen letter-opener right by the nightstand. Later, it occurred to her that the letter-opener might be taken away or used against her, so she saved up some empty tin cans and tied them to the chair, so they'd make a racket if the chair fell over. And she did the same to her window, in case someone tried to climb up through the fire escape and break through that way.

So that made her feel better, though occasionally she still had these weird half-dreams in the middle of the night, where it felt like some stranger had gotten in and was lying on top of her, and she'd try to break free, but find herself paralyzed, stuck in that terrified state for several minutes until she'd manage to thrash herself awake, grab the letter-opener, only to discover the "intruder" had just been her own blanket.

Crazy—the tricks your mind could play on you while you were sleeping. Nothing really to be afraid of. She was certain she'd never told Quintus where she lived. Well, maybe in conversation she might've let something slip that could've been a hint, and he was a reporter, too. He should know how to research people—but even so, that would be a needle-in-a-haystack kind of search in a big city like Dodona. Well, Flynn had her apartment address, but he'd never give that out to Quintus, or anyone who shouldn't have it. He'd turned out to be a jerk, but she should be able to trust him that far. Hopefully.

Chapter 11:

Blackballed

After a week or so off, Joy felt it was time to get back to her life. She updated her resume, typed out a bunch of extra copies to leave with potential employers, and started to make the rounds with the other local papers. The Kallis Chronicle was the Journal's biggest competitor, so she started there. She wasn't fond of their editorial slant, but they did have a reputation for quality, and were most likely to have foreign correspondent positions.

She had a very pleasant chat with the front desk receptionist, who had been working there for years, and seemed to be pretty up on all the latest office news. Obviously she wasn't in any position to make hiring decisions, but her eyebrows went up when Joy mentioned her language skills, and said that she'd heard they'd been looking for Kankulese, Kossar, and Anyan-dialect Xiaish speakers, so she might be able to take her pick, to expect to hear back in a few business days, and to check back at the desk if she hadn't heard anything in a week or so.

Joy walked out feeling better than she had in over a month and hit the rest of her route with a renewed energy. She had nothing but positive interactions with the other papers as well, and she returned home at the end of the day feeling satisfied and hopeful.

Even if the Chronicle didn't have anything, one of the other papers surely would. All she had to do was wait a few days for a letter, or maybe even a courier-message, and then her life could get back on track. She could put this whole mess behind her, and forget it had ever happened.

But a week went by, and Joy didn't hear anything. No interview requests arrived in the mail. Joy tried to be patient, but it was hard. In the meantime, she typed out more copies of her resume, and went through a new round of submissions, broadening her search to include magazines, lifestyle publications, even some specialty-interest sheets, like fashion, theater, and the like.

After two weeks of not hearing anything, she decided to check back with the Chronicle. Joy found the same receptionist as last time, but something felt off. She seemed much cooler and guarded. Her friendliness from earlier was gone, replaced by professional politeness that felt more and more strained the longer the conversation went on. Joy didn't get it. She'd been told to check back if she hadn't heard anything in a week. She'd been encouraged to. But now she was being treated like a nuisance, even though all she'd done was follow directions.

Joy was about to leave, but needed to use their restroom first. As she was coming back from that, she overheard snatches of a conversation echoing down the hallway.

"Got rid of her... didn't seem dangerous, but I guess you can never tell..." That was the secretary.

"...knows people, even if his politics are nonsense... said she loves drama... violent, broke a man's nose..." This was a new voice. Sounded like an older man. Probably someone senior at the paper. The voice had that sort of authoritative boom of a man used to giving orders. Joy moved to one side of the hallway and slowed down, carefully placing each foot so her steps made no noise.

"Heard she was a looker, though. What do you think? Worth an interview for that?" This was the man again.

"I suppose she's pretty enough. I don't think it's worth wasting anyone's time over." The secretary had that strained politeness in her voice again. "Maybe that's it. I've known some women like that—they're used to always getting their way because of their looks. They keep expecting the whole world to work like that."

"She's in for a rude awakening, then," said the man. "Word gets around in this industry. Nobody with any sense wants to hire a viper to poison their office. Maybe she'll learn her lesson, maybe..."

Joy backed away, shaking in anger. She resisted the impulse to run out, confront them, tell her side of the story. But that wouldn't do—she already knew it in her gut. They wouldn't listen. She'd only make it worse. It would be just more fuel for the "Psycho Ms. Fan" narrative.

"Word gets around?" Of course—every industry has networking, people attending the same social functions. This was especially true in journalism. And she was being smeared. How far did this go? How many papers were in the loop on this?

She wandered back down the hallway, hoping there was another exit somewhere that way, so she didn't have to deal with them—ignorant, smug jerks! She was so distracted that she nearly didn't see Quintus.

She froze in pure dread, until she realized he hadn't noticed her yet. He'd fixed his attention on another woman, a short brunette. He was leaning over her and chatting, one hand planted on the wall above her head. It looked like he'd intercepted her coming out of the restroom. Joy thought her smile seemed a bit nervous. Joy turned around and walked back towards the lesser threat of the front desk as fast as she could without running, looking neither right nor left, not acknowledging anyone until she'd made it to safety out the front door.

She found a park bench somewhere to quietly collapse for a while. So, that's how it was. SHE was bad news. SHE was a problem. SHE was violent and unstable and needed to control her temper. But not Quintus, no. Not creepy harasser rapist fucking asshole Quintus. HE was free to move on like nothing had happened. He was allowed to make excuses and put everything on her, and be believed, so he could go right on terrorizing more women out of journalism. Joy had a fleeting thought of that other brunette in the Chronicle building. *Sorry, sister, but there's not a damned thing I can do for you. Ms. Joy Song Fan's got her own problems to deal with. You're on your own. Because your bosses sure as shit won't lift one fucking finger to help you. I can guarantee you that.*

52

Joy returned to Mrs. Jakuba, but she didn't get quite the level of comforting that she'd hoped for, only because Joy had to spend a great deal of energy talking her down from storming the Chronicle offices and giving them a piece of her mind. It left her even more exhausted than when she'd arrived, though it was gratifying to have at least one person on her side.

That was important, because the longer this whole mess went on, the more difficult it became to avoid the nagging suspicion that maybe some part of this was her fault, that maybe she really had done something wrong. She'd been friendly to Quintus at first—maybe too friendly? Had she actually said something to give him the wrong idea? Maybe she should have worn longer skirts. Those thoughts crept around her brain, despite her efforts to dismiss them, or confront them with all her reporter skills, like a hostile interview.

"So, you've been thinking we were too friendly with Quintus at first? Maybe we smiled too much at his jokes, and we playfully slapped him on the arm that one time? Well, answer me this—how many times did we clearly and directly tell him 'No' after that? You can't remember exactly? But that's because we did it so often, right? Give me an estimate—a minimum number?

At least a dozen times? So, which is more important, some subjective interpretation of a minor bit of body language, or the actual words a person says? And writes, as well? Remember that note? Do we or do we not have a written record of us telling him to get lost? Oh, and you want to talk about skirt length? How many other women wear skirts that exact same length?

Did we or did we not a skirt almost exactly that style as part of our KIB uniform? Okay, let's check then… it's an inch shorter, so what? Does that justify assault? Well, does it? That's a yes or no question. Well, then, please describe to me the exact amount of clothing a woman has to wear to make an assault on her person acceptable."

It made Joy furious with herself, that there was a part of her own mind that was like this, that collaborated with the sexist victim-blaming of her enemies, a treacherous fifth column trying to take her down. Joy drew energy from that rage. She was not going to let those bastards beat her. She would not give them the satisfaction.

A few days later, Joy resumed her job hunt, though it had become an exercise in rote repetition. Getting angry could break her funk, at least temporarily, but it did nothing to change the world around her. It couldn't take her off the blacklist or do a thing to improve her job prospects. There weren't many publications left that she hadn't already applied to, and the ones left were a motley assortment of specialist publications.

Joy didn't have much confidence in getting any of the positions, but she felt compelled to make the effort in the hopes that her resume would hit the desk of some editor who wasn't invited to the same parties as all the other cool kids. It turned out that those editors really did exist. They sent back rejection letters telling her she was overqualified.

Apparently there was still something of a labor surplus in Dodona, with the war over and so many soldiers finishing up their tours of duty. Every new position that opened up was met by a swarm of applications, at least according to one recruiter. That made her feel a little better about her difficulties, but it didn't make her job hunt any easier, even when she broadened her search to include stopgap measures like waiting tables. Again, she was informed of her overqualifications, like she hadn't been aware of them when she'd applied.

Joy's only other marketable skill was translating, which she'd looked into. The problem was that the big companies doing most of the hiring for Xiaish speakers mainly produced pro-Kallistrate propaganda for distribution into the occupied Albion-Xia territories. And that... being part of that—the suspension of democracy that appeared to be spreading world-wide, the idea of working to promote that—it made her feel ill. That had to be an absolute last resort. She'd tried looking in the other direction, maybe find a job at a Xia advocacy organization, but most of them had been aligned with Steve Huang's Tranquility party, and had their assets frozen by the State.

The rejection routine had become so ingrained into her that she'd already begun tossing her letter from the Gazette into the trash before the fact that it wasn't a rejection registered in her brain. It wasn't a real employment offer, either. But it was an opportunity to make some money working freelance, and that was something. Joy had been dipping into her savings to make last month's rent, and she didn't have a huge savings buffer to begin with.

She'd practically raced down to the office of the Dodona Gazette to meet with editor-in-chief Garai Sekibo to learn more. Once the interview started, she realized how rash she'd been. She couldn't even remember where she'd seen the listing for the Gazette position and found herself drawing a mental blank as to exactly what type of paper the Gazette was. She'd never heard of it, and was surprised when Garai informed her of how large their readership was. She'd also realized that she still hadn't figured out a decent way to explain how she'd left her last job, but Garai didn't bother to ask. He spent most of his time talking about the Dodona Gazette and how great an independent press was. The big newspapers claimed to be "objective," but this only meant they were blind to their own irrational biases.

Joy found herself nodding in agreement. Yes, she'd just recently figured that out herself. Blind to their own biases? Most definitely true.

Everything went well. Garai was likable, intelligent, and fun to listen to, with a nice musical Axum accent. Garai spoke multiple languages, like her, although the only two they had in common were Kallish and Wuyu Xiaish.

Garai sent her off with a promise to contact her again when he had a good story for her. Joy walked out feeling like a huge weight had been lifted from her shoulders. It wasn't a full job, but she'd be making money doing journalism again, and that was something.

Her good mood lasted until she decided to pick up a copy of the Gazette to get a sense of its standards. The top story was about some explorer, a Dr. Brandt (who she'd never heard of before) trying to fund an expedition to "Naraka, the world of Hollow Vei." What? Joy felt her spirits sinking with each sentence she read. According to the article, the planet Vei wasn't a solid sphere beneath their feet, as most scientists believed, but a hollow shell, with secret civilizations of ancient humans and strange creatures living on that inner surface.

This land was known as Naraka, and was lit by a "Dark Sun"— this was the secret opposite of the regular, bright sun of Yuyi that most people knew. Instead, the Dark Sun, known as "Iyuy"—and that was so painfully stupid that Joy had to quit reading.

Really, just on a linguistic level, that was such nonsense… What kind of newspaper was this? Joy read further, finding stories of ghosts, spirits, fairies, mysterious visitors from other planets, mixed with salacious gossip about popular singers or stage celebrities, scandals of fallen aristocrats and socialites from the nouveau riche classes of industrialists and trading companies, topped off with two pages containing daily horoscopes from five completely different (and incompatible) cultural traditions.

So here it was: the final humiliation. This was the only paper still willing to talk to her: a sleazy tabloid. That's what she'd been reduced to now. This is what all her hard work and dreams had led to. This is what all her grinding and late night college study sessions had earned her. This.

She spent the next few days sitting alone in her room, hoping each day that the mail would bring a response from a publication that wasn't the Gazette, and trying to work out a better option for making rent money other than accepting Garai's offer. But no other offers came, nor did any brilliant money-making ideas, and so began Joy's career as a freelance reporter for the most ridiculous tabloid in Nokomis.

Well, if it was any consolation, it didn't look like she'd be working here much longer.

Chapter 12:

Workin' for the Man

Top of her class at Rouvas, and look at her now—couldn't even hack it at tabloid journalism. Just one more failure to add to the pile.

Couldn't hack it? The thought lit a spark of anger somewhere in her guts. It gave her energy, so she fanned at it. There were few things Joy hated more than being told she couldn't do something, even if she was the person doing the telling. But the assignment really was impossible, or, if not impossible, so dependent on blind luck that it might as well be.

Firstly, the Red Specter had to really exist. If he wasn't real, she'd fail. Secondly, one of Garai's witness list would've had to have actually seen him, and have useful enough info to track him down. If they were all delusional or lying for attention, she'd fail. And finally, even if he was real, (which was super-dubious, but let's just entertain the possibility) and even if she managed to gather enough info to track him down, she still had to convince him to agree to an interview. And if the Red Specter was a real person, he'd obviously taken pains to keep his presence so secret that his very existence couldn't be confirmed. Why would someone like that ever agree to an interview with a newspaper? Of course he wouldn't.

It was impossible. It really was! No matter how she turned it over in her mind, she still got the same result. Nobody could do this. She was being set up for failure!

Joy felt a surge of rage, which she released in the form of a kick directed at the break room trashcan, a corrugated tin monstrosity nearly as big as she was. It made a noise like a thunderclap and began to tip over. Joy had to lunge to catch it and prevent a major gross garbage spill. Joy had been up and pacing around like a madwoman without realizing it. Sheepishly, Joy dragged the can back into its proper place and pushed at its sides until the dent she'd put in it popped out, with another loud bang that reverberated throughout the office.

Joy sat back down. Fortunately, nobody came to investigate the noise. She breathed a sigh of relief. Her temper boiled over so easily nowadays. She didn't used to be like that. At least, she didn't think she'd been. She couldn't indulge in temper tantrums right now. She needed to be able to think.

Set up for failure—why would Garai do something like that? If he didn't think she could cut it at the Gazette, he could have just said he wasn't giving her any more assignments. Why put her through this, then? To jerk her around? For why—laughs? Would Garai do that? Was that consistent behavior for the man, based on what she'd observed while working for him?

No, that didn't fit. Granted, she might be projecting more decency on him than he deserved, like she'd done with Flynn back at the Journal, but she couldn't let that experience poison her against every other boss she'd have in the future. Her gut said that wasting her time with a prank assignment wasn't something that Garai would do.

So, let's go with this assumption: if her assignment was real, then it couldn't be impossible. And if that was the case, then there must be something she wasn't considering. What had Garai been telling her about all her previous stories? It was that she kept failing to tell their readers what they wanted to hear.

Well… okay, but was it her fault that the facts of her stories didn't line up with their wishes? A reporter's job is to report the truth, not make things up…

Something in Joy's brain clicked into place, and everything made perfect sense. Make things up. That was the whole point of the assignment. To see if she could do that. Garai didn't really expect her to be able to track down and interview a modern folktale. He expected her to pretend that she had and submit the results. This was a test to see if she could write fiction.

58

Of course. It was so obvious that it was painful. Granted, it would have been even more obvious if Garai had come out and said that outright, but she supposed that was part of the test here.

But any satisfaction she might've had from solving the puzzle was short-lived. There'd been a reason her work at the Gazette was so half-assed. She still wanted to be a real reporter. She hadn't given up on those dreams. But that wasn't happening in Dodona, because of the whisper campaign against her. She was going to have to move to some other city to escape it. But she couldn't move to another city before securing a job there. To do that, she'd need to travel for interviews. That meant travel costs: train tickets, hotels, food money, etc. And she'd need enough to support herself like that for at least a week, maybe even a month. And she was flat broke. She needed to work to get a job.

But she also needed to impress her new prospective employers with her current work. And she didn't want to attach her name to garbage tabloid journalism. If any legitimate paper saw her name attached to the dreck that passed for "news" in the Gazette, they'd want nothing to do with her, and rightly so. Yet working for the Gazette was her best opportunity to save up enough to get to an interview in the first place.

So she'd tried to walk a tightrope with her Gazette stories, of producing stories that fit within the Gazette's standards, without outright violating any standards for real journalism. So, even if her future employers found out about her tabloid stint, she'd still be able to defend her work. She'd be able to sit up straight, look them in the eye, and say, "Yes, the Gazette is crap, but my reporting wasn't."

In short, she'd been trying to work for a tabloid without really working for one, and Garai was telling her that, no, she didn't get to do that. If she wanted to keep getting money from the Gazette, she was going to start producing "proper" tabloid stories. She had to pick one or the other.

And she really wanted to pick "other," but what would she do then? She'd hoarded up enough non-perishable food in her apartment so that she wouldn't starve right away, but that wouldn't do her any good if she got kicked out for not paying rent, and Dodona rent wasn't cheap.

She could just bite the bullet and translate propaganda. It probably paid okay... but that still felt worse than working for the Gazette, if for no other reason than she'd sort of stumbled into the Gazette by accident. She could plead a case of semi-ignorance to her conscience, which wasn't a *great* case, but it was better than the alternative.

Were there any other options? The only thing she could think of was maybe just going home to her parents, but the thought of it made her feel a bit ill. Her parents already had enough to deal with. She, Dean, Kane, and June had all gotten full-ride scholarships for their military service, but that didn't cover every expense, and it left three more children to put through college, and they'd have fierce competition for full-ride academic scholarships, plus they had Grandma Eu-Meh living with them, and all her medical problems—Joy didn't want to be another burden to them. She was the eldest. She was supposed to set an example for the rest of her siblings. Joy vividly remembered her college graduation, and the looks on her parents' faces. They'd been so proud. She hadn't even told them about getting fired. She couldn't bear to—she didn't even know how she'd explain it. And then to come home, in utter defeat, after all that...

Joy slumped back in her chair and stared at the grungy, faded paint on the break room cabinets, her thoughts stuck in a loop. Finally, she reached her decision. She wasn't going to trouble her parents like that. So she was just going to have to suck it up and do some fake journalism. Just... for a few months. Get it over quickly, save up, start over in a different city, try to put this behind her. She didn't have to put the Gazette on her resume or mention it in interviews. Hopefully, it wouldn't come back to haunt her later, and if it did, she could deal with it then. That was her best option for right now. Which meant that it was time to write a spooky ghost story.

60

Part 3:

The Adventures
of the
Red Specter

Chapter 13:

The Archives

So, how was she going to do this? Well, she was still going to have to go out and interview the people on Garai's list. That was a requirement from Garai. Because people like to see their name in the paper. And then make up some bullshit. But it couldn't be any old bullshit; it had to be bullshit that lined up with her reader's expectations. And she had no idea what that was.

She knew enough about the Red Specter to recognize the name and his outfit: the distinctive gas-mask with the red skull painted on it, and a dark grey trench-coat. Beyond that, nothing.

She had to get familiar enough with the character to make sure her Red Specter talked and acted like the one in her readership's collective imagination. And what would the basis for that be? Was it the one in the comic strip? She was pretty sure that was the most popular version. And, most importantly, that would be the version she had easy access to. The comic ran in the Gazette, and she had free access to the Gazette's archives. So her first task was to go read some superhero comics.

The Gazette's Archives were up on the second floor, a surprisingly large room stacked with years of the Gazette's back issues. Most major newspapers had archives, but Joy had been surprised that a tabloid would care about such things, or would bother with the expense. Who needed a comprehensive historical record of gossip and nonsense? Apparently Garai did.

Joy wasn't sure if it was because he thought the Gazette would be really important for future generations or if it was just a prestige thing—real newspapers had archives, so the Gazette would too. Or something like that. Which meant that any article Joy wrote for the Gazette would likely be preserved for all eternity. Wasn't that wonderful?

Joy strode past row after row of dull gray heavy-duty steel shelves until she found the current month. The past two-and-a-half weeks' issues lay flat on the shelves, unfolded, in a neat stack, with today's issue on top, July seventeenth. Thick leather-bound monthly compilations of the Gazette filled the shelves to the left and above the half-finished July stack, with empty space to the right and below for future volumes. A grand testament to idiocy. Be a shame if something, like maybe a huge fire, were to get started in here and burn it all to ashes, wouldn't it? Joy chuckled to herself, savoring the fantasy of stacks of garbage journalism wreathed in flames—a proper trash fire that'd be.

It would solve her future reputation problem, though. Just one little lit match as a goodbye, after she'd secured a new job, and nobody would be able to prove she'd ever written for a tabloid.

Joy felt a wave of horror at what was going through her own brain. That was awful. It was arson! Garai didn't deserve that. It was wrong. And... and what if the fire got out of control? It could burn down the whole building. There were at least a few offices in here that had nothing to do with the Gazette. Other people would be out of their jobs. They needed to work as much as she did. And if she got caught somehow? Oh, she thought "tabloid journalist" might look bad on her resume? How would that compare to "arsonist," huh? That wasn't her. That wasn't who she was. Knock it off, brain.

She grabbed the bound volumes from the last two months and stacked all the loose papers on top—two and a half months' worth of story. She decided to carry it out to the hallway, where the morning sun streaming through the large windows gave her much better light to read by. She found the Red Specter comic on the inside of the back page.

Joy gave it a quick glance, and couldn't really tell what was going on. It seemed to be the continuation of a longer ongoing storyline. Joy started skipping and skimming backwards through the Gazette issues to find the start of the story, and she got a better idea of how the comic worked. Monday through

63

Saturday the strip was in black and white, and occupied the upper third of a page, but on Sunday, it bloomed into vivid colors, and took over the entire page. Well, it was a neat use of the color press.

Joy found what seemed to be the beginning of the current story on the first Monday of the June volume. She settled in and started reading. Time to see what all the fuss was about.

Chapter 14:

Shiori Rosewing,
Knight of the Caliburn

She'd hoped to get a good sense of the Red Specter character right away, but the early strips in this storyline barely featured him at all. He appeared in the first strip in flashback, as recounted by another character, the elderly Professor Zhang. And even that was just a vague glimpse, with most of the Red Specter's form hidden in shadow—a silhouette for a head and two white circles to represent light reflecting off the goggles of his gas mask.

The Specter brought a warning, that Shiori Rosewing was Up to No Good, and had some nefarious scheme for the town of Zalandag, a small rural community just south of the Goktun Wastelands. Professor Zhang assembled his team, two other men and one woman—Joy assumed they were the regular cast of the comic—and headed out.

The next scene opened with the caption "Edge of the Goktun Wastelands, near Zalandag," with an image of Shiori Rosewing herself, reclining on an ornate divan, and the picture was nothing like she'd expected. This "Shiori Rosewing" had black hair and red skin, and was wearing an outfit that you might describe as a "slinky black evening dress," except most of it was missing, and she was bursting out of what was left. She used an ornate, feathery fan to cool herself. And perched on her shoulder was a scary-cute miniature dragon wearing a dog collar that said "Pochi."

Joy goggled at the image. This was supposed to be Shiori Rosewing? Upon reflection, she realized that she'd seen images of this character before, in various spots around the city—pinup posters in the backs of various nightclubs and bars, that sort of thing. She'd never thought to connect it with Shiori Rosewing.

To be fair, there wasn't much in the way of reliable information concerning the real Shiori. All anyone knew for sure was that she was the Caliburn Knight responsible for the gassing of Brentonsville, and all the deaths and misery that followed.

The Caliburn Order were a strange type of open secret of the old Albion Empire. Everyone knew they existed. In fact, one of the biggest annual festivals in Albion was the Trials of Caliburn, where hopeful adolescents aged nine to thirteen spent a week undergoing various tests, both physical and mental, all leading up to the final challenge, a huge obstacle course in famed Cistonia Stadium, its seats packed to bursting, with over a hundred thousand roaring people.

Thousands of children attempted the Trials each year, but a only a handful made it past all the elimination rounds to be selected as Caliburn Acolytes. Those kids then disappeared, rumors said they were whisked off to the secret island of Arianrhod, and never seen again. Presumably they became Caliburn, but no-one would ever know for sure, as Caliburn Knights swore absolute fealty to the Emperor, to the exclusion of all else. They weren't permitted to have any contact with anyone outside their Order, including family members.

Beyond that, very little about the Caliburn Knights could be confirmed, other than the fact that they existed, and were effective to the point of being terrifying. They'd become more and more important in the years leading up to the Albion Empire's destruction. The existence of Albion's Dragon Knights meant that any straightforward attempt to fight the Empire army-to-army on a battlefield was doomed before it began, so rebels and insurgents frequently resorted to other methods, like taking hostages or hit-and-run banditry-style operations. The Caliburn were the Empire's favored response to such nuisances, if they found they had some compelling reason to refrain from burning the offending city to ashes.

Thus, the Caliburn Knights became weirdly popular, even beloved among the people of the Empire, even in regions that chafed under Albion rule. By surgically targeting and eliminating the actual rebels, something they did with devastating ruthlessness and efficiency, they got credit for "saving" hundreds of thousands of lives.

So the mysterious Caliburn Knights were both feared and revered all across Nokomis as the greatest and most honorable warriors in the history of the world.

Or they had, at least, until Shiori Rosewing put an ugly black stain on their honor when she'd doused Brentonsville with Hemlock Gas. So was that the idea here? To show her as a debased knight? Was that why she wasn't wearing armor? The Caliburn Knights wore plate armor into battle—that was another thing KIB knew about them for sure—even going into stealth missions.

Apparently they had a secret method of crafting plate mail so that it didn't impede their mobility or make any extra noise when they moved. There were plenty of artists' renditions of Caliburn armor, stretching back centuries, but very little consistency or accuracy in those drawings, as most eyewitnesses to a Caliburn mission didn't live to tell about it. The KIB was one of the few organizations that had actually managed to acquire a trove of Caliburn weapons and armor, as a result of the Battle of Cloudkill, but it had all been classified at a level way above Joy's head.

Anyway, the Shiori of the comic was speaking to a tribe of heavily-armed bandit outlaws, and their leader snarled at her, declaring he'd sooner die than take orders from a woman.

Shiori just smiled at him over the top of her fan. "That can be arranged."

Bandit Leader replied to that by drawing a pistol and shooting her in the chest.

Shiori's dragon screamed as pink smoke burst from the wound in its master's chest. It hopped to the edge of the divan and spat a stream of fire at the bandit leader, who dived to the side as three of his subordinates were immolated and fell screaming to the floor.

Bandit leader drew a bead on Shiori's dragon, only to have a tendril of pink smoke engulf his gun hand. The smoke coalesced into a human-shaped form atop Bandit Leader, pinning him to the ground. The form solidified into Shiori, apparently unhurt. She clicked her tongue as she pressed the barrel of the bandit leader's own gun into his temple.

"Oh, that wasn't nice at all. You upset poor little Pochi-kun. Any more stress and he'll start molting early." The baby dragon alighted on Shiori's shoulder, wrapped its tail around her neck and rubbed up against her cheek.

"Oh, it's okay, snookums—Mommy's just fine," she cooed. "Nothing to worry about, just a itty-bitty little gunshot wound. I'm right here, see? See?"

The bandit leader managed to squirm out from beneath her and point up in horror. "What are you?"

"Oh, I'm just me," said Shiori. "But at the Battle of Cloudkill, I had a little accident with my Hemlock Gas—and now I've become much more than a Caliburn knight. No need for any of that hot, uncomfortable armor anymore, either."

Joy rolled her eyes. Oh, so *that* was why Shiori wore that outfit. It was totally practical because magic, Suuurrre it was. Also, Joy would expect that any "accident" with Hemlock Gas would result in a horrible death rather than super powers, but whatever. At least it explained her red skin, sort of.

"Witch!" spat the bandit leader. "You'd be nothing without your powers!"

Shiori smirked at him over the top of her fan. "Oh, you think so? It seems you Goktun barbarians are too ignorant to know what a Caliburn Knight is. Well, I guess I'll have to teach you a lesson."

She beckoned him with her fan. "How about this? One-on-one, you and me, no guns, no gas powers. If you can hit me even once, you win, and you can do *whatever* you like with me. Sound good?"

Joy raised her eyebrows at the last bit, noting the artist had drawn Shiori in an arched-back pinup-pose for that line.

Bandit Leader got to his feet and flashed a broken-toothed leer at her. "That's the last mistake you'll ever make, witch." He drew his scimitar and attacked.

And Shiori Rosewing spent a whole Sunday color page's worth of comic panels kicking the crap out of him, dancing about, batting his scimitar aside with her frilly fan like it was nothing, kicking him in the face with her stiletto heels, tossing him around like a rag doll, and just generally toying with him.

The last panel was a close-up of Bandit Leader's bloodied face, with Shiori's stiletto heel grinding his head into the ground. Her word balloon came in from off-panel.

"Who's the queen of the Goktun Raiders?" she asked.

"Y-you are... Ma'am," said the bandit.

Okay, outfit aside, Joy had to admit that was bad-ass. The black-and-white Monday strip repeated the foot-on-head panel, with the rest of it dedicated to Shiori's sinister-yet-incredibly-vague monologue about how the Raiders were only the first step, for, once her evil plan had been put into motion, she would turn all the citizens of Zalandag into her loyal minions— a new, unstoppable army that would re-conquer all of Albion's traditional Xia territories, CRUSH the pathetic armies of the Kallistrate upstarts, and then, NOTHING could stop her. In the name of the Emperor, she would CONQUER the WORLD!! OH HO HO HO HO HO HO HOHOHO!!!

The artist paid special attention to Shiori's maniacal laugh. The last panel was a close-up of her gleefully psychotic expression, her fan held up to her cheek, but not enough to obscure her wide-open mouth, with all the "HO's" strewn about so they covered the entire background. Well, at least *someone* was enjoying their work.

The next comic featured Professor Zhang's team arriving in Zalandag, only to face resistance and outright hostility from most of the Zalandag villagers, who were used to being subjects of the old Albion Empire. They treated the new Kallistrate "upstarts" with suspicion, dismissing their warnings about Shiori and hinting that they should take their business elsewhere.

Joy tapped at the latest page in irritation. The story wasn't terrible—at least, as far as pulp fare went, but she wasn't reading for fun. This was supposed to be a Red Specter story, but so far, the title character had only appeared for a few panels, and most of him had been in shadow. She needed to get some sense of his personality if she was going to fake-interview him, and so far, she'd gotten nothing useful for that.

Joy tried to speed up by skimming, but reading at normal speed was already tricky enough, what with having to flip past pages and pages of trash Gazette articles. She did her best anyway. No way was she letting some trash comics defeat her.

Chapter 15:

Terror of the Gas-Men

Shiori sent some of the bandits to the village in disguise, pushing a merchant's cart—but Baz, one of the men on Dr. Zhang's team, saw through it and attacked them. Baz was a big, muscular man, with dark skin, a shaved head, and a handlebar mustache. He boasted that petty bandits like them were no match for an ex-Jagdkommando like himself. The strip used a lot of clunky expository dialogue in weird places, like during a fight.

Though, as Joy thought about it, she had to admit it did make sense for something that had to run in serial, where every single chopped-up story bit might be a jumping-on point for a new reader who knew nothing about the characters. So, during the fight, Joy learned that Baz was a seasoned veteran who'd been through a rough patch after leaving the military. He mentioned "crawlin' into a bottle" while punching out one of bandits, but he was feeling "back to his old self" after Prof. Zhang had "cleaned him up."

Meanwhile, Kolton, the other man on Team Zhang, struggled in his fight with another bandit. Red-haired and freckled, Kolton was much younger than Baz—he'd tried to enlist at the end of the war, only to wash out during basic because he'd tried to hide his chronic asthma from the army doctors. He managed to knock out his opponent, noting how well Zhang's "miracle concoction" worked—referring to a traditional Xia herbal remedy, modified to work with an inhaler. But Kolton failed to stop another bandit from grabbing at a small black urn from the cart.

In the following tussle, the bandit managed to shove Kolton away, but broke the urn in the process. Brackish liquid spilled all over the bandit, who screamed as the goo began to vaporize his body. The unfortunate bandit staggered about in a half-solid, half-gaseous state. He lunged at one of his own comrades, seemingly for support, only to have the strange gas-infection spread, so now both of them howled while the thick smoke engulfed their bodies.

"Yehyeh, we have to help them," said Lilla to Dr. Zhang, who held her back. Lilla, the last member of the team, was a pretty blonde woman, so Joy was a bit surprised to hear her call Dr. Zhang "Yehyeh," making him her paternal grandfather. Maybe Lilla got her blonde hair from her mother.

"No! Stay back! It is too late for them," said Dr. Zhang. "They have been infected by Shiori's poison—the same poison they would dump into the well of this village. They have earned the terrible fate they sought for others—trapped forever between life and death!"

As Dr. Zhang spoke, the comic panels showed images of the bandits being consumed by the gas, but instead of collapsing to the ground, they ceased their screaming and began to shamble about.

"It is just as the Specter warned," said Dr. Zhang. "This is Shiori's new weapon. This is the fate she would have for us all—a world of nightmares for her to rule! These bandits are men no more. They've been transformed... into GAS MEN!"

Right on cue, dark patches appeared in the hazy blobs where the bandits' heads used to be, resolving into sunken pits for eyes, and wide slashes for mouths. They were crude mockeries of human faces, like clay dolls fashioned by a child. Darker smoke boiled out these holes, along with a ghostly moan that crawled across the comic page in warped, wavery text: "AaaoOOooOOoooOOOooo!!!"

"Thanks for the lesson, Doc," said Baz, backing away from the lurching monstrosities. "So let's skip to the part where you tell us how to fight these things.""Stay away," said Dr. Zhang. "Whatever you do—you can't let them them touch you!"

"Need a bit more than that, Doc!" said Baz, dodging aside as one of the wraiths swiped at him.

"FIGHTING MONSTERS IS NOT YOUR JOB, BAZ MAN-KARI," came a voice from off-panel. "FOR THAT, YOU NEED A GHOST."

"That voice," said Kolton, "Is that who I think it is?"

"It is!" said Lilla. "Red Specter, where are you?"

"WHEREVER TYRANNY REIGNS. WHEREVER EVIL STRIKES. LOOK TO THE SHADOWS, AND I'LL BE THERE."

And indeed, the next panel showed the Specter's silhouette emerging from the shadowy darkness on a nearby balcony. The Red Specter leapt from the balcony and seemed to float through the twilight sky. He landed right in front of the gas-men, brandishing an odd-looking short spear, and struck a dramatic pose.

"FOR NO INJUSTICE WILL ESCAPE THE WRATH... OF THE RED SPECTER!"

The Red Specter reversed his grip on his spear, the business end of which consisted of a straight single-edged blade about three feet long mounted on top of a fork-like steel tine aligned along the bottom quarter of the blade. And the middle of the spear had a small circular plate for some reason. Joy noted that the Specter wore heavy gloves and had no issue with grabbing the blade of his own weapon. With a click, another set of long blades slid out from the butt end of the spear, only these spread out to form a giant fan, which the Specter used to drive the gas-men back, keeping them pinned against their cart.

Joy couldn't help but giggle a little. She supposed it made sense, but it was just so goofy.

"Uh, that's great and all, Specter," said Baz. "But now what? You just gonna keep them there like—"

"STAY BACK," the Red Specter intoned. "EVERYONE, STAY BACK AND TAKE COVER."

The Red Specter reached into his trench-coat and pulled out a standard-issue Kallistrate Army cigarette lighter. He flicked it on and tossed it at the gas-men, still pinned against the cart by the gust from the Specter's fan. The cart went up in a massive explosion, leaving nothing but a smoking crater behind. The

Red Specter had disappeared as well, though Lilla managed to catch a brief glimpse of a figure in a trench-coat ducking into an alleyway. She chased after him, but when she reached the alleyway, she found it to be empty.

"He always does that," said Kolton.

"Yeah," grunted Baz. "Real conversationalist, that one."

Well, count your blessings, Baz, thought Joy. *It's not like you have to interview the guy, or anything.* Joy sighed and tried to skim faster. She meant to stay focused on just the Red Specter sections, but the rest of the story kept sucking her in. Well, she really did need to pay attention to the general plot, just so she could put any of the Specter's eventual dialogue into context.

Let's see, the heroes on Dr. Zhang's team talk to village elders some more, but still get resistance. Some of the elders accuse the heroes of being the ones to bring this conflict to Zalandag— everything had been peaceful before they showed up. A few more villagers listen to the heroes, they set a perimeter guard around the town, etc., etc. Joy skipped over a couple more strips depicting the night watch and full panels of an empty starry sky and suddenly the Red Specter was attacking a blimp.

Wait, what?

Joy flipped back, and realized that the panels of empty sky hadn't been empty. The blimp had been painted in camouflage to resemble the starry sky, but she could see it now that she knew what to look for. Likewise, other seemingly empty panels actually showed the silhouette of the Red Specter materializing in the middle of the sky. The Specter careened into the side of the blimp's gas envelope, punctured it with his spear, and rode the spear down so it tore a huge gash in the blimp's side. The escaping gas propelled the airship sideways, even as it plummeted, so it veered off-course and crashed just outside Zalandag. More broken urns, more transformed bandits surrounding the Red Specter, who was somehow totally unhurt after an airship crash. The Specter pulls out his lighter again, and... wait, was that supposed to be a hydrogen blimp? Because if it was....

74

The next panel was just one huge, fiery WHOOOOOSH! Nothing left but burnt airship debris, but Zhang's heroes were certain that the Specter must've survived somehow. The whole sequence was ridiculous. Where would desert bandits, or Shiori, for that matter, get a blimp? An airship, even a small one, required maintenance and supplies that....

Whatever, it wasn't important. This was a pulp comic that only cared about the nifty "appear-out-of-the-night-sky" effect. Joy's concern was that she'd just witnessed an entire Red Specter action sequence where he hadn't uttered a single word. It was like the strip was trying to drive her nuts.

Cut to Shiori berating her bandit minions for their incompetence while grinding her high heel into their leader's prone head. This again? Joy was starting to suspect the author (What was his name again? It was at the top corner of every strip. Erik Avakian, that was it.) was indulging a fetish. Or maybe multiple fetishes. Anyway, Shiori finally let the leader up, but he'd had enough. He grabbed a torch from somewhere and prepared to hurl it at her, saying, "You're made of gas, huh? Well, let's see what this does to—YEEEAAAARRRGGHH!!!"

The bandit screamed as Pochi engulfed him in a stream of fire, his torch harmlessly sailing over her head.

"NO, Pochi!" said Shiori. "No fire-spitting without my signal! We've talked about this, haven't we? Haven't we? That was very naughty. Naughty naughty widdle Pochi-kun. Who's a naughty boy? You are! Yes you are!"

Shiori paused from scratching Pochi behind the ears to address the bandits. "Word to the not-so-wise: never wave a torch at a dragon. It means you want to play, and—well... you see what happens."

Shiori sighed as she examined the rest of them.

"Okay, which of you is next?"

The bandits glanced nervously at each other and said nothing.

"Next in command, I mean," she snapped. "Your second-in-com... well, no, it'd be third-in-command, by this point, hmm?

Yes, third-in-command, step forward."

More awkward silence followed, until one raider finally raised his hand.

"He's dead, ma'am. First day you got here, he was standing right behind our old leader when your dragon spit at him, and—"

"Uh, fine," said Shiori. "Fourth-in-command, then."

"Um... he was also standing behind the—"

"Lir's balls! How did you idiots even survive this long?" Shiori cried, throwing her hands up. "If those were your top leaders, you'd think they'd at least know how to dodge better! You people have no standards, that's your problem."

Shiori crossed her arms and spent a few moments in serious contemplation while Pochi nuzzled at her cheek.

"Okay, fine. This is my fault," she said. "I've been expecting too much of you. I see that now."

The raiders all sighed in relief.

"I've been expecting you to think, when clearly that's not what you're good at. So I'll do you a favor and remove you of that burden."

Shiori opened a chest at the foot of her divan and pulled out one of the black urns. By the time the bandits realized her intentions, it was too late. She lobbed the urn into their midst, and their horrible transformation began.

Shiori reclined on her divan as the horrific scene unfolded before her. "Yes, I should've done this from the beginning. Forget all this futzing about with town wells and sneaking around, when I have a perfectly good core for my army right here. Isn't that right, boys?"

From where the Goktun raiders had once stood, a crowd of identical, amorphous gas-men raised their blobby heads and moaned in unanimous agreement.

"That's better," Shiori stood up and surveyed her new troops. "In fact, that's perfect. You're the perfect soldiers for Albion's new army: mindless, relentless, fearless, remorseless! Unfettered by petty human weaknesses, like love or compassion. And, most importantly, this time you shall be following a true leader into battle. I, Shiori Rosewing, shall bring you victory.

We will roll over Zalandag, and our ranks shall swell as we add their fallen to our number. City after city will fall to us, and SOON, yes, so very SOON, the whole WORLD shall be MINE! OOOHH HO HO HO HO HO HO HO HOHOHO!!!"

Chapter 16:

Assault on Zalandag

Joy skimmed forward as Shiori led her army of gas-men on Zalandag. Back at the town, the heroes had convinced a third of the villagers to join their side, but the Anti-Kallistrate die-hards still refused to listen. They met Shiori at the edge of the town to talk things over, and were promptly converted into Shiori's gas minions. After seeing that, all the remaining villagers either joined with the heroes or ran around in a blind panic.

It looked like all would be lost as the gas-men swarmed through the village, but Dr. Zhang's team hadn't been sitting around idle waiting for the invasion.

They'd managed to build three "vaccu-suck" devices, odd contraptions that used high-speed steam-powered fans to suck air through long hand-held tubes with funnel openings on the business ends. They had the bulk of these devices mounted on rickshaws and engaged with the gas-men in a running battle throughout the streets of the town.

They would suck up the gas-men into hollow tanks and trap them there, stopping the gas men without burning down the entire village, though Joy noticed that only the men actually wielded the vaccu-suck weapons. That was weird—you'd think Lilla would be a better choice for running around pulling a rickshaw than the elderly Dr. Zhang.

Joy flipped through the rest of battle, as the heroes raced to suck up the gas-men before they could infect the Zalandag townsfolk with their gas-plague. And surprisingly enough, they seemed to be winning, in no small part because of repeated instances of unusually lucky breaks for the heroes.

Shiori's minions would have a group of villagers cornered, only they'd be hit by a sudden gust of wind, the villagers would make a break for it, and a vaccu-suck rickshaw would show up finish the mindless wraiths off. Horse carts would stampede at just the right time to create a crucial diversion. Wine casks would spill and catch fire in just the right spot to act as a barrier between the Zalandag townsfolk and their attackers.

Joy thought Avakian was just being lazy with all these coincidences, until she noticed something hidden in the shadows of one of the "coincidence" panels—a silhouette of the Red Specter.

She flipped back to each previous miracle and found the same silhouette again. This comic was making it really hard to skim, what with all these hidden pictures.

Too bad there was no hidden monologues from the Specter. No, that would've been too useful, wouldn't it?

The battle raged on, and the good guys kept winning. Gasman after gas-man disappeared into the guts of the vaccu-suck machines, until all that remained was Shiori and her litter-bearers, surrounded by the heroes in the middle of the town square.

"We've got you now, Shiori," said Kolton, as he aimed his vaccu-suck device at the wraiths carrying her divan.

But Shiori was too quick, leaping off her palanquin and rushing Kolton, even as her litter-bearers disappeared into the vaccu-suck's funnel. She laid Kolton out with a kick to the head, leaving his device unguarded.

The Caliburn knight lashed out with her foot, her stiletto heel punching though the vaccu-suck's collection tank. A high-pressure jet of pink gas streamed out and arced high up in the air before gently drifting back to earth, growing thicker as it did.

Inside the growing cloud, *things* began to move.

"No!" yelled Dr. Zhang. "She'll start the whole tragedy over again. We have to plug that hole!"

"I'm on it," said Baz, but Shiori blocked his path.

"Are you, now?" she said, leering over the top of her fan. "You seem more experienced, to be sure—but I've been disappointed by men like you more times than I can count."

"My name is Baz Mankari," he said, drawing himself to his

full height. "And I served six years with the Jagdkommandos, so yeah, I think I'll be more than enough for you, lady!"

Baz lunged at her, and the fight was on. The Jagdkommandos were Kallistrate's best of the best, an elite unit intended to counter the Caliburn Knights. Joy's military combatives trainer, a veteran navy frogman by the name of Kodwo Adachi, had actually taken the Jagdkommando entrance trials, only to wash out on the fourth day of "Hell Week."

Kodwo was the toughest man Joy had ever met. Hitting him was like hitting a tree. And he was one of the ones who hadn't made the cut. Baz had made it, so he fared much better against Shiori than any of the Goktun bandits, trading blows with her and managing to land a few good shots, but the end result was the same, with Shiori felling him with a kick to the head.

Didn't have to use her gas powers, either. Unfortunately, as good as the Jagdkommandos were against regular units, there was no way they could take a Caliburn knight one-on-one, and even this silly comic strip couldn't pretend otherwise.

Baz struggled to regain his senses, as Shiori sauntered past and punctured the collection tank on his vaccu-suck machine, leaving only Dr. Zhang's intact. Shiori faced him and Lilla down, with her army of gas-men re-forming behind her, only their time in the collection tank had changed them. They'd been mashed together, compressed into a tiny space, and now it seemed they couldn't quite remember how they'd been before.

The gas-men had turned into misshapen monstrosities. Some were giants with multiple arms, legs, and heads, while others appeared as co-joined twins, and others were stranger still: bizarre beings composed of spare parts. One unfortunate creature consisted of two sets of legs and hips whose lower torsos flowed into into each other, creating a double-ended beast that staggered about blindly, nearly stepping on a disembodied head that scuttled about on six arms that sprouted directly from its skull.

Even Shiori seemed taken aback by the nightmarish scene. "Yeeesh," she said, before shrugging it off. "Oh, well—it's

80

not like they weren't ugly before. I've worked with worse. No idea how I'll put them in a phalanx, though. That's going to be a challenge."

"You monster!" said Lilla. "Look what you've done to them. Have you no shame?"

"What I've done? I wasn't the one who squashed them all together like that." Shiori grinned and fluttered her fan. "How hypocritical. And typical. Such a shame, really—if you could just see past your pathetic loyalty to your upstart Kallistrate nation and swear allegiance to Emperor Oberon as your forebears did, you'd be so much better off."

"You think us fools, do you?" said Dr. Zhang. "When we can see what happened to your last set of allies, right before our eyes."

"Turn you into gas? No, that's what happens to those who disappoint me," she replied. "And what will happen if you continue to defy me. But you've shown admirable resourcefulness to hinder me so far. Why would I throw that away just to get another shambling gas-soldier if I didn't have to? Do you know how hard it is to get good help these days? Do you? All of you would be far more... useful to me in the flesh."

Joy frowned. Was Shiori staring at Lilla when she said that? Lilla hadn't even done anything useful in the story so far, so why... Never mind, whatever. The heroes made the standard declarations of how they'd never join with her, Kallistrate is the beacon of freedom for Nokomis, etc. Shiori says they're doomed, and—Oh! A hail of bullets hits Shiori from off-panel. It's Baz—he pulled himself together enough to fire his revolver.

"Sore loser much?" said Shiori to Baz, who'd turned incorporeal to avoid the damage, her "wounds" leaving trails of gas that didn't bother her any. "And after I went out of my way to give you the dignity of a fair fight, too. That's gratitude for y— Aiigggh, NOOOOO!!!"

"No, that's smart tactics, witch," said Baz, as Shiori was pulled into Dr Zhang's vaccu-suck. "Just needed you to go gassy so Dr. Zhang could do his thing. Looks like it's gonna *suck* to be you."

The pun was bad enough to make Joy groan out loud, but Shiori disappeared inside Dr. Zhang's device, which he then turned towards the rest of the gas-monsters, as Kolton staggered over to the rest of the heroes as they rallied around the converted rickshaw.

"Wha' happened?" said Kolton. "Did we win?"

"Almost," said Dr. Zhang, looking over the milling crowd of pathetic gas creatures. "Without Shiori to control them, these aberrations have no will. But they cannot be allowed to roam free. This will test the capacity of my vaccu-suck to its limit, but I believe—"

A panel-filling BANG cut him off, as a slight bulge appeared in the side of the collection tank. Another BANG, and the bulge grew larger and more pointed.

"No! Impossible!" said Doctor Zhang, even as the banging continued and the bulge swelled out, deforming the collection tank further. "There's no way... no way she could..."

The vaccu-suck machine exploded as Shiori's stiletto heel burst through its side, followed by the rest of her, along with all the remaining gas monsters.

Shiori's laughter filled the page as she materialized right behind Lilla and seized her by the neck, as the men dived clear of the blast.

"Foolish mortals! Did you imagine your pathetic contraption could contain the magnificence of one such as me, Shiori Rosewing? OHHH HO HO HO HO HO HO HO!"

Shiori brandished her fan, which turned out to hold a concealed blade in one of its ribs, and pressed it up to Lilla's throat, while producing a small black urn in her other hand. She popped the cork stopper off with her thumb and held over her captive's head.

"This is your last chance! You can join me willingly, or become my mindless gas minions, starting with precious little Lilla. Choose quickly, for my patience is at its limit. Will you serve as men or monsters?"

82

Shiori glanced back at the misshapen horde coalescing behind her, and her expression changed a bit. "But while you're here, could you take a look at my back for me?" She shifted around while keeping her grip on Lilla. "I didn't pick up anything that shouldn't be there, like an extra arm, did I? Or someone else's head sprouting out from where I can't see it? I mean, you'd think I'd be able to tell immediately if that happened, but I just want to be sure, y'know?"

"Uh, you look fine," said Kolton. "No extra arms or nothing."

Actually, Joy wished she looked that good from that or any angle, though she had to remind herself that she had the disadvantage of being a real person with real anatomy, instead of a pen-and-ink fantasy pinup drawing.

"Excellent!" crowed Shiori, switching back into full villain mode. "Now, you have ten seconds to surrender before poor defenseless Lilla loses her humanity! Ten... Nine... Eight... Seven... Eh, what?"

Out from nowhere, a familiar silhouette rose up behind Shiori, this time wielding a sword. Before Shiori could react, the Red Specter chopped off her hand, caught the urn before it could fall on Lilla, cut off Shiori's head, and pulled Lilla free of the decapitated villain's grip.

"Red Specter, you saved me," said Lilla, starry-eyed.

"Thank you, Specter," said Kolton. "We sure are glad you're here."

"About damned time," groused Baz.

Shiori's head bounced off the ground while the rest of her body staggered about blindly. She looked annoyed.

"Red Specter!" she screeched. "Where did you come from?"

"WHEREVER TYRANNY REIGNS," intoned the Specter. "WHEREVER EVIL STRIKES. LOOK TO THE SHADOWS, AND I'LL BE THERE. FOR NO INJUSTICE WILL ESCAPE THE WRATH... OF THE RED SPECTER!"

"Ugh, always the same line," she said, as Pochi the Dragon swooped in to pick up her head in his talons, her severed hand held gently in his mouth.

"But this time you're too late. You've meddled with my plans for the last time!"

Shiori sneered at them as her dragon familiar reunited her head with her body. "You face an entire army now! Gas monsters, seize him! Oh, and good work, Pochi-kun. That's a good boy! Now you stay here, because Mama's got a bad, bad ghost man to deal with."

"Specter, what can we do?" said Dr. Zhang. "My vaccu-sucks have all been destroyed—"

"YOU'VE DONE ALL THAT YOU COULD," said the Specter. "NOW YOU NEED TO GET CLEAR. I WILL HANDLE THIS."

The heroes fell back, with Dr. Zhang overriding Kolton and Lilla's objections, while the Red Specter faced off against an army of monsters. He reached back over his shoulder to draw a small buckler with an odd stick-handle that extended well past the edge of the shield. He snapped the buckler to his sword pommel, and Joy realized she was looking at the same spear weapon from before. Apparently it could split into two pieces. The Specter activated the big fan mechanism he'd used before, but it was only a matter of time before the sheer numbers of the gas-monsters overwhelmed him, their multiple limbs wrapping him up, immobilizing him in an upright cruciform stance.

"I've beaten you, Specter," crowed Shiori. "Even you can't stand against all my monsters at once."

"YES," said he, his cigarette lighter appearing in his hand. "ALL GATHERED TOGETHER NOW."

"Minions, NOW!" yelled Shiori, and the gas-monsters shifted their bodies away from the lighter, while maintaining their grip on his arm, yanking it skyward, with the deadly open flame pointing away from their gaseous forms.

"OHHHH HO HO HO HO HO HO HO," Shiori's laugh echoed across the town square. "Did you think you'd beat me again with the same old trick? A master strategist like me, Shiori Rosewing?"

84

Dr. Zhang's group watched this turn of events in horror from the edge of the square. Lilla and Kolton once again having to be held in check by Baz and Dr. Zhang. There was nothing they could do now but believe in the Red Specter.

Shiori strode up to stand inches away from her captive, tapping her fan to her lips while looking him over.

"I must confess, Specter, you... intrigue me," she said, running a long finger across his mask. "Just what are you hiding under there, I wonder?"

The Red Specter didn't answer. He just stood there, silent as the grave, eyes unreadable behind the gaslight reflections on his goggles.

Shiori just shrugged. "Well, we'll find out soon enough." Her smile was predatory. "But first, one little thing. Fire is dangerous. Not a toy. So, we'll be taking that away —"

Shiori reached up to grab the Red Specter's lighter, only to have the Specter display a surge of strength — not enough to break free, but he managed to pull the lighter out of Shiori's reach.

Shiori rolled her eyes and tried to grab it again, but the Specter did the same thing, and again until he was waving his whole arm back and forth in the air, just managing to keep her from getting it.

Shiori crossed her arms and glared. "Well, now you're just being childish. You realize I've got a whole world to conquer, here? I've got better things to do than stand around playng silly games with —"

Shiori's eyes went wide, and for the first time, her face showed an expression of sheer terror.

"HEEEEEERRRE POCHI-POCHI-POCHI-POCHI..."

"NO! No, Pochi-kun, no playtime now, no... oh crap!"

Shiori dived to one side, gas jets from her feet shooting her along like a rocket, as Pochi spit a stream of molten fire into the massed army of gas monsters, and the Zalandag town square exploded into an inferno.

Dr. Zhang's crew huddled down from their safe distance, trying to peer at the flames without being blinded. About twenty yards away, Shiori sprawled in the dirt. Her stiletto heels had caught fire, so she kicked them off and stamped her bare feet in the dirt. Pochi landed on her shoulder and licked her face.

Shiori grabbed him by the scruff of his neck and waved a finger at him. "No, no, no! Bad Pochi! Bad! Mommy's very, very angry. No treats for a week!"

The baby dragon stared at her with huge, liquid eyes. Shiori scowled, but allowed him to perch on her shoulder again. "Being cute won't make up for destroying my entire army, so don't think I've let you off for that. But it's not all bad. At least you got rid of *him*, didn't you? That persistent thorn in my side, that menace who's foiled every single one of my plans, that pompous, dour, self-righteous meddler, that fool in a mask who calls himself—

"Red Specter!" cried Lilla, her expression joyous.

"What? Impossible!" Shiori turned back to the town square. Most of the gas had burned off in the initial fireball, leaving smaller bonfires of burning debris in its aftermath. Visible in largest, central fire was a black silhouette. This dark core of the bonfire stirred, struggled to its hands and knees, and staggered to its feet. It took one step forward, then another, a man-shaped phoenix.

"No," the witch gasped, shrinking away. "The heat from that explosion was… it's impossible! No one could survive that. Not even you. This can't be happening. This isn't real."

But it was. The Red Specter advanced on her, step by step, as the flames diminished and went out. And the Red Specter stood there unharmed, with barely a scorch mark on his trench coat.

"What are you?" she breathed. She held up a hand to point at him, or maybe ward him off, and the artist put a bunch of wavy lines around her hand to show how badly it was shaking. She wasn't laughing this off. "Why won't you die? What does it take to kill you? WHY WON'T YOU DIE?"

86

"DO YOU WANT TO KNOW?" The Red Specter intoned. "DO YOU REALLY WANT TO KNOW THAT? BECAUSE I CAN SHOW YOU. I CAN SHOW YOU TERRORS OF THE COSMOS THAT DRIVE MOST MEN INSANE."

The Specter brandished his odd composite spear at her, and she staggered to her feet and backed away, unwilling to even try to use her Caliburn combat skills against him, for what good would it do?

"No—stay away! Stay back," she said.

"JUDGMENT COMES FOR US ALL. JUDGMENT IS IN-ESCAPABLE. NOW YOU FACE YOURS," said the Specter, closing the distance between them.

"Is that right?" said Shiori. "I wonder just how committed you are to your 'Judgment.' Enough to let an innocent die? Let's test that, shall we?"

She pulled out one final black urn, the smallest one yet, and hurled it to strike Lilla Zhang full in the chest. Lilla looked down in shock as the urn shattered and spilled all over her. Her eyes rolled up and her knees buckled.

At this, the Red Specter took his eyes of Shiori, who turned into gas and flew up into the sky, staying just close enough to deliver one last taunt through her disembodied face.

"Poor little Lilla. Pray that your precious hero can offer you any comfort in your last moment. Good luck seeking warmth from a cold corpse. You're so good at slaughtering my gas-men, Red Specter—so I'll leave you with one more to dispose of. And remember this, Red Specter! Remember the price you pay for ever daring to defy me, Shiori Rosewing!" And then she jetted off into the night, carrying little Pochi with her, leaving only mocking laughter behind.

"OHH HO HO Ho Ho Ho ho ho ho..."

All the men rushed to Lilla's side, but the Red Specter got there first, taking her in her arms as she gaped in horror at her own body, as the outlines of her hands started to blur as pink vapor streamed off them.

"No!" cried the Professor. "That's the first stages of the trans-formation! My adopted grand-daughter... is turning into...

"A GAS MAN!"

To Be Continued... was what it read at the very bottom of the panel. And that was today's paper. Joy was all caught up. Aiyah! What a place to stop. What were the writers thinking? Didn't they have any consideration for their readers?

Now she would to spend a whole day on pins and needles wondering what was going to happen to poor Lilla. Well, granted, it wouldn't be the worst loss to the team, since Lilla hardly did anything, and that had been getting on Joy's nerves. But that didn't mean she wanted to see Lilla die or anything. Interesting, that last line, though: adopted granddaughter. So Lilla wasn't ethnic Xia at all. That was a bit disappointing, but whatever.

And beyond that, she'd wasted a huge amount of time. The whole point of this had been to get a good idea of the Red Specter's character... and she hadn't done that! She'd read two month's worth of strips, and she still barely knew anything about him. He'd only shown up for short action sequences and had very few lines when he did. How was that a Red Specter comic? Misleading title much? She'd need a much better sense of his character if she was supposed to fake-interview him.

Maybe she hadn't read enough. The strip had been going on for a while. Maybe this last story was just a fluke, a change-up of POV. She should check out more strips to be sure. She'd just read the past two months' worth. She could go back another four months... no—six months. She just needed to exercise more discipline with her reading. She didn't need to mess around with any more of the hidden-object schtick that the artist was so fond of. She only needed the parts where the title character showed up and had lines. It was as simple as that.

Joy gathered up all the loose newspapers, along with the monthly bound volumes, and returned them to the archive shelves. Only after she'd put them back in place did she stop to wonder why she'd done that. She stared long and hard at the past two-and-a-half's months' worth of papers, realizing that all her work for the Gazette was contained right there, and that they were certainly the only archived copies of that work in existence. And if those volumes were to just walk off and disappear, so would any evidence that she'd ever worked for this sleazy tabloid. Forget any stupid ideas about arson—all she had to do was sneak off with a few books. Granted, they were large, bulky books, so sneaking anywhere with them would be tricky, but still, she should still be able to...

Joy shook her head. This wasn't helpful. And she really didn't like this train of thought at all. She was a good person—or, at least she always tried to be. The fact that she was thinking about stealing and burning other peoples' property worried her. What had gone wrong with her life, that she was seriously considering committing a crime, even a really petty one? Something could go wrong. Something she hadn't thought of.

And anyway, thinking about how to destroy her shameful tabloid reporting now was pointless. She was about to do a whole lot more of it, wasn't she? Because she had no other choice. At the very least, she should wait until she'd finished her last Gazette article and was ready to jump ship to a real paper. Then she could weigh the pros and cons of stealing Gazette archives. Agonizing over it now was a waste of mental energy. She needed to get back to her research.

She returned to her reading bench in the hallway with another three archive volumes. The next story was more of the same. Well, the villain was different, a "Doctor Clockwork" who used rogue analytical engines to make a platoon of Steam golems go berserk. But it was still the same formula—Zhang's team tried and failed to stop the villain, Lilla got captured, and then the Red Specter swooped in at the last minute to save everybody, and Dr. Zhang capped it off with a pat moral about the dangers of technology and the need to use it responsibly.

The Specter barely had any lines. Joy had learned next to nothing about him, though she had learned that Lilla's last name was Lemko. Dr. Zhang was a family friend who'd taken her in after her parents had been killed in the Great War.

Joy sighed and decided to take a break. She yawned and stretched, feeling a few things pop around her neck and shoulder. It was hard to get the heavy archive volumes into a comfy reading position on the hallway bench. Even skimming, she'd let herself get sucked into the story, and forgotten to move around at all. She paced about the hallway for a minute or two to work the kinks out before hauling the volumes back to their places on the shelves.

She looked back at the previous two months. Should she read another? Her sense of the character was still really thin. Was it enough to write a fake Red Specter interview?

She thought over all his grim lines in their spooky, heavy font, all the hints he'd dropped about the darkness of his life, which normal people were "better off not knowing", his "stuck between life and death" shtick, and an image of the Red Specter did form in her mind. Unfortunately, it was an image of a mopey teenager holed up in his room, dressed all in black, with the back of his hand permanently stapled to his forehead, writing pages and pages of terrible poetry in his journal, all about how life was nothing but suffering and pain and emptiness and not only did Susie Horvath not know he existed, but she'd even started going out with that turdball Chet Lazlo, and ALL WAS DARKNESS!

Joy had to steady herself against the steel shelves until her giggle fit passed. Okay, she doubted that was characterization Garai was looking for. She had to remember, it needed be just the right kind of nonsense. All right, she'd read one more story arc—see if that turned up anything useful. She pulled down two more months' worth of archives and hauled them back to her reading bench.

The next, or rather, previous story was a big change-up in narrative style. Not only did this story barely feature the Red Specter, it had few of the other heroes either. It seemed to be going for a gritty noir thriller from the viewpoint of a Triad boss by the name of Yajin Jang, a.k.a. "Diamond Jang, King of the Underworld." Diamond Jang started selling a new drug called "Dreamtime," and his business began to suffer one mysterious mishap after another, while the Red Specter's silhouette appeared in the background. Finally, the Red Specter sent Jang a direct warning: stop making Dreamtime, for the drug "blurred the line between this world and the next," or else the Specter would take his organization apart, piece by piece.

Of course Jang didn't listen, and the stakes escalated. As his situation grew more and precarious, Diamond Jang's mental state deteriorated, until he finally resorted to taking Dreamtime himself.

The next bit of the comic got really bizarre, with Jang ascending up to the Pure Land, before meeting the Red Specter, who chased him down to the Abyss, the cold void outside the cosmic Great Wheel, full of nameless Things that would devour and un-make the souls of the truly despicable.

But then Jang woke up to the sound of the police busting down his door, setting off an extended action scene, culminating in a confrontation with the real Red Specter that ended with Jang being carted off to a mental hospital, his mind broken, as the heroes reflected on the Moral of the Story, and the Red Specter... here we go... the Red Specter uttered a few pithy lines, repeated his catchphrase, and flew off.

Joy sighed. Once again, the Red Specter barely appeared in his own comic strip, and half the time he wasn't even himself— just a hallucination in a drugged-out mobster's mind. Though, Joy had to admit, her earlier impression of the Red Specter as a mopey, over-dramatic teenager didn't seem as apt as it had before.

Some of the imagery in this story had been legitimately creepy—especially the bits with the Abyss. Joy knew most of the teachers at her temple didn't take ideas like monsters in the Abyss or even the Pure Land very seriously. They chose to put their emphasis on Lir Kovidh's teachings of awareness, kindness, and morality, over those more fantastic elements. Still, she could never be totally sure those tales weren't true—that there might be some horrible punishment lying in wait for the spirits of wicked people, to snatch them up before they could reincarnate.

Joy shivered just a tiny bit, inadvertently tugging at one of the pages, pulling it partially free of its binding—about three inches worth of page separated from the spine. Joy cursed under her breath and pushed it back into place. She closed and opened the book. It looked like the rest of the pages held the torn page in place pretty well. It wasn't all that noticeable. And really, who would notice anyway? Even at legitimate newspapers, most archives went unread. And these were tabloid archives. She could tear out every third page and probably no one would even notice...

Joy sat bolt upright as the full implications of her musings hit her. She could really do that. She really could. Forget stealing a volume—all she had to do was flip through the archives, neatly tear out every single one of her stories, stuff them in her purse, take them home and burn them, and no one would ever be the wiser. She'd be leaving the overwhelming majority of Garai's property untouched. She wouldn't be destroying anybody else's work—just her own. Joy turned the idea over in her head, looking for a downside, and not finding much of one. The odds she'd get caught doing it seemed incredibly low, as long as she was smart about it. The odds that anyone would discover it after the fact were even lower.

Realistically, they were practically nil. So why did the very idea make her nervous. Especially with all this business of wicked souls getting cast to the Abyss. No—that was silly, no one would be sent to the Abyss over a little newspaper vandalism. Or would they?

She shook her head to clear it, stood up, and stretched. This was all pointless right now. She couldn't do anything until after she'd finished her last Gazette article, anyway. No, check that—she'd need to wait until the month after her last article. Because if there was one time they might notice missing pages, it would be when they were cutting and trimming the loose papers for binding. Time to focus on the now.

And right now, she'd read enough comics. Sadly, Joy still didn't feel like much of a Red Specter expert. The character remained nearly as confusing as he had before. She didn't have any confidence that she could write a bunch of fake interview responses for him. But it was getting late.

Joy looked over the witness list and sighed. Might as well see who she could track down. Maybe one of these witnesses might have something interesting or coherent to say. Maybe they'd give her a jolt of inspiration for her fake interview. Or, if not, then the Gazette archives with their Red Specter comics would still be here tomorrow. But considering how unreliable some of Garai's contacts could be, if she waited a day there, her witnesses could disappear to some other city or country overnight. Time to hit the streets.

Part 4:

Legwork

Chapter 17:

A Holiday For Everyone Else

Joy emerged from the dark foyer of the Gazette offices and stepped out into the street. The sun was painfully bright. Even though she wore her sun hat, still she had to stop and squint until her eyes adjusted. Everything seemed extra-vibrant and extra-loud today. Everyone was gearing up for Liberation Day tomorrow.

The red and gold national flag of Kallistrate hung everywhere, along with assorted draperies and trim. The street vendors seemed to be in a competition as to who could be the most obviously patriotic, and even the ones who weren't going all-out would have at least a small flag mounted somewhere on their kiosk. Because it wouldn't do to not have anything. Folks might think you weren't patriotic, and you could lose business.

That reality bothered Joy, but the delicious smell of roasting meat from one of the street vendors drove that thought right out of her mind. Her stomach complained at her, so loudly that she was surprised when no heads turned to check out the commotion. Her donut breakfast was not sustaining her all that well. She wanted something hot and savory, and for a minute she mulled over the option of getting a simple meat-bun to tide her over—just one!

But no, she knew exactly how much money she didn't have in her wallet, and would continue to not have until she finished her ridiculous assignment. She was just going to have to tough it out until she made it back to her apartment for dinnertime. She had food there—stockpiled from a military surplus sale. She'd bought an entire pantry's-worth of canned goods: beans, preserved fruit, canned corn, canned tomatoes, packed tins of shredded fish and crab meat, and, uh...'Victory Meat.'

Victory Meat was another of Kallistrate's wartime industrial triumphs, specially engineered to alleviate food shortages. Victory Meat was... well, it was a square-ish tin containing a block of pink meat that was... ham, basically? It kinda tasted like ham. Ham-ish? Ham-adjacent? She was sure there were pig parts in there somewhere. Well, the point was that a sealed tin of Victory Meat would keep forever, and she'd been able to get stacks of it for cheap. And she had three huge burlap sacks on her makeshift pantry floor, surrounded by a minefield of mousetraps. One sack of dried noodles, one sack of uncooked rice, and one sack of potatoes. She'd been giving the potatoes priority lately, since some of them were starting to sprout. But anyway, all she needed to do was pick a staple, cook that, pick one or two of her tinned meats or veggies, heat those up, combine and add with a little salt and pepper, and you had a hot, filling meal.

It wasn't a great meal, but it was free (or rather, she'd already paid for it—same difference) and it didn't taste awful. Most days, it didn't. The monotony was the real issue. Her standard budget meal wasn't something to look forward to, but she'd found that waiting until she was really, really hungry before starting mealtime helped flavor her food like nothing else would. So by saving money and not eating now, she'd be making her dinner that much more awesome, ha ha.

Hahhh...

Gods curse it all to the coldest reaches of the Abyss—she had really been looking forward to some fucking pancakes today.

Joy shook herself and started rifling through her purse until she found her notebook. None of her bellyaching was going to solve any of her problems. She needed to focus. She found her notes flipped to the contacts she'd transcribed from Garai's mess into her own neat, precise handwriting. That was a key skill—there was nothing worse than losing a key piece of data because it was too messy to read. Who was closest? Joy found an address that, given the street name and house number, was an estimated ten-minute walk from here, listed as... Madame Zenovia, Medium Extraordinaire!

Joy sighed. Just reading the name caused an image to pop into her head: of a certain type of insistently credulous evidence-resistant person, a type that she'd come to know quite well after two months of working for the Gazette. It was exactly the sort of person she really didn't want to deal with today.

But no, she shouldn't think like that. That was pre-judging. Maybe this Zenovia person would be full of insights, and her story would be really interesting, and give her some solid ideas for her fake interview. That'd be fantastic, as Joy sure didn't have any ideas for that now. And maybe, just maybe, Madame Zenovia might have actually seen something real—something that could make a legitimately interesting story. It wasn't impossible, after all—just highly unlikely. As a reporter, keeping an open mind was important—but not so open that you let your brain fall out. Listen to everything, but try to verify everything.

Or, that would be the correct approach for a regular news story. This case was different. This time she'd be writing fiction.

Joy felt her spirits sink as she trudged past all the festive holiday decorations, feeling weirdly disconnected from the world around her. It felt surreal, this victory celebration. Maybe it was because, technically speaking, the war had never ended.

Granted, the remnants of Albion's grand army hadn't been seen in years, but Emperor Oberon had never issued a surrender, either.

Blame the 13th and their botched capture mission for that. They'd been ordered not to damage the palace, which was so ancient it pre-dated the Sidhe empire, and was one of the most iconic and treasured structures of the world. And they were not to harm the royal family, either. They were to be taken hostage and used to force a surrender from Emperor Oberon. That was the plan.

With the Terrestrial Royal Family dead, General Yagcha had lost the leverage he'd needed to force a surrender, and the remainder of the Albion troops began an organized retreat on a massive scale, fleeing to the northwest Nokomis coast, crossing the treacherous northern straits on huge naval transports to reach safety in the Hybrassil Islands, the ancestral home of the Sidhe and Emperor Oberon. What's more, the sea lanes going into Hybrassil were subject to horrifically violent and unpredictable weather. Albion mariners had some secret knowledge of dealing with this, which the KIB had spent years failing to discover. Without that knowledge, any naval invasion of Hybrassil was impossible.

So, instead of a decisive end to the war, the world was left with a stalemate. The Emperor never surrendered, vowing vengeance instead, both sides either unwilling or unable to continue the fight. Technically, the war was still going on even now, though President-Dictator Hardwicke had declared victory after the last Albion soldier had fled across the sea, and neither army had fired a shot at each other since then.

General Yagcha had retired his commission after the cease-fire, and removed himself from public life, refusing to give interviews.

His seclusion was frustrating for Joy as a reporter, but as a person, she found it admirable, and for the thousandth time wished that the Kallistrate Plenum had appointed General Yagcha as Dictator, instead of Hardwicke. The founders of Kallistrate had clearly intended for the Dictator position to be temporary — to be used only in the direst possible situations, for emergencies that threatened the Republic's very existence.

Unlimited power could only be trusted in the hands of people who didn't want it — people who'd drop it like a hot iron the very second it was no longer needed. It should never have been given to someone who was already President. What had the Plenum been thinking?

And, since hostilities had never officially ended, Hardwicke had never relinquished his dictatorship, claiming the emergency had never ended. The hypocrisy of the triumphant banners snapping in the summer breeze galled her. How could you hold a victory holiday while simultaneously insisting that the war was still on and we hadn't won yet? Make up your mind.

But Joy bet Liberation Day would've felt strange regardless. It was an all-consuming holiday that hadn't existed until three years ago. It had no traditions. Nobody had any warm Liberation Day memories from their childhood. Maybe it just needed time. Maybe in twenty years Liberation Day would be her favorite holiday. Not this year, though. This year she'd be skipping the parades and the street fairs. They'd only make her want to spend money she didn't have. She should stay in, work on her Specter story, and heat up something from her pantry. Hey, she could have a meal of Victory Meat on Liberation Day—that'd make her *extra*-patriotic, right?

Joy's route to Madame Zenovia took her right past the entry-way to The Golden Banquet, and she couldn't stop herself from slowing down just a bit and glancing through the large windows separating the diners from the street. She could plainly see the waiters and waitresses wheeling their little carts around with the baskets of steamed dumplings and various other goodies. It reminded her of when her parents used to take the whole family on day trips to Varvara City, and all the fun she'd had.

Varvara really had a way of leaving an impression. From the second you entered Rumi Janda Central Station, with it's palatial, soaring marble columns, every corner of the city contained something amazing. There was the museum district, or the walking tour of the ancient city-state's medieval fortifications, the famous aqueduct-fed fountain-gardens, the two-hundred-year-old original Xiatown district, and, best of all, the one month her parents had relented and taken them to Pika Island Fairgrounds, with the roller coasters, Ferris wheels, crane drops, haunted houses, and all.

Unfortunately, she had never been able to appreciate these trips as much as she would've liked—she had to keep her attention on the rest of her siblings. There were six of them besides herself, and, as the eldest, it was her job to help her parents watch out for the younger ones, and make sure nobody got swept away in the crush of all the other people swarming all over RJ Central. Because heavens help her if she actually lost track of anybody—she'd get such an earful for it.

But the finishing touch to any trip to Varvara City was dinner at the Imperial Plum. That was another order-off-the-cart-style restaurant, just like the Golden Banquet. Looking back, Joy knew it wasn't super-elegant or anything, but it had felt like high-class fine dining at the time. The main hall was airy and open, with huge mirrors on opposing walls that made it seem like it stretched on forever. Once they'd wrangled everyone into their seats around one of the big round tables, everything else was so easy. There was no waiting, just flag down a cart and pick something out. There'd be something for everyone, no matter how picky anyone was feeling. They'd all worked up some serious appetites, but the carts just kept on coming until they'd all stuffed themselves silly. Herding everybody back to the train station after dinner was always much easier than it had been in the morning. They'd gorged like such greedy little butterballs that they'd become docile sheep at the end. Dad liked to joke he could just roll them all home if they got tired of walking. Most of them fell asleep on the train headed home to Gortyn. Those trips had been so much fun, despite some of the aggravation that came with being in charge of the younger kids.

She wondered how they were all doing, her family. Mom's last update letter had been a few months ago, and—well… she hadn't replied to it yet. She really supposed she should. But— that would be such a hard letter to write. She would have to tell them about Quintus and getting fired. Just thinking about it made her nervous. Admitting that she'd gotten fired, even when it wasn't her fault. It felt shameful, not like her. She was the eldest, the model for the rest of her siblings. She was the one who helped everyone else fix their problems. She wasn't supposed to be the problem. And stressing over a letter home to Mom and Dad was always less productive than filling out another job application, or trying to turn one of her Gazette stories into something decent. It felt like this whole mess would be a lot easier to talk about after she'd already fixed on her own. There was no need to burden them with it, so she'd ended up not writing anything at all.

And that really wasn't acceptable—the bit about not writing anything. She should at least send a note or something. Letting them know she was still alive. Just a quick letter—it didn't have to include much detail. She could do that. After she'd finished her Red Specter story. So she could pay rent. The note home would be the first thing after that.

Lost in thought, Joy left the comforting scents of the Golden Banquet to fade away at her back as she trekked off to meet a witness to a phantom known as the Red Specter.

Chapter 18:

Meet the Medium

Madame Zenovia's office was a tiny little hole in the wall, extremely easy to walk past, if not for the gaudy sandwich-board sign propped up on the sidewalk, which said "Madame Zenovia, Aetheric Medium Extraordinaire, Palmistry, Aura Readings, Divination, and More!"

It did take Joy a while to decipher the sign, as the words had been painted dark green over a dark purple background, in an odd, swirly font that was supposed to look 'cosmic' or something, and the whole sign had been peppered with various mystical symbols from a dozen different religions, all outlined in gold, so they stood out more than the actual message of the sign.

Joy knocked at the door, waited a minute or two, knocked again, still no response. Joy stared at the door another minute or two, looking up and down for some notice listing Madame Zenovia's normal business hours, and finding nothing. Joy sighed and started checking her address list against her city map, trying to figure out if it'd be worth it to go to one of those and come back later, when she heard noises from inside. It sounded like footsteps.

Joy swung the brass door-knocker a third time and called out, "Madame Zenovia? Are you there? Hello?"

Finally, the door opened a crack and a suspicious brown eye glared out at her. "Who's there? What do you want?"

Joy switched on her friendliest, most inviting smile. "Hello, Madame Zenovia? I'm Joy Song Fan, from the Gazette. I'm here to listen to your story."

"What story?" The eye narrowed. "What are you talking about?"

"Um, excuse me," said Joy. "You *are* Madame Zenovia, correct?"

"Says so on the sign, don't it? Can't you read?"

Joy bit back a response about how it was possible for more than one person to live at the same address, and it was really hard to identify a person from just their eyeball. She needed to keep this on track.

"Good, then you're the one who saw the Red Specter down by the docks..." Joy took a quick glance down at her notes. "...Three nights ago."

The eye went wide. "How do you know about that? Have you been following me?"

Joy checked her notes again. "Um, you wrote it in your letter to the Gazette. That's why I'm here. I'm following up on that."

Joy tried to keep her smile as reassuring as she could, as it seemed like a single wrong word or gesture could spook the woman into slamming the door. This was surreal. Joy was not used to having anyone act afraid of her. She was five-foot-two and on the thin side—thinner than she liked, partially thanks to her "tins n' staples" diet—so the concept of Scary Joy was ridiculous. Just a tiny, inoffensive Xia girl come to see you—nothing to worry about here.

"Yes, I know the Gazette. Only paper in this town worth reading. That's why I picked them to get my letter. Still full of gossip and lies, though. Just last week, they had some idiot claiming that the Weeping Mithras was just a leaky drain. Can you believe that?"

"Really?" Joy said, grateful that she hadn't let Garai run her picture along with her article, like a lot of the regular contributors to the Gazette did. Score one for journalistic integrity. "Oh, I remember that story now," she said. "I'm pretty sure they fired that guy."

"Well, good."

The eye seemed mollified by this, but didn't move.

"So..." Joy said. "Would you like to tell me about what you saw?"

"Saw what?"

"Three nights ago, down by the docks. Did you see something strange?"

The eye turned hard again. "I'm not crazy!"

Joy kept her smile in place as best she could and took a long, deep breath, wondering if she was wasting her time here. And why would Madame Zenovia be so suspicious of anyone knocking on her door? Wasn't this a storefront? How did she run a business like this? Shouldn't she be greeting customers...

Ah! Joy got a flash of inspiration. "Crazy? Of course you're not. You're Madame Zenovia, the medium, aren't you? You have... special powers of insight, isn't that right?"

"Madame Zenovia sees much that is hidden." Was the voice a bit less wary? Joy thought so.

"Oh, that's great. You see, I'm in a real pickle and I could really use your help. I've been working on this Red Specter story and I'm completely stuck, as I don't really understand this, uh... aetherology or spirit world stuff at all. I really need some expert advice, from someone who really knows what they're talking about. Madame Zenovia, could you help me, please?"

The door clicked shut, and Joy's heart sunk for a second, until she heard the rattling of a door-chain to see Madame Zenovia's weathered tan face in full, as it peered her over speculatively.

"Not just stuck on your story," she said. "You're stuck in your whole life. Your aetheric aura is way out of balance. All green-shifted."

"Oh dear, it's green-shifted? Is that bad? And I really have been feeling stuck in my life lately. How did you know that?"

"Madame Zenovia sees much that is hidden. Your aura needs a full cleansing and rebalancing. I can take care of that. Come on in."

The rest of the interview proceeded on much more friendly terms, but not with any more coherence. This wasn't the first time she'd gone to see a fortune-teller. Aetherology was big in vogue, and had been for a while, so nearly every fair or festival would have at least one occult-ish divination booth or spirit channeler somewhere, and they usually had long lines in front.

Back when she was still attending Dodona University, one of her investigative journalism speakers had invited a guest speaker, the stage magician known as the The Great Phantasmo. When the class started she'd wondered what a stage magician could have to do with journalism. At the start of the class, he met with each student privately and gave them each a "crystal reading," meaning he waved a piece of blue quartz over her head while humming for a minute. Then he told them the results of the reading while they wrote it down. Joy didn't remember all the details of her reading, just the feeling of shock at its accuracy. Stuff like: "At times you are extroverted, affable, sociable, while at other times you are introverted, wary and reserved," which fit her pretty well. One bit stuck out in her mind: "Your sexual adjustment caused you some difficulty," which was a weird thing to have some strange man tell you, though it was true.

Her parents hadn't told her anything about sex, other than she was going to a good college—so she'd better not ruin that by getting pregnant. She had her future to think of, and she needed to set a positive example to all her younger sisters, who all looked up to her.

So she'd taken that advice—really, it was nothing she hadn't already decided for herself. But she hadn't counted on how difficult sticking to that resolution would be. She didn't date often, but now and then she'd get into situations where things got…heated, and remembering all that other stuff got difficult. There'd been one relationship she'd cut off entirely, because she'd gotten to the point where she couldn't trust herself. That had felt awful. Inessa had found her sobbing into her pillow in frustration, and when Joy had explained why, she'd given her a look like she'd sprouted another head. Inessa sat her down, and patiently explained to her that there were multiple forms of safe birth control, and the campus had a clinic that would hand them out to students for free.

Joy had been floored. All that stress and worrying and agonizing—over something that had such easy solutions, if only she'd known about them.

Anyway, Joy had been amazed that the Great Phantasmo could tell all that from a crystal reading. When the class lecture started up, Professor Gelfland asked everyone if they thought their crystal reading was accurate. Most hands went up, including hers. The Professor then asked for a volunteer to recite their reading to the class, and one young man, much braver than her, did so. When he did, Joy couldn't stop herself from bursting out laughing, for his "personal" crystal reading was word-for-word identical to hers, and to everyone else in the class. *Everyone* could be "extroverted, affable, and sociable" *sometimes*, while being introverted at other times. And, apparently, everyone thought they had problems with their sexual adjustment, even the guys. The trick was to use language that sounded specific, or deeply personal, but was actually vague as hell, and most people would fill in the actual details themselves.

The Great Phantasmo led the rest of the class, and demonstrated more feats of "spiritual power." He told people to pick a number at random and then told them what number it was— correctly. He brought out a "seance table," had volunteers link hands around it, and made it jump and "levitate." Some of the tricks he explained, (like the table trick—which was a matter of leverage, pushing on certain points on the surface of the table, sometimes sneaking his foot beneath the table leg to make it jump) others he didn't. The point to that was to demonstrate that, no matter how smart they were, they could be fooled by a trick they weren't familiar with. Extraordinary claims required extraordinary evidence to back them up, and should never be accepted uncritically.

In the Q and A that followed, the Great Phantasmo told them about how he'd gotten involved in debunking aetherology and related frauds. His wife had died suddenly a few years back— taken ill in Dodona during a rough portion of the war, and supply shortages left her unable to get enough of the medication they needed. After her funeral, he'd gone to the aetheric mediums seeking solace, only to be outraged when he found nothing but charlatans doing tricks that a trainee magician would scoff at.

Someone asked Phantasmo if maybe the mediums might be doing some good, if they gave grieving people some kind of closure. He admitted that was a difficult question, but all too often the aetherics wouldn't stop there—they'd use the emotional connection they'd forged with their victims to bilk them out of as much money as they could. And he'd found cases even worse than that: one family had gone to a medium to confirm that their daughter, a gunner for an Iron Crawler platoon who'd gone MIA, had definitely died. The medium said she had, and the family went into mourning, only to have their daughter interrupt her own funeral, still very much alive, after surviving a harrowing experience at a remote holdout POW camp. This was the danger of lying to people "for their own good"— though he felt that was giving these scammers too much credit. And besides which, wasn't pretending to speak for a deceased loved one the worst form of slander? We all hate it when people who don't know us make things up about us. We hate it worse when that gossip spreads and becomes confused with the truth. Now imagine how you'd feel, if you'd passed on, and some stranger began telling all your loved ones that you'd said and done things that you'd never had. It was awful. There were better, healthier ways to deal with grief.

The Great Phantasmo ended the class to a standing ovation, and Professor Gelfland had a terrific follow-up class the next week, talking about how a lot of what the Great Phantasmo told them applied to journalism, of how those same principles applied to investigating non-supernatural claims, or of dealing with vague, dubious claims from politicians.

So she hadn't been surprised that Madame Zenovia had accurately told her that she'd been stuck in her personal life. That was a typical starting point for most aetherics: like Phantasmo's crystal reading, it was broad enough that it could apply to everybody.

Joy followed the medium into her home. That was clearly what this was—a townhouse where the main living room had been converted into an aetheric studio. Black curtains covered the windows, shutting out the bright mid-day sun. The only light came from various candles set around the edges of the room, scattered about among all sorts of mystic-looking bric-a-brac: shelves full of mandalas and statuettes next to wall-scrolls covered with arcane-looking symbols from many different cultures and belief systems, mashed together with no apparent rhyme or reason.

The center of the room held a circular, three-legged table, covered by a deep red cloth, with an actual crystal ball on the center of the table. Joy sat across from Madame Zenovia, who instructed her to put her hands on the crystal ball, so the "aura cleansing" could begin. Joy started to comply, but something occurred to her.

"Wait, is this a service you charge money for? Because that's actually not why I'm here. I was interested in your story from three nights ago—"

Well, that didn't go over well at all. They went back and forth a few times, with Madame Zenovia claiming that her aura was "so green-shifted it was disturbing the spiritual field of the whole room." It was so bad that it was "blocking her connection to the aether." Joy found it awfully suspicious that Madame Zenovia needed an aetherial connection just to use her normal memory, but Madame Zenovia said this was the burden of being gifted as she was—you became sensitive to such things. Oh, and Joy's aura was getting worse by the minute, darkening to a putrid olive. This was clear signs of a curse. Madame Zenovia must fix it, or dire consequences awaited her. Joy breathed in and massaged her temples. Maybe her life really had been cursed. It would explain so much, though she doubted that Madame Zenovia could actually do anything about it. Never mind that she didn't have any money to spare on aetheric services, this was starting to sound like pay-for-play, and as a journalist, that would be a breach of ethics...

Ethics? Had she forgotten who she was working for? Journalistic ethics? Oh, that was hilarious. She cracked herself up—pretending like she was still a real journalist, even now. If she was going to dive into the gutter for pay, better go all in. Wasn't that the whole point of this assignment?

Joy wrote out the address to the Gazette office in her notepad, tore the sheet off, and handed it to Madame Zenovia. She could bill the paper—send it to the desk of editor-in-chief Garai Sekibo.

Madame Zenovia didn't seem too happy with that and started going on a tangent about the mystic connection created by the exchange of coin, a bond of great significance to the spirits, but relented when Joy explained that she didn't have any cash on her. It turned out the spirits could live with billing instead of coin. Joy got a small amount of amusement picturing Garai receiving a bill for an aetheric cleansing. Hey, it was a business expense, right?

Joy and Madame Zenovia both put their hands on the crystal ball, and Madame Zenovia began to guide her through the "aura-cleansing process." Joy was instructed to visualize her aura, a color surrounding her, a projection of her larger aetheric self, and to describe it to her. Joy did as she asked and was a bit surprised when something came to mind.

"I see it—it's this dark, splotchy bluish-purple, like a bruise. But there's something beneath it—it's a wide pattern of hairline fractures like in a cracked glass window. They're this angry, deep red—And they're pulsing, throbbing like blood through a vein, and—"

"No, no, no—that's wrong," snapped Madame Zenovia. "You're not looking correctly. I can see it, and it's dark green. It's the curse, fouling the vision of your third eye. Listen to Madame Zenovia, or you'll never get through this."

110

Joy swallowed her irritation and played along, forcing her visualization to turn green so she could get this nonsense over with. She remembered one question directed to the Great Phantasmo during his presentation: while he'd shown that some aetherics were definitely frauds, that didn't prove that every single one of them was. Could it be possible that a few might really have true spiritual powers? The magician admitted that he couldn't prove the total nonexistence of aetheric powers, but no medium he'd investigated showed any ability that couldn't be explained by either psychology or trickery. He *had* found a few mediums who seemed to genuinely believe their powers were real—and they tended to be terrible at their jobs, going off on their own delusional tangents, instead of cultivating and exploiting the delusions of their clients. Joy was starting to suspect that Madam Zenovia was this second type of aetheric.

The rest of the aura cleansing went smoothly enough, as Madame Zenovia filled the crystal ball with her own aetheric energy of clean light blue, like a cloudless summer sky. Joy was instructed to pull that energy into herself, feel it happen with every breath. There were other bits of business along with that, but Joy recognized what was going on here—a simple type of meditation, very similar to exercises she'd been led through at her Kovidhian temple growing up, only with more bells and whistles thrown on top.

At the end of the "cleansing," she really did feel better, and she thought maybe Madame Zenovia might not be so bad, though she still didn't approve of the fact that the medium was charging money for something anyone could get for free at a temple.

Joy wanted to get onto the interview, but Madame Zenovia wasn't done yet. Joy's aura was clean, but they still hadn't dealt with Joy's curse. That was still mucking things up. They needed to contact the spirit world to solve that. They held hands, Madame Zenovia began her reading, and said she could feel "three names coming to me: Wong, Tan, and Zhang. There's a strong aetheric connection there."

Well, of course—the medium had taken one look at Joy and picked three of the most common Xiaish names out there. The odds of her knowing someone with one of those names was pretty high. On a whim, she mentioned her "Yehyeh Zhang, the scientist and inventor who'd taken her in after she'd been orphaned at the age of eleven, and spent the rest of her reading by substituting the life story of Lilla Lemko from the Red Specter comics for her own. The spirits of the aether didn't notice. Joy struggled to keep a straight face, it was so ridiculous. But then Madame Zenovia went into a trance and began to talk to her "dead" father, never mind that he was still alive. And, was it her imagination, or did the phrasing of Zenovia's quotes from her dad sound a bit off? Just a bit sing-song-y, with some occasional broken grammar? Her dad didn't talk like that! The whole thing was so insulting. Then Madame Zenovia began to relate all these things from her "father;" vague warnings and predictions, nonsense instructions for removing her "curse," and then personal stuff—about how she was his only precious daughter, and he was so proud of her. This was disgusting. As Phantasmo said, the worst form of slander. It wasn't fooling Joy—but only because she'd been lucky enough to have met the Great Phantasmo, and come forewarned. What would this be doing to someone who really believed it? Joy had to tune out the medium's nonsense in order to remain calm.

She let Zenovia drone on in her fake non-accent while she let her attention wander to the mystical decorations about the room. Some of the symbols were Xiaish characters: earth, water, fire, metal, wood, spirit, and so on. Most were posted up in isolation, but she did notice one small sign that had an entire phrase. It stood out because it formed the centerpiece of its own little altar, surrounded by red candles and flanked by a pair of holy temple lion statuettes. The script itself was striking, the characters weren't so much written as sculpted—embossed to the point of bas-relief. They shone with metallic gold paint against a bright red background, surrounded by a border of more intricate patterns of embossed gold.

112

The sign said, "Service Entrance to the Rear."

Joy snorted, and had to bury her face in her hands to hide her hysterical laughter. She wasn't sure why that was the thing that got her, or that it was really all that funny, but she was cracking up and couldn't stop.

"There, there," said Madame Zenovia, rather woodenly, while patting her on the shoulder. "Contact with the other side can be painful, but know that your parents are always with you."

Joy nodded, grateful that sobbing and laughing could look so similar from the outside. She made a special effort to sound like she really was sobbing, but her own fake laugh-crying, and the fact that Madame Zenovia was totally buying it, only elevated the ridiculousness of the whole situation, making her crack up worse, so it was a while before she could regain her composure.

Joy wiped her tears from her eyes, blew her nose, and tried to get down to business finally, only to have her witness try to insist she needed to do past-life regression to get past her obvious trauma. Oh, come on! It was obvious that Zenovia was just trying to run up the bill. They went around in circles for a few times, until Joy insisted that she was too emotionally drained from talking to Yehyeh to do something as intense as visiting a past life, and maybe she could do that another time. Finally, Joy got Madam Zenovia to focus on what she'd come here for: the story of how she'd seen the Red Specter.

Chapter 19:

Spirit Walk

Three nights ago, Madame Zenovia had been performing aura-balancing and past-life regression for some "very important client, very confidential." The way she'd said it made it clear that Joy should find this impressive, but she'd clammed up when Joy asked for more details, citing "client confidentiality." That was a thing with aetheric mediums? She did mention they'd met in a "very ritzy, very impressive conference room in one of the hotels in the downtown theater district on Chontos Blvd.

Anyway, she'd finished up her work for Mr. Big Mysterious Client, but she wasn't quite done. She'd still been sensitized and attuned to the flows of the aether, wandered into a special "harmonic convergence of ley lines," and proceeded on a "linked aetheric spirit walk." She was particularly proud of this, declaring that she was the only person she knew of who could do it. All other aetheric mediums had to sit still in order to send their spirits into the aether, but she could leave her body while still maintaining control of it, walking it around like a dog on a leash.

That's what she was doing three nights ago, when she sensed a negative energy nexus down by the docks—a black vortex that threatened to disrupt the harmonic balance of the entire city, and it was up to her to put a stop to it. Her spirit flew across the city skyline, confronting the demons of Mara who scuttled across the rooftops. They were popping out of the energy vortex, a few at a time, but the portal was growing, and more and more of the demons slunk their way into the human world as it did. They trailed lines of darkness out of the vortex—not darkness as a mere absence of black, but a foul anti-light that stuck to everything it touched. The demons darted back and forth across the docks, not randomly, but in pre-determined patterns that traced out a mystic web that, when completed, would multiply the anti-energy of the vortex tenfold, creating a permanent rift for the demons to pour through forever.

Even as she watched, a great Demon Queen began to push its way through the black portal, though it didn't yet have room to make it all the way through, just two of its gargantuan arms—spindly, yet powerful, like an insect's, with wicked three-fingered claws at the end of each—and its bulbous head, which was mostly covered by a single compound eye. With every breath it took, it expelled a black miasma, and its pure malevolence was so intense that it hit Madame Zenovia like a punch, like a gale-force blast of wind, pounding at her through the aether.

So Madame Zenovia fought them, not directly, for that was not wise, but in a battle of weaving. She gathered to herself all the energy of the aether, aided by the native energy contained in the ley lines of The Great Wheel. They formed a new net of shining gold, and whenever it contacted the anti-light web, the darkness evaporated like shadows before a lantern. The demons were many, but she had power they didn't, and she felt it grow as her real body approached the docks.

She'd remained linked to it the whole time by a silver cord tethered to her navel, and as the cord shortened, her power grew. She'd reached the point where she'd covered most of the warehouse district in golden light, and the vortex's expansion had ceased, its evil energy pent up by the borders of her web, and the demons howled and gnashed their teeth, but they couldn't approach her mystic net, for its powerful positive aetheric charge would sear their otherworldly forms like a hot poker.

But then one demon, far more clever than the rest—it must have been a demon prince—it figured out a way to bypass her net. It flew down to the ground and into the body of a human, a man working at the docks, an innocent bystander whose limited senses did not even perceive the mighty spiritual battle raging over his head.

115

Clad in human flesh, he was able to approach her frail corporeal form without fear. The other demons saw the prince's gambit work and followed suit. The demons wearing human skin surrounded her real body, and she was powerless to stop them. They seized her and shook her, and she felt her astral body waver as her concentration did. A serious enough trauma to her real body in this state could sever the silver cord, and then her spirit would be forever lost, unable to return to her real body, wandering between the boundary of life and death forever. Such a fate was worse than death, and she fought down the instinctive, primal panic to end her spirit jaunt. If she did that, the whole city would be overrun. She had to finish the web first, but her concentration was shot. She felt the silver tether pull at her painfully, stretch to the point of snapping....

And then a presence flew into the midst of the possessed and scattered them. Madame Zenovia let her body slump against the wall of the alleyway, as her spirit-self poured a final surge of energy into her net, choking off the vortex until it was just a mere trickle, but closing that would require care, not brute force.

She wove the threads of light in a slowly narrowing circle, for the pressure behind the geyser of anti-light grew stronger as it was forced to pass through a tighter hole. She spared a glance back at the interloper who saved her, and nearly miswove her bindings, so surprised was she by what she saw. The human-riding demons scrambled about, trying to fight a new figure, even stranger than they. His head was a red skull with glass disks for eyes, he wore a long coat, wielded a short sword and shield, and most bizarre of all, he had no aura at all.

Here Madame Zenovia had to stop and give Joy an impromptu lecture about the universal nature of aetheric auras and how exceedingly strange it was for any being to not have one. Joy nodded, did her best to look impressed, and tried to prompt the medium to get back to the story. The last thing she needed was for Zenovia to lose her train of thought now, when she was finally describing something that actually sounded relevant to

116

her Red Specter story. Joy had sat through so much bullshit that it was straining her to the breaking point. If she had to listen to a repeat version of Zenovia's aether-weaving battle she was going to tear her own hair out.

Fortunately, Madame Zenovia did return to her story. Yes, the red-skulled stranger's lack of any kind of aura was truly unprecedented. It was as if he was not actually in the same world as the rest of them—like some kind of projection, except then there should have been a silver cord, or some similar trail leading elsewhere.

The stranger faced down the possessed dock-men and danced through their ranks, fading away one second to surge back and strike like a viper the next. The demons tried to use their numbers to their advantage, but the stranger was too nimble, and could fly up walls to escape them, only to dive down on their heads. He continued the dance until he'd smote every demon to the ground, though Madame Zenovia couldn't watch too closely, as she'd drawn her net of light around the vortex like a noose, strangling the Demon Queen as it thrashed its giant clawed arms. The mental strain of the exertion dizzied her. The whole world rocked and swayed like a ship in a tempest, as little red spots swam behind her eyes. The rift let out one final, desperate pulse of resistance, and she felt it collapse back to a tiny, pencil-thin hole, as it had been before.

Exhausted, she snapped back to her body, to see the glassy-eyed skull-man hovering over her, and though he'd saved her, she couldn't help but recoil as the impossible figure reached out to her, and she was terrified, for his lack of any type of spiritual presence was an even bigger affront to the universe than the demons had been, his simultaneous existence and non-existence confounding her senses. She didn't want him near her, but her throat was so sore, her scream came out as only the barest whisper. The stranger's presence expanded to fill her whole world, and she'd awoken in a horse-drawn cab outside her own door, as the cabbie helped her back to her couch, where she fell into a deep slumber and didn't wake until early evening the next day.

"And did you remember anything else about the Red Specter? Any specific details that stood out to you, besides the lack of an aura? Did he say anything to you?"

"What? What specter?"

Joy fought down her frustration. "The man with the red skull and glass eyes. You said—"

"That's not a specter. A specter would've had an aura—this stranger was something else."

"Oh, I understand that—I think. I was just calling him that because that's what everyone does. In the papers and the comics. The Red Specter."

"What? Comics? This isn't some joke. Don't be mixing matters of spiritual import with comic-book nonsense. Are you making fun of me?"

"Oh, of course not! I'm investigating the truth behind the legend—the person... spirit... whatever—the entity they based the strips off of."

"Name's all wrong," muttered Madame Zenovia. "A specter would have an aura. Don't put any stock in funny strips. Waste of time. An apparition like that is nothing to joke about."

"Well, they're not really joke strips—"

"Then why are they called *comics*? It's disrespectful, making jokes like that..." and Madame Zenovia went off on another tear, about the fools who scoffed at matters Beyond Their Ken, and how it would all catch up to them eventually, but the significance about what the medium had just said took a second to really register with her.

"Wait a second, Madame Zenovia—I just want to clear something up. Are you saying you don't read the Red Specter comic strip?"

"Of course I don't. I thought I told you—"

"But you read the Gazette, right? And the Red Specter comics run in the Gazette."

"I told you, I don't read comics."

118

Well, that was unexpected. Or maybe not. Joy had already talked to Madame Zenovia enough to realize how faulty her memory could be. She'd probably seen an image of the Red Specter in the Gazette while skimming past it and then forgotten about it. Anyway, her story was obviously delusional, but there were bits that seemed like they might intersect with reality. Maybe Joy could actually verify some of those. She asked Madame Zenovia if she could remember anything special about the cab or cab driver? Any names? Identifying marks? Apparently, the cabby had a strong, masculine blue and silver aura. Well, that helped a lot. The few physical details she got contradicted each other.

"Why are you going on about the cab driver, anyway? You're missing the most important part of the story. Are you sure you're a reporter?"

"I'm sorry," said Joy. "It's just that I'm still pretty new at dealing with these, uh... topics of advanced spirituality. That's why I need your help. What point am I missing?"

So then Joy had to spend the next half hour listening to Madame Zenovia expound at length on the topic of the mysterious stranger. (Apparently Madame Zenovia still didn't care for the term, "Red Specter.") She was convinced that the apparition she'd seen used to be human, some shaman of great power, who'd overreached, or been pushed past his limits—perhaps by a similar invasion of the forces of Mara—until his silver cord had snapped. This was catastrophic, certain to kill the shaman's physical body, and likely to shred his spirit to pieces, in the worst type of eternal oblivion. But somehow, the spirit-half of this shaman had survived, bereft of his body, and unable to find peace. He wandered the breadth of the Great Wheel in a state of limbo, neither alive nor dead, seeking justice or vengeance—who could say. Such were the dangers of astral travel, the risks that mediums like herself undertook for the good of all.

Joy nodded and jotted this all down in her notes, and tried to take it as seriously as she possibly could, until she was able to nudge the conversation back to the dock workers who'd assaulted her. Any memorable details or identifying marks about them? Would she be able to recognize any of them if she saw them again?

"What difference does that make?" snapped Madame Zenovia. "It wasn't them that shook me, it was the fiends possessing them that are dangerous. I could describe them if you like, but it'd do you no good. There could be one staring eye-to-eye with right now and you wouldn't see it, for all the sensitivity you have. You haven't the gift. I can tell these things."

"Oh, that's too bad. Then it's fortunate I have you to help me. But I wonder, would I be able to feel a demon's presence if it possessed me? Like, those men from the docks—do you think they'd remember anything from when they were possessed? If I could find one and interview him, maybe I could learn some more about what happened that night. Maybe I could even learn some of the demon's plans. Did you get a good look at any of the dock men from that night?"

Madame Zenovia peered at her a long time. "You're smarter than I thought you were. Might be hope for you yet. Stay here."

Madame Zenovia pulled herself to her feet and disappeared to a back room separated by a beaded curtain. The air was suffused with some kind of pungent incense. Joy had been able to ignore it before, but after being in here so long, it was becoming oppressive. She felt a dull pressure in her sinuses that was threatening to turn into a headache. Her stomach squirmed around in a weird way. She wasn't sure if it was nausea or just hunger. One of the small tables along the wall held a tarnished tea set, along with a few small tea cakes arranged on the platter. Joy couldn't help wondering how long those cakes had been there, whether they were still edible, whether they were for guests or not, and whether it would be acceptable etiquette to help herself without being explicitly invited.

"You want some?" said Madame Zenovia, stumping back into the room. "Go ahead. They'll get stale otherwise."

120

Joy crunched into one of the cakes. Yeah, it was a bit late to stop them from going stale. She didn't stop eating, though. That would be rude. Plus, she found that if she sucked on it the dry, cake-like material in her mouth enough, it'd start to moisten and dissolve, enough that she could get it down. She hoped her poor stomach wouldn't punish her for this later.

"It was dark that night," said Madame Zenovia, "So I didn't get a good look at those dock-men. Was using my second sight to get around. But during the struggle, I grabbed something off of one of them. And when I woke the next day, what did I find clutched in my hand but this—" And with a big, dramatic flourish, Madame Zenovia slapped an oblong piece of metal into Joy's hand.

Joy stared at the object, which could be best described as one half of a patterned metal eggshell. Smooth on the concave side, patterned on the convex side, Joy wasn't sure exactly what it was. It could've been an amulet, but she didn't see any spot to attach a cord or chain. It was too big and the shape was too odd for it to be a coin, but it was too small to be a belt buckle. And the design on the convex side was like nothing she'd ever seen before.

It was a picture of a very strange figure. Its head was some bizarre cross between a parrot's and an octopus', except it had three eyes on each side of its beaked, oblong head, and they were each on their own jointed stalk, like the eyes of a crab. Tentacles fanned out from behind the head like a ruff, twining across the borders of the piece, and Joy noted that while most of them were regular octopus tentacles, some of them terminated in five-fingered, almost human-looking hands. Below the head was a humanoid torso with lobster claws instead of arms, and below its knees the legs transformed into two separate fish-tails.

It was naked, and very male. There were all sorts of religions across the world who had gods with animal aspects to them, but Joy couldn't remember seeing one that looked like this one. Usually they weren't so creepy.

Well, that was a bit rude of her. There were all sorts of faiths practiced by various peoples throughout the former Albion Empire, some of which could have some rather odd traditions, but just because something was strange, didn't make it bad, necessarily. Still, she shuddered at the idea of people worshipping the creature on this medallion-thing. It was just too strange. The eyes, especially. Cold and blank, with too many sets all pointing in the wrong direction. There were faiths that worshipped gods with animal heads, but the eyes were always human. This thing was grotesque. It had to be some sort of adversarial figure, like a demon. But why carry around an embossed image of something like that?

Well, whatever it was, it was the only piece of physical evidence from Madame Zenovia's grand spiritual adventure. Joy asked her if she could keep it, and Madame Zenovia offered to sell it to her for a hundred dollars. Oh, for the love of....

Joy flipped over a fresh sheet of paper in her notebook, pressed the object between the pages, and rubbed her pencil over the top sheet. The end result was a passable copy of the image, though the curved surface of the amulet made for a bit of distortion on the rubbing. Now it looked even creepier. Joy tried to hand the amulet back to Madame Zenovia, who recoiled at the sight of it.

"Get that thing away from me, it's tainted—cursed. Can't you feel it?"

Joy stared at her. "But I got it from you. You were just trying to sell it to—"

"Like I'd keep something with that in my house? You need to get rid of it, right away. Ill fortune will follow you everywhere if you don't. Take a boat into the middle of the ocean and hurl that thing into the sea. Then burn all your clothes and scour your skin with salt. Then come back to Madame Zenovia. I can cleanse your aura from your curse-sickness. I can see it now. Putrid olive green."

Joy gave up. "Yes, I'll definitely do that," she said, and tossed the weird demon-medallion into her purse before taking her leave. "Thank you so much, Madame Zenovia. I really appreciate your taking the time to talk to me. And for... um, saving the whole city from that Demon Queen."

"Not just the city, most of the Kallis Coast," declared the medium. "You sure you don't want more tea-cakes? They'll go stale if nobody eats them."

Joy stared long and hard at the two remaining bricks of dry sandstone that Madame Zenovia referred to as "tea cakes." Her stomach was of the opinion that they technically counted as food, and there was room for more. Joy thanked her host, wrapped up both cakes in a handkerchief, tossed them in her purse, and made her escape to the outside world.

Chapter 20:

Taking Stock

Joy found a bench nearby and took long, deep breaths of the clean air outside, trying to clear the incense from her lungs. Even though she'd spent the past hour sitting, she still felt exhausted. She'd wrapped those tea-cakes up for later, but her stomach asked her why she was bothering to wait, and she had no good answer. She crunched down on one of them while flipping through the names and addresses of the remaining "witnesses," and wondered if the rest of them would also be nuts.

Joy still had no idea what to make of Madame Zenovia. At points it seemed like she really believed what she was saying, but Joy had caught her using blatant con-artist tricks, too. Was it a case of mental compartmentalization? Con people to pay the bills, because that worked better than her "real" stuff?

Speaking of mental compartments, how much space did Zenovia even have? During the whole ordeal, there'd been stretches where she'd seemed lucid and cognizant of what was going on, and other points where she seemed unaware of what had happened the moment before.

And yet, she seemed to function well enough—she was apparently able to run her psychic business, despite having one of the worst methods of greeting customers Joy had ever experienced. And certain things seemed to stick in the medium's mind—she'd never gotten confused about who Joy was, or why she was visiting. And somehow she'd managed to write a coherent letter to Garai about spotting the Red Specter, even if she'd forgotten about it later.

Actually, Joy really wanted to see that letter now, to see if it actually contained the words "Red Specter," since Madame Zenovia didn't use it during their interview.

Thinking about the state of Madame Zenovia's mind made Joy feel guilty for some reason. Maybe she was being too harsh to an old woman dealing with senility, apparently alone and abandoned. That could happen sometimes, and it pissed Joy off.

How could anyone just toss their parents aside and shirk their responsibilities like that? Granted, she could easily imagine how dealing with someone like Madam Zenovia on a daily basis would be draining. There'd been days where having Gramma Euh-Meh around the house had felt confining, on top of Mom and Dad and all her siblings, but that was family. You had to do right by family. Granted, the Fan family had been lucky—on Dad's side, anyway. Every one of them had survived the Great War. There were a lot of families that couldn't say that, and Joy knew her parents were grateful for it. Dad made sure to give thanks at every family gathering, ever since that first Liberation Day, that all of them were still there.

Maybe Madame Zenovia hadn't been so lucky. Maybe she didn't talk about her family because they'd passed to the "other side" themselves. Maybe Joy could've looked past her own irritation to show more concern for a lonely old woman suffering from dementia.

Joy had a sudden impulse to get back up and knock on Madame Zenovia's door—take a closer look and see if she was okay. But another thought delayed her. Something about her assumptions nagged at her… old woman with dementia. How old was Madame Zenovia, anyway? Joy tried to remember details of the medium's face. She actually wasn't remembering much in the way of wrinkles. Why did she assume she was old? Was it the way she dressed, with the elaborate headscarf and all those layers of flowing fabrics she wore? Had it been the way she walked? The more Joy thought about it, the more uncertain she felt. Madame Zenovia could be anywhere from early forties, to—heck, who even knew? Joy knew how unreliable appearances could be when determining someone's age—Joy was twenty-six, but sometimes she had people mistaking her for a teenager.

But what did it matter, anyway? Even if Madam Zenovia did need some type of material help, Joy was in no position to offer it. She could barely take care of herself. That was just the cold reality of the situation. That was why she'd come out in the first place. She needed material for her article. So, what did she have?

Joy flipped through her notes from the session, as her jaw worked to grind down the stubborn tea cake, and felt her spirits sink. "A shaman of great power" who'd "let his silver cord snap." This was just like her story about Kiona the dragon-girl princess. (With a tail!) It was nothing like the comic. It wasn't what people expected or wanted to hear. She could already picture Garai giving her the lecture. That whole interview had turned out to be a complete waste of time.

Joy gave herself a minute to feel disappointed before getting back to business. Persistence was a reporter's best friend. You had to keep plugging away at every lead until you finally got the one that broke the big story. Joy checked the remaining three addresses against her city map. Two were within walking distance. The third was way off in the northwest corner of the city—she probably wouldn't be able to get to it today. Joy headed off to the first address, which turned out to be an ugly, dilapidated rowhouse with boarded-up windows.

Chapter 21:

The Soler Family

Joy knocked on the door and yanked on the pull-chain for the apartment number, to no avail. She double-checked the address against her notes, then pulled out Garai's original paper, to make sure she hadn't made some kind of transcription error. This was the right place. Joy tugged on the pull-chain again, then tugged on the ones for the other three apartments, just to see if she could find anyone to talk to.

After ten minutes of this, she had to admit defeat. Either the building was abandoned, or everyone was out. She moved on to the next address, another rowhouse—but this one was in much better repair.

A tired-looking woman with a baby on her hip answered the door. Joy introduced herself and asked for the name on her list, a Thiago Soler. He did live there, but he wasn't in.

"Said he needed to get out, be by himself—away from the kids," she said. She wasn't sure when he'd be back. Probably really late, maybe past midnight.

"You don't know when he'll be back?" Joy asked.

The woman pulled away from her, her expression guarded. "This time of year is really tough on him. This Liberation Day business. It reminds him of his brother. They were in the same unit, you know. Thiago saw him go. That would be rough on anyone, wouldn't it? Well, wouldn't it?"

"Yes, of course it would," said Joy, silently cursing at her foot-in-mouth disease. Two sentences in, and already she'd created a hostile interview. "I'm sorry, I didn't mean to imply anything. I just wanted to schedule an interview, and—"

"Mom! Mom!" A small, dark-haired little boy bounded into view and started tugging on the woman's skirts. "Mom! Mom!

Rosa won't stay on her side of the couch. She keeps bothering me, and I told her to stop, but—"

"Did not!" An even smaller girl, otherwise a mirror image of her brother, stomped into view, face screwed up in righteous indignation. "I was not on his side."

"Was so!"

The woman tried in vain to explain to her kids that mommy was busy and she'd get to them in a moment, but they were unconvinced. This matter of territorial incursions into mutually agreed-upon zones of non-aggression on the living-room couch was a matter of the utmost seriousness, requiring immediate dispensation of justice from the sole available officer of the peace. Could she not see that? Was she going to be negligent in duties? Joy could see that said peace officer was about ready to lose her shit, so she decided to offer some emergency mediation.

Joy leaned over to bring her head down to their level, and favored them with her brightest smile. "Oh, look at this! What an adorable pair of children. Hello there, you little cuties. What are your names? My name's Joy."

Both of them ceased their pleas for arbitration and stared at her, noticing her for the first time. Rosa was able to say her name, though she had a hard time looking right at her, sort of squirming around while she talked, with her hands behind her back. The boy wasn't able to do so well. He retreated to the safety his mom's skirts, peering out at her from behind her leg. His mom had to answer for him. His name was Mateo.

"Well—Rosa, Mateo—how'd you like to play a little game with me?" Joy didn't bother to wait for an answer. She'd already been digging through her purse for the hook. "If you win, you know what happens? You can get a special lucky coin."

Joy produced the quarter, and both sets of eyes locked in on it. She had them. "Okay, the game is called 'Who Can Stay Quiet the Longest.' You need to put your hands over your mouths, like this...."

Joy demonstrated, and they both copied her, attention held by the lucky quarter. "Good job! Now you just stay like that, and don't make a sound. And whoever does that for the longest time wins the game and gets the lucky quarter. But that's not all! Because guess what?"

Joy thumbed another coin from her palm out into view. "Today I happen to have *two* lucky fortune coins—and if you both manage to stay quiet for long enough, you *both* get a quarter. Sound good?"

They both nodded, and Joy pretended to start the timer by glancing at her wristwatch. If they'd been her younger siblings, she'd have used something cheaper and more creative than a "lucky fortune coin," but this would do in a pinch. Anyway, the mom, whose name was Kanda, seemed much friendlier now, and was able to answer some questions, thanks to the quiet game. Joy made sure to periodically jingle or flash the quarters in her pen hand, to keep the kids' attention on the reward. She'd really prefer it if they both managed to win the "contest."

But back to business: Thiago had enlisted immediately after the call went out, very early in the war. Now he worked hard in one of the steel refineries, commuting upriver every day on the ferry to the northern edge of Dodona. He'd told her about seeing the Red Specter, down by the docks. He'd been standing on the roof of one of the warehouses, a dark outline against the starry sky. Then he'd leapt from rooftop to rooftop, until he'd actually taken flight, soaring in a long, graceful arc, until he sunk out of view behind some buildings a few blocks away. Thiago and his drinking buddies had taken off into pursuit, only when they'd gotten close to the point where they'd seen the Specter drop out of sight, they'd heard crashing, yelling, and even a gunshot or two, and had wisely turned around and ran the other way.

Joy found the claim of gunshots rather startling. Shouldn't something like that have been in the news? Well, maybe it had— Joy had a hard time forcing herself to read any of the Dodona newspapers these days, though she knew she was only hurting herself by doing so. Joy asked for more details about the man Thiago saw on the roof, but Kanda didn't have any. She'd have to ask Thiago that next time he was home.

"You said he was out with his drinking buddies when he saw this?" Joy tried to put as much of a neutral, nonjudgmental tone to the question as she could. Kanda had already shown that this was a touchy subject for her.

"Yes, and if you're asking if he was really seeing straight—I don't know." Kanda looked more defeated than angry now. "You should know—this wasn't a problem before the war. Those gas masks—I don't think they stop everything. Sometimes he gets the shakes—I've seen it—and a shot of whiskey is all that stops the...."

Kanda trailed off, glancing back to her two young children, standing with covered mouths, but wide-open eyes and ears. Mateo noticed the adults were looking at him, and Joy saw his hands come off his mouth. She gave her coins a sharp jingle, reminding him of the game, and he clapped his hands back in place, quivering with alarm over his near-fatal blunder.

Yeah, there was a limit to how long you could run the "let's-be-quiet" game with kids their age before their patience ran out and they exploded like overheated steam kettles. Joy glanced at her watch and pretended to count down.

"Three... two... one... Dingdingdingding!" she said, throwing up her arms. "Congratulations! You both win. Yaaaayyyy!"

The kids cheered and bounced around the foyer, though they had to settle down for Joy to hand them their prizes. Kanda prompted them to say thank you to the nice young lady, and they did.

"Now, let me tell you a special secret about these lucky fortune coins," said Joy.

"There's a way to make them even luckier. Want to know how? You go find a spot—it should be somewhere in your house—that's a special place that only you know about. Under your pillow will work, but if you can find someplace even more secret, that's even better. That's how you get the best luck, and you want to do it right away."

The kids nodded, and both ran up the stairs, where Joy guessed their rooms were, the whole dispute over the Great Couch Incursion all but forgotten. Joy figured that'd occupy them for at least five minutes, maybe more.

That left the adults to talk about adult things. Joy was able to confirm that Thiago was drinking way more than anyone should, but it really did sound like it was partially in response to some type of chronic condition that'd he'd developed during the war. Joy suggested seeing a doctor at the Veteran's Hospital—maybe they'd have some medicine for his "shakes" that worked better than whiskey.

But they'd already tried that. They'd gone in, filled out some forms, and been told to expect a reply in four months. That had been six months ago.

"Six months?" Joy couldn't believe it, but Kanda was adamant. Thiago's symptoms weren't bad enough, they said. Thiago retained all of his faculties. He could move around on his own. He could go to work at a factory every day. There were others who weren't so lucky, who'd been left permanently paralyzed by the Hemlock Gas. They would be treated first. Thiago would have to wait his turn.

So, what could they do? And, there were reprieves—times when it wasn't so bad. But right now, they were running up to the anniversary of Matias' death. Yes, that was his brother, and little Mateo was named after him. They'd all been so close. If the situation had been reversed, and Thiago had been killed, she would've married Matias instead. Thiago would've wanted that. The years went by, but it didn't feel like it was getting any easier. It was so hard sometimes.

Joy was at a loss for what to say. She remembered back to her time at the KIB, seeing a pamphlet for state-provided mental counseling for veterans. She tried to bring it up, but Kanda got annoyed with her again. Thiago wasn't crazy!

Joy had a hard time explaining how this kind of mental coun-seling wasn't just for crazy people. As soon as the words left her mouth she realized that was the wrong way to phrase it. Maybe she'd be able to find one of those counselling pamphlets for when she came back in three days at seven o'clock in the evening. That's when Kanda thought Thiago would be available to talk. Mission accomplished, sort of, and Joy managed to part on good terms.

Joy began to walk back the way she came with no particular destination in mind. She felt a twisting in her stomach, a sense of dread that had been rising ever since she'd left Madame Zenovia's. What was she supposed to do now?

Chapter 22:

Echoes Of War

She had one name left on her list. She wasn't going to get to it today, and tomorrow was a holiday. She wanted to get this story done, but she didn't see what more she could do now. She had an anxious sense that her actions were being judged; that she was being watched. The feeling was strong enough that she even looked behind her to see if someone was following her, but of course no one was.

She stared down at that last name and address and sighed. Would they even be home tomorrow? Or would it be another abandoned building? That would be a long distance to walk for nothing. Joy felt her heart sink at the thought of it. She knew she needed to check. Real journalism was something like ninety percent perseverance, sifting through dozens of false leads until you got the one that broke the whole story wide open. She knew that, but right now she was finding it next to impossible to summon the energy for any of it. Not for this stupid story.

Joy tried to occupy her brain by reviewing the interview with Kanda. Actually, there was a lot to unpack here. Joy wasn't sure what Thiago's "shakes" were, but they sounded serious. Certainly they were bad enough to be seriously affecting his home life—making him turn to drink to numb the symptoms. And to be kept waiting for over six months to see a doctor about it? Outrageous! Certainly, priority should go to veterans suffering from paralysis, but that was no excuse to not treat veterans like Thiago at all.

Was the Veteran's hospital so badly overwhelmed? Well, if so, they needed to pour more resources into it—hire more doctors, expand their facilities, even add new locations, if that's what it took. It wasn't like triumphant Kallistrate was hurting for money.

Poor Thiago and poor Kanda—Joy couldn't stop wondering about his "shakes." What were they? Kanda claimed it had been the hemlock gas, and that could be possible. As far as Joy knew, although Kallistrate scientists had figured out countermeasures against the Rosedeath—gas masks and an emergency antitoxin cocktail—they still had no idea what it actually was. No one had ever managed to gather a sample of the stuff. Even if you siphoned it into an airtight container, it would disappear in a few hours. Not dissipate, not break down—disappear, leaving no trace elements behind. That was supposed to be impossible, but it happened again and again. Who knew what the effects of long-term exposure were.

Or maybe the "shakes" were a psychological problem. Joy had seen first-hand how the state of someone's mind could affect their health. Take her weeping statue story: that veteran had been adamant that he felt worlds better after the statue "took his pain from him." Of course, there were limits to the power of suggestion. It couldn't regrow a leg. But the implications were profound. Thiago had lost his brother in the war. He'd seen it happen. What might that do to a person, to see your own family die in front of you? Could it make you physically ill, to the point where you got seizures, or panic attacks?

What if the circumstances of Matias' death had been especially tragic or horrific? It wasn't like horrific deaths had been uncommon in the Great War, especially towards the end. Golems, mines, new types of high-powered artillery and rapid-fire weapons, all deployed in hostile cities with cramped streets where you had no idea who was an enemy and who wasn't. Prolonged exposure to that level of stress, day in and day out—what could that do to the mind of a human being. The "shakes" were probably the least of it—just the most obvious symptom.

Thinking about it gave Joy a twinge of guilt. She'd never had to go through anything like that herself. The Kallistrate military had determined that she'd be best suited shifting through intercepted communications in foreign languages, safely behind

134

a desk at the KIB. She'd been prepared to take on a riskier position, like a field agent or something. She'd mentioned that to her family, and Dad made a huge show of how relieved he was to have her out of danger. "That just shows how Central really knows what it's doing, Joybear. They figured out that if they let you anywhere near the front, you'd get it into your head to try to slay a dragon single-handed, and then you'd get eaten, and then where would we all be?" That got a huge laugh from the rest of the family, though Joy didn't think it had been at all funny. She wasn't a reckless kid any more. She was very sensible and level-headed.

June had served too, but she'd entered service towards the end of the war, and she'd been a medic. Medical personnel were rarely targeted by anyone, since they had a policy of treating the injured on both sides of the conflict. June had come through fine.

Kane had also entered service towards the end of the war and hadn't actually seen much fighting. According to him, his unit's average "engagement" had been to roll into one town or the other and accept the negotiated surrender of the local garrison.

Dean's service had been far more harrowing, crewing one of the armored "Spikefruit" cargo ships in the Kallistrate navy. That had been terrifying because death could be so sudden and random. One of Albion's Sea Dragons could surge up from beneath the waves at any time, at point blank range, and torch the entire ship, along with its crew. Kallistrate's only counter was to create cargo ships that doubled as floating grenades. The iron spines on the spikefruit ships would blast out, mortally wounding any dragon who ignited their shaped charges, but it wouldn't save the crew from being cooked alive. Kallistrate could make that trade-off. They could replace ships and crew faster than Albion could raise new dragons. But no-one could replace Joy's brother.

Joy had a hard time envisioning the courage involved to crew one of those ships, knowing how it worked and what would happen if you got attacked, and still saying "Yes, sign me up."

But thousands of sailors had done it anyway. One time she'd tried telling Dean how brave he'd been, and how proud she was. He'd gotten embarrassed. He didn't want to accept any praise. He said he didn't think he was brave. He didn't like to talk about his experience much, other than to show her some of the pages in his sketchbook—drawings of his convoy and the sea, taken from the crow's nest, or detailed renderings of the ship's interior. Joy knew his convoys had been attacked multiple times, but each time some other boat had been the target.

That had been a relief for Joy and the family. They'd been so lucky. But now Joy was starting to worry about Dean. He must've had to watch his fellow sailors drown, or be burned alive, helpless to stop it. She wondered if Dean ever got "the shakes." And if he did, would he be able to see a qualified doctor about it?

And that soldier who'd gone to the Mithras statue—was it possible he'd done that because the Veteran's Hospital hadn't been giving him adequate treatment for his phantom pain? She'd been so focused on the "miracle regrowth" part of the story that she'd neglected to check on that angle. The more Joy thought about it, the more she suspected that there were quite a few Thiagos and Kandas out there—people still suffering from the after effects of the Great War, and Kallistrate was failing in its responsibility to care for the men and women who'd sacrificed so much for the good of the nation.

This was a real story, with real consequences and import. This was one of those times where a real, dedicated journalist could expose the truth and make a difference.

Too bad there wasn't anybody like that here. Ms. Joy Song Fan was busy tracking down some ghost sightings to pay her rent. No one in Dodona was going to accept a serious, important story if she was the one writing it.

It left a bitter taste in her mouth. It was so hard to stay enthusiastic about creating a plausible fake interview with a ghostly folkloric figure who barely spoke, when there were these other issues that demanded attention running around her brain. Kovidh's meditations were supposed to help you deal with out-of-control thoughts and help you stay present, but Joy found they weren't working so well for her right now.

She decided to just relax and let her brain do whatever. Her bench was in the shade and a sudden breeze brought some relief from the oppression of the hot summer air. All the Liberation Day flags and banners fluttered in response. Joy noticed that this street had a lot of posters dedicated to various heroes of the revolution, rendered in the new art style a lot of these posters used, bold and simple: Partholon Hardwicke, General Bonami Yagcha, members of the 13th Steam Golem Company, the Red Specter and his crew, and....

Wait, what? Joy sat up and double-checked to make sure she wasn't seeing things. She wasn't. She was staring right at a poster depicting the Red Specter, posing heroically in the background, with Lila, Baz, Kolton, and Dr. Zhang in the foreground, gazing up with admiration. This was a bunch of fictional characters being posted and lionized in the exact same manner as a bunch of real ones. Was this a prank?

Joy walked up close to the poster so she could compare it with the regular ones, and had to conclude that if the Specter poster was a forgery, it was so skillfully done that it might as well be official. Why would anybody do this? And were there more of these posters around town? If so, that could explain all the Red Specter sightings right there.

Well, maybe for Madame Zenovia, it did—one of those posters could have filtered in through her psychotic break, to mix in with her hallucinations about demons running rampant, but Thiago had claimed to see him standing on a rooftop, silhouetted against the night sky. That couldn't have been a poster.

And it was interesting that both Thiago and Madame Zenovia had reported both a Red Specter sighting and some kind of large fight (with gunshots, even?) three nights ago at the docks, by the warehouse district. Actually... Joy checked her notes from

"Trench," which said, "night before last," in the same area. But when had Garai interviewed him? If it had been yesterday, that would line right up. It could easily be a coincidence, and that still left a huge area to cover, but still—was there any reason not to do a quick canvas? Just head down to the docks and ask around—see if anybody saw anything? Because it really did seem like something strange had happened. All she needed was one good, detailed account of it. Maybe it would even provide a useful context for Madame Zenovia's ravings, and that weird amulet-thing she'd found. The Red Specter comics did seem to occasionally veer into some spooky-mystic territory, like during Diamond Jang's Dreamtime trip. Maybe she could wring something useful from that interview after all.

And it wasn't like she had anything better to do today. Might as well make use of all the daylight hours of high summer. Yes, she had to think positive. She was going to get a break, and she'd use it to turn in the most entertainingly garbage-tastic piece of nonsense Garai had ever seen, and then she'd do it again on the next story, until she'd earned enough to quit the Gazette, and leave this city for a better one, whose serious newspapers weren't infested with misogynist creeps and their enablers, so she could finally start her life for real.

She headed off back down towards the docks, her resolution gaining a new level of urgency as she passed by the Golden Banquet again, the smell of hot, sweet, and savory food hitting her like a wave. Joy had to grit her teeth and think of the future, a time where she had a secure paycheck and would never have to settle for Victory Meat again.

Chapter 23:

The Magic Lantern

Joy got on 5th Street and made it all the way to Chontos Blvd before she decided to take another break. She could've kept going, but it made sense to pace herself. It felt so good to sit down and stretch her legs out. She was wearing the wrong shoes for hiking all over the city. She hadn't been expecting to be doing any legwork today. She'd been hoping to turn in her anti-Hardwicke rant and take the rest of the day off. Ideally, she'd have been using pedi-cabs to cover this distance, but that wasn't in the budget right now. Even the fares for the cable-trams were too much. The only cost to walking was time and energy. But her supply of those things wasn't unlimited either, and the fact that she was getting hungry again wasn't helpful. Joy remembered that she still had Madame Zenovia's last tea cake, but as hungry as she was, she wasn't that hungry yet.

Thinking of Madame Zenovia reminded Joy that she had to be pretty close to the starting point of the medium's "spirit walk." Joy wondered if she'd have any chance of retracing Madame Zenovia's steps if she headed to the docks from here. As soon as the thought crossed Joy's mind, she spotted a potential landmark, about a half-block down from where she'd been sitting. She got up to take a better look at it. There, in full-color glory, was the Red Specter himself. He stood ten feet tall on a theater billboard for the "Legend of the Red Specter" Magic Lantern show.

Magic lantern shows were the latest rage—traditional shadow puppetry mixed with new materials and analytic-engine techniques. It used a powerful electric lantern beamed through a diorama of translucent acetate cutouts to project a moving image onto a huge screen at the front of the stage: a window into another world.

But Joy recognized something about the Magic Lantern that most people didn't; it was actually an outgrowth of military technology used to create a pilot simulator for steam golems. She'd gotten a taste of it in one of her supplemental courses—the final boss in a simulated mission, designed to "kill" the trainee to teach them to respect just how complex the golems were, and how difficult piloting them was.

Joy had spent two months on that course, mostly studying a manual and taking turns on a "dummy table": an elaborate mockup of a steam golem control console, before getting one chance to do one simple mission on the simulator, running it in gimp mode. "Gimp" was short for GMP: General Mobility Protocol, a setting that allowed one person to run most major functions of the steam golem, albeit in a limited and sub-optimal way. Normally a steam golem ran with a team of three: Pilot, Gunner, and Combat Mechanic. GMP was for driving a steam golem around base, from one hangar to another, or for emergencies where the Combat Mechanic had become a casualty. Joy came out of the experience with a sense of awe of the skill of a real golem crew. She'd had enough trouble mastering the gimp controls—she couldn't imagine dealing with the full version—which was more complex by several orders of magnitude.

Joy stared up at the huge poster of the Red Specter and wished she could afford a ticket. She'd heard that the Magic Lantern productions kept getting more and more advanced. Freed from the restrictions of building generic scenery that had to constantly adapt to input from a pilot, the designers could focus their energies on making specific elements look as cool as possible. Apparently, there were portions of the show where the hand puppets would be replaced by an acetate reel with hundreds of individual paintings of the character, that scrolled across the screen at such high speed that it appeared to be moving, like a flip book or a zoetrope, only better. She'd really like to see that, even if it was for a cheesy Red Specter story.

140

It had just started this week, and would be running for the next three months, at least. The show didn't start until eight PM, and the tickets didn't go on sale until four, which was… in ten minutes, according to the clock above the box office. Already there was a huge line stretching outside the front of the theater. Part of that had to be holiday traffic, but still, people seemed really excited to see this show. Joy wondered if maybe she could find room in her budget for a ticket after she got paid for her story. She decided that the answer was no. Money coming in from freelancing was too unreliable. She had to save in the flush times to prepare for the lean times. And she had to save up enough to pay for her relocation. She couldn't forget that.

And she couldn't forget why she'd come here in the first place. On a whim, she went up to the box office to ask if anyone there had been working the evening shift three nights ago and had seen someone matching Madame Zenovia's description walk past at any point. It was a bit of a long shot, but a woman decked out in a bright headdress and tons of gaudy costume jewelry wandering around talking to herself might leave an impression. The answer was yes, one of them had seen her, but it took a while to reach that point.

First Joy had to listen to the attendant's spiel about how tickets weren't on sale yet, and anyone under the age of sixteen would need a parent or legal guardian's permission to see the show. It had annoyed Joy enough to slap her military ID up against the glass, even though it didn't matter, since she wasn't buying a ticket. And the attendant (who was certainly younger than Joy — she'd bet ten cans of Victory Meat on that point) didn't have much useful to add, other than he'd seen a strange woman matching Zenovia's description acting weird and wandering off on Chontos heading south.

Joy stomped away from the box office in a terrible mood, wondering if the meager diet she'd been on lately was to blame for being mistaken for a teenager. That had been the third time this month.

Joy knew there were some women who would love to look younger than they were, but she hated it. Growing up, she remembered flipping through her mom's fashion magazines, during her meager downtime between studying and watching over her siblings, looking in awe at the gorgeous, sophisticated, curvy women displayed therein. She wanted to be like them someday. But, at twenty-six, she had to face the truth that she'd done all the developing she was going to, and she'd fallen way short of her intended goal. Mom said that her breasts would get bigger when she got married and had kids, but Joy didn't find that comforting at all. Why did she have to wait to get boobs until the point in her life when they'd be the least fun to have? The way things were now, she had a nagging fear that she was unintentionally attracting pedophiles. Ew.

Speaking of which, Joy realized that her angry haze had distracted her from noticing some guy trying to get her attention. He was being persistent about it, too. Well, that was the last thing she needed right now. She was about to ignore him and head off to the docks when a hand clapped down on her shoulder. Joy whirled around to tell this creep off, and found herself staring face-to-face with Professor Gelfland, her favorite teacher from Dodona university.

Chapter 24:

Professor Gelfland

Professor Gelfland was a huge cuddly bear of a man squeezed into one of his appropriately stuffy tweed jackets, despite the summer heat. He had a slightly squashed bulbous nose, an infectious smile, and eyes that radiated intelligence.

"Oh! It's you, Professor," she said, letting out a sigh of relief. "Hello. It's good to see you."

"Good to see you, too. I'm sorry if I startled you, but you seemed lost in thought, and I didn't want to miss the chance to catch up with one of my best students."

"Oh—thank you, Professor," she said, though the compliment felt odd, like it applied to someone else. She felt a weird disconnect from Joy the academic. That Joy had been competent and successful; nothing like the person she was now.

"But I'd give any credit there to my teacher," she said. "And speaking of which, how's that been going? Any more disrespectful kids giving you trouble?"

"Nothing I can't handle," he said. "But how about you? I remember you were going to start up with the Journal, right? How's that treating you? Flynn hasn't been giving you a hard time, has he?"

Joy felt the whole world drop out from beneath her feet. He didn't know. He hadn't heard. Whatever social club had been used by all the Dodona editors-in-chief to blackball her didn't include her old professor, or at least they hadn't mentioned it around him.

And now she had to explain it? The whole embarrassing mess? She didn't have time for that now, or the energy. She was right in the middle of something, and if she had to stop and explain the entire story, about getting assaulted and then getting fired for being assaulted… Well, it could lead to a messy sobbing breakdown right in the middle of the street, with a huge line of people as witnesses. Already she could feel the wave of emotion bubbling up, threatening to spill out of control. She had to put a lid on it. She couldn't deal with this now.

"Oh… No! He hasn't… well…" Joy struggled to organize her thoughts. "I'm… I decided the Journal wasn't the best fit for me. I'm freelancing now."

"Oh, I see," said Professor Gelfland, although she thought he looked a bit confused. "Well, that's got its upsides. You definitely have more freedom that way. Have you sold many stories? Anything I might've heard of?"

"No, um… nothing you'd have heard of," said Joy. Because if there was one thing Professor Gelfland had always emphasized in his classes, it was the civic and moral duty that journalists had: to serve as watchdogs for the Republic, to keep the public informed and hold the powerful accountable. She'd loved that about his classes. But there was no way she could tell him that she was freelancing for the Gazette, not without going into her whole sordid backstory.

"But enough about me," she said, "What about you? How have you been? Any major changes since I left?"

"Fortunately, no," he said, looking relieved. "For a while there was this push for all textbooks to require certification from one of Hardwicke's agencies—not for accuracy, but to screen for "dangerous ideas.""

"Ugh, that's awful," said Joy. "But you said it didn't go through?"

"Fortunately, there are still some folks in the Plenum with enough guts to stand up to Hardwicke's overreach, and a few newspapers with the guts to report on it," said Professor Gelfland. "We dodged a bullet for now."

…but who knew if they would the next time. He'd left that bit unsaid, but Joy could fill in the blanks. She felt another twinge of guilt. She hadn't heard anything about this. She hadn't been

144

paying attention. She was so wrapped up in her own problems that she'd lost track of the rest of the world. That wasn't like her. Something had gone wrong with her. She didn't feel like herself any more. She hadn't felt like herself for months.

"Joy, are you feeling alright?" Professor Gelfland asked. "You look a little out of it."

"Oh, It's... It's nothing," she said. "I think I'm getting a little hungry. I haven't had much to eat since breakfast."

"Well, I'd be happy to treat you while we catch up, but then I'd lose my place in line, and I wouldn't expect you to wait for food until we get our tickets, because that could be a while."

"You're in line for the show, Professor?" Said Joy.

"Of course," he said. "Going to see it with my son, Hugo."

Joy looked over to where he was pointing to see a tow-headed kid far back in the line waving back at them. She smiled and waved politely.

"Well, that makes sense," said Joy. "Is he looking forward to the show?"

"Not as much as I am," said Professor Gelfland.

Something about that startled Joy more than anything else that had happened that day. "Professor Gelfland! You're a Red Specter fan?"

"Is that surprising? It's a very popular comic," he said. "And, you know Joy, you've graduated already. It's okay for you to call me Dan."

Joy ignored his suggestion, too blasphemous to even consider, and focused on the first bit. "Well, Professor, I know that it's popular, but I didn't expect something that cheesy to be popular with you."

"Professors aren't allowed to enjoy cheese?" He said, eyes twinkling. "I never agreed to that. It doesn't say that anywhere in the faculty handbook. I checked. Specter fandom isn't limited to just young people like you."

"Me? I'm not a Red Specter fan."

"Eh? Then what were you checking at the box office?"

"Oh, I was researching a story." The words popped out of her mouth before she had a chance to think.

"A story? Like, for the entertainment section? Interviewing the cast and crew?"

"Ah... no. This is..." Joy had a burst of liar's inspiration. "This is for a fictional story. A short story for a magazine."

Actually, that wasn't stretching the truth too far. A good number of the Gazette's front-page stories were so over-the-top ridiculous that she had a hard time believing that anyone took them seriously, even the Gazette's readership. She suspected that a lot of people bought the paper purely for laughs. She hoped it was most of them.

"Oh? I didn't know you wrote fiction, Joy," sad Professor Gelfland.

"Well, this is a bit new, so I thought I'd try my hand," she said. "But the magazine said they specifically wanted a story about the Red Specter, so I'm trying to do some research on that—like what the character is about, what the audience wants from a Red Specter story."

"Hmm..." said Professor Gelfland. "You know, that's not a good approach for fiction, or any kind of writing, really. It's best to write what *you* want, so your voice comes through. Otherwise—"

"Well, great, but my *voice* is telling me I need to sell a story if I want to pay my rent this month," Joy snapped. "Following my bliss or whatever sounds great, but I'm gonna have a hard time doing that if I'm out on the damned street lugging my typewriter around in a rucksack, now aren't I?"

Professor Gelfland withdrew as if stung, and Joy had to collect herself. "Oh, I'm sorry, Professor. I've been in a rotten mood lately, and—"

"No, no—it's my fault," he said. "You know, you get tenure and you build a nice comfy nest in academia, and it's easy to forget how it is for young people out in the real world. Of course your rent takes priority."

146

"Thank you," said Joy. "Sorry."

"No problem," he said. "You should see how cranky I get when I'm hungry. Say, there's a bunch of decent sandwich shops around here—why don't you grab a late lunch and meet us back here. We can get tickets for the show, and maybe it'll give you ideas for your story. My treat for the lunch and the tickets."

"Oh! Thank you... but I'll have to pass," she said.

Both those things would've been fantastic under other circumstances, but hanging out with her old college professor right now meant she'd have to be lying to him the whole time. It would ruin everything.

"I still need to check out some Red Specter sightings down at the docks while it's still light."

"Sightings? People have seen him?"

Joy winced. "Well, some people *think* they've seen him. What they've actually seen is anybody's guess. But it does seem like there was... some sort of incident by the docks three nights ago. Probably it wasn't really the Red Specter, but... I don't know... I just—"

"Well, you never know," he said. "Maybe you can get a story idea from whatever happened. That's how the Red Specter folklore got its start, before it became a comic."

"Oh, really? The real-world sightings of the Red Specter actually did start before the comic, and not the other way 'round?" Garai had said as much, but Joy had every reason to doubt him as a reliable source.

"Oh, definitely. That's been confirmed many times over," he said, with a level of confidence that killed any doubts Joy might've had. Professor Gelfland wouldn't repeat information if it hadn't been credibly sourced. Actually, this could be a real opportunity.

"You sound like you've done some research on this, Professor," she said.

"Well, folklore is a hobby of mine. And the Red Specter is a very special type of folklore."

"Special, how?" Joy asked, while pulling her notebook out of her purse. "Actually, is it okay if I pick your brain for a bit, Professor Gelfland?"

"Sure," he said. "Well, I'd say he's special because he's the first mythic hero of Kallistrate."

"Hmm?" That sounded odd to Joy. "How would he be the first? Dodonus or Jul Varva have been around for hundreds of years, at least, and—"

"Ah, but those are heroes of the Kallis Coast," he said. "They don't mean anything to a Strata farmer or a Goriack highlander. But the Red Specter is a hero of Kallistrate, the entire country."

"Oh, I see what you mean now," said Joy. Kallistrate was a new country, cobbled together from a patchwork of historically independent city-states, squabbling feudal lords, and barbarian tribes from the north. And the Kallis cities were even more diverse, populated by all sorts of ethnic groups whose cultural roots went elsewhere, to Xia or Axum or Zipang or Kosstan or someplace even more remote. Interesting.

"It's because he's associated with the war, isn't it?" Joy said. "The one major event that everyone in Kallistrate went through."

"That's it exactly," said Professor Gelfland. "His costume is a gas mask and the trench-coat of a Kallistrate infantryman. Without the war, neither of those things exist. And answer me this—what ethnic group does the Red Specter represent?"

"Well, that's..." Joy had been about to say that he must be a Kallisian, the light-haired, pale-skinned peoples who'd founded the Kallis cities and settled all of Strata, but no sooner had the thought crossed her mind than she realized the problem with it. "We don't know. We never see his face—well, I didn't in any of the strips I read. Is that true for all of them?"

"Yes, that's consistent throughout the series," he said. "You never see his face. So, not only does he represent the whole country, he could literally be anyone. There's no one in Kallistrate who couldn't see themselves as the Red Specter."

148

"You mean, there's no *man* in Kallistrate who couldn't see themselves as the Specter," corrected Joy. "We women are stuck with Lilla Lenko."

"Ah... yes, you've got a point there," he said. "Uh, you don't like Lilla?"

"She's nice enough, but she never actually does anything. She just stands around watching the guys, just killing time until she gets held hostage and has to be rescued. Who'd wanna be her?"

"Oh," said the Professor. "Well, Shiori is a powerful character, and—"

"Yes—and she's naked and evil," Joy retorted. "Those are my choices?"

"That is true," said Professor Gelfland. "Well, do you like any of the characters? It's going to be hard to write a Red Specter story if you don't. Which is your favorite?"

Her favorite? Joy hadn't even thought about that. She ran through the cast list and found each of them falling short. Lilla was a wuss, Kolton was a milquetoast, Baz too stoic, Dr. Zhang too old. The Red Specter had his moments, but he was so absent from from his own series that he was barely a character. Really, if she had to think of a fun character, one who stole every scene they were in, it'd have to be...

"Ugh. Shiori Rosewing would have to be my favorite, if I have to pick," she said. "Because she's the best character. Not because I'd ever want to be her," she added, in response to her professor's raised eyebrow.

"Well, you're not alone. Shiori is really popular, for various reasons," said Professor Gelfland. "It's a big part of what I'm looking forward to in the Magic Lantern show. They're saying that the actress who plays her is a blast; just tears the roof of the place."

"Well, yippee," said Joy, though that actually did sound like fun. She kinda wanted to hear what that OH HO HO laugh sounded like. But Joy found the whole turn of this conversation disquieting, like they were doing something wrong. It took her just a second to realize what it was.

"Isn't that a problem, though? That there's this character called Shiori Rosewing who's this fun sexy villainess who everybody likes?" Joy said. "Shiori Rosewing is a real person. A mass murderer and a war criminal."

"Well, I can see that," he said. "But that's what we have historians and reporters for—to give future generations the ability to separate myths from reality."

Which was the opposite of what she was about to do. Joy felt her spirits sinking, but Professor Gelfland didn't seem to notice.

"And when Shiori Rosewing first appeared in the comic, she was very different from the character you see now. She was vicious and humorless and not nearly so sexy. All those attributes developed over time as she became more popular. I can actually show you."

Professor Gelfland opened his rucksack and pulled out three books, slim at their spines, but the covers were broad and tall—tabloid-sized. A familiar gas-masked figured gazed up at her, beneath the title: *Adventures of the Red Specter*.

Joy flipped it open to find row after row of the newspaper strip, conveniently laid out, with no need to keep flipping through page after page of unrelated news stories. And what was more, every single strip had been colorized, not just the Sunday ones. And even aside from the color, the art looked much better here, crisp and clean—the result of using higher quality paper, as opposed to cheap newsprint. This would've come in handy earlier.

Joy flipped through the pages until she found Shiori's first appearance, though Joy didn't recognize her at first—her face was pale, not red, and she was wearing a fantastical suit of armor. She and the Red Specter were fighting a duel high in the Cloudkills, on a plateau surrounded by a sea of pink gas flowing down towards unsuspecting Brentonsville. The Specter won the duel, impaling Shiori through the gut. Mortally wounded, she fell off the plateau to disappear into the gas, cursing the Red Specter as she did.

150

The Specter flew off to warn the city, but Shiori wasn't done. A vision of a Sidhe witch appeared before her. She said her name was Morrigan, and she could grant Shiori new life and new power to continue to fight in service of the Emperor—but at the cost of her immortal soul. Shiori agreed, on condition that she be allowed to wreak vengeance upon the Red Specter, and the deal was struck. The witch cast her spell, the vaporous Hemlock Gas flowed in through the cracks of Shiori's armor, dissolving her old body and leaving an empty suit of plate armor behind like a discarded shell. The gas coalesced into the familiar red-skinned figure, with her slinky black evening dress, only most of it was still there.

"Wow, they didn't shy away from Brentonsville at all with that origin," said Joy.

"Well it makes sense," said the Professor. "That was where the largest number of Red Specter sightings happened, and that's where his legend really took off. There are even a few photos."

"Photos? Really?" Joy hadn't heard that. "Have you actually seen—"

"Front of the book," he said. "In the Introduction."

Joy found what he was talking about. She frowned. "These are awfully blurry," she said. She supposed that if you squinted, you could make out a figure with a trench-coat, and a shadow that resembled the Red Specter's forked pole-arm. But this was hardly conclusive evidence.

"I've heard that they've invented cameras that can take decent pictures on just a second's worth of exposure now," said Professor Gelfland. "But even without that, there were quite a few eyewitnesses who claimed that the Red Specter visited them and warned them to evacuate the town—high profile civic leaders, too—the mayor, the chief of the town guard, major religious leaders. Most of them recanted later, but not all."

"Do you think they really saw what they claim?" said Joy. "I remember how the Great Phantasmo warned us about how people's perceptions can be fooled. Could it have been mass hysteria?"

"That's definitely possible. The biggest counterargument to that is that someone had to have ran through the city warning them of the oncoming gas cloud. That part has been confirmed. My theory is that it was actually a group of people that did it, likely a Jagdkommando or other special forces unit."

"I guess that's plausible," said Joy. "Is there a Jagdkommando unit that paints their gas masks red?"

"Not that I know of, but you know how much the Hardwicke administration loves secrecy," he said. "So, there could be one, but it also means my theory is going to remain speculation for now."

"Ah, too bad," said Joy. She went to hand the book back to him, but he offered to let her borrow them, as research for her story. She liked that idea, but the books were too big to fit in her purse, so she got his address to pick them up later. "Any other juicy Red Specter rumors I should know about?"

"Well, I don't know if this helps your story, but there's one conspiracy theory about the Red Specter that I actually find plausible: that the Red Specter comic is actually government propaganda."

Joy snorted at that. "Propaganda? Really, Professor?"

"You don't think so?"

"It doesn't read like propaganda at all," said Joy. "It's not... real propaganda is easy to spot. It's super on-the-nose. Sure, there were a bunch of pro-Kallistrate themes in the stories I read, but nothing outside of normal patriotism."

"Yes, it's subtle," said the Professor. "And maybe it doesn't meet the formal definition for propaganda. I just can't think of another term to describe it. But it is consistent with how Hardwicke thinks. Most tyrants revel in crude bluster and overblown self-aggrandizement. They have to, in order to whip up the mob. But Hardwicke knows how to work within the system—and he doesn't need to bluster. He demonstrated his strength by defeating the greatest empire in the history of the world. And one of his greatest strengths is his ability to get the best work out of talented people—even people who would normally be against him. I think Mr. Avakian might be a prime example of that."

"Okay," said Joy. "But I'm hearing a ton of speculation here and no evidence."

"I was getting to that," said the Professor. "You know how popular the comics section of the newspapers has gotten. There are even some people who buy the papers primarily for the comics and barely glance at the actual news."

"What?" Joy said. "You can't be serious."

"Not flattering to our profession, but I assure you, it's true," he said. "So it makes sense for each paper to try to cultivate their own, exclusive comic strips to draw in readers. But there's one strip that runs in every major paper, and most smaller ones— tabloids, magazines, even some specialist and hobbyist rags. Guess which one it is."

"The Red Specter?" Joy said. "Are you saying these papers are all being pressured to run the Specter comic by the government?"

"Oh, no—nothing like that. No coercion is needed. Because any periodical publication that's been in operation for at least six months can obtain the rights to publish the Red Specter for free."

"What, really?" Joy said. "You've confirmed that, Professor?"

"Of course," he said, "It's no secret either. Check this out."

He handed her one of the compilation volumes and asked her to note the price, printed on the back cover.

"Five dollars!" she said. "For a hardback with color printing? That's insane."

"Only if you care about making money," said the Professor. "If your goal is to distribute your message as far as possible, it makes perfect sense."

"But that's a huge expense," Joy tried to mentally calculate all the money lost on an operation like this. "Well, I guess it could be a government agency secretly bankrolling it, but it could also be some eccentric industrialist as well. Wouldn't that make more sense? I think Hardwicke's got more important things to worry about than comics."

"You could be right, but this actually does fit in with some of Hardwicke's obsessions about forging a unified national Kallistrate identity. Case in point: Liberation day coming up tomorrow—a brand-new holiday, associated with the war, that applies to everyone, not just specific ethnic groups, like the Kallisian Jolner festival or the Xia Lunar New Year."

Joy was about to argue that both those festivals seemed perfectly unifying to her. She'd grown up with Jolner presents around the tree every winter solstice, and everybody turned out for the lion dance parades at the Lunar New Year, with tons of blonde Kallisian and dark-skinned Axumite kids running around with red envelopes of lucky money. But then she remembered her trip up to Knittlefeld. Yeah, she couldn't picture any lion dances up there.

Liberation Day would encompass the entire country. Joy paused to take in all the holiday decorations covering the theater district, the banners and flags in red and gold. Who was paying for all this? Joy wondered if Knittlefeld and other towns out in the Strata countryside had perhaps received a shipment of similar decorations, with patriotic posters of Kallistrate's war heroes. Including one of the Red Specter and his crew, just like the one she'd seen before?

This whole business was making her head spin, and more importantly, she didn't see how any of it was going to help her fake an interview. "Ugh, so that's the secret of the Specter's popularity, then? Just cheap, widespread war propaganda?"

"Oh, heavens no," said Professor Gelfland. "If that was all there was, I sure wouldn't be spending my Sunday waiting in line for tickets to see a show about him. It's a great story with a great character."

"Great character?" Joy found that description odd. "Well, the stories are fun in a pulpy kind of way, but in the stuff I read he was barely a character at all. He just shows up at the end as a deus ex machina, saves the day, says a bunch of cryptic, spooky lines, wraps it up with his catchphrase about nothing escaping

154

the Red Specter's wrath, and runs off. Is there more to him in the earlier stories?"

"Hmm... well, not really—in the sense that the formula you've described doesn't vary much throughout the series," he said. "With this type of pulp, what makes it good isn't the same as a literary novel—it's the way it can tap right into the heart of the hopes and dreams of an entire culture. And I think the Red Specter succeeds there, to a phenomenal degree."

"You mean with the supernatural-slash-ghost thing?" Joy asked. "Like, I guess that's in tune with the aetherology craze that's been going on lately. Is that it?"

"Well, that's related, but I'm speaking to the underlying cause of both these things."

"The war," said Joy, and as soon as she said the words she realized how obvious it was. "A lot of good people were lost, a lot more were injured or permanently maimed, and even more families and loved ones were left behind with their grief. So you're saying that reading Red Specter comics is a way to help people deal with that?"

"That's part of it, but there's still more," said the Professor. "Tell me, from the parts that you've read, can you tell if the Red Specter character is actually a ghost? Is he alive or dead?"

"Umm..." Joy played all the details of her morning reading binge back through her mind. "I'm not sure. He kept spouting a lot of nonsense about how he's both and neither. Didn't make any sense to me."

"Oh, but it does make sense. In fact, that's the point," he said. "Because it's not just grief that people are dealing with—it's uncertainty. Because in addition to all the soldiers listed as killed, a huge number of them were declared MIA, and have stayed that way for years. Remember when I said that it could be anyone behind that mask?"

"Oh—I see," she said, as everything fell into place. "And that anyone includes those who are alive, dead, or missing. Caught between life and death and all that. But he's not suffering... well, maybe he is… but he's continuing on as a hero, not as something pathetic or malevolent, like most ghosts. And if you're one of those people who's lost someone, just the concept of a lost spirit who fights for justice, that could be a comfort—just the idea that it's possible."

"That's it," said Professor Gelfland. "You always caught on quick."

Joy thanked him, but her old teacher seemed lost in thought, and a weighty silence descended over their conversation.

"Your family didn't lose anyone, did they?" he asked. "I think I remember you mentioned that once."

"Yes, we were lucky," she said. "I knew some people who died, back from my high school. It was sad, of course, but they weren't close friends. How about you?"

"My family is small, and most of us were either too old to fight, like me, or too young, like Hugo," he said. "I just had a lot of talented students who never came back. I'm glad you weren't one of them."

"They put me safely behind a desk doing translation," said Joy. "No dangerous secret agent business for me." For some reason, that sentence came out sounding much more bitter than she'd intended.

"Secret Agent Joy?" Professor Gelfland was grinning now. "Don't they have a height requirement?"

She knew he was just teasing, but something about that rankled her.

"Hey, don't laugh," she said. "In a different lifetime, I could've become a Caliburn Knight."

She saw his eyebrows raise incredulously, and kept going.

"I'm serious. We had a quite a few summer trips to visit my mom's family in Suiren, and there wasn't anybody who could touch me on the Caliburn courses," she said, referring to the extensive obstacle courses, erected in every city of Albion by the Empire, where aspiring young knights could hone the skills that would allow them to pass the real trials held every year in Cistonia Stadium. "I could blast through them, backwards and forwards, faster than anyone."

"Really," said Professor Gelfland. "Now, that's something I never knew about you. I hadn't realized you were such an athlete. And I—oh, wait…"

He paused, looking back towards the ticket line. "Hugo's waving. He looks annoyed—and he's right; we've been leaving him out. You should let me introduce you and we can continue the conversation with him."

"That sounds nice, but actually, I should get going while it's light," she said. "You can introduce me some other time, maybe when I come over to borrow your Red Specter books. And thanks for that insight into his character. It's going to be really helpful for my story."

"Good luck with that—though let me make one suggestion," he said, "If you're writing pulp, you might want to use a pen name. If you do decide to return to journalism—and I definitely hope you do—you won't worry about any anti-pulp writer prejudices hurting your career."

Joy's mouth dropped open. A pen name! That was brilliant. She'd use a pen name. Why hadn't she done it already? Well—of course, because journalists don't do that. But that was her whole problem—that she still imagined herself a real journalist while working for the Gazette. Garai wouldn't care about what name she used. Why would he care, so long as she produced a good story? "Professor, thank you! That's a great idea," she said, and hugged him.

"Oh, no problem," he said. "That's what we elders are here for. Tell me your pen name when you think of it. I'd like to read your story."

"Uh… sure, when I think of it," said Joy, "Though I don't think you actually want to read it. I don't expect it to be any good. Just collecting a paycheck until I can save up enough to move."

"You're moving?" Professor Gelfland asked. "Where to?"

"Not sure yet," she said, feeling a rising urge to escape as the conversation veered onto dangerous territory. "Someplace where it's not... not so competitive. I need... I need a break, that's all. Just have to save up a bit first."

"Well, if money's an issue, why I don't I just loan you some?"

It felt like the whole world dropped out from beneath her. "What?" was the best she could manage. "You can't do that. It's too much. You can't... waste your money on—"

"I won't be wasting anything. This is an investment. And a good one," he said. "The real waste is someone with your talent grinding away at something she's not passionate about."

"No—I... I'm sorry. Thank you, Professor. I have to go. Enjoy the show. Goodbye!" And Joy fled the scene as fast as she could, lest she have a complete breakdown.

Chapter 25:

Joy Is A Liar

A few blocks later, Joy stopped speed-walking at a shady alcove with white marble pillars. She leaned back up against one of the pillars and took long, deep breaths, until she could deal with the reality of what a bunch of warmed-over garbage she was.

She couldn't believe she'd done that—stood in front of her favorite teacher and lied through her teeth. She lied about what she was doing, who she was working for, and for a while she'd imagined herself to be so clever at hiding it. "Yay, pen name!" Now she could do an even better job of concealing how she was betraying every sacred value of good journalism that Professor Gelfland had taught her to cherish. And, at the end, he'd offered her money. Said it was a "good investment."

What a joke. Her?

She should've told the truth. Right from the beginning, she should've owned up to what happened. Why hadn't she? Because the thought made her nervous? Really, what did she think Professor Gelfland would say?

She remembered their conversation. "Flynn hasn't been giving you a hard time, has he?" That was one of the first things he'd said, jokingly. The expected answer was "no," or "working hard, learning lots," or something. Flynn Hartmann had been one of Professor Gelfland's star students who'd made it big. He'd recommended him to her and vice-versa. Professor Gelfland had known Flynn for years longer than he'd known her. If she told him that Flynn had been a moral coward and a shit boss, would he have really believed her? Or would he make excuses, say she'd gone too far in defending herself from assault. Would he ask her what she'd been wearing?

Joy had to quell another wave of anxiety, mixed up with hefty doses of panic and despair. Lir's balls, why was she still like this? Some asshole tried to shove her into a broom closet and she'd decked him and gotten fired and that had been months ago so why oh why was she still acting so fragile? Was she going to let that ruin her life forever? She needed to toughen up. Rise above. Don't let the bastards win.

The anger gave her a spark of energy, enough to climb out of the cauldron of boiling emotion and put the lid on, though she still couldn't rid herself of any of it. Standing around feeling sorry for herself wasn't going to help her with anything. What had she just learned? She could use a pen name to protect her reputation for the future; she wouldn't have to torch the Gazette's archives when she quit. Yippee for her.

What else? Someone, maybe the government, was pushing the Red Specter character so hard that they were willing to do it at a loss. Interesting, but did it help her story? Not that she could see. Maybe those compilation books could help, but, even as ridiculously cheap as they were, she couldn't spare the funds to buy them. She still had the Professor's address, and she could try to swing by later and borrow his, but, aside from the potential awkward disaster that could turn into, he'd already told her that the Red Specter's character wasn't going to be significantly more developed than in the stories she'd already read.

But that was by design. The Specter's character was kept intentionally vague, so people could subconsciously project themselves or their lost loved ones into him, and if that was true…

…If that was true, then the whole idea of trying to corner him for an interview was misguided. A good interview dug deep into the heart and mind of its subject, drawing out specific, memorable details about their lives. But any specific detail she revealed about the Red Specter's character would lessen his appeal. People would read her story and come away feeling dissatisfied, even if they couldn't say why, because whatever details she invented were sure to fall short of their projected hopes and dreams. She'd

160

be revealing how the magician did his trick, which even The Great Phantasmo wouldn't do, not even to prepare them against frauds. "All I'd show to you is that magicians are blatant liars, neither as skilled or clever as you imagine," he'd said. "I'd ruin magic for you forever, and I won't be responsible for that." No, leave that task for Ms. Joy Song Fan.

So, the assignment was impossible, after all — or impossible to do well, which was just as bad. She was being set up for failure, yet again. She leaned back against the pillar and put her head in her hands. What had she ever done to deserve this? Was she being punished for something she'd done in a past life or something?

Lately it felt like the whole world was conspiring against her, looking down and judging. Joy felt a prickle down her spine, like someone really was watching her. She snapped her head up, looking around at the milling Sunday crowd, but nobody seemed to be paying her any mind.

Well, of course they weren't. Everybody was occupied with their own business. They had better things to do than mess with her. The world wasn't out to get her. It just didn't care about her, one way or the other.

So, if that was how it worked, why should she care, either? Why was she killing her feet and driving herself nuts running around for this stupid damned story, or for anything. It was garbage fake news — everything she didn't believe in, and the story would flop anyway, no matter how much work she did, and she was so tired, and fed up, so maybe she should pack it in, and admit defeat, instead of —

No! By every misbegotten abomination of the Abyss, no freakin' way!

Once again, a hot undercurrent of rage came to her rescue. It blasted through her mind and cleared out a heavy fog, one that she hadn't even realized was there. The entire street scene snapped into a heightened focus — scents became sharper, sounds became crisper, colors more vibrant.

And her mind snapped into gear, like an analytical engine that had just been fixed. And her mind told her that she could never quit.

If she quit, they would win. They could never say they'd beaten her as long as she didn't give up. She wouldn't let them win—not Quintus, nor Flynn, not anybody who'd ever doubted her and told her she couldn't do something. She didn't care how rotten and nonsensical this stupid Red Specter story was—she was going to finish it and she was going to get fucking paid and she was going to leave this lousy city and find a real newspaper where she could do real news and she was going to become the best fucking reporter that Kallistrate had ever seen.

Something weird had really happened down by the docks three nights ago, and, as a reporter, she was going to find out what it was—for the sake of practice, if for nothing else. Then she would track down Thiago and the last person on Garai's list, and if she still had nothing useful....

...Well, at the very least, she could return to Garai with what she had and explain why a Red Specter interview was actually a terrible idea—maybe they could switch the focus of the story to something better. The idea of asking Garai for help and feedback felt new and different. She realized she'd been thinking of him purely as an obstacle, but maybe that didn't have to be the case. Maybe she could learn a few things from him, even if they would never apply to her later career as a real journalist.

Head buzzing with renewed ideas, Joy pulled her city map from her purse, plotted a course to the docks on the south side of Dodona, and started walking, leaving the glitz of Chontos Blvd. behind her.

Part 5:

Chaos at the Docks

Chapter 26:

Dockside Blight

Forty minutes later, Joy reached the dockside district facing out into Dodona Harbor. Her feet were killing her, so she searched for a resting-place. Lately Joy had grown accustomed to walking most places throughout the city, but today had been a new record for her, and her calves and thighs were making their complaints felt.

And she wasn't seeing any convenient place to sit down. There were plenty of crates and barrels that could potentially be used as seats, but those tended to have large men in sea-stained clothes either hauling them away or stacking other crates on top of them.

And most of the decent resting spots she'd seen on the way over tended to be occupied. The hidden and not-so-hidden areas of this district were home to scores of men and occasionally women camped out in all the spots that might afford a bit of shelter or respite. They tended to be skinny, wearing dirty, raggedy clothes, with long, unkempt hair and beards, sometimes twisted into thick, ropey strands.

Some of the more organized among them had constructed makeshift shelters for themselves out of abandoned boxes and crates. Most were not that organized, and many didn't appear to be organized on any level whatsoever. They lay motionless, the whites of their eyes showing both above and below their irises, small pipes made of glass or porcelain clutched in their fingers, stained with some tar-black residue. Spike pipes. She tried to give them as wide a berth as she could, but the clutter of refuse choking the sidewalks sometimes forced her close enough to notice that some of the poor wretches were wearing the tattered remnants of Kallistrate military uniforms. She couldn't tell if these were actual veterans, or if they had simply acquired surplus uniforms as clothing.

On two occasions she saw men stalking around on random paths zig-zagging across the street, muttering curses, carrying on a vicious argument with no-one she could see, shaking with a fury whose cause she couldn't know, and whose target she couldn't guess. But even those weren't as dangerous as some of the hangers-on, single men lounging around and trying to get her attention as she walked past, sometimes yelling out catcalls. She stayed alert, didn't engage, and kept moving. Fortunately, no-one tried to follow her for more than a block.

The speed at which the streets of Dodona switched from being a vibrant urban culture to a cracked-brick wasteland dizzied her. It had gotten rough barely a block after she turned off Chontos and got worse the further she went. That lasted right up to the point where she crossed the train tracks, as sharp a demarcation as she could imagine. Instantly dissolution was replaced by industry, and the presence of people engaged in productive work, toiling on the arteries of the shipping lines drawing sustenance into the city. They had lives—something to strive for, and something to potentially lose.

She couldn't say that with any confidence about the pitiful lost souls she'd passed on the way here. Walking past those alleyways had been like traversing the land of the dead, or the half-dead, maybe. Part of her felt guilty for fearing those poor wretches, the ones lying zoned-out in their tiny homes of makeshift garbage, but exactly what would she have done? She barely had enough to feed herself, as the growling of her stomach reminded her, and she didn't have the platform to do a real expose on the situation.

Resting would have to wait. She started her sweep down the busier sections of the dock. As she passed by groups of laborers, some of them started yelling catcalls as well, but this time Joy plastered a polite, professional smile on her face, and headed over towards them. Groups of bored dock workers were much less dangerous than single roaming mashers. Most of them seemed rather startled as she introduced herself and started asking questions. It was almost like yelling random crap at passing women was a terrible way to get them to talk to you, to the point that they didn't even expect it to "work."

However, once they got over the awkwardness of having to deal with her as an actual person instead of a piece of passing scenery, she was able to start asking real questions, but unfortunately she wasn't getting much that was useful. Most of them didn't remember seeing someone matching Madame Zenovia's description, and the few who did couldn't say much, other than she wandered off to the west. She had less luck when asking about some sort of incident three nights ago, like a fight or a riot. The guys either didn't know, or pretended they didn't know, or hurriedly tried to hush up anyone who started to say anything about it.

When she pressed further, she got warned that her line of questioning was "dangerous," and "some people" wouldn't like it. After a few attempts, one worker let slip that "some people" meant "Mr. Ben Li Fang, one of the more colorful figures of post-war Dodona, a former pirate who also went by the name "Benny the Shark."

During the Great War, the specialized, defensive nature of the Kallistrate navy meant that Central Command had to get creative when it came to naval offense, harassing shipping lanes between the various Albion territories, particularly the ones to the Sidhe homeland of Hybrassil. Rather than divert resources from the spikefruit convoys, Hardwicke's government issued Letters of Marque to private ship captains, turning them into "Privateers," authorized to attack any ships sailing to supply Albion territories and keep the spoils of their attacks from themselves. In short, it was legalized piracy.

Joy had never been keen on the practice, even though the military analysts said it had been effective. She didn't like the idea of ruthless pirates attacking and looting civilian ships in

Kallistrate's name, because who but a pirate would become a privateer?

Benny the Shark was a prime example. She hadn't seen pictures, but apparently the man had an unusually large jaw, and during his tenure as a pirate, he'd filed his teeth into sharp points, all the better to terrify the crews of the ships he'd boarded, hence the name. After being legitimized by his Letter of Marque, he'd settled down in Dodona, rich beyond imagining from all his legal plunder, his jagged smile covered in gold caps. Further rumors suggested that he hadn't reformed at all, and now functioned as the local head of one of the Triad crime syndicates, trying to make inroads into the major trade cities of the Kallis Coast. Given the dock workers' reactions to the mention of his name, Joy would guess those rumors to be true.

Joy tried explaining that she wasn't planning on starting any trouble with Mr. Fang; she was freelancing for the Gazette on a Red Specter puff piece, but that didn't have the reassuring effect she'd hoped for. Most of the dock workers were sure that the Red Specter was real, and were scared of him. If anything, he scared them worse than Benny the Shark, and that was something.

Joy managed to get a few ghost stories from some of the laborers. The Specter was a harbinger of death—the merest sight of him would spell your doom. He'd bide his time stalking you. No matter how far you ran—flee to Axum, flee to the northernmost edge of the frigid Dagan Sea, flee to the tiniest, most remote island in the Kotu Ring of Fire—it wouldn't make a shred of difference. The Red Specter would hunt you down, and you would never be seen again.

Of course, there were skeptics and scoffers, who claimed everyone else was just seeing things. The situation left Joy in a bit of a pickle. Those who believed in the Specter seemed unlikely to talk about actually seeing him, for fear of invoking his "curse," and even got nervous when she said his name, while those who didn't believe in him obviously hadn't seen him. She tried asking them if they knew anyone else who claimed to see the Specter, but didn't get anything solid. Still, the more people she talked to, the more Joy had a feeling that something was up. In each conversation, she could feel it, an underlying tension, like a giant invisible clock spring beneath their feet, getting wound a notch tighter every time she asked about what happened three nights ago or mentioned the Red Specter.

On something like the eighth or ninth round of this Joy managed to get a scrap of new information: the fracas from three nights ago had occurred on the pier where a ship named the Joanne Spaulding was moored. The name sounded familiar, though Joy couldn't remember where she'd heard it from. A famous opera singer, maybe? She'd tried asking for the pier number, but instantly everybody clammed up, claimed they couldn't remember.

Joy decided to move on and see if she could find the ship on her own, since she'd hit the point where her interviews were just giving her the same information, over and over again. She drifted over towards the sea side, scanning the prows of the larger ships for their names. Joy assumed the Joanne Spaulding would have to be one of the big ships in order to qualify as a landmark. But a fluttering in her stomach disrupted her concentration, as she realized that someone was following her.

Joy picked up her pace and continued west, but the feeling didn't subside. She steeled herself and glanced back. It was one of the laborers from her last interview, a lanky man with a dirty, scraggly goatee. During the interview, he'd said next to nothing, either to her or to his co-workers, and had stared at her constantly like a starving wolf chained up outside a butcher's store.

Joy recognized that look. She'd seen it on Quintus' face right before he'd pushed into the supply closet. Regardless of what this man might know, she could not allow herself to be alone with him. All her instincts were screaming "danger," and she'd be a fool not to listen to them.

Joy wasn't going to mess around here. She needed to get rid of him, before this situation could escalate. Disrupt whatever

168

plan he had before it started. But how? Joy thought of Madame Zenovia, and it gave her an idea. She began muttering to herself, starting soft and getting louder. Then she added a head twitch, and batted at the air around her head, like swatting at invisible flies. She whirled around and directed a furious "Shh" at the empty space right next to her, tried to walk away from it, repeating "Not in public! Told you not in public. Stop talking to me!" She stumbled around, then walked in a circle, maintaining her weird argument with no-one. Stalker-boy had caught up to her, but now he looked confused. Joy whirled on him.

"You," she said, presenting him with a rictus grin. "You followed. Do you see it? You do, don't you! Not like the others they didn't understand, couldn't tell, but you—you see them crawling, hopping, swarming everywhere, everywhere, everywhere infestation webs: glowing lines from the rooftops to the sky to the spider-mother, the one in the spaces between worlds between walls between the folds in your brain reaching in and they take take take everything, every memory soul-scrap-shard spirit to him, he's the one he pulls the threads the Specter Red Specter all praise him none but me knows the truth, I know the truth, I KNOW IT'S YOU RED SPECTER!" Joy screamed back at the warehouses and was pleased to see some droplets of spittle flying off in that direction. "I KNOW! I KNOW! I KNOW YOU'RE THERE! MASTERMIND, FOUL! You don't belong! You don't. NOT FOR YOU, THIS WORLD! GET OUT! GEEETTTT OOUUUUUUUTTT!"

Through her peripheral vision Joy noted that her shrieking was attracting attention from around the docks. Not that she expected anyone to actually do anything besides stare, but she doubted that Stalker Boy appreciated the audience. She kept up her ranting, while cycling through different languages for added effect, as Stalker Boy shook his head and muttered "crazy bitch," before wandering back the way he came. Joy dialed down her volume, but kept up her act for another minute or so, until she was sure she'd lost her stalker, and she could go back to normal.

Generally speaking, nobody wanted to deal with a crazy person. Even a predator would think twice about going after prey that was so completely unpredictable. That was her hope anyway, but he'd kept staring, even as she'd gotten more and more incoherent, and she'd been worried that it wasn't working—that she'd have to rely on her combatives training again. Joy had a feeling he might've still tried something if it hadn't been broad daylight and people had been watching.

It's not like craziness was a perfect defense. Madame Zenovia had been walking around acting crazy three nights ago, and someone had tried to grab her—though as Joy thought about it, she couldn't be sure it had actually been an attack. Maybe someone had been trying to restrain her from wandering into a dangerous area. That matched up better with the fact that someone had hired a pedi-cab to take her home. But she couldn't be sure of anything until she managed to find a genuine witness.

Joy forced herself to keep walking at a brisk pace, even though her knees felt wobbly. She clutched her purse tight to keep her hands from shaking and took long breaths as she began to cross Shackle Bridge over the Ala-Muki. The stiff breeze coming over the bay helped clear her head, and the scenery was nice as always, with small recreational outrigger sailboats cutting across the blue-green waters, steering clear of the larger flat-bottomed paddle steamships carrying passengers and cargo deeper into the continent. Even the steel struts of the Shackle had been decked out in red and gold for Liberation Day, flags snapping out taut from the wind.

Steel rails separated the pedestrian walkway from the train tracks that were the primary justification for the Shackle's existence. Joy appreciated that the bridge set some clear boundaries for everyone to follow. The world could use more of that. Back when she'd been working at the Journal, before everything had gone pear-shaped, Joy remembered one of her male colleagues complaining about the advantage she had as a pretty woman:

she had such an easy time getting attention. Folks would line up to talk to her.

She'd decided to thank him for the compliment rather than launch into a lengthy correction that he probably wouldn't get. He wasn't totally wrong, either. She didn't doubt that those laborers' initial eagerness to talk to her had a lot to do with how she looked, and she wasn't above batting her eyes to get a story. The problem was that so much of the attention she got either wasn't helpful, or actively hindered her, to the point where she was having to waste energy doing improv theater performances in the middle of the street to get out of it.

All she wanted was to do her job, and somehow she'd been forced to devote half her time and mental energy fending off stupid male bullshit. She wondered what it would've been like to have to work a little harder to get attention but not have to deal with any of that other garbage—for just once, to be able to purely focus on her work, only that and nothing else. Right now, it sounded like paradise.

Chapter 27:

Guards' Lives Matter

It took Joy about twenty minutes to cross the Shackle. She'd forced herself to try to enjoy the hike over, let the stiff breeze clear out some of her stress, and she hadn't had to wait for the drawbridge at all. The west side of the docks continued on in much the same manner as the east, and Joy prepared to resume her search, but something felt wrong. She had that same anxious sense of being watched, and she glanced back at the Shackle, worried for a second that Stalker Boy really had followed her across the bridge, but of course that was ridiculous.

She'd checked numerous times on the way over. Stalker-boy wasn't magic, able to materialize out of thin air, like he was the Red Specter or something. No, something else was bugging her. What was it? It was the bridge — had Madame Zenovia mentioned crossing the Shackle on her spirit walk? Joy didn't think so, but did that mean the medium hadn't made the crossing, or just hadn't mentioned it her story? That'd be a weird detail to leave out, but Madame Zenovia had been a weird person, so maybe that's what happened.

Or else Joy, in her eagerness to put the Ala-Muki river between her and Stalker Boy, had rushed right past the Joanne Spaulding and was now looking in the completely wrong area. Joy stared back at the long steel span of the Shackle, thinking of how far she'd have to walk to double-check all this, and saw the massive leaves of the drawbridge section begin to rise, reaching up to the sky. Well, that was perfect, wasn't it?

With nothing else to do, Joy started to wander off west. This would be so much easier if she could just get someone to answer a simple direct question. Maybe the dock workers on this side of the river might not be so skittish? Joy looked around for

172

potential interview subjects and saw a reassuring sight: a patrol of four Dodona City Guardsmen, decked out in their vests of hardened black leather over their navy-blue uniforms, peaked steel-and-brass skullcaps, small steel bucklers rimmed with polished brass on their arms, and solid truncheons at their sides. Here were some people who wouldn't be intimidated by ghost stories or Benny the Shark or whoever.

Joy walked up to them, opening with her warmest smile. "Excuse me, officers, but do you have a minute? My name is Joy Song Fan, freelance reporter. I was wondering if you could answer a few questions about an incident—some sort of fight or small riot—that occurred on the docks three nights ago, somewhere in the vicinity of a ship called the Joanne Spaulding."

The four guards turned to face her, tense and wary. "What was that?" said one of them.

Joy was taken aback at their tone, but she repeated the question and got a row of hard, unfriendly glares in return. What the Abyss was going on here?

"What do you know about that?" said one of the guards.

"Um, very little beyond what I just told you," said Joy. "That's why I was asking. Is there anything you can—"

One of the guards started to say something, but another of them, an older man with an air of authority about him, cut him off with a gesture. "I'm afraid it's against department policy to comment on ongoing investigations," said the older man.

"There's an investigation?" Joy asked. "Well, what can you—"

"No comment, which is what I just said," The senior guardsman spoke in careful, clipped tones. "You do understand Kallish, yes?"

"Of course I do," said Joy, biting back the rejoinder: *and that should be obvious, since I'm clearly speaking it right now.* Instead she tried to clarify. "But I wasn't asking for specific details of the investigation. I just—"

"Miss, this is a dangerous area," said the leader. "If you don't have any business here, we're going to have to ask you to leave."

"What?" Joy felt like she'd stepped off the bridge into some crazy warped mirror-world. "I do have business here; I'm a reporter. And what's so dangerous here that I have to leave?"

"There's a lot of unsavory types hanging around these docks. And this area is in a heightened state of alert, due to reasons I am not at liberty to divulge," said the leader. "A delicate young flower like yourself shouldn't be wandering out here by yourself."

"I can handle myself," said Joy, reminding herself to keep smiling, no matter what. If she lost her cool, it'd all be her fault.

"Miss, I'm afraid we must insist that you allow us to escort you to a safe location, for your own good," said the leader as all four of them formed a semi-circle around her, an impenetrable wall. "And you need to keep away from this section of the docks, or else—"

"Okay, wait—you can't do this," said Joy.

"Miss, as an officer of the law, I have the authority to—"

"You have the authority to cordon off a specific hazardous area or crime scene to everyone, but it needs to be clearly marked," she said. "You can't chase reporters out of a huge public space like this. Freedom of the Press means—"

"Freedom of the Press," sneered one of guardsmen, "That's the term you people use to justify the lies and abuse you rain on the Sleywie Anden—"

"Brannock!" said the leader.

"—while we risk our lives to keep you safe, nattering gossips of the Journal, hiding safe behind your desks, launching attacks on a faith you couldn't begin to understand, not a bit of guts among the lot of—"

"Brannock, that's enough!" The lead guardsman punctuated his admonition with a solid rap of his knuckles to the side of Brannock's helmet, hard enough to rock him a bit.

The sudden violence made Joy jump, though she recognized that Brannock's helmet prevented any damage from the blow—it had only been intended to shut him up. But his rant had given her a useful context; it seemed that she'd blundered into the middle of someone else's argument.

"Um, I think there's a misunderstanding here," she said. "I'm not with the Journal. I'm freelancing for the Dodona Gazette, and I'm not interested in attacking anyone. I'm just trying to do a puff piece on Red Specter sightings. And maybe get an interview."

"You want an interview with us?" said the leader.

"No, with the Red Specter," she said.

All of the guardsmen stared back at her in confusion, except for the youngest-looking one, who burst out laughing.

"The Gazette! You said you work for the Gazette, right?"

"I'm freelancing for them, yes," Joy said.

"MacInroy, what's this about the Gazette?" said the leader.

"The Gazette is a joke paper," said MacInroy. "My Mom follows it regular. It's hilarious. I've shown it to you a couple times, Chief, remember? They had that story of the two-headed goat whose turds could tell the future. And the one about the hidden lycanthropy outbreak sweeping Dodona—they even had a quiz for that one: Ten Signs You Might Be a Secret Werewolf. It scored you at seventy percent werewolf, Chief—remember that? Had us worried we might need to put you in lockup next full moon."

The chief rolled his eyes while the other guards snickered. "Yeah, that'll be the day. The same day as the lizardmen stage their invasion from the sewers. What did they call that one?"

"Kobolds Ate My Baby?" said Joy. That had been the leading front-page story in the same issue where her weeping saint story had run. The kobolds had been way more popular.

"Yeah, that. So, MacInroy, all those ridiculous articles you shove under my nose are all from the same paper? Can't believe they actually print that crap. No offense, Miss."

"None taken," said Joy, though inside, a part of her was yelling, *they print that crap because people will* pay *for it. Garai doesn't give a fig if they do so ironically, as long as they buy it.*

On the other hand, she did find it comforting to find more of the Gazette's subscribers who were savvy enough to spot the nonsense. It gave her hope for humanity.

"But what I don't get is what this Red Specter business has to do with three nights ago, or the Joanne Spaulding," said the chief.

"That's where and when several witnesses spotted the Red Specter."

"Spotted him? Isn't he a character in a comic strip?"

"Apparently, the Red Specter was a folklore figure before the comic started," said Joy. "And trust me, I've spoken to a lot of people today who are certain that he's real."

"And they said they saw him three nights ago," said the chief. "How many witnesses?"

"I've got five names," said Joy, "but I've only been able to get any info from three of them."

"Were they drunk, on Spike, or just plain crazy?" MacInroy asked.

"Um..." Joy took a second to mentally review her sources. "...one of each?" All the guardsmen chuckled at that.

"Well, I can't comment on the case, but I can tell you I was in this area at the time, and there were no comic-strip folklore ghosts running around," said the chief, and....

...Wait. The guardsmen kept calling him "Chief?"

"Um, sorry," said Joy. "But is 'Chief' a nickname, or are you actually Chief Gallach, the head of the City Guard?"

"You've got me," said Chief Gallach. "That a surprise?"

"Yes, I'm surprised you're out on foot patrol, instead of coordinating everything from behind a desk."

"Oh, I do that," said Chief Gallach, "But spend too much time behind a desk, and you lose touch with the day-to-day realities of the streets. So, every now and then, I hit the beat with all my boys. Keeps me grounded."

"That does make sense," said Joy, though something about it nagged at her. Apparently he'd been doing that same work

176

three nights ago, and very late? He'd just said so. That seemed like a bit much for keeping "grounded."

Well, it wasn't her concern. She had to stay focused on ghost-hunting.

Speaking of which...

"Well, since we've established that I'm not here to slander you or interfere with your investigation, am I free to go?" Joy said. "I really could use the pier number of the Joanne Spaulding—see if I can find any better quality Red Specter sightings."

"You really need to do that?" said MacInroy. "I thought you just made everything up."

"We do real interviews," said Joy. "People like to see their names in the paper. My boss is big on that."

"Wellll... here's the thing," said MacInroy. "We're not saying this area is dangerous just to give you a hard time. You know who owns the Joanne Spaulding? It's Ben Li Fang, otherwise known as—"

"Benny the Shark," said Joy. "Yes, I've heard the name. Is that a problem, though? That he owns the ship?"

"To be sure. He's Triad, Miss, through and through," said MacInroy. "And he's the bane of this city. Smuggling, gambling, prostitution, drugs—it all goes back to him. Keeping it all under control is like bailing out the sea, though that won't stop us from trying."

"You know he's doing all this, but you can't arrest him?"

"It's not what we know," said Chief Gallach. "It's what we can prove in a court of law. Benny's got sharp lawyers and connections. You'll be surprised, Miss, at how eager these posh high-society types are to pal around with a gangster—so long as he has money. They throw out all notion of decency, while spitting on honest flatfoots like my boys here. And Benny knows it. He's shrewd, trying to use the papers to turn the public against us."

"He's using the papers?" Joy said, astonished. "Do you mean the big ones, like the Journal and the Chronicle?"

"That's how it is," said MacInroy. "For the past few weeks, not a day goes by that some bit of lies doesn't get printed about us: we're corrupt, we're thugs, we're foreign cultist loons. Benny's the one profiting off this city's misery and suffering, but to hear the Journal tell it, we're the bad guys."

"Wow," said Joy. She'd really lost track of current events. She needed to get over her resentment and start reading the papers again, at least once a week, if she didn't want to keep getting blindsided like this. "Wait, you said they called you foreign cultists?"

"It's discrimination," growled Brannock, looming over her. "You reporters call yourselves 'objective,' but you're full of your own predjudice—the fastest to slander that which you don't understand. You—"

"Whoa, Brannock," said MacInroy, stepping in between them. "It's not her, now. In fact, I'd say her Gazette is the most honest of all the papers. Better to tell a tall tale so outrageous that nobody but a fool would believe it, than a lie clever enough to cross the ocean before the truth has finished tying its shoes."

"Uh, thanks," said Joy, though she wasn't thrilled with that defense. "But I was surprised they were calling you foreign. I thought you were all Kallisians."

"We were all born in this country," said Chief Gallach. "But our parents or our grandparents came over from the Vannin Isles, and a lot of us joined the City Guard—turned into something of a family tradition, and now the papers are trying to make it sound like some sort of takeover, like it's only Vannish people allowed, which simply isn't so."

"Oh, so you're Vannish. Ethnically, I mean," said Joy, but something from earlier nagged at her. "Wait, didn't you say you were something else, earlier? Sley-something?"

Brannock started to say something, but a gesture from the chief silenced him. All the guardsmen kept their eyes on Chief Gallach and his stony expression. Had she said something wrong? Been unintentionally insulting, like the Knittelfeld citizens complimenting her on her Kallish? She wondered if she should apologize, but the chief spoke first.

"Sleywie Anden," he said. At least, that was as best as she could make out. She'd studied enough languages to recognize when she heard something that followed a different set of phonetic rules, to the point where her brain just wasn't geared to hear it properly. She'd seen it when her Kallish-speaking friends tried to get her to teach them Xiaish words and phrases. They always mangled the tones.

"Sleywie Anden," Joy repeated, though she was certain she'd botched the pronunciation somehow. She fished her notebook out of her purse. "Could you spell that for me? I'm sure I'll get it wrong otherwise."

"I'm afraid I must decline," said the Chief. "Those words describe our faith, and it's part of our beliefs to avoid public declarations of faith. True piety is a matter between the individual, the church, and God. And it doesn't have anything to do with your ghost story, does it?"

"Oh! Well, no," said Joy. "I was just asking for myself, really. Linguistics are an interest of mine, and I hadn't heard that language before. I don't want to disrespect your religion or anything."

"The Journal should follow your example, Miss," said MacInroy.

"Call me Joy," she said, "And, if you don't mind, I really could use the pier number where I can find the Joanne Spaulding. I promise I'll be careful."

This earned her some wary looks, but, after a couple more rounds of back-and-forth, she managed to wheedle them into revealing that the Joanne Spaulding was a large paddle-wheel steamship with a red hull, berthed by Pier 25. They also handed her a "safety whistle" on a lanyard, which she should use to signal them if she got into trouble. Joy thanked them and tucked it into her purse as she readied to go, but MacInroy wanted her to wait a second while he pulled his chief aside and had a hushed conversation with him.

Joy didn't catch any of it until the end, when the chief nodded and said, "Yeah—that's not a bad idea."

"What's not a bad idea?" said Joy, hoping this wasn't something else that would get in her way, like an official escort.

Chief Gallach produced a piece of paper from his pocket and unfolded it to reveal a pen-and-ink sketch of a girl with straight black hair and almond-shaped eyes. "We've been looking for a runaway. Name's Sue May. She was last seen in this area about three nights ago. Her family's real worried, and, you know, a young girl like that in a place like this—it'd be real easy for her to get mixed up with a bad crowd. Like, maybe the type that wouldn't let her get away so easy."

Joy examined the picture, wondering at what would make this girl run away from her family. "How old is she?"

"About fifteen, we think. Anyway, we've been scouring the docks with no luck, but maybe you might do better. The uniform makes us stick out. It could be spooking her into hiding when we come around."

"I could see that," said Joy. All that jet-black leather did make for a rather frightening presence. "Do you really need all that armor? Aren't you roasting in there?"

"More like steam-cooking, Miss Joy, like one your Xia dumplings," said MacInroy. "Except we don't smell so nice, as my wife would tell you. Can't get so much as a peck on the cheek from her until my leathers are in the basement. But it's regulations. Part of the job."

MacInroy was married? So young. And she'd thought that he'd been acting a bit flirty…

Well, whatever. She wasn't looking to start a relationship either. "Well, every job has it downsides. I'd be happy to help you look for this girl. I can ask around while—"

Joy tried to take the picture, but found that the Chief wouldn't let go of it.

"This is our last copy," he said. "Handed out the rest of them already."

"Oh, I see," she said, though that seemed like poor planning on the Guards' part. And wouldn't it make more sense to post these fliers up where everyone could see them, rather than handing them to individuals?

Well, whatever. Joy had her own problems to worry about. She settled for an intent examination of the artist's sketch, trying to burn the image into her brain. "I'll just keep an eye out for lost girls in addition to comic strip ghosts."

"Still say you're wasting your time," said Brannock. "You won't get so much as a peep out of anyone here. There's no-one in the world more superstitious than sailors, and it bleeds over into all the dock-men like you wouldn't believe. Add that so many of them are Xia, and that only triples the effect. No offense."

"None taken," said Joy, making sure not to let her smile waver. Brannock had tossed off his perfunctory "no offense" in a manner that made it clear that it would be ridiculous for her to actually take offense. While he wasn't exactly wrong about a lot of the Xia dockmen being superstitious, she found it richly ironic that he could be so cavalier about other people's beliefs, while he flew off the handle at any perceived insult to his precious Sleywie Whatever.

"Well, good luck with your story, Miss Joy," said MacInroy. "And, if you could, it'd be great if you could mention how helpful the City Guard were to you. We could use some good press somewhere."

"I'll try to fit it in," said Joy, "But I'm not sure if it'll help much. If it's printed in the Gazette, nobody will believe it."

That earned her some chuckles as she headed off to Pier 25. Finally! That had been a lot of effort for a tiny bit of information. All she'd needed was the pier number for the Joanne Spaulding, and maybe some solid information about exactly what had happened here three nights ago. The pier number was all she'd gotten, and that was only after several minutes of haggling, trying to convince them that she could handle herself like an adult.

And that was only after she'd convinced them she wasn't from a serious paper, trying to "smear" them.

Actually, the more she thought about that, the more troublesome it became. Even if it was true that the Journal and Chronicle were libeling the Guard, that didn't excuse the Guard's initial behavior. They shouldn't be using their authority to try to intimidate reporters just because they didn't like their coverage. And it wasn't like these were just low-level Guardsmen acting on their own — Chief Gallach had been with them.

Joy wondered exactly what the major papers had been printing about the Guard. Something about foreign Vannish cultists? That was odd. From looking at them, she didn't see any obvious physical markers to separate them from ethnic Kallisians, although MacInroy had a reddish tinge to his hair, which you didn't see very often.

Maybe they could tell the difference? But Joy didn't expect that any of the Vannish guardsmen would feel the need to walk around Knittelfeld with a sign explaining how they were born in Kallistrate.

She supposed it must be their religion that set them apart. Joy had never heard of the Sleywie Anden, but she knew very little about the cultures of the Dagan Sea. It was such a remote area — she hadn't even realized that so many immigrants from that region had made it to the Kallis Coast.

Could that be the source of the hysteria? Joy remembered Brannock's accusation about journalists — that their claim to objectivity was a self-delusion that made them blind to their own biases. Well, she'd seen that firsthand with Flynn, so maybe the Journal really was smearing the City Guard in their coverage. And why should she care if the Guard was retaliating against the major Dodona papers? Those papers had done nothing to defend her when she'd needed it. Why should she stick her neck out for them? They could take care of themselves. She already had more than enough to deal with just making rent. And it was time to get on that.

Joy picked up her stride and headed off for Pier 25, heels clicking across the pavement, hoping to finally find something she could use to build a decent story.

Chapter 28:

The Triad Ship

Joy had barely walked for a minute before she found Pier 25 and the Joanne Spaulding, but both were overshadowed by the titanic creature that attended them: a huge, steam-powered monstrosity rearranging stacks of cargo along the docks like a giant infant playing with blocks: a crane golem. Kallistrate had spent decades developing steam golem technology in secret, but as the project neared completion, they'd needed a way to test their technology in the real world, and to build huge factories capable of mass-producing the gigantic war machines without alerting the Albion Empire what they were up to. Just as the technology for the steam golems' feet had been adapted to create the Iron Crawlers, the tech for the arms had been used to create crane golems.

Of course, they hadn't been called that when they'd first come out. They'd been given some boring moniker, like claw-arm cranes or something. But everyone called them crane golems now. Compared to the later military steam golems, which looked roughly like knights in plate armor, the crane golem cut a bizarre figure. Instead of a broad, armored prow of a chest, the crane golem had a narrow one-person cab encased in planes of glass, with the bulky, powerful shoulder mechanism protruding out behind, seemingly disembodied as it all got perched atop a skeletal steel pylon that was mostly empty space, a crisscrossing triangular framework stretching down to the ground, next to the steam engine that ran everything, sending all power up to the shoulders through a heavy central drive shaft.

The crane golems' arms were unnaturally long—almost spindly, but the three-fingered claws at their ends were thick steel that radiated power and strength. Joy watched the golem work, pivoting in place and picking at the various cargo containers strewn about the docks. She found something about it deeply unsettling. Maybe it was the way the arms were bent, with their elbows pointed up to the sky. It didn't look human. It was like a cross between an ape and a praying mantis, or some kind of spider. The glass panes of the cab windows definitely lent it a bug-eye sort of feel.

Wait a minute, hadn't Madame Zenovia mentioned something like that; a spider-monster sticking its head and arms through a dimensional portal? As hallucinations went, that wasn't too far from reality. Joy watched it reach for the deck of the Joanne Spaulding. The claws inched down in fits and starts, pausing when a cry rang out and sailors swarmed on the ship's back, bearing ropes and hooks that they threaded through the massive steel fingers, tugging and yanking to make sure everything was secure. Then came another cry, and the sailors scrambled back to whence they came.

One sailor waved up at the golem cab, yelling something she couldn't make out, and the spider arms began to rise, so carefully that Joy might have called it dainty, as the ropes all stretched taut, and all the barrels and crates left the steamship deck in one great mass, caught up in the web of a huge cargo net.

The whole thing swayed back and forth as the crane golem swung it about to an empty space on the docks and began to lower it down. Again the crane became hesitant as it neared the ground, as another mass of sailors converged on that spot, waving and shouting at the pilot. Joy saw him pulling the control sticks inside the cockpit as he safely deposited the cargo bundle on the docks, and the sailors disentangled the carry ropes from the claws.

Well, that was something you didn't see every day. Joy strolled over to see if any of the dock workers might have noticed anything odd three nights ago. But unfortunately, none of them had any time for her. They were heads-down in their work, and Joy overheard enough to gather that they were behind schedule.

As soon as she got close they started barking about how she was in the way and needed to clear the area, and no amount of eyelash-batting would compensate for it.

Joy wandered off to the very edge of the dock, where she was out of everyone's way. Maybe if she hung around long enough, she could catch a brief interview with some of the workers when they went on break. She leaned up against a tall mooring post and took this chance to get a good look at the Joanne Spaulding. It really was a pretty ship, though it had seen better days. The hull was a rich red with a wide black stripe just below the first deck, trimmed with gold, though that trim had faded quite a bit.

The ship's name was up at the prow, faded red-and-gold letters in an ornate style. Joy wondered if the ship's owner had intended to be patriotic, in addition to being an opera fan. Joy let her gaze trail aft, along the nice, elegant lines and a neat feminine curve where the deck of the ship flared outwards to cover the side-mounted paddle-wheels. The ship designer hadn't covered the top half of the paddle-wheels entirely. There were some ornate cut-out sections on the sides that left the spokes of the wheel partially visible. She wondered if that was purely for aesthetics of if there was some practical reason for it. She wondered how it would look when the wheels started turning.

Joy studied the paddle wheel, with its slats and spokes dipping into the water. Paddle-wheels always made her think of ladders. She'd always wanted to try climbing one—to swim up to it and ascend to the deck. It really looked like you could do it. The trickiest part was where the cowling formed a barrier between the wheel and the deck, but Joy bet she could squeeze through some of those ornamental cutouts on the outside and grab the railing. If only she was a kid again and could get away with climbing over everything like she used to. Combine that with a nice dip in the water, and it'd be the perfect break. Too bad she was a grown-up now.

Well, even when she was a kid, she was too chicken to try something like that—not that she was frightened of the climb.

It was getting yelled at for messing around with a dangerous machine where she wasn't supposed to. Messing around in dangerous areas was one of the few places where she might try disobeying her parents.

Joy still felt her cheeks burn with shame remembering the last time. She'd been fifteen, walking Hugh home from school, when she'd decided to check out the new rows of houses going up next to Perun Lake. She was supposed to be watching Hugh, but he was eight frickin' years old already. She'd had a rough day, her homework load was light, and she wanted to blow off some steam—do something just for herself for once. Hugh could look after himself. She'd been able to do way more than that at his age. She'd told him that in no uncertain terms—just stay put and he'd be fine.

And maybe she was a bit old to be climbing around like a monkey—certainly she was too old for the Caliburn courses, but she still had an itch to climb. Joy tried channeling her energy into gymnastics, but she couldn't stand her school's coach, Mrs. Sun, whose only method of instruction was a relentless drilling of poise and posture fundamentals, to be mastered before the student did so much as a forward roll. Oh, that and an unhealthy focus on her charges' weight, which she checked weekly, in front of the entire team.

Joy didn't need that aggravation, so she quit, but kept doing a lot of the stretching and calisthenics on her own. She'd been at it for a month before the day she'd told Hugh to stay home while she went to explore the construction site at Perun Lake.

She felt the results as she set herself between two vertical beams that made the unfinished skeleton of one of the new houses and pressed out in both directions with her hands and feet, just like one of the wall-climbing sections of the Caliburn courses. This was easier than it had ever been, as she ascended to the second floor, finding cross beams to practice pull-overs, going up to the rafters and back down again, running along the apex ridge-beams, stopping to enjoy the view from the top, looking down over Perun Lake and the rest of Gortyn, feeling happier and freer than she'd had in years.

It didn't last long. A crash and a scream broke her reverie. Hugh hadn't stayed put like she'd told him to. He'd shadowed her from a distance, and tried to keep following her into the unfinished houses, except somehow he'd fallen into the "moat" that surrounded the foundations, and he'd landed on a spike long enough to pierce his calf and come out the other side.

Joy had to carry him on her back into the nearest neighborhood until she found someone who could call a doctor. Then her parents came, and she was in the worst trouble she'd ever been in her entire life. Her dad slapped her. That was the only time she could remember him doing that. Because of course this was all her fault, never mind Hugh was the one who didn't stay home like he'd been told to. No, it was all her fault for setting a bad example. Hugh got waited on hand-and-foot while he recovered, and of course, most of his chores had fallen to her in the three months she'd been grounded.

Some days that was easier than others. He really had hurt himself, and she felt bad about that. And sometimes she did feel guilty about what happened, before she remembered to be mad over the lack of sympathy she was getting. No-one understood why she'd been climbing around a construction site, no matter how she tried to explain it, because nobody bothered to really listen. She got zero credit for figuring out how to rescue her injured brother from the bottom of a six-foot ditch, by using a spare wooden plank as a ramp while carrying him on her back. No, anything that ever went wrong was her fault, and she just had to endure it. That's how it always was.

There were times where it was enough to make her dream of running away from home. In her dream, she'd sneak out in the middle of the night, board a ship to Cymru, and rush her way to victory in the Trials at Cistonia stadium. The fantasy always ended with a huge crowd of people cheering her on, while the rest of her family had to sulk at home in despair, full of remorse at all the demands they'd made, all the pressure they'd put on her. They'd be sorry, then—but it'd be too late, and they'd have to make do without her.

Of course, she'd never gone through with it—and even if she had, it wouldn't have worked so neatly. You couldn't just waltz into Cistonia stadium and sign up for the Trials; there was a whole system of regional preliminaries you had to work through to even get that far. And the Trials were an annual event she'd have to wait for.

Her resentment could never survive that long. Hugh would do something cute, or Dad would do something goofy, or June would come to her for advice, or Family Game Night would kill it off if nothing else did. The fantasy had only ever been that—a mental escape when she got stressed out. She'd never have run away for real.

But some kids did more than dream about it. Joy remembered the ink sketch that the Guardsmen had shown her. This Sue May—maybe she was much less sensible than Joy had been at her age. Or maybe she'd been smitten with a rotten louse of a boyfriend who'd dragged her into this. Joy remembered a near miss with Belle on that front, one that ended only when Belle realized he'd been cheating on her. It had taken some careful maneuvering on Joy's part to lead her to that revelation without appearing to, but she knew Belle wouldn't have believed it if she or June had just straight-up told her. Maybe Sue May didn't have big sisters watching out for her.

Or maybe Sue May's family was even worse than that. Maybe there were drug or alcohol problems at home, and that's why she'd left. Maybe she'd been abused. Joy hoped it wasn't that. It shouldn't be—Sue May's family cared enough to contact the Guard and distribute those fliers. The Guardsmen had said the family had been very worried, hadn't they? Even if there were problems at home, surely it was better to stay and try to work them out, rather than starve out the streets. Yes, Joy would definitely keep an eye out—

"Having trouble finding something, Miss?"

Joy started and spun around to find two broad-shouldered men standing right behind her. They were too well-dressed to be sailors or dockhands, but not nearly well enough to be gentry. They had small bruises and adhesive bandages on their faces and hands, and their expressions were anything but helpful. Everything about them screamed "Triad Thugs."

Chapter 29:

Disrespect

"Oh, hello," said Joy, resolving to be polite and friendly, despite the men's appearance. "Actually, I could use some help. I'm a freelance reporter, working for the Dodona Gazette, and I just have a few questions—"

"Well, I don't answer questions," said the man. "All queries related to Mr. Fang's businesses gotta go through official channels. That means you gotta go downtown and speak with Miz Chow. So, Miz Reporter, why you nosing around here instead, huh?"

"Ah. Um... so you two work for Mr. Ben Li Fang, then?"

"I didn't say that. Don't you go printing that I did," said the first thug, eyes narrowing. Joy got the immediate impression that she was not dealing with the sharpest tack in the drawer. Well, at least he made up for it by being big and mean-looking.

"Oh, you're right," she said. "You didn't say that. Well, I didn't know about needing to go downtown, but since I'm here, maybe you could help me out, just a little bit. I was looking for—"

"Ain't answering no questions from no reporters," he said.

"Yes, I understand," she said. "But these aren't questions about Mr. Fang or his business, it's about an incident from three nights ago—"

"What? What do you know about that?" The thug advanced on her, forcing her to backpedal to keep a safe distance. His partner hung back, leaning against another mooring, looking bored, but it was a dangerous sort of boredom, like a jungle cat lounging in a tree, pondering on whether it should pounce and rip out your throat, or just take a nap instead.

Joy needed to keep everyone calm. There was no reason not to be calm. "I don't know anything about three nights ago," she said. "No one will answer my questions."

"Yeah? Well, they better not, if they know what's good for 'em," said the first thug. "And if you know what's good for you, you'll quit asking. In fact, that's what you will do. You're trespassing on Mr. Fang's private property. You need to leave."

"What?" Joy said. "This is private property? I didn't see any signs."

"Well, you're seeing one now," said the thug, tapping at his chest. "I'm the sign, and the sign says, 'Scram!' You got a problem with that?"

"It's not that I have a problem, or rather… it's not that I don't believe you," Joy lied. "But without a sign—a regular sign, I mean—it's hard to know where the borders of Mr. Fang's property are. So I can know when I'm trespassing and when I'm not. And, besides—"

"Oh, I can help ya there," said the thug. "Look to your left."

"Okay," said Joy, and looked left.

"Now look to your right."

Joy looked right. "Okay."

"You see all that?"

"Um, yes," she said.

"That's all Mr. Fang's property, and you're not allowed there. Now, beat it!"

Joy closed her eyes and took a long breath. This was absurd. She was absolutely certain that she was not on private property, and that Benny the Shark did not own the entire waterfront, east to west, and that these goons had no legal right to chase her off. She was also certain that neither of these assholes gave a single shit for what her legal rights were. They only knew that they were bigger and prepared to be violent and that meant they were right, no matter how ridiculous their arguments were. And she was getting so tired and fed up with big, loud, aggressive bully-boys showing up and arbitrarily dictating where she could go and what she could do and who she could talk to and making her entire life a hundred times more difficult than it needed to be. She was so fed up and frustrated with the whole business that she could scream.

But she wasn't going to scream. She couldn't do that. Because, in the end, however fed up and frustrated she was didn't matter one bit. No amount of anger from her would make these thugs any less big or potentially violent or impervious to reason. She could just take her rage and eat it, because she had no other choice.

Maybe she could change the conversation?

"Okay, listen," she said. "I think we've had a misunderstanding here. All I want is—"

"Only misunderstanding here is you not leavin' when you've been told to," said the thug. "Now, are you clearing out, or will you be needing an escort from us?"

"No, no escort is necessary," said Joy. "But first, I just need to check—"

"Okay, escort then," he said, seizing her by the upper arm and dragging her along. Joy felt it cutting off circulation to her hand and forearm. That really hurt.

"Ow! I—wait!" Joy said, trying to dig in her heels, to no effect. Bits of her combatives courses from her supplemental training were popping back up into her head, but part of her was sensible enough to know that escalating this situation would be a terrible idea. Trying to actually fight them would be a last resort, one that almost certainly wouldn't end well.

But the sort of half-resistance she was doing only served to irritate the thug. He stopped pulling for a second, only to shake her.

"Right, you're gettin' on my last nerve, lady. I'm gonna say this one more time, and—"

"Lir's Balls!" Joy snapped. "I'm just a tabloid reporter tracking down Red Specter sightings. There's no need for any of—"

The thug just sneered at her. "Bitch, I don't care if you were the—"

"Wait! What did she say?" For the first time, the skinnier thug spoke, appearing at the bigger one's side.

"Who cares, Chen?" the first thug said. "We just gotta—"

"No, Yang—I heard her say it. You did too. You heard it."

"Who cares what she said," said the bigger thug, whose name was Yang, apparently. "It's a bunch of—"

"I care," said Chen. "And if you had any sense, so would you. We must hear this. You, say it again."

Joy took advantage of Chen's distraction to pull her arm free from Yang's grip. Chen was staring at her with a feverish intensity that made her wonder if this was actually a positive development.

"Um, all I said was that I was trying to interview people who've spotted the Red Specter—"

"You see! You see! You hear that?" Chen rounded on Yang, crowing in triumph. "He is real. He is here. People have seen him. He's the one behind all of this. Will you admit it now?"

"Bullshit," said Yang. "She don't know nothing. This is—"

"She is a reporter," said Chen. "From a *newspaper*. You tell me that isn't proof? Would they print it if it wasn't true?"

Of course they would, thought Joy, though now didn't seem to be the best time to point it out, not while Chen was the only thing between her and Yang's vise-grip.

"I don't care if they put it up on Chontos in flashing lights ten-feet tall," said Yang. "Ain't no way I'm gonna be pestering the Boss with your half-baked funny-pages ghost story bullshit."

"Ignorant fool," snapped Chen. "Your blindness will be the end of us all."

"Oh, so I'm ignorant? I'm just dumb gutter trash, not like you, Chen," said Yang. "You think you're better than me, is that it? I notice you don't call me *Lao* Yang. Don't think I haven't noticed that."

"You are not older than me," said Chen, in precise, clipped tones.

Joy tried to edge away from the two men without being obvious about it. They were both staring eye-to-eye, inches away from each other. Apparently just mentioning the Red Specter's existence was enough to set off some long-standing beef between the two men. She wasn't sure if this was going to improve her situation or not.

194

"Oh yeah, that's right," said Yang. "You're used to being a big shot, aren't ya? Back in the old Imperial Army. What was it again? Lieutenant? Major? Well, guess what—it don't mean shit any more, does it? Imperial Albion is gone, and now you're nothing more than a common dirty criminal, just like the rest of us. You get that, Chen?"

"I am aware of my rank, and I am aware of who I am now," said Chen. "But also I am aware of who I was, and what happened in the war. Unlike you, I remember what it was like for a unit that caught the attention of the Red Specter, and it was exactly like this—everything begins to go wrong.

"Supplies, rations begin to disappear. Then your informants go, and the locals become too frightened to be seen with you. Then soldiers disappear. No bodies—they just vanish into thin air. And all the while, you can feel it happening; the Specter's wrath—the force of his hatred. It is a constant, oppressive feeling of eyes on the back of your neck; a gaze that will leave you cursed. It the same as what I feel now. I try to warn you, but you—"

"Hey, maybe you wanna shut the fuck up now, Chen?" Yang said, glancing in her direction. "Since we've got a *reporter* here, and—"

"No, I will not 'shut the fuck up,' Yang. I am tired of your foolishness—"

"I'm foolish? You're one shooting yer dumb-ass mouth off in front of—"

"No—we are going to deal with this now. I say you are a fool because only a fool would ignore the wisdom, hard-won in the field, that I try to give you," said Chen. "But you know nothing of this, nothing of the real strength of your Xia culture. You have no inner strength, no true pride. I see it when you kowtow to Ah Nei Wei."

"Kowtow? Bull," said Yang. "And what do you care about that? You're the one who's all 'rah-rah Albion Empire." Wouldn't she have outranked you, even in your old job?"

"That woman is a disgrace. She brought great shame to the Empire," said Chen. "She was one of their great mistakes, one of the mistakes that led to their end, and she will do the same to us. It is her presence that draws the Red Specter. It is all her fault. She will—"

"Oh, really?" Yang said. "Well, if that's what you really think, why don't you try saying that right to her face? I'd love to see that. You gonna do that, Chen? Walk right up to Ah Nei Wei and call her a shameful mistake that ended the Empire? You gonna do that?"

Chen glared back at Yang, but said nothing in response. His face was like a stone statue.

"Yeah, I didn't think so," said Yang. "You make out like you're some kinda big shot, but you don't fool me. You're scared of her, aintcha?"

"I am not scared," said Chen.

"Yeah, you are. You know she'd wipe the floor with your punk ass if she wanted to. Just admit it. Admit that all your War Hero bullshit is just that: bullshit, and the truth is you're nothing but a coward who—"

The word "coward" proved to be Chen's breaking point. He shoved Yang hard in the chest, Yang shoved back, and then the two were at each other's throats.

"nicetalkingtoyouguysseeyoulaterbye," murmured Joy as she turned on her heel and left the scene at a brisk walk. Don't run, not yet. Predators were attracted to running prey. She remembered that from somewhere.

Unfortunately, the brawling thugs blocked the only escape route that didn't lead into stacks of cargo crates, which formed a gigantic maze. These were huge piles of stuff wrapped up in netting, or massive boxes that were bigger than her apartment. Joy assumed this was a holding area for cargo waiting to be transferred elsewhere, and the scale of it managed to send a tiny sliver of awe through her rising panic. Amazing what that crane golem made possible. But her primary concern with the huge

196

stacks was their use as cover, so she could get out of sight of the dangerous men and circle around to flee the area. She had almost reached the corner of one of the stacks when she heard a shout behind her. She broke into a run as one of the thugs yelled, "She's getting away!"

Chapter 30:

Secret Cargo

Joy sprinted around the corner and down an aisle made of stacks and stacks of trade goods. Her heart rebounded against the inside of her rib cage as her heels clacked against the concrete. Joy had some practice at long-distance running as part of Kallistrate basic training, though as non-infantry, she'd gotten the abbreviated version of that, but this was the first time she'd ever had to run for her life. Her legs felt like they weighed nothing. She was practically flying. She tore her way through the cargo-maze, skittering on her pump heels as she took the corners, using her arms to push off the cargo-piles, trying to keep an internal sense of which way was which until she could lose those Triad thugs.

Why in the world were they chasing her, anyway? Did they even know? Well, she wasn't going to stick around and find out. She heard them in the stacks behind her, yelling at each other, and screaming abuse at her, and what they'd do when they caught her. That sounded like Yang, and it only made her more determined to not get caught. Not getting lost was another story. There was so much stuff here. You'd think it'd be better organized, but as far as she could tell, it had been strewn about randomly, with no rhyme or reason to the pathways through all this junk. Maybe there was a system she wasn't appreciating while running through it full-tilt.

A part of her had to wonder just what was in all these casks and crates, though from the smell of one really unpleasant aisle, she guessed that at least some of it was fertilizer. Or, since she heard mooing from between the slats of one of those huge room-size crates, maybe it was just cow manure. How long had those cows been cooped up like that? Poor cows, but she had her own problems to deal with.

She emerged out into a nexus of sorts, with a choice of three aisles going forward, one straight ahead, and two more to the left of it; two more aisles on her left going back the way she'd come; or she could just go left and keep going and… wait, was that the way out? That looked like a view of the street from here. Joy turned towards the exit just as Chen ran out from the center aisle to stand right in front of her, and then turned the wrong way, running over to check the exit, and the two far left aisles. His back was towards her, but he was blocking the way out.

Joy froze for a second, held her breath, did the fastest tiptoe she could manage across to the rightmost aisle, and resumed her sprint as soon as she was out of sight. She heard a shout from Chen, followed by the slaps of his shoe leather striking concrete. Had he heard her? Had he seen her? She had to assume so. Ahead of her she saw a T-junction, and a flash of movement on the ground go off to the right. She'd spooked a cat. On an impulse, she followed it. Maybe it knew the way out? She turned right at the junction, to get a glimpse of black fur at the end of the aisle as it darted left and disappeared. She chased it down to find….

…A complete dead-end junction, with a huge stack of broken or empty barrels ahead, a barrier of cargo-netted packages to the right, and a solid wall of those room-sized containers to the left. This was a dead end. She heard shouts behind her. Chen and Yang. They'd be around the corner any minute. She was trapped.

The stray cat was there with her. It looked back, meowed at her, and scampered up a lumber beam to the top of the cargo wall, where it hunkered down and stared at her. Joy looked at the beam. One end had fallen off a larger stack of lumber to hit the ground, while the other remained at the top of the pile.

The base had wedged itself between random piles of bric-a-brac. The beam had been stable enough to support a cat, but would it handle a small Xia freelance reporter? Only one way to find out.

Joy hopped on the beam, starting off on all fours, straightening up as she ascended. Just like a balance beam, only this one bounced and wobbled under her feet with every step. She had to be precise when she planted her feet: straight up-and-down, with no sideways shear. She increased her pace as she approached the top, as she saw the upper end of the beam start to skid from its resting-place, and she had to make an emergency leap to reach the top of the pile, as her walking-beam clattered to the pavement below, followed by several of its brothers, and the black cat darted away, down to the next aisle.

"What the… She's a damned monkey," came a shout from below.

Joy didn't bother to look back. She crawled to an adjacent pile, one lashed in place with ropes, grabbed a handful of rope, swung down to hang from it, and let go, landing into a forward roll to break her fall, just like a Caliburn course. Only she forgot she still had her purse with her, and she felt the contents painfully as they got squashed between her back and the hard ground.

She regained her feet and instantly realized she'd made a huge mistake. Why did she jump down? She should've stayed on top for as long as she could, so she could see her way out of the maze. This wasn't an obstacle course. Now she'd trapped herself in another cul-de-sac. The thugs were going to catch her, as soon as they ran around the wall she'd just climbed over.

Another meow caught Joy's attention, and Joy caught a glimpse of yellow eyes from the shadows before they vanished entirely. Wait, where had they gone? Joy ran to the spot where the cat had disappeared. She got down on her hands and knees, forcing herself to stay calm and focus, and then she saw it. What had first appeared to be just a shadow was actually a thin tear at the corner of one of the big container's panels. Just enough for a cat to squeeze through. But not her.

She stifled a scream of frustration and pounded at the offending super-crate, startling herself at the way it jumped in response. The whole panel was loose. She seized it, yanked on it as hard as she could, and the gap widened to bigger than cat-sized. Was it Joy-sized? Today seemed to be her day for trying new things. She wrenched the panel outward as hard as she could and jammed herself into the hole.

The panel snapped down on her, and she muffled curses as she shoved with her legs to force her way in, as the rough wood edge snagged her clothes and hair and scraped her skin. She had a bad moment where she was sure she'd been trapped, but she fought down the panic, and, through a mix of wiggling, sucking in her belly, and pushing against the panel from the inside, she finally wormed her way into the big container-crate. The panel snapped shut, and she was in the dark.

She tried to hold herself perfectly still and make no sound whatsoever, but that proved impossible. The feeling of weightlessness from earlier was gone now, and her thighs felt like they'd expanded to twice their normal size. She could feel her pulse pound through her body, traveling in a great wave originating from her chest. She heard it each time the wave crashed past her ears. Her breath came in huge gulps, and she couldn't will herself to stop or slow down, or stop shaking. She pressed herself against the side of the huge crate with her ear to the wall, tried to listen to the outside world, and hoped that the racket her body was making wasn't as loud as she feared.

She heard footsteps outside, and a voice raised in anger and disbelief. It was kind of muffled, but she could recognize Chen's voice, saying he knew she was in there, and she'd better come out if she knew what was good for her. Joy stayed where she was as the voice came closer, grew more menacing, making it harder and harder to control her breathing. He could hear her! Any moment now it would be over. There was a great crash, the snapping of splintering wood... but the loose panel stayed where it was. The noise was coming from outside, accompanied by some sloshing sounds. Chen must've thought she'd tried to hide in one of the barrels, and he was tearing his way through them. And not finding anything.

This went on for what seemed like forever, with the thumping of the barrels being overturned, or knocking into each other as

Chen worked his way through them. It felt like it took forever. How much time did he need to realize that nothing was there? Why couldn't he just give up and go away, already? What had she done to deserve this level of scrutiny, anyway? Didn't he have better things to do? Joy sent out a fervent prayer to Lir Kovidh, to the spirits of her ancestors who might still be around, to any higher power that might be listening, just do something to make this man go away.

Yang arrived instead. He and Chen got to arguing again. That went on far longer than it needed to, as far as Joy was concerned. The yelling reached a crescendo, but the last phrase she was able to make out sounded like, "Okay, FINE!" and the two of them took off, but not before one of them took a hard, frustrated punch at the wood panel she was leaning against. The whole thing shook, and it was like someone had fired off a cannon straight into her ear. She nearly had a heart attack right there, terrified that they might notice the loose corner of the crate, but they didn't stop running. She put her head back to the crate wall, and heard their footfalls recede into the distance. Finally, she was alone.

Slowly, her breathing began to return to normal. Sweat poured out of her hair and formed a small rivulet that ran down her forehead and dripped off her nose. Large patches of her clothing were soaked through, and beneath that her clothes pinched at her and itched. The skin on the backs of her heels had been rubbed raw—she could just tell. She really wanted to take her shoes off, but decided against it. She remembered reading something about your feet swelling up and not being able to get them back on later. That had been in one of her field manuals, she was sure of it. She felt an unpleasant stiffening in her calves and thighs, and forced herself to her feet, suppressing a groan as she did. She shuffled around in a circle, as quietly as she could, trying to loosen up.

The air in the cargo container was hot and stifling, despite the dark. She wanted to go outside, or at least stick her head out for some fresh air, but she didn't dare. She wanted to wait a good long time, until she was sure her two new bestest buddies had definitely given up on her. She still had no idea what she'd done to even make them want to chase her, other than exist and be witness to their petty little dick-waving contest.

Joy sighed and remembered the warnings of the Guardsmen. She supposed this section of the docks really was dangerous, after all. Oh, and she still had a whistle to summon them, which she'd tossed in her purse and completely forgotten about when she'd needed it. She looped the lanyard around her neck. Better to do that now, when it was fresh in her mind.

Also, she should write down what the fuck just happened, while that was also fresh in her mind. The longer you waited, the more subjective and unreliable your memories were prone to become. That was a key tenet she remembered from one of her college courses. Though in college, she'd never had to take notes while she was this sweaty, and in the dark.

She found a spot on a nearby crate, illuminated by a beam of light creeping in through a crack in the container wall, where she could prop up her notepad and write without dripping on it too much.

What had she learned from that bizarro encounter?

1. The Triad leadership, namely Ben Li Fang, aka "Benny the Shark," didn't want any reporters poking around "their" territory, particularly the Joanne Spaulding.

2. They really didn't like anyone asking about the event from three nights ago, and expected that any eyewitnesses would keep quiet "if they knew what was good for them."

3. One of them, Chen, was certain that the Red Specter was real, and he was also certain that the Red Specter was acting against the Triad, but indirectly, from the shadows. Why had he thought that? Because Chen was an out-of-work officer from the old Imperial Army, and he saw similarities between what had happened during the war to army units targeted by the Red Specter and what was happening now to his new gang.

Joy tried to sort through her agitated mind to remember what Chen's evidence for that had been. What had he actually said? People going missing, things going wrong....

That had been it, hadn't it? If you laid it out like that, it was a pretty weak case. Joy jotted it down in her notes anyway. No wonder Yang didn't take it seriously. The only compelling evidence for Chen's case was his own conviction that it was true. He'd said he could feel the Specter's presence, with total certainty.

But Joy had been working for the Gazette long enough to see that same level of conviction in people who believed in things that turned out to be utter nonsense. Yang was probably right to dismiss Chen's worries, though that created a simmering resentment between them, one that blew up as soon as she mentioned the Red Specter's name. Actually, it had to be about way more than that. Chen seemed to fancy himself a man of honor—career military—and was finding any standards of honor that the Triads possessed to be beneath him.

Joy had to wonder if the oppressive presence the veteran complained of—that constant sense of being watched, of being judged, and found lacking—was really the Red Specter. Because, to her, it sounded a lot like a little something called a guilty conscience. Joy had been feeling a bit of that lately herself. The thought made her pause, as she found herself sympathizing with Chen. But no, it wasn't that similar. Tabloid reporting wasn't breaking the law. And she was going to quit as soon as she could, and Garai wasn't going to send goons after her to break her legs when she tried to leave. So it wasn't the same thing.

She was getting off-topic. Focus, Joy! What else had the thugs said? Something about another Albion army vet in the Triad, higher-ranking than Chen, a woman named Ah Nei Wei. Joy scratched the name out in Kallish characters, as she wasn't sure which Xiaish characters were the right ones. And was it Ah Nei Wei or Ahn Ei Wei? And had she heard that right? It could be a regional dialect she didn't know. It was such an odd name.

Though she was one to talk, with a name like Joy Song Fan. A lot of ethnic Xia here tended to give their kids a Kallish first name and a Xiaish middle name, which they could reverse if they went abroad, but Joy's parents had decided to be different and tried to give their kids Kallish names that would easily convert to Xia phonetics, an idea they'd given up on by the time they'd got to Belle. They'd wanted to call her Jen, but that would've meant the Fan sisters would've been Joy, June, Jen—which was too many J's in the family. They could've used May, but there were already a bunch of May's and Mei's on their block, and how could they think of having May follow June—that would look ridiculous.

Joy was glad Belle couldn't see her now; she'd have laughed herself silly. Every time Joy fell short of living up to her title as the role model, Belle was there to rub it in her face. Well, it wasn't like Joy had ever asked for that job, but she had it anyway, for as far back as she could remember. She wasn't allowed to misbehave. Her worst rebellion had been her expedition to Perun Lake. Funny how the skills she gotten from her most disreputable habit had been the exact thing that had saved her ass just a few minutes before.

Joy sighed and rubbed at her temples. What was she doing, dredging up childhood resentments at a time like this? That wasn't going to help her with anything. She needed to focus on the now.

She studied her meager notes from her encounter with the Triad goons. Not much here, and she wasn't going to get anything useful from anyone in this area if she had to deal with the Triad chasing her around all the time. Was there a way to get them to leave her alone? They'd said something at the beginning—Joy managed to concentrate enough to remember: "Go downtown and talk to Benny's secretary—Ms. Chow?" Was that right? Joy scratched the name out on her notepad.

Well, that might work. Mr. Ben Li Fang maintained at least the pretense of being a legitimate businessman, so there would have to be some sort of real office that she could contact to clear this up. Granted, Joy had some misgivings about bringing herself to the attention of a gangster. The very idea made her nervous. But she couldn't shy away from those risks. Part of being a good reporter meant incurring the ire of dangerous people in search of the truth....

Wait, what truth? What was she talking about? She'd forgotten where she was working again. This was a stupid fake story for a stupid fake newspaper and she'd already wasted too much time and effort on it already. Nothing about this nonsense was worth crossing the Triads over. What was she even thinking? As soon as it was safe, she would go straight back to her apartment and never come anywhere near Pier 25 ever again. She would make up some bullshit about whatever it was that happened three nights ago that nobody wanted to talk about, and have the Red Specter creep out of the shadows at the last minute to toss off some cool-sounding cryptic garbage that the Gazette's readers would eat right up.

Yes, that was exactly right: an "interview" that consisted of a few terse exchanges, uttered by a mysterious figure in the darkness, who warned her not to get too close. That was perfect and fit in exactly with who the Red Specter's appeal. Only problem would be figuring out exactly what those exchanges would be. She was drawing a blank here. Why was that? Maybe it was because, despite all her work, she barely had any idea what was really going on here. She had a ton of loose threads, but the meat of the story was missing.

She supposed she could just make something up, but she found herself drawing blanks every time she tried to think of specifics. Eventually she decided to quit trying. As soon as she felt the coast was clear, she was going to go home, make herself a mediocre meal, organize her notes, and go to sleep. Maybe a fresh day would giver her ideas. And she still hadn't spoken to Thiago directly—and she still hadn't checked last name on Garai's list. All she needed was for either of them to give her enough detail to make up something decent.

206

So now she just had to wait. Idly, Joy took note of her surroundings: a huge box filled with smaller boxes, with enough free space in the center to form a narrow aisle. Joy edged through that aisle, looking at all the boxes piled up to the ceiling, wondering what was in them. She tested a few and found them nailed shut. Just as well. She really didn't have any business poking through them just because she felt like it.

The crates didn't seem to be labeled with anything useful — just some random numbers and an odd, swirling sigil that seemed familiar somehow, but she couldn't quite make out the details. The interior of this container was dimly lit, by sunbeams coming in from cracks in the walls and ceiling, but they weren't hitting the most convenient spots to let her see what she wanted. Maybe she could use her compact mirror to redirect the sunbeams.

Joy started fishing through her purse when a high-pitched noise, something like a cross between a squeak and a chirp, emanated from the darkness around her feet.

Joy got on her hands and knees to look around, and saw two amber eyes looking back at her. It was the cat from before; a big beautiful short-haired black cat with little white patches on its feet — little "socks." It was lying on its side on the floor, in a "cave" created by a long crate lying on top of two shorter ones, and it was covered in kittens.

Even in the dim half-light, she could tell they were adorable. She counted five of the little darlings, and she had to count tails because their heads were buried in their momma's belly, except for one who was crawling over the rest of its siblings, who was making all the noise.

Momma cat alternated between licking the heads of her babies and staring at her with a steady gaze. Joy wished she could get a closer look, but that probably wasn't a good idea with a strange cat that was nursing. She heard they could get really protective of their kittens.

She began to wonder if maybe she might be too close. There wasn't a whole lot of room in here, and she didn't want to spook

Momma Cat into moving her kittens when she didn't have to. Joy tried to stand up, but she grazed her head on the long box that formed the "ceiling" of the cat's cave, and had to swallow a curse. No startling the kitties!

But as she cleared her head to look down on the offending box, she noticed the lid had been knocked loose. No, the nails on this one had been pried out. She could see inside where a bit of polished wood poked out from the shredded straw packing material. Was that a sculpture of some kind? Well, if the lid was already off, it wouldn't hurt anything to look. Gently she pulled off the top of the crate and set it aside. The wood bit she'd seen was the only exposed portion of the object, the rest being wrapped up in an oilcloth bundle along with three other identical bundles laying right next to it. She untied the twine holding the cloth in place, knowing she could re-tie it later, and pulled off the wrappings to reveal...

...A nice, shiny, brand-new fully-automatic submachine gun, exactly like the Kallistrate military would've used. Actually, she was sure it was the same model, straight from the Matev factory in Sarpedon—see, there was the maker's mark burned into the stock.

Joy had gotten a general overview of firearms for some of her supplemental field training courses. This model was called the Manticore, and it was the first of its kind—an automatic rifle small enough to be carried and fired by a single infantryman, as opposed to being mounted on a tripod or a larger machine, like a steam golem or iron crawler. Joy dug through more of the straw packing and found the disk-shaped high-capacity ammo drums that went with the rifles. This was no joke. This was the complete package.

It made Joy's blood run cold. She'd been given a turn with a Manticore once on the firing range. All you did was squeeze the trigger, and the monster roared to life, spitting out bullets in a continuous tongue of flame, shuddering and jerking against her shoulder like it was trying to buck free of her grip. She had a hard time keeping the muzzle pointed down at the target, and she couldn't believe how quickly the bullets ran out. She finished her turn feeling shaky and exhausted... and just a little bit exhilarated. But the destruction they caused when they hit their target—they had no business being used by anyone who wasn't in the military.

Which meant that their presence here, outside an official military depot, was very, very illegal. Like, capital-punish-ment-level-treason-against-the-state illegal. There was no way this was a legitimate shipment. With a shaky, nervous sensation in her stomach, Joy realized why those Triad thugs had been so confrontational and eager to drive her off. It was to keep her from finding this. And, in doing so, they'd driven her right to it. Lir's balls, she'd come here to do a silly puff piece. Why was that so hard to understand?

Joy felt the solid, lethal weight of Manticore, the black metal cold in her hands somehow, despite the stuffy heat inside the container. This was a serious weapon. And this was serious news. The type of story she'd dreamed of breaking open back as a student in Professor Gelfland's classes. But it was easier to sit in a safe, comfortable classroom and read about heroic acts of journalism than it was to be faced with the reality. Telling anybody about this would make some dangerous and powerful people very angry with her.

Joy held the stock of the Manticore up to her shoulder, braced against it like she'd been trained to, and sighted down the barrel. She remembered what had happened to the targets when she fired. Cheap planks of wood, painted black and shaped like rough silhouettes of people, with concentric white ovals on them to track shot accuracy. The Manticore would tear huge chunks out of them. With a little practice, you could even saw them in half with a constant stream of bullets. Joy shuddered. No way could she stand by while a criminal organization like the Triads gained access to this kind of firepower. She had to do whatever she could to stop them.

She needed a full inventory of this whole container. How many guns were we talking about here? She pulled out her compact, using the mirror to reflect the beams of sunlight where she needed them. Finally, she got a good look at the sigil, and recognized it immediately. It was the same as the design on Madame Zenovia's trinket, of the octopus-headed man-thing. Joy still had the amulet, so she double-checked it to be sure. The amulet was more ornately detailed, but it was the same design.

So, was this a Triad symbol, then. Or maybe a personal symbol of Benny the Shark. He'd started his career as a pirate, after all, and this was a nautically-themed deity. Was this what Madame Zenovia had stumbled onto on her 'spirit walk?' Something to do with illegal arms deals? Amazing that she was alive, then. Or maybe her incoherence had saved her—she was too crazy to take seriously, so "disappearing" her would've have drawn more attention than quietly subduing her and sending her home. Joy didn't think she'd be able to act crazy enough to get the same treatment, not at this point.

Joy started tearing her way through the various crates, using the tip of the Manticore gun as a crude wedge until she found an entrenching tool in one of the crates that worked better. Why the Triads were stocking up on entrenching tools was beyond her, but that was the least disturbing discovery she made in her little inventory sweep. Lever-action repeating rifles, more Manticores, pistols, cases of ammunition, rockets, mortars, land mines, bayonets, machetes, grenades, and dynamite. Lots and lots of dynamite. Joy tried to picture what might happen if this crate managed to catch fire. There'd be nothing left save for a smoking crater in the ground, for sure, but how big would that crater be? The blast would send deadly flaming shrapnel flying off in all directions. There'd be a larger fire, and what if there were more cargo containers carrying explosives?

The more Joy thought about it, the more likely that option sounded. What were the odds that a cat would randomly lead her to the one single container holding illegal contraband? An image popped up in her mind of a chain reaction of multiple dynamite crates in the cargo maze going up one after each other, all throughout the huge cargo maze, obliterating everything and everyone. It was horrifying.

Joy felt her knees shaking and had to sit down. Momma cat turned her head, keeping an eye out for any funny business. *But don't worry, Momma,* Joy thought. *No funny business from me here. Right now I'm the least of your worries. I just want to look at your babies for a few minutes.* Kitties were calming. Kitties were relaxing. Nothing could be too horribly wrong in a world that also contained cute kitties. She had to remember that. It helped her deal with the fact that she'd stumbled into the most insane situation she could imagine.

This weapons cache was ridiculous. She had no idea what the Triads were plotting, but it was something huge. Pimping, selling drugs, shaking down shopkeepers for protection money—none of those things required this kind of firepower. This was like a preparation for an armed takeover. Did the Triads plan to overthrow the government? She'd say that was insane, except for the fact that she was sitting smack in the middle of the evidence for it. Whatever it was, there was no way she could ignore this now. She had a duty to report this to the authorities straightaway, no matter what the consequences were. It was settled.

A high-pitched mewing snapped her out of her reverie. Two of the bolder kittens had wandered up to investigate her. Joy took a short glance at Momma, who seemed pretty nonchalant about things, and slowly extended her hand for the little guys to check out. They darted away at first, but returned to sniff and bump their little heads against her nails. That progressed to attacking her fingers with their claws and she got one of them comfy enough to sit in her lap, which her skirt could turn into a kitty trampoline, such that the other mewed at her until she brought it up to join her sibling. It was remarkable how calming this was. Joy sent a sincere thank you to whatever god had created kittens and small furry animals in general. The kittens did wonders for her sanity, playing with her for a good long while until they finally got bored and wandered back to Momma.

Joy stood up to do one final sweep, not that she really needed to find any more weapons to know this place was awful. But maybe she could find something like an invoice or inventory list that she could show to the authorities. She picked her way over to the far end of the shipping container, where she hadn't checked yet. There was another empty space back there where it looked like some crates had been shifted over. It could be another major find. She squeezed through the aisle to shine her mirror into the alcove.

A person was in there. They shrank back and cowered from the light. "No," she said, "Please don't hurt me," followed by a high-pitched babble that Joy couldn't quite make out.

Chapter 31:

Missing Person

Joy jerked back and managed to swallow a yelp of surprise. This had to be the busiest shipping crate in the whole docks.

The girl huddled against the wall of the shipping container, curled into a little ball. She flinched as the light from Joy's compact hit her, and there was a metallic clinking as she did. Her eyes peered out from beneath a black curtain of long, dirty, stringy hair. They were wide with terror, and the contrast of the whites of her eyes with her black hair and grubby skin made them look huge.

When she spoke, it was in halting Wuyu Xiaish, but with an odd rustic accent that Joy had a hard time parsing. "Please. Don't take me back to the Triad. They'll punish me for leaving. Please don't take me back."

Joy felt her fingers clench around the edge of her compact so hard that for a second she thought it might shatter. No, now wasn't the time for that. Anger would only frighten this girl. She had to remain calm.

"Don't worry, I won't take you back to them. I'm a friend. I want to help you," she said in Xiaish, picking short, simple sentences to prevent any miscommunication, while smiling and putting as much reassurance into her voice as possible.

"Help me?" The girl eyed her warily. "Why would you help me?"

"Because if I was in your place, I'd want someone to help me," said Joy. "And besides, that's what people do."

The girl just stared at her, still wary, though she relaxed her huddled stance, opening up just a tiny bit. As she did Joy caught a bright reflection from her compact light. The girl had a thick collar of some type around her neck and matching cuffs around her wrists. When the girl caught her staring at them, she turned away, and Joy heard metal clinking again. This time she recognized it as the chains connecting the collar to the shackles. Joy could practically hear the unspoken rebuke: *If people are so good about helping each other, how did this happen?*

Time to take a different tack. "Oh, but please, excuse my manners. I was so startled, I didn't introduce myself. My name is Fan Joy Song. What's yours?"

More staring, but Joy forced herself to be patient and keep smiling. This girl had to want help. Eventually, that need would overpower her fear. That's what she hoped anyway. The silence stretched on until Joy decided to try saying something else, but that's when the girl murmured something. Joy asked her to repeat it.

"I am Wong Hsiu Mei," she said.

Hsiu Mei, which sounded like Sue May to the Guardsmen. Just as Joy had suspected, this was the runaway they were looking for—and she'd definitely gotten into some trouble.

"Well, Hsiu Mei, lots of people are very worried about you. Your family wants you to come home."

The fugitive girl narrowed her eyes. "You're lying. My parents are dead, and my grandparents too. I have no home to come back to."

Joy blinked. "What?" she said. The guards hadn't mentioned that. They'd said… wait, what had they actually said? Joy could have sworn they'd said that Hsiu Mei's parents had been looking for her, but maybe they'd actually said "family," and she was misremembering it.

"Do you have other family besides your parents and grandparents, who might want to look for you? Uncles, aunts, cousins—that sort of thing?"

"All dead in the Barbarian Uprising," she said, using the Albion term for the Great War, "except for…" And then she raised her head for a second, before shaking it in denial. "No, that's impossible."

214

"What's impossible? What is it?" It had only been a second, but Joy had seen just a flash of something wonderful on Hsiu Mei's face: hope. She had to keep that going.

"My aunt and uncle—well, the brother of the man my mother's youngest sister married. Uncle Tan is a scholar in Genyen Province. I heard there was no fighting there. But that is so far away."

"Genyen might be far, but it's not too far," said Joy. "Not in the world of steamships, railroad, and telegraph."

"But he barely knows me. I was four the last time he saw me. He couldn't—"

"Doesn't matter. All family is precious, especially in hard times," said Joy, and something else occurred to her. "And by 'scholar' do you mean, 'Scholar of the Celestial Empire?'"

Hsiu Mei nodded, so Joy continued. "Impressive. You know a Celestial Scholar is not allowed to neglect his filial duties, right? Doesn't it make sense that he'd want to make sure all of his family is taken care of?"

Hsiu Mei blinked. She started to straighten up a little. "M… Maybe? But it's been years—"

"The Great War caused all sorts of chaos. They might have had a rough time sorting things out, but most of the Celestial Scholars retained their positions in areas that surrendered peacefully. It might've taken a while, but if I were in your Uncle's place, I'd be moving heaven and earth to find you."

"Really?" she said, hesitant, the voice of someone afraid to hope again.

"Absolutely," said Joy, and climbed up into the little crate alcove so she could look Hsiu Mei in the eye. "I don't know what you've been through, but I know this—you are a very brave young woman, and you are going to be just fine."

For a second, Hsiu Mei just looked shocked, then she scrunched her face up and buried it in her hands. Joy closed the distance between them, managed to get her arms around her. The girl stiffened for a second, then crumpled against her and started sobbing. Belatedly, Joy remembered how the Fan family could freak out her Mom's relatives with how huggy they were, but this was a barbarian custom they stood by. Everyone needed hugs sometimes, and this was definitely one of those time. Joy let Hsiu Mei stay like that a while, until she calmed down, and pulled back again.

Hsiu Mei looked back at her, then ducked her head and mumbled. "I made a mess on your nice clothes. I'm sorry."

"Don't be. You are more important than clothes," she said, and besides which, after squeezing through the rough edges of the shipping container's secret entrance and busting open a bunch of grimy weapons crates, this outfit was basically ruined anyway. But never mind that.

"And speaking of which, are you injured anywhere? Can you walk okay, chains aside?"

Hsiu Mei nodded, "Yes—they had orders not to 'ruin the goods' in any way before sale. If they did, they would have their heads cut off and be thrown in the sea."

"Oh. Well, good," said Joy, breathing a sigh of relief, glad that the runaway had been spared at least a little trauma. Those chains had made her worry. Then the rest of that sentence caught up to her. "Wait, they were going to ship you off and sell you?"

"They were going to sell me here," said Hsiu Mei.

"Here? Really?" Joy felt her mouth drop open. This story kept getting crazier and crazier the more she dug into it. She couldn't believe this was all going on in modern-day Dodona.

"Yes. They were going to show me to the buyer first. As a preview. But there was some kind of fight, and I escaped instead."

"A fight?" Joy repeated. "Wait, did this all happen three nights ago?"

Hsiu Mei nodded, and Joy couldn't stop herself from pressing further. "Did you see the fight? Or hear anything?"

"It was too dark to see much. I was on the boat and the fight was on the docks."

"What did you see? Actually, just tell me what happened from the beginning. In your own words."

216

Hsiu Mei took a deep breath, gathering her thoughts. "Three nights ago, they took me from the cell where they kept us and brought me down to the dock."

Joy had her notepad out. "Where was this cell?"

"On the boat."

"Which boat?"

"I don't—I could not understand the name." Hsiu Mei flushed a bit.

"That's okay. What did the boat look like?"

"It was big and red. With wheels on the side."

"Was it docked near a huge machine with giant metal arms?"

Hsiu Mei nodded vigorously. "Yes, that's right."

"Thought so. So, what happened next?"

"Well, we waited until the buyer showed up."

"Did you see him? Did you get his name?"

The girl shook her head. "They did not bother to tell us much, generally. They only told me that this was an important buyer, and I should behave myself, or I would be punished. I should smile and look pretty, and consider myself honored that I was being shown first."

Joy took another careful look at Hsiu Mei. Get the girl some rest and a nice hot shower, and she could be a model. Made sense they'd use her to sell the rest. "How many other girls were they going to sell?" she asked.

Hsiu Mei snapped her head up in surprise, "What?"

"You said they were showing you first, and before that you said they took you out of a cell where the others were, so I figured that meant they'd taken a bunch of you. Is that wrong?"

Hsiu Mei stared down at her fingers in her lap, while she twisted and twined them together. "No," she mumbled. "There were six others besides me."

"Mm-hmm," Joy said, trying to keep her tone encouraging. Hsiu Mei didn't like this subject for some reason. They could go back over it later. "Did the buyer show up? Did you get a good look at him?"

"I saw him from far away. The men were all talking there, before they would give him a good look at me. But he looked anyway. He kept staring and staring. I did not like it."

Hsiu Mei shuddered and hugged herself, and Joy felt her own skin shudder in sympathy. She knew that feeling, but the thought of poor Hsiu Mei having to go through it made her grit her teeth, and had a sudden vision of tracking down that fucking creep and putting an end to his staring with her entrenching tool, just swinging it over and over and over...

Whoa! Joy tamped down her rage and tried to breathe deep. That wasn't what anyone needed right now.

"What did he look like?" she said instead.

"He was not Xia. He was one of the barbarians. Big eyes and nose. Hair like wet straw."

"Do you think you would know him if you saw him again?"

Hsiu Mei nodded. "I would not forget that man. Ever."

Joy hoped that wasn't true. That soon enough she could reunite Hsiu Mei with her uncle and they could live happily and forget any of this ever happened.

"But you escaped, right?" Joy said. "How did you do it?"

"The men were interrupted before they finished talking. There was a strange voice in the night. It was a woman's voice, I think. But it was strange. It droned on and on, like it was coming from far away, and it kept getting louder. I did not understand anything it said. Some of the men went off, to check on it, I think. Then the drone of the voice became a screech. It was so loud, all the men went off towards it, except one remained to watch me. Then the men started shouting as well, and there were loud bangs, and the sounds of things breaking. And the shrieking continued, getting louder. Some of the men shouted things I didn't understand, but then someone yelled out in Xiaish, and they repeated it: 'Red face ghost.'"

Joy gaped at her. "They said what?"

"Red face ghost."

"They really said that? You're sure that's what they said?"

218

Hsiu Mei nodded. "Yes, because when the man guarding me heard it, he got scared. His face went white and he ran away. I was standing all by myself. At first I was scared to run, because I thought, 'If I run and they catch me again, they will be angry and they will do horrible things to me.' But then I remembered the way that barbarian was looking at me and I decided that I will try to run anyway.

"I ran into the piles of cargo where I thought they wouldn't see me so easily. I ran and ran, looking for a safe place. Then I hear a meow by my feet, and I see a cat, and—"

"And followed it in here," Joy finished. "Hsiu Mei, while you were running, you didn't happen to see anything of the fight, or who was doing all the screaming, or anything that looked like a ghost?"

She shook her head. "I was too scared to look that way."

About what she figured. Anyway, that story could wait. There were more important things to deal with now. "And you've been holed up here ever since?"

"Yes," said Hsiu Mei. "I took the chance to run when I had it. I had no time to think of what next. I don't... everything here is strange. I don't know anyone. I have no family here. I know staying in this room is no good, but..."

Her voice broke under the weight of her desperation. Joy reached over and rubbed her on the shoulder. "Don't you worry. I'm here now. From here on out, I'll be your big sister, all right? I'll be taking care of everything."

As soon as Joy said it, she knew it felt right. Hsiu Mei needed comfort and support. Joy remembered when Mrs. Jakuba had insisted on being called Tishka. It had really helped.

Hsiu Mei blinked. "Big sister? Why would you do that?"

Joy shrugged. "Well, I've got three real little sisters, and three little brothers, but because of my job, I've had to move around a lot, and I don't see them often any more. But I'm just used to being the big sister, and right now, I think you need one. So I just can't help myself."

"But, you can't," said Hsiu Mei. "If you help me, you'll be in trouble, too. You can't—"

"Well, that's backwards, actually," said Joy. "Because we're in Dodona now, and it's against the law to sell people. And all these weapons in this room are against the law, too. When I report this to the city officials, the Triads are going to be in so much trouble you won't believe it."

Hsiu Mei shook her head, frantic. "You don't understand. The Triads are vicious. And they're everywhere. I seen them... and it's not just the men. There is this one woman with them, with terrible scars. She is the worst... she told us all what she'd do if we ran. She said—"

Joy shushed her with a gesture, while taking a mental note of this mention of a woman—it must be that Ah Nei Wei, whom Chen didn't like. "Don't worry about it. I know they're scary, but that's no surprise. That's how they control people. By scaring them, so they won't fight back."

"But—"

"I said not to worry. You've had more than your share of worry, and now you need to stop. You've been a very, very brave young woman, but you don't need to do that any more. You just leave everything to me."

Hsiu Mei hugged her knees and let her hair fall over her face. Joy had to strain to hear her next words. "Not brave. All I do is run and hide."

"You escaped, and that's more than brave enough. That's braver than a lot of people in your situation would've been, take it from me."

The teenager sniffled and shook her head.

"You may not believe me now, but one day you'll look back and see that I'm right." Joy gave Hsiu Mei one last squeeze and started to back out of the alcove.

Hsiu Mei looked up. "Where are you going?"

"To get help. Don't worry, I won't be long."

"Don't leave me! I'm scared."

220

"I said not to worry." Joy kept her voice gentle. "I'd take you, but you've got those chains on, and they'll rattle and draw attention. You've been nice and safe in here for three whole days. You'll be just as safe for another hour or so. Though I doubt it'll be that long."

The sunlight leaking through the cracks in the shipping container was fading. The goons chasing her would've had to have given up by now. "I'll be back with help and you'll be back with your aunt and uncle in no time, trust me."

The poor girl gazed at her desperately. "I don't... why are you doing this? You don't even—"

"Because," said Joy. "I'm a big sister, and it's my job to look after my little sister. It's just what we do."

Hsiu Mei just stared at her.

"You just sit and hold tight," said Joy. "I'll be right back." And she turned and eased her way to the little entrance crack at the other side of the huge crate, and prepared to rejoin the outside world.

Joy had intended to just stick her head out through the crack to make sure the coast was clear, but that didn't give her the field of vision that she wanted, so she stuck her shoulders out too. That was better, and the coast was clear, so she tried to pull herself back in so she could exit feet first, but the loose panel grabbed at her like a pair of jaws, and she didn't have the leverage to push it open and pull herself back up at the same time. In the end she had to just surrender to gravity and slide all the way out headfirst, and she ended up in a heap on the ground with a painful bruise on her hip, but basically okay. And there hadn't been anyone around to see that, thankfully.

She dusted herself off as best she could, noting the irreparable damage to her outfit with dismay. Nothing to be done for it, though. She reached back up through the crack in the shipping crate to retrieve her purse. All she had to do for now was avoid the Triads long enough to track down the guards. She still had their emergency whistle, which had managed to remain on her neck through her little tumbling act, but she didn't want to use it unless she absolutely had to.

Joy started to creep along the side of the cargo aisle when a metallic clinking behind her made her jump. She turned to see Hsiu Mei slide out of the cargo container and stumble towards her.

"Hsiu Mei! What are you doing?" Joy said. "I told you to stay inside and wait—"

"Please," the girl gasped, and Joy stopped short as she saw Hsiu Mei's face. There were fresh tracks through the grime where her tears had been falling, and her face scrunched up in a rictus. "Please, you have to save the others. The others on the ship. The ones I left behind."

"Well, of course we will. We're going to save everyone. I didn't forget—"

"But I did! I forgot about them! I saw my chance to run, and I did, and I left them behind. I was only thinking about myself."

Hsiu Mei clutched at her, and Joy staggered a bit. Standing up, they were nearly the same height. Joy needed to get her calmed down. "That's okay, Hsiu Mei. You did—"

"No, it is not okay! I left her behind! I left my sister behind!" Joy blinked, "Your sister?"

Hsiu Mei sniffed and nodded. "My little sister Lin Lin. She was on the boat with me. I am supposed to take care of her. I was the only one she had left, and I abandoned her."

"Hsiu Mei, listen," said Joy. "Listen to me carefully—you did not abandon her. You did—"

"No, I did. I left her. I ran away and left her alone. And then... and then..." Hsiu Mei stared up at Joy with big, watery eyes as she struggled to catch her breath. "I knew if I ran I'd be punished if I was caught.

"But I didn't think... I thought only of myself. They still have Lin Lin. Since they can't punish me, they'll punish her instead. It's been days! They've probably been doing it for days, while I cower and hide. And I'm supposed to be the big sister! I'm supposed to be the one protecting her. But instead I... I..."

Hsiu Mei made a pathetic whimpering noise and buried her head in Joy's chest. Joy made shushing noises and stroked her hair, but she couldn't be as reassuring as she wanted. Unburdening Hsiu Mei's guilt wasn't a trivial thing, but this was a really bad time for it. Joy supposed she hadn't helped earlier with all that "leave it to Big Sister" talk. She'd been inadvertently twisting the knife. But she hadn't known! She'd assumed that Hsiu Mei was an only child. Actually, something about this whole situation was nagging at her, like she was missing something, some important detail. But she didn't have time to think about that. She needed to take control here.

Joy grabbed Hsiu Mei by the shoulders, shoved her out to arm's length, and gave her a firm shake. "Hsiu Mei! Look at me," she said, but the girl shook her head and kept her eyes low.

"No, I need you to look at me. I need to see your eyes. C'mon, little sister." Joy understood the shame that kept the girl's gaze fixed on the dirt, and that was exactly what she needed to break.

Slowly, Hsiu Mei raised her head. Joy finally got a bare glimpse of her pupils, though they seemed to be pointing somewhere around her collar, and was about to launch into her best impromptu pep talk, when she was interrupted by the worst thing possible.

"Well, look at this," crowed Yang. "I look for one and got two."

Joy whirled around, searching for him, then finally looked up, to where he was perched—on top of the stack of cargo-netted crates. They'd stolen her trick! She'd given them the idea.

"Chen! I got them! Over here!" Yang waved over towards the center of the maze, then turned to leer at them. "You've had some fun playing hide and seek, girls. Well, playtime's over. Time to come home to Daddy."

Chapter 32:

Catch As Catch Can

Hsiu Mei's eyes went wide, and she lunged back towards her hidey-hole. Joy seized her by the arms before she could get far.

"No, they've seen us," she shouted, pulling in the other direction as hard as she could. "That won't work. We've got to run! C'mon!"

They lost precious seconds in that tug-of-war while Yang descended on the cargo net, but Hsiu Mei gave in and they both sprinted for freedom, only to see Chen round the corner to cut them off. They tried to rush past him anyway, but he was too quick, catching hold of the chain hanging from Hsiu Mei's collar, and then grabbing Joy when she tried to free Hsiu Mei. Joy managed to twist free of Chen's grip, but by then Yang caught up with them and it was too late.

Joy struggled in Yang's grip. "Let me go," she yelled. "This is kidnap—"

The blow caught her off-guard, as the back of Yang's hand caught her across the cheek. She'd never taken a hit like that. It was nothing like the slap she'd gotten from her father that one time. They'd never gone all-out in her supplemental combatives practice. Even with Quintus, it had been more of a wrestling match than anything. Her ears rang and her knees went wobbly, but Yang hoisted her up by her collar, so she'd choke if she let herself fall.

"Shut your fucking mouth," he roared, and gave her a hard shake. "You've given us more than enough grief today, and I ain't taking any more from you."

Joy gasped and struggled to regain her balance. Right now she was more aware of the fact that she had a left cheekbone than she'd ever been aware of anything in her whole life, and that was because it was screaming at her. She felt stinging tears leak from her eyes and tried to blink them away. Okay, that hurt, but that's all it did. She had more important things to worry about now. This was an emergency situation, and she'd have plenty of time to curl up in a little ball and whimper later. She forced herself to ignore the pain and found, with some surprise, that she could.

"Just looking for the Red Specter, huh?" Yang snarled, and pointed at Hsiu-Mei. "Tell me, does *she* look like the Red Specter to you? Hey, Chen—be careful there, she might be your devil-ghost in disguise or whatever."

Chen rolled his eyes and snorted. He was controlling Hsiu Mei with one arm, yanking upward on her collar, so she was forced to stand on her tiptoes to take the pressure off. Terrified didn't even begin to describe her expression.

"Don't look like Chen buys that, does he? Looks like you didn't find any Red Specter. Seems like what you found was a filthy little whore, ain't that right, Chen?" Yang said this all in gutter-level Xiaish, just so Hsiu Mei could understand it.

"Please," said Joy. "Please listen to me. She's very young and she's lost her parents. It's not—"

"What part of 'Shut the fuck up' do you not understand?" he screamed in her face. Joy cringed as he did, but fortunately, he didn't bother hitting her again. "Bitch, I saw which of those crates you came out of. You just poked your nose in the wrong shit. You are so fucked right now, you'll need to—"

"Sir, please," Hsiu Mei choked out. "Please let big sister go. It is my fault. I am the one who ran away. So please punish me instead. She will promise to say nothing and I will go with you. Please let her go."

Joy was terrified that Yang would deck her for interrupting him, but he looked more confused than angry. "Let Big Sister go?... Oh, wait. You mean *her?*" he said, pointing back at Joy. "*She's* your big sister?" Yang found the idea ridiculous enough to burst out in a fit of nasty, braying laughter while Chen just looked bored. "She's not big anything. But I'll tell you what, little whore. You've been getting a nice easy ride so far, from what I hear. You're valuable goods. Except now it's starting to look like there ain't gonna be no deal at all, so it looks like you're gonna have to earn your keep some other way.

"Well, I got some ideas about what you can do, you and your big sister can…" and then Yang proceeded to spew out the most vile torrent of sadistic and obscene sexual practices, all in graphic detail, while Hsiu Mei started bawling.

And Yang kept going. He kept piling more and more twisted details on. The jerk had already won, but he just wouldn't stop.

But of course. That's how it always was, wasn't it? It was never enough. The assholes of the world would do whatever the fuck they wanted, and no amount of reasoning or begging or pleading would stop them until they got what they wanted, and then they'd take even more. Because they felt like it. Because they thought it was fun. And, most of all, because they could.

So, of course they'd never stop. How long had it been like this? Quintus at the office. Flynn who pretended not to take a side, thus enabling Quintus. The Guardsman who ignored her report of assault. The mashers and stalkers all along the docks and throughout the streets of Dodona. Everything wrong with her life: her rotten job and her crap apartment and her hunger and her worry. Every single fucking little detail was all because of them, because they never let up, not once, and she was just so *sick and fucking tired of it she could scream*.

And something in Joy's head went 'click.'

"Hey!" she said. "Asshole!"

Yang reacted as he had before, he whirled around to snarl in her face, except Joy had anticipated it, had thrust her own head forward, spine straight, power coming from her entire body, neck and shoulder muscles braced for impact. Yang ended up bashing the softest and squishiest part of his own face against the hardest and thickest portion of Joy's skull.

226

Joy felt the impact hum through her whole body, felt the opposing force yield with a crunch. Yang clutched at his face and yelped, staggering back, and Joy followed, measured the distance, and channeled every ounce of her fury into her leg, firing it off in a kick that went straight into the asshole's crotch, striking clean and true.

Yang croaked and doubled over, trying to clutch at her, but Joy managed to squirm free, trying to get enough space to knee him in the head, pulling the thug's jacket over his head and shoulders in the scuffle. It was an accident, but she went with it, throwing her knee into the space where she knew his head was.

Yang actually managed to pull back from the blow a bit, but Joy felt it connect, and Yang staggered backwards, wobbly-kneed with his arms thrashing around wildly as he tried to get his jacket back on right.

Joy had a second to worry that her best shots weren't enough to put this gorilla down, when she heard a frantic yell from Hsiu Mei. Joy spun to see Chen's charge, and she reacted without thinking, sitting straight down while planting a foot in his gut and catching hold of his lapels. Chen felt like he barely weighed anything as she rolled back and sent him flying off her foot, most of the power coming from changing the direction of Chen's own energy. He sailed through the air, upside down, and crashed into Yang, who had just managed to get his jacket back on straight. One of Chen's heels whipped into Yang's bloody face, and Chen landed mostly on his head. Joy couldn't have aimed that better if she'd planned it. Yang fell back onto a crate, which broke, and they both ended in a dazed heap, tangled up in the debris.

Joy stared at the two Triad thugs in astonishment. That had worked. All that stuff from her combatives courses. She couldn't believe that had actually worked. She caught Hsiu Mei staring at her, eyes like saucers.

"You beat them up," she breathed.

Joy felt a weird electric thrill run through her, like her whole body was humming. That had been so satisfying. Amazing what could happen when you got so mad you forgot to be scared. Then she noticed that Yang and Chen weren't knocked out, not by a long shot, and were struggling to their feet. Rage and luck would only get her so far.

"Enough fighting, time for running," said Joy, as she grabbed Hsiu-Mei's hand and half-led, half-dragged her off to sprint for the exit of the cargo maze.

Yang and Chen yelled and gave chase, but the girls had a nice head start on them, and Joy was riding an adrenalin surge for the second time today. She was sure she'd outrun them this time, but Hsiu Mei was holding her back. Joy urged her to keep moving, but from the look of things, she was already pushing past her limits, staggering and gasping, and Joy realized Hsiu Mei had been hiding in a weapons cargo crate for three days. What had she been eating in all that time? She couldn't have much energy left. Nothing they could do about it now, though. Joy pulled at her, exhorted her to keep moving. Sheer willpower could do a lot. They just had to keep going for a little while longer.

She heard the Triad thugs yelling behind her, getting closer and closer. She couldn't let them catch her before they reached the end of the maze. The exit was about fifty yards away. Joy clutched at Hsiu Mei and tried to double her running for the both of them. They passed another stack of giant crates, and from the corner of her eye, Joy saw it wobble.

There was a huge crash right behind her, followed by terrified cursing from Yang and Chen. Joy and Hsiu Mei both jumped, and neither could resist looking behind them to see what happened. An entire column of supply crates had just tipped over to block the path behind them, and the ones that had fallen furthest had split open, spilling their contents all over the storage yard. Potatoes and sugar—or was that salt? What a shame to waste food like that. And why had they just fallen over? Joy looked to where they'd been stacked up, and thought she saw a flicker of movement. Then she heard a thump, and saw one of the thugs' hands reach over the top of one of the crates. No time to waste.

Joy dragged Hsiu Mei out of the cargo maze and into the railyard, frantically searching for any sign of the city guards. The street was on their left, and she veered towards it, slowing down long enough to pop the guard's whistle into her mouth and start blowing. It made a piercing high-pitched noise that echoed across the docks, possibly the most annoying sound Joy had ever heard. Good. She blew hard enough to hurt her own eardrums, and the guardsmen ran into view in the street a hundred yards away, summoned as if by magic.

What luck! Something today was finally going her way. Karma was smiling on her finally.

Joy slowed her pace to give poor Hsiu Mei a breather, down to a walk. Those thugs wouldn't dare try anything in full view of the City Guard. "Look," she said to Hsiu Mei, who was gasping and bent over double. "We're saved. Those are the officials who have been looking for you. We've done it. You'll be back with your aunt and uncle in no time."

Hsiu Mei managed to straighten up to peer at the guardsmen hustling towards them. She stared at them a few seconds and then her eyes went wide in horror. "No," she gasped, and started to back away, back the way they came. "No," she repeated, though heaving lungfuls of air.

"Hsiu Mei, what's wrong?" Joy said. "These aren't bad men. They're here to help—"

"You work for them? How could you?" and the look of betrayal on her face was wrenching. "You said you'd be my big sister. I trusted you."

"You can trust me. I just want to help you. What's wrong, I don't understand. Please, you have to believe me."

"No, no," with a look of anguish, Hsiu Mei turned to run, but Joy grabbed her shirt. They struggled for a second, and Joy managed to push her up against a wall of shipping containers and pin her there. They were a few yards away from the maze entrance. Hsiu Mei sobbed and struggled, and Joy fought to make eye contact.

"Hsiu Mei, talk to me. I need to know what's wrong. I can't help you if you don't tell me what's wrong. You're on your last legs. You can't run forever. You need to trust me. I'm not going to hurt you. You have to believe me."

"Need some help there?" said Chief Gallach.

"Um, yes. And I am so glad to see—"

Hsiu Mei went rigid and pointed right at Brannock. "That man!" she cried. "That is the man who showed up three nights ago. That is the man who was going to buy me. Don't make me go with him. Please, I beg you."

Chapter 33:

Dirty Copper

Joy whirled around in shock. "What? Are you sure? Are you absolutely certain that's him?"

Hsiu Mei glanced over at Brannock and looked away, shuddering. "I do not forget that stare."

Joy looked over and had to concur. Brannock was creepy stare guy, all right, just like before. Only now it was directed at poor Hsiu Mei.

Oh no.

And that was when it clicked into place—little details that had felt wrong ever since she'd found Hsiu Mei in the shipping container. Hsiu Mei's distant uncle crossing a continent to look for her in Dodona—that *was* a stretch, wasn't it? And if Hsiu Mei *and* her sister had gone missing from home, why had the guards only mentioned Hsiu Mei and not Lin Lin? But that made perfect sense if the people searching didn't need to find the younger sister—because she'd never escaped.

"What's she on about?" said Chief Gallach. "What's she saying? You need us to—"

"No, it's fine," said Joy, grateful that the guardsmen couldn't understand Xiaish. That gave her some wiggle room. "She thinks you're scary. With your armor and weapons. Just give me a minute."

MacInroy gave her a winning smile, which he then directed over to Hsiu Mei. "Scary, us? That's just because you don't know us. 'Cause if you did—"

"—You'd know what a bunch of creepy, chickenshit cheats you're dealing with," said Yang, having finally caught up to them. He stood there with his squashed, bleeding nose, and his suit was covered with splinters and sawdust from the broken crate. He squared off against the guards, with Joy and and Hsiu Mei off to the side, a wall of cargo at their back, cut off from escape in either direction.

"Words are hurtful, Yang," said Chief Gallach. "But I'll over-look that for now, seeing as you're clearly having a bad day. But this is City Guard business, so—"

"Yeah? Well it's Triad business too. And the Triad doesn't stay in business letting punks walk away with merchandise they ain't paid for yet—ain't that right, Chen?"

Chen didn't answer. Chen wasn't there. Everyone stared at Yang, who spun back towards the labyrinth of cargo, confused.

"Chen? Hey, get out here. Hey, Lieutenant General Whatever—this ain't funny. Get your ass over here, you big coward! Hey—"

"Looks like Chen's got more sense than you, Yang." said Chief Gallach. "It seems he can count. There's four of us and one of you, so why don't you just back off and—"

"Fuck that! She ain't going no place," snarled Yang, and drew a long knife from a sheath hidden somewhere behind his back. It was practically a sword. Joy gulped and thanked Kovidh she'd had the sense to run when she did. The Guardsmen reacted instantly. They drew their batons and rapped them against their bucklers, making a horrible racket. The sound carried across the docks, and when the Guardsmen stopped, there was a faint echo as other groups of the City Guard in the area beat their shields in response. Reinforcements were on the way. Normally that would be good news, but now Joy wasn't sure. Maybe it was just Brannock. If he was the one bad apple, and she could expose him to the others...

"Hey, Joy," said MacInroy. "C'mon and bring Hsiu Mei over to us. Tell her we're gonna take her to see her family."

"How long would it take?" Joy asked. "Between the time she leaves here and the time she could see her parents?"

"Oh, not long," he said, all earnest smiles. "They're staying in a hotel right near the guard station. We send a runner ahead, they could probably meet us there. Maybe fifteen, twenty minutes."

232

Joy felt her stomach drop out of her. She hoped she managed to not let it show. She had to make sure. "You mean they're here in Dodona? You've spoken to them?"

"Oh, yeah—they're great people," he said, with perfect sincerity. "And they're super worried about their only daughter, too. I know they'll be thrilled when they see her again. So c'mon and bring her over here, won't you?"

"I'll tell her," said Joy, backing up so she could speak to Hsiu Mei without taking her eyes off either Yang or the guards.

"What's going on?" Hsiu Mei said. "What's happening. I don't understand anything."

"Hsiu Mei, I'm sorry," said Joy in Xiaish. "The men with the shields and armor are the city guards, but they're corrupt. I didn't know that when I spoke with you earlier. They lied to me, and I didn't realize it."

But she should have. From the very moment she'd met the Guardsmen, their behavior had been strange and suspicious. Intimidating the press, the Chief out on a foot patrol, followed by every detail of Hsiu Mei's story that didn't fit—why hadn't she seen it?

Because she hadn't wanted to. She'd wanted so bad to be rescued, for things to be easy. She'd wanted to have kind, just authorities to turn to, who'd step in and make everything right. She'd wanted it so bad that she'd ignored every sign that warned her it wasn't so. And now they were screwed, and it was all her fault.

"But what do we do now? What about my uncle?" Hsiu Mei wailed.

"I'm going to get us out of this, Hsiu Mei. Just stay by me and wait for my signal. Big Sister is going to take care of you. Trust me. You are going to be okay."

"What's going on?" said the Chief. "Why's she getting upset?"

"It's 'cause your boy sucks at lying, and he just got caught," said Yang. "You pigs just got made, so how 'bout we drop the bullshit, huh?"

The Chief gave MacInroy a sidelong glare, who replied with a sheepish, aw-shucks grin. "Whoops," he said.

So casual. Like it was no big deal. They were treating people like property and acting like this was a playground argument about whose turn it was on the swing.

Joy felt her lips pull back from her teeth in a snarl. "You people are disgusting. All of you. It makes me sick. How you can look me right in the eyes and lie to me—"

"*I* told you her family was missing her, and her new family does miss her," said the Chief. "Brannock's service to the Sleywie Anden has earned him a second wife, and you've done us the favor of finding her for us."

"Second wife? She's barely fifteen, you sicko," Joy snarled. "When Central finds out about this, you're gonna—"

"Central will not be finding out anything about this from you." The Chief said. "We will make sure of that."

Joy felt a chill, like her blood had been replaced by ice water. He couldn't possibly...

"Hey, Chief," said MacInroy. "Do we have to kill her? Because I still don't have a second, and I—"

"You ain't taking nothing," roared Yang. "You don't get what you ain't paid for. You don't do that to Benny the Shark."

"And I've told you, we have paid," said the Chief. "So we will be taking the property we've paid for. This one today, and if Benny keeps holding out on the rest, we're gonna—"

"Try something stupid? And maybe suicidal? Sounds fun. I'd like to see that," said a new voice, a ragged alto, as an armored figure emerged from between two railcars, followed by two men dressed in suits similar to Yang's.

The interloper crossed the rail yard in long strides, appearing at Yang's flank in seconds, without seeming to expend much effort. The armor she wore was strange, consisting of multiple small steel plates sewn together in overlapping segments with thick cords, kind of like a lobster's tail. The helmet she wore had a similar design, and had a short crest on the forehead of

234

a beetle with huge horn mandibles stretching to the sky. A wide, garish piece of cloth hid a great deal of the armor's design from view. It was somewhere between a cape and a tabard, tucked into the belt on the right hip to wrap around the left shoulder and secured to her back somehow. This mantle was mostly black, except for some pattern Joy couldn't make out due to the wrinkling of the fabric, and because the outline of the pattern was in an eye-bleeding hot pink. The interloper had an odd-looking pole arm, a slim, slightly curved sword blade fixed on the end of a staff, which she casually rested on her shoulder. She fixed the guardsmen with a huge grin, utterly devoid of warmth, that caused the numerous scars criss-crossing her face to stretch and warp. The city guard tensed, brought their guard up, and Joy couldn't blame them.

Joy was reminded, growing up, in her school, there'd been a group of nasty little boys, the type whose idea of a good time was tying firecrackers to the tails of stray cats and setting them off. Her parents told her to stay away from them, and she did, as those nasty little boys turned into dangerous and unstable young men.

Because you knew, deep down, that those cats had just been practice. You could see it their eyes, and Joy could see it in this woman's eyes, that to her, all of them were nothing more than stray cats, and she had a full supply of fireworks.

Chapter 34:

Enter Shiori

Chief Gallach narrowed his eyes at the newcomer. "So…
you're the one everyone's been talking about. What was it again?
Ah Nei Wei?"

The woman actually looked shocked for a second or two,
then began to laugh, a harsh, braying sound that carried across
the docks.

"Was that funny?" said the Chief. "Do I have the wrong person,
then?"

"Nah, that's me," she replied. "But hearing you guys call me
that is hilarious. 'Ah Nei Wei,'" she repeated, mimicking Chief
Gallach's accent, and broke out in more guffaws."

"Well—what should I call you, then, if not that? Who are
you, really?" asked the Chief, maintaining his calm, even as
his troops bristled at the woman's tone.

The woman straightened up and grinned. "Who am I, you
ask?" she said, like the Chief had offered her present, and it
wasn't even her birthday. Yang blew out an aggrieved sigh.

"Well, I've been told to keep that on the down low, but if you're
asking me, then I guess I've got no choice but to tell you, yes?"

She swung her pole arm with a flourish that made the Guardsmen flinch, while Yang and the other Triad men stepped back
to give her space.

"My name is a dangerous name; dangerous to hear and even
more dangerous to say. Numerous are my titles, each one feared
and outlawed coast to coast: the Butcher of Brentonsville, the
Hemlock Witch, the Terror of Yaolun, Last of the Caliburn,
Inheritor of the legacy of Keelia Rosewing—"

As she spoke, the woman punctuated her statements with
flourishes of her spear and her cape, allowing Joy to get a good

view of the banner draped over her back; a stylized icon of a rose with petals that were barbed like thorns, hot pink on a pitch-black field. That was the Rosedeath banner, the insignia of the secret Albion forces whose weapon was poison and whose reputation was atrocity. And this woman was wearing it as a cape. She was proud of it.

"I've killed men, women, and children, too many to count, so best mind your manners when talking to me—Shiori Rosewing!"

Shiori finished her introduction with a final sweep of her spear and struck a martial pose, while baring her teeth at the city guard, before returning to rest.

The whole display might have looked ridiculous on another person, but Shiori Rosewing—the real article, the actual person, holy crap—she carried herself with a presence that said she could back it all up. Joy felt Hsiu Mei tense up and cower behind her at the sight of the woman. The City Guard were all on edge. Even her Triad allies seemed wary around her.

"Yes, Shiori Rosewing," said Chief Gallach. "So those rumors are true after all. Very well. I am Chief Gallach, and these are—

"—A bunch of pigs making a racket in Triad territory. Yeah, I can see that." She turned to the two men trailing her. "You two—go back and round up every available body you can get. When pigs start squealing, more will come swarming. I've got these four."

"Yes, Ah Nei Wei," barked the two Triad men who'd come with her, and ran off in different directions.

"Shiori Rosewing," said Chief Gallach. "You were a Caliburn knight—supposedly a champion of the virtues of old Albion Empire. I believe respect and honor were among those virtues. There's no call for flinging insults."

"Oh, pig's an insult?" she said, "I thought it was a fun nickname. And you're lucky I'm being generous enough to start with insults. Let's talk about what you've done to Yang. That wasn't smart. How you plan to make amends for that, hmm?"

The guards all looked over at Yang, and the blood pouring

out of his nose. "We didn't do that," said MacInroy. "We never touched 'im. He was like that when we got here."

"Oh, please," said Shiori. "You think I'm stupid? What happened, Yang? They trying to throw their weight around?"

"Uh..." Yang hesitated in his reply. "Uh, yeah. That's what happened. Got me by surprise."

"Oh, you big, stupid, sexist liar," said Joy. "Is getting beaten up by a girl that embarrassing? You're pathetic."

All eyes turned to her. Whoops. Did she really want their attention on her? Or maybe... You know what? Fuck it. She was angry and tired and fed up and sick of their shit. All of it.

The Guardsmen looked between her and Yang and started smirking. Even Shiori looked amused.

"Yaaannngg," she said. "Who broke your nose? And roughed you up? Was it the guards? Or was it the little girl over there? Fess up now—you know how much your Aneuwei hates it when you lie her."

Joy noted that Shiori's Triad nickname sounded different when she said it, but Yang's reaction was more remarkable. He squirmed under her gaze like a guilty toddler.

"She... She just got a cheap shot in, that's all!" he finally blurted out.

The city guard started laughing at that, and Shiori just shook her head.

"Hey, fuck you guys!" Yang said. "You didn't see it! She's like a little wolverine. Bitch is psycho."

"Oh pul-lease," said Joy. "You big bully thugs are all the same—You think you can do whatever you like, and that's good and normal, but when a woman does it back, she's a psycho bitch, and you turn into whiny little toddlers. Why can't you just suck it up and take your ass-kicking like a man for once?"

Yang snarled as the Guardsmen guffawed, but Shiori held him back.

"Okay, I don't know who the fuck you are," she said to Joy, "But I like you already. Sure hope I don't have to kill you."

The off-hand way Shiori tossed that out put a chill on Joy's rage. Shiori wasn't talking figuratively. Joy had to play smart to get out of this. She had to think of something.

"She's dead," said Yang. "Me and Chen caught her snooping around. She found the runaway *and* one of the munitions crates, and then she went running straight to the Guard. I think they sent her to do their dirty work for them."

"I'm a reporter," said Joy. "And I'm not working for the Guard. And I'm not interested in any of your business. I'm freelancing for a tabloid, and all I was looking for was—"

"Hear that?" said the Chief, talking over her. "Not working for us, and of course she's not. Why would we hire someone to investigate our own merchandise? That doesn't make sense."

What? Their own merchandise? So the Triad wasn't stockpiling weapons—they were selling that to the City Guard. Why in the Great Wheel did a local police force need that kind of firepower? Were they actually plotting a coup?

"Oh, it doesn't?" said Shiori. "Well, if she's not one of yours, then you won't mind if we take both of them back for a nice, long chat? Problem solved, and you can put your little sticks away and clear out of our territory."

"You get the reporter," said the Chief. "The other one is ours. We paid for her."

"Aww, but Chief, I wanted the—" MacInroy's whine was cut short by an elbow to the chest from his superior.

"You ain't paid for shit," said Shiori. "Seriously, do you idiots think you can stiff Boss Fang and get away with it?"

"We did not stiff you guys!" said MacInroy. "We delivered it to your boys right where we were supposed to—"

"—Like hell you did," said Yang. "More like you jumped 'em, kept the money, dumped the bodies somewhere, and come to us with—"

"So, they disappeared?" countered MacInroy. "Just vanished into the night, huh? With six crates of gold bars. Sounds like your own people decided to cut and run to me. That's your own

239

discipline problem, and no way are the Sleywie Anden gonna foot the bill for—"

"Enough!" snapped Chief Gallach. MacInroy shut up and stood to attention.

Joy's mind raced as she tried to catch up with what was happening. She needed to figure it out quick if she was going to have a chance of getting her and Hsiu Mei out of this. The City Guard was buying girls and weapons from the Triad, but the deal had gone sour because the payment had gone missing, and both sides blamed the other. Chen had said something about that: "Things going wrong, people disappearing." And where was Chen, anyway? Why hadn't he shown up yet?

"Yeah, enough of your yapping," said Shiori. "I'm fed up with it. Those girls are ours. You want them, you can pay for them. Otherwise, scram. And you're lucky we're leaving it at that. Boss Fang is way more patient than I. I'd have carved you all up and put your heads on pikes the first time you crossed us."

The Guardsmen tensed, but Chief Gallach kept his cool. Guardsmen had to remain calm when dealing with agitated, potentially violent people. Chief Gallach might've been a decent cop once—well, good at his job, anyway.

"Well, that only shows why Mr. Fang is the boss," he said. "You should learn from him. You should realize that he didn't earn a nickname like 'Benny the Shark' for being squeamish. He didn't try that because he knew there would be consequences. We're the Dodona City Guard. Kill any one of us and uproar will be like nothing you've ever seen."

Shiori narrowed her eyes, but didn't say anything. The Chief pressed on.

"This deal, the original deal, is a good deal," he said. "We both stand to profit, and we both want it to go through. We both want the same thing."

Joy watched the Chief defuse the situation, and realized that the last thing she wanted was for the two sides to come to terms. Neither side would let her walk away with Hsiu Mei. Her only chance was if the two sides came to blows, letting them slip away in the chaos.

"The money is out there somewhere," said the Chief. "If it's really true that your men disappeared with the gold, then the City Guard has methods of tracking them down that the Triad doesn't. If we pool our—"

"Don't believe him," said Joy. "It's just more lies. He's trying to trick you like he tricked me."

"No one's talking to you, girl," said the Chief. "Now, like I was saying—"

"No! They're... they're fanatics!" Joy remembered how touchy the Guardsmen had been about their religion. Maybe honing in on that could piss them off. "They're all part of some weird cult. Sleywie whatever. And they won't even say what god they worship—maybe it's really Skakul. They could be a bunch of evil Skakul cultists."

Of course, that was a ridiculous accusation. Despite occasional bouts of hysteria in publications like the Gazette, Joy doubted that Skakul cultists really existed outside of pulp fiction and comics like the Red Specter. It was just the most insulting thing she could think of to say about them.

None of the looks the Guardsmen gave her were friendly, and Brannock was trying to murder her with his gaze, but they didn't explode like she'd hoped.

But Shiori chuckled and said, "Nah, nothing that interesting. Their god's some weird little small fry from up north named Nibiru."

That got a reaction. All of the Guardsmen flinched, save for Brannock, who started screaming, "Blasphemy! Blasphemy! You dare invoke the King of the Deep by name, you infidel?" He said more, but it was in some weird language Joy didn't know. Was it Vannish? Was that the actual name of their language?

Chief Gallach yelled something in the other language that shut him up, and Joy seized the opportunity to fan the flames some more.

"Nibiru? What's a Nibiru?" she said. "I've never heard of it."

"Of course you haven't heard of Nibiru," said Shiori. "Like I said, Nibiru is some insignificant, minor sea god from the Vannin islands. He's not even the main sea god, that's somebody else. So even Vannish sailors don't bother with Nibiru, that's how unimportant Nibiru is—"

"Excuse me," said Chief Gallach, crisp and controlled. But it was overly controlled, requiring considerable effort. The taunts were working. "In our culture, it is considered very inappropriate, very disrespectful, very unlucky, to refer to the Lord of the Depths by name. It's—"

"Really? Well, I ain't part of your silly Sleywie cult, so I can say Nibiru as much as I like, I think. Nibiru, Nibiru, Nibiru," she said, enjoying the twitchy reaction of the Guard.

Joy noticed the Chief's neck muscles turning into hard cords from the effort of keeping a straight face. "Childish taunts are beneath you," he managed. "Our culture—"

"Yah, yah, culture whatever," said Shiori, who turned to Joy and said. "Don't let 'em fool you. You know why there are so many Sleywie bastards all the way down in Dodona? Because everybody else in Vannin hates their fucking guts. Can't stand 'em."

The Chief glared. "It's true that Kallistrate's principle of tolerance—"

"Yah, tolerance," Shiori snorted. "Don't buy it. They'll go on about *tolerance* as long as it suits them, but the instant they get a whiff of power, they'll use it to force Nibiru on everyone. Make everybody bow to Nibiru, every waking moment, and suck all the joy out of life. It's true—I heard it from a Vannish sailor just the other night. A Sleywie town has no smoking, drinking, whoring, dancing, music—some of them even ban laughing. He couldn't believe we let any of 'those Sleywie cunts' sign up to the City Guard, much less run it. Thought we were crazy. Said the only solution to a Sleywie infestation is to burn it out, like roaches—"

242

"That's enough! That's more than enough," said the Chief. The entire City Guard had their hackles up and Chief Gallach laid his baton across Brannock's chest, in the manner of a dog trainer preventing a charge. But even the Chief wasn't looking so calm right now. She had to keep pushing.

"Wow, that's crazy," said Joy. "Who ever heard of banning laughing? Nibiru is the weirdest god I ever heard of."

"Looks weird, too," said Shiori. "Bizarre fish-octopus-crab-looking motherfucker with a huge swinging dong."

"*That* thing?" Joy said, remembering the figure on Madame Zenovia's trinket, and on all of the crates. "I think I've seen it. On the… um…"

Joy cut herself off before she could remind everyone that she'd seen all the illegal merchandise, but Shiori didn't pay any mind to that.

"Course you have," said Shiori. "These whackos put images of their 'secret god' on every damn thing they own. And I mean everything, including *her*."

Shiori pointed at Hsiu Mei, and Joy noticed something about her shackles, something she'd missed before. The chain link right below the collar wasn't a chain link at all, but a solid piece of metal about the size of an egg, and the image of Nibiru embossed on the outside.

Joy leaned in to get a closer look at it, and Hsiu Mei whispered, "Big Sister, what's going on?"

Joy straightened up and murmured in her ear, as she did. "I'm goading them into fighting each other. We'll have a chance to run when they do."

"Yeah, those aren't ours, those chains," Shiori continued, turning back to Joy and Hsiu Mei. "Some local member of their cult met the seller in Gancheol with them and insisted that all the girls get cuffed before they went aboard. Said it was ceremonial. Wouldn't even give us the keys."

"Ceremonial shackles?" Joy said, taking another look at Hsiu Mei's chains, noting that they didn't actually restrict her movement all that much. "Do they have some bondage fetish? Now that's creepy. Don't you think that's creepy?"

"Yah, sure. Creepy, perverted, deranged—"

"Enough! Woman, you test my patience," said Chief Gallach. "You seem to mistake my restraint for a license to toss out endless insults. That's a mistake you'll come to regret."

Shiori just grinned at him. "Oh, I'll regret it? How's that gonna work? You gonna do something about it?"

"Yes, I will," said the Chief. The Guardsmen, picking up on some unspoken cue, raised their batons and shields, and began to fan out, looking to surround the Caliburn knight, who just grinned, not bothering to go into any sort of defensive stance.

"We will be taking the girl, the one we paid for," he said. "You will keep the reporter, to question as you like. We each get something. Very fair, yes?"

Shiori snickered, her eyes glittering. "Ah, Chief—you're so sweet, it's almost cute. Like watching mice dictate terms to a tiger."

"So arrogant," said the Chief. "Shows what happens when you let a woman carry a blade." The guards had her and Yang surrounded on all sides now, though they kept their distance. Shiori still hadn't bothered to go into any kind of fighting stance, and she frowned as Yang went back-to-back with her.

"Hey, Yang," she said. "No crowding. Give me space, here."

Yang grimaced, but he followed orders. He kept his guard up and shuffled out through the widest gap in the circle of guards, who let him pass after a nod from the Chief. Yang stood outside the circle, weapon lowered, demoted to a spectator. Shiori faced the guards alone.

"You've made a huge mistake, woman," said Chief Gallach. "Killing any of us would cause an uproar, but there's nobody who will mourn your death, war criminal. That's the fate of a cowardly poisoner. The survivors of the Brentonsville eviction will cheer us. They'll give us medals. We'll be heroes."

"…Said the mouse to the tiger, before being eaten," said Shiori.

244

"You know, I have a daughter," said the Chief. "In fact, by the ineffable will of the Deep King, I have no child but that daughter."

"So it's Nibiru's fault you're firing blanks?" Shiori said. "Weird reason to keep wor—"

"And you know what else," he said, talking over her provocation even as he glared murder at her. "My daughter is a widow, widowed before she could bear me a grandson. Because of you. Because of what you did, I had a useless burden move back in with me. Because of you, I'll be stuck with her, for the rest of my days. But the machinations of the Fathomless One are mysterious and profound, and today He has seen fit to grant me the gift of revenge. I will give my family satisfaction. I will bring my daughter your head!"

Joy tensed and grabbed onto Hsiu Mei. "Get ready," she whispered.

"Bring it," said Shiori.

Chief Gallach flicked his baton, and all the guardsmen rushed her at once.

"Now!" said Joy, and yanked Hsiu Mei's arm. Both of them bolted toward the street full-tilt. But Joy had barely taken three steps when a foot-long sliver of black steel whistled by to lodge itself in the wall of cargo crates in front of her, bare inches from her face. It stuck fast, vibrating from the shock, and Joy nearly ran into it face-first. She shrieked, stopped short, and Hsiu-Mei crashed into her from behind. The two of them had to cling together to keep each other from falling.

"And where do think you're going?" said Shiori. "You're not going anywhere. You're going to stay where you are and behave, or the next one goes in your skull."

Joy stared at the razor-sharp piece of steel half-buried in the wood. It was a slim and simple design, like a needle with an iron ring for an "eye." No guard at the hilt, with red cord wrapped around the grip. You couldn't help notice details like these about something that was a few inches away from your eyes. But Joy's favorite feature of the throwing-knife was how it was not imbedded in her temple. She absolutely did not want that to change.

Her whole body trembled and her breath was coming short and fast. She had to tamp that down. She might scare Hsiu Mei. And just what had happened? Shiori was supposed to be distracted. Joy followed the trajectory of the throwing knife back to Shiori's outstretched hand, and gasped at what she saw.

The guards were in complete disarray. MacInroy crouched protectively over Brannock. MacInroy's helmet was missing, and one side of his face was covered in the blood oozing from from a huge gash in his scalp. Brannock was whimpering and clutching at his arm, also leaking red all over the place. What happened to it? It looked odd. Oh—that was because it was missing below the elbow. No, check that—it wasn't missing. It was right over there, lying on the ground a few feet away, still clutching its official City Guard baton. Joy fought down a wave of nausea because she did not have time for that right now, dammit.

The other guard, whatshisname, groaned and tried to push himself to his hands and knees, but Yang swept up behind him, put the point of his long-knife to the back of his neck, pushed him to his belly, and collected his buckler and baton. And then there was Chief Gallach, lying flat on his back at Shiori's feet, gloved hands around the curved blade of Shiori's polearm, trying to push it away from his throat, and failing at that task. Joy felt like the victim of some kind of an illusion, like one of the Great Phantasmo's sleight-of-hand card tricks. She'd taken her eyes off them for a mere second. How could the fight be over already? That just wasn't possible. It wasn't!

There was a rustle of activity, and the men Shiori had sent off for reinforcements returned, each with a dozen Triad members trailing behind them. Everyone else had cleared the area, apparently sensing trouble. The railyard section of the docks was free of the usual worker activity, although—oddly enough—the crane golem was still going, as it lifted a massive cargo container aloft. Apparently no one had bothered to climb the ladder and tell the operator to clear out.

"'Bout time you idiots showed up," Yang barked at the reinforcements. "Not that we needed you, with Ah Nei Wei hogging all the fun to herself." He hauled his captive to his feet and shoved him over to join MacInroy and Brannock.

"Chief, Brannock's really hurt, said MacInroy, trying to wipe the blood from his face. "He's not... I can't get him to answer questions."

"Pack the stump, put pressure on—urk!" The Chief's voice sounded strange with Shiori's blade pressed up against his throat. "Okay, you can stop—guhhh... enough! You've won already."

"Oh? Have I?" Shiori's eyes were wide enough that Joy could see the whites above the pupils. She had a manic expression as she gazed down at her captive. "Seems like my enemies are still breathing. Does that count as victory, I wonder?"

"Ahhh... fine, You... won. I... I was wrong. You keep the girls, we get nothing. No... reason to—uck!"

"No reason? What do you know about it, pig-mouse?" Shiori snarled, baring her teeth at him. "You want me to forgive you? Well, I don't feel like it. That's all the reason a tiger needs."

"Insane... you—I'm Chief of the City Guard. Kiill me and... consequences would be—"

"Consequences!" Shiori howled. "You don't get it, do you? Bitch, I'm Shiori Rosewing! The Hemlock Witch. The Terror of Yaolun. Shiori the City-Killer. You think I give a fuck about your petty politics? You think I give a fuck at all?"

The Chief went pale, as did the rest of the Guard. Even Yang did a double-take. "Uh, Ah Nei Wei," he said. "Maybe we oughta ease up a bit. Killing a guardsman really does cause a lot of problems, so—"

"Yang!" Shiori fixed him with a vicious glare, making him shrink back a step. "You questioning my orders?"

"Oh, no, Ah Nei Wei. I wouldn't do that."

"Great. So shut your mouth while I handle this." A clatter of boots hitting gravel and concrete drew her attention. "Oh my, look who's here."

The Guardsmen's shield-bashing signal from the very beginning of the confrontation had finally worked, as two squads of four came running up from the street, with a third squad rounding the corner coming from the other direction.

"Chief!" said the leader. "What's going on—"

"Everyone! Hold... positions and stay calm! That's... order—urk."

"Actually, I'm giving the orders here," said Shiori. "And I was just deciding whether killing your commander would be fun enough to be worth the hassle. What do you think?"

There was a loud click, audible even over the chugging of the crane golem's steam-engine, as two of the city guard produced heavy black revolvers and leveled them at Shiori. Joy's jaw dropped open. Since when did the City Guard carry guns? Then she remembered the huge cache of weapons and realized she shouldn't be surprised.

"I think it won't be fun for you at all," said the guard leader. "Now, drop your spear and put your hands on your head."

"You know, when you say that, it just makes me want to swing my spear even more. This just gets more fun by the minute. I'm so torn." Shiori shifted just a bit, and Joy noticed she had a sheath on her wrist with more of her deadly throwing knives. She showed no signs that she was willing to drop her polearm. Joy stared at Shiori's feral expression and the full realization hit her—of the type of person it took to create the legend of Shiori Rosewing, and she was not what you'd call sane. Except Shiori just might have the skills to make reality bend to fit her insanity. Joy wondered if Shiori could actually dodge bullets or if she only thought she could. She wasn't sure which possibility scared her more.

The two factions stared each other down from opposite ends of the rail yard, each poised on a hair trigger, as the arms of the crane golem swung overhead, oblivious to everything else going on.

"Everybody, wait," gasped Captain Gallach. "Just... Knight Rosewing, why are you doing this? What do you want? Right now, just tell us that, and maybe we can... we can work—"

"Oh, you think so?" said Shiori. "Work things out? But what if what I want is your head on a platter?"

A ripple of tension ran through the City Guard. "Chief, we've got a clear shot—"

"Hold," croaked the Chief, holding up one hand. "Listen—"

"No. I am sick of hearing you talk," Shiori. "You yammer on and on. You think you're being so patient, and so reasonable, parading about before the tiger, believing it should pay close attention to you, like your squeaking is of great importance. You only show that you understand nothing. All of you."

Shiori directed that last bit at the Guardsmen pointing guns at her. "It's nothing but mouse after mouse—this whole city is full of 'em. Legions filling up the houses, eating and breeding 'till they spill out on the streets, swarming all around me. And they're so stupid. None understand their place. None are smart enough to even understand that they are mice and the tiger is a tiger. Just like you, Chief. And just like all you pathetic City Guard."

The Chief looked like he wanted to answer, but he could only make vague choking sounds, as Shiori had grown more and more agitated throughout her tirade. But the next time she spoke, her voice was quiet, just barely loud enough to carry over the sound of the steam crane.

"And you know what? I am so very tired of being patient. Because I really hate mice like you, Chief. I hate you more than *anything*. And I think it's time you were all reminded just what happens when a tiger gets angry." And her smile was a psychotic mask, the face of someone so wrapped up in their own world that all else was trivial. The face of someone who just didn't care about what happened next. It was the face of someone who might do anything.

"Benny the Shark!" Joy called out. "Shouldn't you check with him first?"

Shiori turned to glare at her, and Joy struggled to keep from wilting under her glare. Joy needed chaos in order to escape, but... not like this! She didn't want to see a human being get their throat sliced open. There had to be another way.

"I mean, this kind of blow-up really would be a big deal," she continued, trying to keep her voice steady. "So, um... I was just thinking... maybe before that, you might want to—"

"You. Who were you again?"

"Um, I'm a reporter—"

"A reporter-mouse," said Shiori. "Who thinks it's more clever than it is. You thought if you got the other mice to fight the tiger for you, then you could run away to your little mouse-hole."

Joy tried to keep a straight face, but apparently she failed, because Shiori smirked at her reaction.

"What?" she said. "Did you think you were clever? You weren't. Of course I saw what you were doing. It's a strategy that's common as dirt. Mice too weak to fight their own battles try to play the stronger off against each other. I see it all the time."

Joy should've been terrified, but Shiori's words resonated inside her mind. Everything that had happened so far, combined with little details she'd been half-noticing all day—Shiori knocked them all loose, and they fell together to form a complete picture.

"Yes, that's it!" she cried. "You're exactly right."

"Of course I'm right," said Shiori. "You think flattery will—"

"No, not about that," said Joy. "I mean—yes, you were right, but that's not the main thing. I mean what you said about it being a common strategy. That's what's happening, before I even got here. Someone is playing you against each other. The Triads and the City Guard. They couldn't fight either of you directly, so they're trying to get you to fight each other."

Everyone was staring at her now. "What nonsense are you talking?" said Shiori.

250

"Nonsense, yes, tabloid nonsense. That's what I thought, too—but look at the evidence. People disappearing. Things going wrong. That's what Chen said, and where did Chen go? Where is he now? And those crates? Why did they just fall over, all of a sudden? Wouldn't trained laborers stack them up better than that? That's when you lost him, isn't it, Yang?"

Yang just stared at her like she was crazy, and Joy realized she was babbling. Well, whatever. Nothing to do but plow through, though Joy had to raise her voice to be heard over the noise of the crane golem, as the huge railcar-sized container it was toting swung over in their direction.

"And that missing payment, with all those missing people, isn't that a convenient thing to fight over? Something where both sides suspect the other, and neither can afford to back down? And exactly what in the Abyss actually happened three nights ago? I know there was some kind of riot, but what set it off? I've been up and down these docks trying to get a straight answer to that, but nobody will say."

"And why won't they say? Because they don't know, or won't think anybody will believe it," Joy had to shout now, because of the crane, combined with something else, a chorus of lowing coming from the container it carried. Must be a livestock shipment, judging by the glimpses of movement she could see from between the slats in the sides of the container. Oh, and the smell.

Joy kept going. "Yeah, everyone would think they were crazy, or delusional, or superstitious, or seeing things, but what if they weren't, not this time? What if it was true? What if it was really true?"

She had everyone's attention, though she didn't know if she was convincing any of them.

"Would you get to the point already," said Shiori. "What are you talking about?"

"I'm talking about the only person who'd dare to go up against a corrupt City Guard and the mob at once," said Joy. "I'm talking about the only person who could, doing it the only way he could: staying hidden from his enemies, never showing his face; striking from the shadows, only to disappear back into them; picking you off one by one, and letting superstition and fear eat at your morale. Does that sound familiar? Well, it should—if you read the comics page. Because there's only one man who could do all that, and that's...."

Joy paused as a shadow fell over her. The huge cattle container was blocking the light of the setting sun as it stopped in a position directly above them, centered on Shiori and the Chief. The mechanical whine of the crane golem changed pitch as the massive crate began to lower, and Joy realized that the golem operator wasn't going to stop.

"...COWS!" Joy yelled, pointing overhead.

Chapter 35:

When Cows Fly

Everybody looked up, following her finger, except for Shiori, who narrowed her eyes in a 'you-don't-seriously-expect-me-to fall-for-that-do-you' glare. She stayed focused on Joy, even as the container continued its descent in fits and starts, even as the golem's giant claw-fingers began to open, causing the cables that held up the container to slip down toward the massive steel fingertips, and the huge crate to jerk about mid-air. A chorus of distressed moos echoed out over the railyard, and a light shower of... cow detritus rained down on the warring factions. That finally got Shiori's attention, and she looked up just in time to catch a faceful of the product of a particularly anxious cow. It struck dead-center with a wet, juicy splat.

Most of the Triad and some of the Guard froze in horror at the sight, while those with more presence of mind started waving and yelling at the crane operator, to no avail. Joy noticed one idiot bursting out in hysterical giggles. Oh, wait—that was her. Shiori wiped her eyes clear and fixed Joy with a glare that promised her a slow and horrifying death.

Fortunately, one of the left claw-fingers lost its grip, and the huge container jerked midair again, dangling precariously from the two remaining fingers. Yang cried out and tackled Shiori, while the guardsmen darted in to grab the Chief by the ankles. Everyone scattered for safety as the livestock container descended to a height of about five or six feet above the pavement and the golem claws opened fully, releasing its cargo, which fell to the earth with an earsplitting crack.

The sides burst and the cattle spilled out, fat, shaggy, and disoriented. Joy winced as they hit, expecting total carnage, but all of them seemed to regain their feet immediately, milling about and mooing. Joy turned her gaze up to the crane operator, but the sun was reflecting off the glass. Who was that—this third party who dared step right in the middle of a Triad/Guard brawl? Could it be?

"Big Sister, look out!" said Hsiu Mei, seizing Joy by the wrists and hauling, yanking her along and forcing her up a pile of cargo. Joy spared a second for a backward glance, only to see a wall of brown hairy flesh bear down on her. She jumped up enough so Hsiu Mei was able to hoist her the rest of the way, as the massive animal crashed sideways into the cargo pile, where she'd been standing mere moments before.

"Whoa, that was close," breathed Joy, before realizing what had just happened. "Hey, that cow just tried to kill me. What the hell? Bad Cow! No grass for you!"

"They're upset," said Hsiu Mei. "It's a strange place with strange people and strange noises."

"Being upset is one thing, but that's no excuse for attempted murder. Aiyah!" Joy glared at the disgruntled bovine prowling the perimeter of the crate. "You hear that! I hope they grind you into meat buns, you cow asshole!"

The cow snorted and paced around the crate, along with all its brethren, tossing their heads and rolling their eyes, Joy was so frustrated she wanted to scream. This was the perfect time to flee, but they were stuck here with no way out. There was a loud clamor from one side of the railyard, as the guardsmen tried beating on their shields again. The cows didn't seem to care for that much.

Hsiu Mei winced. "They shouldn't do that. The cows could stampede."

"Stampede?" said Joy. "What a great idea! C'mon, Hsiu Mei. We're taking the mad cow train outta here. Jump on my signal." Joy waited for the asshole cow to get close enough so they could leap on its back.

Hsiu Mei stared at her. "What? That's crazy. If we fell—"

"You want those men to catch us? You have a better idea?"

"N-No, but…"

"Great! On my mark. One… two… three… jump!"

254

They did, and landed square on the huge animal's back. It bellowed in protest, and bucked a few times, trying to throw them off. Joy pitched forward, lying flat and grabbing handfuls of shaggy hair to stay on. This cow did not have the stampede concept down at all. It needed a lot less vertical motion and way more horizontal motion. Despite her intention to dig her heels into the beast's flanks, she was getting way less purchase with that than she'd hoped. Every time it bucked, it was liked being gut punched by a fist that was bigger than she was. And Hsiu Mei was clinging to the back of her jacket and inadvertently collar-choking her.

Joy tried to turn her head to say something to her, just in time to see Hsiu Mei twist her grip enough to put both pinkies in her mouth and make the loudest whistle Joy had ever heard.

And then the herd was off. The whole mass of them moved as one, crashing forward like a tidal wave, completely unstoppable. Men shouted curses, ran for safety, and Joy heard gunshots ring out. That only made the herd run faster. Out of the rail yard and onto the main thoroughfare of the docks, a hundred hooves beat at the concrete as the shaggy cows made a concerted break for freedom. Joy held on for dear life. Though having a cow run was an improvement over the bucking, it still wasn't comfortable by any means. Now she knew why people generally rode horses. The cow's back was angular and uncomfortable, and the forward-and-back rocking motion hadn't gone away. But it was easier to deal with, and she was able to raise her head enough to get a sense of her surroundings.

The stampede was charging full-tilt into the Wharfside Arcade, the nice touristy section of the harbor district. Just in time for one of the luxury ferries to be dropping off distinguished visitors to the fair city of Dodona. They got a welcome they wouldn't soon forget, as a hundred tons of angry livestock bore down on them like a tsunami. Men screamed, women shrieked. All around her, Joy saw wealthy dandies wearing suits that probably cost more than her entire apartment building scramble up light poles or decorative trees to get away, while elegantly jeweled and coifed women scrambled for cover anywhere they could get it, some of them forced to dive under stone benches or even to leap into the harbor.

It could easily have been worse; so far everyone seemed able to get clear of the deadly hooves, and all the shrieking seemed to divert the cows' path just a bit, but not before the cows tore through the outside seating areas for La Belle Terrasse, a five-star restaurant with reservations on a year-long waiting list, just to sample their custom-raised beef. The cattle wreaked terrible vengeance for their departed and tasty, tasty brethren, overturning tables, sending expensive sterling silver utensils and exquisite crystal wine glasses flying, trampling the pristine tablecloths, and smashing the chairs to splinters.

From the porches and store fronts of all the elite boutiques, people stopped and stared in astonishment as a full-blown cattle stampede tore through the Wharfside Arcade, where that sort of behavior was generally frowned upon. Joy really hoped no-one she knew recognized her. She'd never live that down.

But that wasn't the worst problem. She was getting tired. Maintaining her grip on her cow was getting harder and harder, but falling was not an option. Falling meant going under the herd and getting mashed to a pulp by a barrage of iron-sharp hooves. That image stuck in her mind and gave her a surge of energy, letting her hold on for longer, but the constant bouncing worked to dislodge her grip, bit by bit.

She felt herself sliding to one side, with no respite to let her re-adjust, Hsiu Mei trying to pull her back upright, but beginning to succumb to the same problem herself, and they both kept slipping... and slipping....

There was a mighty crash as the cows tore through a sweet-meat vendor's kiosk, and their cow swerved to avoid it, charging down a dark side-alley, separated from the herd.

This was their chance. "Jump!" said Joy, and while what happened next was not much of a jump, they managed to get clear enough to avoid being trampled, and landed in a pile of junk. Which turned out to be someone's house.

"Oh! I'm so sorry," she said, staggering to her feet and clearing the detritus off herself, Hsiu Mei, and the poor unfortunate they'd landed on. "I swear that was an accident. Are you okay? You're not hurt anywhere, are you?"

"Oh nnnooo…" said he, after Joy cleared enough garbage to get a good look at him, and rather wished she hadn't, finding a man with long, unkempt hair sprouting from his head and face. His jacket had partially disintegrated, though enough remained for Joy to recognize the army surplus fashion. His eyes had an eerie disconnected quality to them, and he clutched a smoke-stained glass pipe between fingers that looked like they hadn't been washed in a month. Joy realized she was talking to a junkie in the middle of a high. "I'm feeling no pain, man. And muh spell worked. Finally summoned a pixie."

"Well—good for you, then," said Joy. "Well, if you excuse us, we've got some really terrible people to run from, so—"

"No, no, no, no! Can't do that," whined the junkie, and seized her by the wrist. "Can't fool me—catch a pixie, get wishes. Them's the rules. Gotta follow rules. Gotta follow them. Rules are rules."

Oh. When he'd said pixie, he'd actually meant her. She was supposed to be the pixie. Joy decided she was fed up with dealing with everybody else's nonsense today.

"Ok, fine! You've caught me. Now it's… Wish Time!" She plastered a huge fake smile over her face and threw her arms skyward in a celebratory gesture that also freed her arm. "Ala-Ka-zoom, Ziggity-Splat, we'll grant your wish in no time flat!"

The junkie smiled and cackled, "I wish… no, wait. Gotta do this—"

"And when pixies grant wishes, we listen to the truest, most secret wish of your heart," Joy kept going, "And your heart tells me that its truest wish is to quit smoking your brain out through your lungs, clean yourself up, and get your life back together.

257

Wikkety-Woo, Flurpetty-Flurp, Ding-a-Dong Doodle, and Bin Bong Bam. Wish... Granted!"

As she cast her fake spell, Joy performed a series of magical poses, ending with a kick that knocked the junkie's glass pipe out of his hand to shatter against the brick wall behind him.

"Ah! Shit!" he said, ducking to the side and shielding his face with his arms.

"Our contract fulfilled, we pixies must be off, back to Pixie-land. Zippity-Doo, Jiggity-Jam; you're motherfucking welcome."

And without missing a beat, she turned, grabbed Hsiu Mei's hand, and marched out of the alleyway.

She'd been prepared to run if she needed to, but the only thing that followed them was a resentful murmur.

"Man, pixies are *assholes*."

Part 6:

Home Base

Chapter 36:

Kossar Hospitality

Joy managed to get Hsiu-Mei back to her apartment building without drawing any undue attention, or at least that's what she thought. It could be hard to tell sometimes. Joy had taken her jacket off and had Hsiu-Mei carry it so it was covering most of her chains, but there was nothing much to be done for the rest of their appearance. Joy had been wearing simple-yet-stylish business attire, but after a day of squeezing into cargo crates, brawling with gangsters, and cattle rustling, she was no longer office ready. She was covered in sawdust, had multiple runs in her stockings, a major rip in her blouse from that damned cargo crate, and the side of her face where Yang had backhanded her felt stiff and swollen. She was sure she looked hideous, and had spent most of the trip home fighting an urge to pull out her compact and check.

She didn't, though, because there wasn't any time for that. They had to get Hsiu Mei safe and off the streets before either the Triads or the City Guard caught up to them. They stuck to back alleys and side streets, and when they did cross big public avenues, Joy tried to walk as briskly and confidently as she could, and the fact that she looked like she'd been through a war zone was beside the point, and none of your beeswax to boot, so how could you be so gauche as to even bring that up?

It seemed to work. At least, nobody stopped what they were doing to gape at the obvious fugitives. Actually, things went really easily. Dodona was a huge, cosmopolitan city. Weird stuff happened all the time, and people just shrugged and went about their business. For right now, Joy was grateful for that, enough to give Hsiu-Mei some leeway to gape at the sights from the Lenart Memorial Bridge as they went back across the Ala-Muki in the twilight.

Their anonymity lasted up until they reached her apartment building. "Yoo hoo! Joy! How are you doing?" The voice belonged to Mrs. Jakuba, leaning out of the windowsill on the first floor, as usual.

"Hello, Tishka," Joy replied, speed-walking to cut the distance between them. She doubted that they'd been followed, but she still wanted to keep Hsiu Mei's presence here quiet.

"Out late this evening? And you have a friend. I don't believe we've—" and Mrs Jakuba's expression switched to alarm as they got close enough for her to get a good look at them. "Goodness gracious! What has happened to you! Has there been accident? Are you okay?"

"Oh, we're fine, Mrs. Jakuba. Don't worry about—"

"You do not look fine to me. Come in so I can look after you. I need to check for myself that you are fine."

Joy tried to refuse, but Mrs. Jakuba wasn't the type to let an opportunity to fuss pass her by. Besides which, the more Joy thought about it, the more sense it made. Mrs. Jakuba was a lot better prepared to deal with starving refugees and really hungry journalists than Joy was on her own. At the very least, she'd have something in her stewpot. And her apartment had more places to sit down. Joy's apartment was the very definition of small and spare—just shelving, her bed, a dresser, a writing-desk that was basically a wood plank set over some crates, and a second-hand office chair that was literally coming to pieces.

Seriously, her chair had a rip in the seat cushion wide enough for the stuffing to leak out. She'd patched it up with packing tape, but the tape had a habit of peeling off in wads that stuck to her skirt while she was typing. There'd been days where she'd ended up walking around in public for hours with tape stuck to her ass before she'd noticed. But even back when she'd been making a decent income at the Journal, she'd never bothered to put any money into furnishings.

She'd been expecting to be assigned to a position abroad, so why bother?

Mrs. Jakuba, on the other hand, had one of the nicer apartments on the bottom floor, and it was set up for entertaining. Mr. Jakuba had been an accountant with a Kossar trading company that brought him to Dodonna. Never a senior position there, from what Joy had been able to figure out, but he must've done reasonably well and invested wisely for his widow to live as comfortably as she did. The whole apartment had that comfy lived-in feeling and was covered in family history, and Joy always felt welcome here. She hoped Hsiu-Mei would get that, too.

Joy started right into the introductions.

"Hsiu-Mei, this is Mrs. Jakuba, but I usually call her Tishka, which means Auntie," she started off in Xiaish, "She's my neighbor and my good friend. We can definitely trust her. Say hello and I'll translate."

Joy relayed Hsiu-Mei's nervous introduction, complete with apologies for intruding in her home.

"Oh, is no trouble. I love having people over. Sue May, yes? How is it Joy has not brought you over yet?"

"Well, we just met today," said Joy. "Actually, she's been having a really bad time lately, and I think we could use your help."

Joy felt guilty roping Mrs. Jakuba into this mess, but she'd didn't see any way of accepting her help while hiding what was going on, and she didn't have the energy to try. She convinced Hsiu-Mei to lower her jacket to let Mrs. Jakuba see the chains and collar that they'd been hiding.

"I was investigating a story, and I managed to get her away from some bad people," Joy explained.

Mrs. Jakuba's eyebrows shot up at the sight, but she recovered admirably. "Oh, you poor thing. This is terrible to be happening in Dodonna in this day and age. And your parents, they must be so worried. What are those idiot guardsmen doing, to allow this to be going on?"

"Um, I'd say the City Guard definitely aren't going to be any help here," said Joy, "So I was thinking—"

"No help at anything, the City Guard! Mashers can accost decent women at work, and do they do anything? No—they sit on their butts and file reports. Same thing when old Matya's store got broken into. Was the thief caught? Of course not, though Officer Blackerby made sure to file a report. And now this. Look at you—you look half-starved. And filthy. We need to get you clean. And fed. Come, sit! I will take care of this."

Mrs. Jakuba gestured for Hsiu-Mei to sit on the couch, which she did, after a nod from Joy, who was wishing that their host would slow down and stick to one subject so she could have a chance to translate.

She got a brief opportunity when Mrs. Jakuba bustled off to the kitchen, just enough to explain to Hsiu-Mei that their host was upset about Hsiu-Mei's mistreatment and was bringing food, when Mrs. Jakuba came back in with a small half-loaf of bread and a salt shaker to go with it.

Hsiu-Mei's eyes lit up at the sight of food. She started to reach for the bread, but stopped herself midway, a chagrinned look on her face. She smiled at Mrs. Jakuba and shook her head.

"Eh, she doesn't want it?" Mrs. Jakuba said, turning to Joy. "Should I get something else—"

"No, no—it's fine," Joy turned back to Hsiu Mei, "She says, as your host, that she insists you accept her—"

That was all Hsiu Mei needed to seize the bread and start tearing off chunks. Joy had been impressed that she'd remembered her manners at all, considering how hungry she must be. Actually, now Hsiu Mei was wolfing her food to the point where Joy was about to step in to keep her from making herself sick, but Tishka beat her to it, scrubbing at her hands and face with a damp washcloth—so important to do before eating, and tsking over the barbarity of the manacles getting in her way here. What kind of monsters do this to a young girl?

These chains would have to come off right away.

It was right about then that Mrs. Jakuba noticed the egg-shaped lump of metal dangling from Hsiu-Mei's collar, the one with the Nibiru insignia engraved on it, and proceeded to freak out like Joy had never seen from the normally unflappable woman.

She jumped back from Hsiu-Mei like she'd been burned and started yelling in Kossar. At least, Joy thought it was Kossar, but it was coming out in a torrent and she couldn't keep up with it at all. She was maybe able to pick out every fifth word, but the rest of it was a jumble. The words for 'evil,' 'unclean,' and 'cursed' seemed to recur a lot. Joy spent the next five minutes between trying to get Mrs. Jakuba calmed down enough to talk to her again, and trying to keep Hsiu Mei from panicking in response, reassuring her that it wasn't anything she'd done—the symbol on her amulet was bad luck, and Tishka was upset about that.

Finally Mrs. Jakuba calmed down enough to make sense. "You say she's in with bad people? Who are these people and how is she in? How does she have that... *thing* on her neck?"

Wow, her hands were actually shaking, and when she pointed at the amulet, she turned her head to one side, like she was afraid of looking at it directly.

"Hsiu Mei doesn't know anything about it, I'm sure," said Joy. "She's a war orphan, she got caught by the Triads to be sold to the, um, Nibiru cultists in—"

Mrs. Jakuba cut her off with an ear-splitting shriek and another torrent of crazy Kossar, before grabbing her by the shoulders and shaking her. "Do not say that name. Terrible luck will you bring with that. It is not to be spoken. Promise me you will not."

"O-okay, Mrs. Jakuba. I'm not saying it. You can calm down now."

"I will be calm when you promise. I did not hear promise."

"Okay, I promise. I promise that I won't say Nib... I mean, the name you said not to say." *While I'm in earshot of you,* Joy mentally added. "But what do you know about it, Tishka? Why's this... um, Deep King so bad?"

Mrs. Jakuba glared at her. "It is best not to be talking about that. Only bad things will come of it. But did you say there are cultists of... of *That*... in Dodona?"

"Yes, and um… they include Chief Gallach of the City Guard and most of his lieutenants, I think—"

"Aigh, no wonder they're so awful," she said, rubbing her temples. "This is very, very bad."

"I know," said Joy. "And I'm sorry to get you wrapped up in this—"

"Oh, nonsense. Your problems are my problems, didn't I say I was your Tishka? People need to stick together, or we all fall apart. First, we are getting those chains off, and out of my apartment. Very bad to be bringing that in where you live, not that I'm blaming you, dearie. Mr. Tanno down the hall, he has cousin who is a locksmith. I think we can get him over when I explain is emergency."

"Oh, you don't need to do that—"

"I most certainly do! That is terrible symbol, and is very bad for your friend as well. Not to mention just having any chains on her—how terrible a thing, for a young girl! No, we must—"

"No, I agree about the chains," Joy moved quickly to forestall another rant. "I meant we don't need to call anyone. I can get them off quicker. I can pick the lock. I was KIB during the war, remember?"

"Eh," said Mrs. Jakuba. "If you can get those chains off then why have you not done it already, you silly girl? Think of your poor friend."

"Well, my lock picks are up in my room—"

"In your room? And what good are they up there? All the schooling you have, and sometimes I wonder at your sense."

Well, you wouldn't be the only one, Joy thought to herself, but she was getting a bit annoyed at the criticism.

"For goodness sakes, Mrs. Jakuba, I don't carry them with me. How—"

"And this is my point," said Mrs. Jakuba. "Such useful tools, and you leave them lying around. Then time comes when you need them, and do you have them, huh? What good is that fancy purse you carry always, then?"

"Umm..." Joy hadn't considered this at all. She couldn't remember the last time she'd needed to pick a lock. It never came up. She thought of explaining this, but Mrs. Jakuba was already shooing her to the door.

"Go! Get your picks and come right back. Hurry."

"Where are you going? What's going on?" said Hsiu Mei, who, of course, hadn't been able to follow any of the whole conversation.

"I'm just going to get tools to get those manacles off you," said Joy, switching back to Xiaish. "I'll just be a minute or two."

Hsiu Mei's gaze passed from her to Mrs. Jakuba. It looked like the thought of being left alone with the crazy shouty lady didn't appeal much.

"Don't worry. It's just the image of the strange god on your chains that upsets her," Joy explained. "Normally she's very nice. And I'll be right back. Oh, and if she offers you any more food or tea, you can go ahead and say yes the first time. It's not considered rude in this country. Anyway, I'll be back in a minute or two."

Joy had to go up three flights of stairs and down two hallways to get to her room. All the small rooms were up on the top floor. Walking into her apartment she was struck by just how spare and shabby it looked compared to Mrs. Jakuba's. It was more than just the furnishings. Mrs. Jakuba's place had an important feel to it; it was a home, a place where someone had constructed a life for themselves. Joy's apartment was the opposite. It was just a location with the bare necessities for living, sleeping, and eating, and no more. But it was always like this after going to visit her neighbor, the contrast always gnawed at her. Fortunately, she was too busy to dwell on this today.

She had to go into her closet and dig through her trunk to find her picks. Thankfully, it was right where she thought she'd left it, in with a bunch of her old military stuff, like her different uniforms, workout sweats, old field manuals—actually, she was surprised at all the junk she'd kept. There was stuff from academy, and her old high school, too—but she didn't have time to be organizing or tossing things out. She grabbed her picks and returned to Mrs. Jakuba's apartment, where she found Hsiu Mei polishing off the last of the bread while Tishka was puttering around in the kitchen. She emerged as soon as Joy came in, asking about the picks.

"Right here," said Joy, holding up the soft leather case, with individual pockets for each tool, and unrolling it. The design was such that it could be easily concealed, worn under clothing. And Joy supposed it could even fit in her purse easily enough—maybe Tishka had a point about that.

"And you are sure you can get those chains off?"

"Oh, no problem," Joy reassured her. "I had a look at those locks and they're nothing special. Plus, I'm good at this. I scored one hundred percent on the exit exams on the field course for lock-picking, and the instructor said—"

"Yes, very good. You start work now."

Joy sighed as she found herself led over to Hsiu Mei on the couch. Lock-picking had been her favorite part of the supplemental field training. It was like every lock had its own special secret, but one that could be discovered. There was an unshakable logic to how a lock worked. All you needed was training and tools, and it would open for you. Too bad the rest of the world didn't work like that.

Hsiu Mei's eyebrows went up as Joy unrolled her pick case on the empty bread dish. "Can you really free me with those?"

"Yup," said Joy. "Here, give me your wrist."

Joy started in on the lock. It took her a bit longer than she'd have liked to remove, considering how simple the lock was. She was a bit rusty, though thankfully the lock wasn't, ha ha.

No-one was timing her, but it felt like maybe a whole two minutes might've gone by before she heard the telltale click, and the rod keeping Hsiu Mei's wrist captive fell away. That was a pretty poor time for her. She did much better on the second.

Hsiu Mei rubbed at her wrists, which had been chafed raw in a few spots. Those would need to be cleaned and bandaged.

"Big Sister, who are you? How is it you know all these things?"

Now the adulation was getting embarrassing.

"Oh, I worked for Kallistrate Intelligence during the war. That's where I learned this. It's not really that difficult. I could teach you, if you like."

"You mean you were a spy?" Hsiu Mei sounded even more awestruck. "Is that how you were able to beat those men up?"

"Well, yes," Joy admitted, squinting to get a closer look at the collar. It was the same easy lock as the manacles, but the angle made picking it a little trickier. Still not a huge challenge.

"Actually, I take that back," said Joy. "The part about being a spy, I mean. I was an analyst, not an agent. Mostly I was sitting at a desk—Ah! There we go," said Joy, as the collar clicked open, and she was able to pull those nasty chains completely clear of the girl. "Now we've got you—"

The chains were ripped from her hands by Mrs. Jakuba, who threw them on a piece of scrap wood she'd laid on the floor, and started smashing away at the weird emblem of Nibiru with a cast-iron meat tenderizer, continuing the assault until the raised image of the weird god was an unrecognizable mess.

Whoa. Mrs. Jakuba sure didn't like Nibiru at all. Joy noticed Hsiu Mei trying to hide behind her, and she couldn't blame her. This wasn't the normal Tishka she was used to. Her reporter's instincts told her there was a story behind all this, but whether now was a good time to try to follow up on it—

Mrs. Jakuba glared at the marred mess of the Nibiru emblem, like she was expecting it to make a break for it or something, before deciding there was no point taking chances, and rained down with a single, focused finishing blow. There was a brittle crunching sound, mixed with something new, a high musical chime, as the Nibiru emblem crumpled flat, and something shot out to the side in a flash of bright blue and landed spinning on the carpet at Joy's feet.

268

It was the largest glittering blue gem Joy had ever seen, bigger than a walnut. Mrs. Jakuba yelped when Joy picked it up, but Joy didn't pay her any mind. She was surprised at how round and smooth the sides were. She'd expected it to be faceted by the way it glittered. But, upon closer examination, she realized that all the facets were actually strange structures beneath the gem's surface. How did they do that? Were those actually facets? The more she gazed into the jewel's depths, the more complexity she found. It had its own odd geometry, fascinating and beautiful.

A stream of rapid, mostly unintelligible Kossar snapped Joy out of her reverie. She managed to get the gist of it, though. Tishka wanted her to put the gem down.

"Do you know what this is?" Joy asked. "Have you seen something like this before?"

"No, but if it's related to the Abomination, then nothing good can come from it," she said. "Everything it touches, it taints. So put that down. We must destroy it."

"This is evidence," said Joy. Though evidence for what, she didn't know. She tried to remember everything she'd learned so far.

"Hsiu Mei, have you seen this before?" she said, switching to Xiaish, and holding it up for her to take a closer look at. "Did you know this was hidden in your collar?"

Hsiu Mei stared at the gem in awe, but she shook her head. Joy pressed further. "Do you remember when they put your manacles on? Was there anything unusual about it?"

You mean, aside from being chained up like an animal? Joy mentally added, kicking herself at the phrasing of her question, but Hsiu Mei didn't seem to take offense, brow furrowed in concentration.

"There was a foreigner there. He put the chains on. He chanted and gestured and waved a scepter around. And he even poured some red liquid on each of the symbols. Noriko said it was blood but I don't think it was. It smelled wrong.

"But I couldn't understand anything he said. It took a while and the guards were annoyed with him. It was strange. Does that help, Big Sister? It's all I can remember."

Hsiu Mei was so eager to please, it made Joy feel bad for putting her on the spot. But this was important. Any information could be helpful.

"Anything else about his appearance that stood out? Do you think you could recognize him again if you saw him? Was he the same as the Guardsmen?"

"I... He was wearing foreign clothes. But not like those uniforms. I... I think I would know him if I saw him. I could try to remember..."

"Don't worry too much. It's not critical. But if there is something else you remember, make sure to tell me, okay?"

Hsiu Mei nodded, but Joy doubted there'd be much else to come out of this. Of course the Sleywie Anden wouldn't be wearing their guard uniforms while engaged in illegal human trafficking. But now there was a whole new element to this story. Jewel smuggling on top of everything else. One was a cover for the other. But why do that? The Sleywie trusted the Triads to transport illegal weapons and slave girls, but not these jewels. These, they had to hide.

"Joy?"

"What? Oh—"

"I do not like that jewel in my house," said Mrs. Jakuba. "And I do not think you should have it either. It is bad luck, I think."

"Well, I'm not going to keep it. It was being smuggled into the city, so it's probably stolen or something," she said. "I have to find out who it really belongs to, and of course I can't turn it in to the City Guard."

The mention of the corrupt Guardsmen set Joy's thoughts into a whirl. The law in Dodona was being enforced by criminal fanatics. How was she going to deal with this?

She caught Tishka's concerned look. Well, the last thing she wanted was to worry her friend and host.

"Don't worry, though," said Joy. "I'm going to take care of it. I haven't worked out exactly how, but—"

"You are going to be taking care of it?" Mrs. Jakuba put her hands on her hips and stared at her. "Whole City Guard versus you, and you will take care of them. Who are you now, the Red Specter?"

"Tishka, you've heard of the Red Specter?"

"Of course. Is in funny pages and also lantern show. Everybody knows this. You think old people are so out-of-touch with new things, eh?"

"Oh, you're not old, Tishka—"

"Ah, enough of this. No changing subject. You are not fighting whole City Guard department now. You are both filthy and tired, and have you eaten anything? You—" she said, pointing at Joy. "You go take shower, and hide that jewel somewhere, if you insist on keeping it. While you—" pointing at Hsiu Mei "—are getting hot bath, which I think has been a long time for you. Then we are going to sit down and have a proper dinner, and then we figure out what next on full stomachs, so we can think straight, yes?"

Well, that did sound like a good idea, so Joy left Hsiu Mei in her care, after giving her a quick rundown on the situation, and a super-fast lesson on the Kallish words for "Yes," "No," "Please," "Thank you," and "What is this called?" which she hoped would be sufficient for the time it took to clean up and get back.

Chapter 37:

I Do My Best Thinking in the Shower

Absentmindedly, she rolled the weird blue gem between her fingers as she climbed back up to her apartment. Why hide contraband in contraband? Surely, that had to be more trouble than it was worth. Joy went back to the most obvious reason— they didn't trust their couriers enough to let them know. That was weird when you considered all the things the Sleywie had trusted the Triads with, but if you accepted that premise, the rest sort of made sense.

Hide the gems in symbols of your faith on girls selected to be bride-captives. If anyone questions it, say it's part of your religion, which is obscure and hated, but still feared. Both the girls and the jewels would get a degree of "protection" from a creepy symbol sanctified by some bizarre ritual. Superstitious sailors would be wary of invoking a deep sea-god's curse and stay away from them. The girls would unwittingly guard the gems twenty-four-seven. If anyone tried to tamper with the symbol, the girls would know about it. And the girls themselves would be guarded closely because their buyers would be expecting them to be delivered "intact," because patriarchal scumbags had a thing for purity. So she supposed the plan did make sense, as long as the captive girls didn't try to flee, like Hsiu Mei had. And even that had been a freak occurrence, with her guards panicking over a...

"...Red Face Ghost."

Joy thought about that. And thought some more. Was she really going to consider this? It felt weird. Every other supposed miracle she'd been sent to investigate always turned out to be delusions and nonsense, though sometimes they seemed impressive at first. That statue really did weep, and it did have her wondering if she'd found a miracle for a few hours before the contrary evidence began to pile up, culminating in the leaky drainpipe.

But she also remembered what she'd said to Shiori, about how there must be a third party acting against them, the Sleywie and the Triad. Everything she'd blurted out then still felt true, and obviously someone had been operating the crane golem when it dropped a herd of cattle on them. But could that golem pilot really have been the Red Specter?

Joy was so busy mulling it over that she nearly walked right past her apartment door—which was easy enough to do, as it looked just like every other one on this floor—and then tried the wrong key twice before finally getting in. Stripping out of her clothes brought her back to the present. Her outfit really was ruined. Well, the skirt could maybe be salvaged. The rips there were on the smallish side, and maybe those stains would come out. Maybe. But her blouse? And her stockings? Total casualties. And that had been her really nice professional outfit. And it hadn't been all that nice. But it was something she could put on and feel confident as a serious, professional newspaper reporter, even if she wasn't one. How was she supposed to do her job now? And if she couldn't do her job, she couldn't get the money for new clothes. She needed a brand-new ensemble to afford a brand-new ensemble. Arrgh!

Disgusted, she tossed her skirt on her bed and chucked her blouse in her trash can as she trudged off to her tiny bathroom for a shower. At least she had running water and a functioning shower head. Granted, it consisted of little more than a curtain and a drain in the stained tile floor—but it did work. And, given the weather and how overheated she was, she didn't require the water to be much above lukewarm. She relaxed as the jets of water scoured her skin, washing away all the nasty she'd accumulated from her day of insanity.

It was nice to have one thing go right for her today. It was a little thing, but she decided to be inspired by it, and turn her mind to the big puzzle at hand—the mystery of the Red Specter. As the rivulets of grime disappeared into the drain she engaged in a thought experiment. Her entire day had been spent collecting stories about a mythical hero called "The Red Specter." The stories came from various sources: Garai, the comic strip, Madame Zenovia, Kanda Soler, Professor Gelfland, the dock workers, Chen the Triad goon, and even Hsiu Mei, indirectly.

Taken individually, nothing she'd seen or heard was conclusive evidence of a real Red Specter. In each individual case, there was a more plausible explanation than a ghost hero in a gas mask. But all of it, together? What if she was letting her experiences reporting on fake nonsense bias her against the simpler explanation—that everyone had been telling the truth about a person who really existed and who they'd actually seen? Was that even possible? It didn't seem so—if for no other reason than that some of the things she'd heard were mutually contradictory. Still, she felt like she was on to something.

Suppose the Red Specter was a real person, one who went to great pains to keep his existence secret, but acted directly enough to make the creation of at least a few eyewitnesses inevitable. But those eyewitnesses only got brief glimpses under high-stress events. Wouldn't that create the exact situation that she now found herself in? Sure, that was possible, but it didn't exactly help her separate truth from fiction. Any of the wild stories she'd heard about him could be true, or none of them might be. That left her no better off than from when she'd started in Garai's office this morning.

So, forget everyone else's account—what had *she* seen? She'd definitely seen an unknown person drop a herd of cows on her. That had definitely happened. And... when she and Hsiu Mei had been running from Yang and Chen in the cargo maze, she'd caught a flicker of movement right before a huge stack of crates and junk fell over to slow up her pursuers. Why did that happen? You'd think the dock workers would know their jobs well enough to stack boxes so they didn't tip over—not without some other force acting on it, and with such convenient timing to slow up Yang, and to make Chen... Wait—Chen had outright disappeared! He'd never turned up for the showdown with the Guards. He'd vanished, just like he'd said others in the Triad were vanishing, and then it had happened to him.

Well, she couldn't be sure he'd really vanished. He could have just decided enough was enough and deserted, though Joy had a hard time picturing the proud Albion veteran running from a fight, and at such an odd time. Maybe he could, if he realized what his conscience had been telling him....

That was still assuming the "oppressive feeling" Chen had complained of actually was his conscience, and not what he'd claimed it to be: the gaze of the real Red Specter, always watching, always judging. Joy had felt it too, she realized—a feeling she'd been having all day, ever since... since when? Madame Zenovia's, that was right. She'd been feeling weird ever since then. Had the Red Specter been tailing her this whole time?

Aiyah—now she was getting paranoid. But that could be by design, part of the Specter's plan. Get the Triad paranoid, so they'd start making mistakes... and then what? She still had no good information—was it one man, a Jagdkommando like Professor Gelfland said, or a whole unit of them? Was he/ they working under government sanction or had he/they gone rogue? Were they the source of the myth or were they copying the myth? So many questions and no good answers.

Well, put the Specter to the side for now. There were two evil factions at loggerheads in Dodona, and they both had reason to find her and shut her up permanently. But Joy was sure she'd lost them in the chaos of the stampede. There was no way they'd been followed home, she was sure of it. But could they track her down eventually? They knew her first name and what she looked like, and what else? What else had she let slip? Had she told them her middle or last name?

Joy ran the day's events back through her head. She couldn't remember giving out her last name—but she'd told everyone that she'd freelanced for the Gazette! All they had to do was swing by the office and they'd know where she lived. They could be on their way right now. Either the Triads or the guard—or that vicious Rosewing woman. They could come busting down the door any minute. She had to warn Tishka and Hsiu-Mei. They had to run!

Joy's stomach flipped over, and she shut off the water, grabbed a towel and began scrubbing herself dry in a near-panic before her logical self had a chance to reassert control. Logical Joy reminded her that since she was a freelancer, the Gazette didn't have her tax information. She was expected to track and pay that herself. Did the Gazette even have her address? He never sent her paychecks by mail. She always had to pick them up in person and wait for him to write them out by hand. But Garai must have her address somewhere. She was sure of that, but could the bad guys find it?

Joy remembered hearing his secretary kvetching about it. Garai's system for written records consisted of grabbing whatever scrap of paper was handy and scribbling on it, resulting in multiple unrelated bits of information on a single sheet of paper, with bits of text going in different directions, often in different languages, all organized by date and shoved into a huge filing cabinet.

It actually functioned better than you'd think, because Garai kept so much organized in his head. He could remember the date when he'd encountered any important info to within a few days, so he could find what he needed... mostly. But without him, his records were worse than useless.

Joy checked her clock, surprised to see that it was nearly nine PM. So much had happened today. The Gazette offices would be open, the paper being readied for the presses, to make sure the latest bogus news would arrive at the stands the next morning. But Garai wouldn't be there. He worked long hours, starting in the early morning and ending by early evening, usually between six or seven o'clock. She was safe for now. She let out a long sigh of relief and allowed herself some time for self-care.

276

She'd been walking and running so much in the wrong shoes that she'd rubbed both her heels raw, so she took the time to wrap some clean gauze around her feet and bandage up her skinned knees. She grabbed the first presentable thing she could out of her closet, which happened to be the blue-grey skirt and blouse to her old Kallistrate military uniform, which hung a bit loose on her, threw on a pair of comfy cloth sandals, and was about to head back down to rejoin Mrs. Jakuba when she remembered the glittering blue jewel lying on the top of her small dresser.

Yet one more thing to make a complicated situation even more complicated. A huge gem like that, and somehow she'd never heard of it. Well, the Sidhe nobility had ruled a vast empire for over a thousand years, so that was plenty of time to amass hoards of riches in their various palaces, to get dumped into the black market when those palaces got sacked by Kallistrate, Zipang, or emboldened insurgents. Still, this jewel was something else. It seemed to glow a faint azure in the dim light of her apartment, though it might just be collecting and refracting the available light—she couldn't be sure either way.

And there were a bunch of these gems being smuggled using the girls as cover—or were they? Joy realized she didn't know for sure that the other shackles contained hidden gems—the other ones might be decoys. But what were the odds of Joy rescuing the only girl with a gem? What were the odds on any of this?

Enough. Joy was keeping Mrs. Jakuba waiting. She grabbed the jewel and stuffed it into the middle of her sack of potatoes, which seemed like the best hiding-place for it at the moment. She felt a weird electric thrill as her skin made contact with the cool, smooth surface. It made her hesitate, reluctant to part with it. She shook it off and headed downstairs for dinner.

Chapter 38:

Chowtime

Joy found Hsiu-Mei chowing down at the kitchen table. Mrs. Jakuba had one of those open kitchens that was big enough to fit a dinner table, so it served both as a kitchen and a dining room. Mrs. Jakuba declared this to be the best idea ever, since it cut down on the time it took to transport the food to hungry people, plus everyone got to see for themselves just how hard their cook worked. Hsiu Mei looked worlds better. Her skin had a nice rosy glow from being scrubbed, and her jet-black hair had been shampooed, de-tangled, and brushed straight. Joy recognized some of Mrs. Jakuba's hair clips keeping her locks out of her face while she ate. She was also wearing one of Mrs. Jakuba's nightgowns, which hung on her like a tent.

Hsiu-Mei beamed at her when she came in, and Joy was taken aback a second. This girl was going to break some hearts when she got older. Then Joy remembered that there were people out there right now who weren't bothering to wait for Hsiu-Mei to age properly before trying to marry her off. Looking at the poor fugitive swimming in Tishka's nightgown, with the sleeves rolled up five or six times just to keep them out of her stew, it was apparent how much of a child she still was, and Joy had to fight back her fury, to keep from ruining dinner.

And Joy wouldn't dream of ruining one of Tishka's dinners. Even though their host kept apologizing for how simple their fare was, as she wasn't expecting company. But of course this was ridiculous, as the hearty, rich beef stew that had been simmering all day was enough of a meal for everyone, what with all the peas, carrots, potato chunks, thick short noodles, and fatty hunks of tender beef in it. Hsiu Mei certainly wasn't complaining—she was slurping it down like there was no tomorrow, and that worried Joy. The girl was going to make herself sick gorging like that on rich food after barely eating for several days. Joy had to step in and force her to start taking breaks. And besides which, in Kallistrate it was bad manners to pick your bowl off the table like that, so Joy started to teach Hsiu Mei proper etiquette—use the spoon for everything. It forced her to slow down, and she needed to learn that anyway for future dinners. She got so focused on it that Tishka had to chide her for not touching her own food. Joy complied—oh, man, did that hit the spot right now—and for a few minutes the kitchen got quiet, with everyone's attention fully occupied by eating a warm, savory, delicious meal.

It couldn't last forever. Hsiu Mei reached the bottom of her bowl and began to bawl, prompting Tishka to wrap her up in a hug, while Joy hovered over her, trying to pick out something intelligible through the sobs. Eventually it came out.

"She's feeling guilty about enjoying such a wonderful meal while her little sister and the other girls are still being held captive in a cage," said Joy.

"Agh, such a shame," said Tishka, rocking Hsiu Mei. "Not your fault, child. All the bad men's fault. A disgrace, our City Guard is. Something must be done."

"We'll have to expose them," said Joy, who'd been able to sort her thoughts out during dinner. "All the local authorities are either corrupt or suspect, so we'll have to contact the national ones." Joy repeated this in Xiaish, so Hsiu Mei could follow her.

"National—like your Intelligence friends from when you worked there," said Mrs. Jakuba. "They even have office in Dodona. Perhaps we could go after dinner. That would be safest, yes?"

"They're not open right now. Nobody will be there." said Joy, and then had to alternate between translation and forestalling Mrs. Jakuba's indignant rant. "An intelligence bureau is all about actively looking for emergencies before they happen. They're not set up to go rushing out fighting crime at all hours of the night. It's not their normal job. I think they will help us, once I explain the situation, but it might take some time for them to figure out how to deal with this. Probably they'll have to coordinate with the army. They might even have to call troops from other cities. At any rate, there's no way I'll be able to contact anyone until their office opens at nine o'clock the day after tomorrow, because of the holiday."

"And in the meantime, we are having to fend off police and gangsters ourselves," said Mrs. Jakuba, and paused for a minute. "You don't think they could find us here, do you?"

"They know my first name and that I work at the Gazette," said Joy. "I expect they'll be able to get my address from my boss, by either threatening or tricking him, and if not, they might be able to find my address from that old crime report I filed against Quintus. I expect that to take them at least a day or two. But we should find someplace else to hide ASAP. Umm..."

"We will go to Temple" said Mrs. Jakuba. "Reverend Hayashi is a great priest, very good man. I am seeing him every Sunday, and he always says, any problems you have, bring it to the Temple, so there we will go until the government sorts out these gangsters."

"That... could work," said Joy. Actually, it was a great idea. The Prakasa Mandira was a huge structure with high walls, one of the oldest and largest of its kind in eastern Nokomis. Its seven spires dominated the western Dodona skyline. The city had many temples, but when locals talked about The Temple, everyone knew what they meant. Most holy places had a tradition of providing sanctuary, and it didn't matter how tough the City Guard or Benny the Shark thought they were—trying to strongarm the Temple was a bad move. The depth and breadth of the outrage that followed would make their lives very unpleasant. People would get so angry that they'd forget to be scared.

But could they really trust Rev. Hayashi? Joy hadn't gone to Temple herself in ages, as the Prakasa Mandira was a Susanvada Kovidian temple, and she was Vienijanti. She'd gone in for a few services with Tishka, and found herself scratching her head at some of their ideas, and the answers the priests gave her didn't help much, so she'd begged off after that. Sure, the Reverend did seem like a nice man, but her experience with the Mithras priests had taught her that it was easier to present an appearance of wisdom and holiness than to actually be wise or holy. They could be repeating her mistake with the Guard—trusting an authority only because they wanted a rescue so badly, only to be let down when that authority proved to be fallible.

But it wasn't like she had a better idea. There wasn't any way they could get through this without help. They'd have to roll the dice and confide in somebody sometime. If everyone was corrupt, they'd be screwed no matter what they did.

"Yes, we should all go there tonight," she said, and translated the plan to Hsiu Mei.

"Tonight, after dinner—which you are letting get cold," said Mrs. Jakuba. "Maybe we should also feed this to Hsiu Mei. She certainly knows how to appreciate good cooking."

Joy looked down and realized her bowl was still half-full, and Hsiu-Mei was indeed eyeing it hungrily. Between all the watching over Hsiu Mei and the explaining and the translating, she'd ended up ignoring her own bowl. "Sorry, Mrs. Jakuba," she said, and went on to fix that problem while Mrs. Jakuba refilled Hsiu Mei's bowl. Everyone was quiet for a bit as they tended to the business of eating, and it was Joy's first truly satisfying meal in ages, though Mrs. Jakuba's warning was correct. She'd allowed her stew to drop down to lukewarm, and it wasn't as good as when it was hot. Still, she got a little extra enjoyment tearing into the beef chunks, imagining it as revenge on the killer cow from the docks. Who's top of the food chain now, you bastard?

She was showing Hsiu Mei how to mop up the stew remnants with a dinner-roll, and looking forward to maybe refilling her bowl with a nice hot one from the stewpot, when a comment from Mrs. Jakuba changed everything. She was reassuring Hsiu Mei through another bout of guilt over abandoning her younger sister, with Joy hovering over her shoulder translating.

"You had no other choice, dear," Tishka said. "If you hadn't run, what would be happening now? Those rats would have the both of you, and how would that be any better? This way we can get help, and we get her back for sure."

"I hope so," said Hsiu Mei. "But—but what if they move her? Those guards we were supposed to be sold to—they aren't paying like they should. If this goes on much longer, the Triads will ship them elsewhere to be sold. And I'll never see Lin Lin again."

"I'm sure that won't happen," said Joy. "Shipping all of you over here had to be expensive, and then shipping you elsewhere with no sale—they lose money that way. The Triads have waited this long, I'm sure they'll wait a few days longer to try and settle with the Guards. Everything is going to be fine, you'll see."

Hsiu Mei sighed. "If you say so, Big Sister. But I know they won't wait forever. I heard the guards talking the night I escaped. They said Boss Fang is getting impatient. That he is thinking of cutting his losses, and that if those foreign devils do not pay up by midnight on the eve of Liber Day, they would ship us out first thing next morning. When is that, do you know?"

Joy tried to keep her face neutral. Based on Hsiu Mei's reaction, she probably failed at that.

"You do know!" Hsiu Mei clutched at her and her voice rose an octave. "When is it? When do they ship her out?"

"What is it?" demanded Mrs. Jakuba. "What is going on?"

Joy ignored Hsiu Mei and translated into Kossar, mostly as a way to stall until she could gather her wits, which didn't calm Hsiu Mei at all, and Tishka didn't hide her reaction to the news well, either. Joy found herself caught between competing sets of demands in two different languages, with Mrs. Jakuba insisting that she track down someone from Kallistrate Intelligence tonight, explain that it was an emergency, and Hsiu Mei tugging at her shirt and demanding to know what was going on, none of which was helping her think.

There was no point trying to be clever. Joy held Hsiu Mei by the shoulders and looked her in the eyes. "Okay, Hsiu-Mei. I want you to listen to me, and I need you to stay calm. You have to understand that everything is going to be okay."

"When is it? When is Liber Day? Is it tomorrow? They're not shipping her out next morning, are they?"

Joy could not lie to this girl. "Yes, they are," she said, "But don't wo—"

But Hsiu Mei wasn't listening. She burst out in tears and buried her face in her hands.

"What did you say?" said Mrs. Jakuba. "You didn't tell her, did you? Oh, you did! What on earth are you thinking?" Mrs. Jakuba swatted her on the arm hard enough to sting, enfolded Hsiu Mei in her arms, and rocked her with shushing noises that needed no translation.

Joy rubbed her arm and paced the room, trying to gather her thoughts. Maybe she could've handled that better, but maybe not. She really wasn't a fan of lying to people for their own good. It seemed like it always ended up worse in the long run. But that wasn't the important thing here. What in the Abyss was she going to do now? Joy could talk about her Intelligence background, but she'd just been a low-level translator. It was enough of a connection to get her in the door during business hours, but that was it. And even if she somehow managed to find the local KIB director's home address and beat down their door, she doubted there was anything they'd be able to do on just a few hours' notice.

Intelligence was mostly about sifting through reports, analysis, and paperwork. It wasn't like the local KIB had a commando team stationed in the basement. She didn't see how they'd be able to deploy a rescue team in time. Who would they get— a squad of analysts, with maybe a half-dozen supplemental courses among them?

Sheesh, she had more training than that. The sad truth was that she was the most qualified rescuer that anybody would be able to find before morning. And she wasn't qualified for this. There was no way she could....

The thought darted through her head like a mouse scurrying for cover. She grabbed it by the tail and dragged it back for a closer look, ignoring its desperate attempts to wriggle free. There was no way she could just go out and rescue the girls herself, now was there? Was there? Everything Joy had seen and heard throughout the day ran back through her mind—the docks, the maze of supplies, the exact position of the Joanne Spaulding, and more—the special swimming and snorkeling lessons from Warrant Officer Adachi. He'd explained to her exactly how to sneak up on a boat from underwater, just like a real Navy frogman. And then what? Joy turned the budding plan over and over in her mind, prodding at it with contingencies and what if's, trying to remember how long it took her to pick the really complicated locks....

Another part of her grabbed her by the shoulders and shook her, and told her she was crazy. This was not going to work and she was going to get herself killed. And what then? What would that do to her parents, to have their child die before them? Maybe she should think of that, what it would do to them to have her body just show up in the city morgue, or—worse still—disappear without a trace. The worry would kill both of them, eat away at them for years. It would be even worse than how she was behaving now, barely any contact with them at all for half a year. She couldn't be that selfish.

Joy looked over at Hsiu Mei, face still buried in Mrs. Jakuba's bosom. Joy's family was important. Her parents meant the world to her, even if she didn't always show it. But their family wasn't the only one in the world. There were other families out there, too, who'd lost a lot more than theirs' had. There had been a war, and men and women had gone out to fight it. A lot of them hadn't come back. They'd marched off into the teeth of terrible danger—rifles and cannon, vicious dragons on one side, and merciless steel titans on the other. There were families all over the world missing their sons and daughters. And then there were children like Hsiu Mei, who were missing their parents.

Joy's family had gotten off light. Everyone had come home at the end. Joy never had to worry them at all—she'd been working at a desk, far behind enemy lines, taking combat courses out of sheer curiosity. Of course, her work as an analyst had been important and saved lives. And it had been the best way for her to contribute to the war effort. Central Command had said so.

But at the same time, she knew she was privileged, because she'd never had to look out across the battlefield and see a monster approaching. A monster that could kill them with barely a thought, and whether you lived or died that day depended on luck, on whether or not that monster happened to turn your way at the wrong time. Dean had faced it. He'd spent two years of his life sailing on a boat that was also a bomb, never knowing if a dragon would burst up from beneath the waves, to kill itself and everyone aboard in a fiery explosion.

It was insane—yet people did it. Hundreds of thousands of them. She'd asked him once how he managed to do it—how did he convince himself to get on that boat so many times, knowing what he did about how it could kill him, and do it again and again. He'd stared at her a bit, shrugged, and said he did it because he felt like there was no other choice. Someone had to do it, to protect their home, their family, their country. And if someone had to, it might as well be him. He couldn't fob it off on someone else. That wasn't right.

And now it was Joy's turn. It might've been rash, but she'd made a promise to Hsiu Mei to protect her and to protect her family. She'd invited her to think of her as a sister. And this was where it all came down to brass tacks. Because this time it wasn't a case of just stumbling into a huge mess by accident. This was deliberately marching off into a gangster's den—killers who would not play nice with her if she got caught. And why would she do something so insane? Well, someone had to do it. And right now, she was the only one who could. That made it her responsibility, whether she liked it or not. So the only question was this: would she shoulder her burden, or shrug it off?

Joy went back over to Hsiu Mei, whose crying fit was dying down under Mrs. Jakuba's ministrations. She got her attention and told her she had a new plan, and her sister was going to be fine. In fact, if all went well, she could expect to see Lin Lin at the temple tomorrow morning. Hsiu Mei gave her a look like she wasn't sure whether to believe her or not, but she had some hope back. Joy was sure of that. But to do that, Joy would need her help.

She proceeded to quiz Hsiu Mei about everything she could remember from her time on the Joanne Spaulding. Where had she been kept on the ship, what had the room looked like, how were they guarded, etc.

Unfortunately, Hsiu Mei had been so caught up in her own confusion and fear during her captivity that couldn't give her much in the way of specific details, but at least Joy got a general picture of what was going on.

The girls were all kept in a single cage somewhere in the cargo hold. They weren't guarded directly, but a guard would pass by to check on them every half hour during the day, and once an hour at night, or at least that was her best guess. Being locked up in a cage with no access to direct sunlight made it hard to gauge time, with day and night blending into each other. Joy would have to take that estimate at face value.

All the while they were speaking in Xiaish, Mrs. Jakuba watched them intently. Normally Joy would never be so rude as to exclude a non-Xiaish speaker like this, but she knew that if Mrs. Jakuba heard the types of questions she was asking, she might guess what Joy was planning. That would be another argument that she didn't have time for. And partly, she was afraid that Tishka might win the argument.

Joy didn't have much faith that her courage could withstand a determined assault from Tishka. Joy was having enough trouble keeping it propped up against her own self-doubt. Joy wrapped up her interview, because she had run out of useful questions, and it was clear Hsiu Mei didn't know any more.

"All right, that's it," said Joy. "I've got to put my plan in motion. You stay here and finish your dinner, then Tishka will take you to the Temple of Kovidh, where you'll both be safe."

"What is your plan, Big Sister?" said Hsiu Mei, eyes wide.

"I'd tell you, but there's not enough time," said Joy. "I have to get everything done by tomorrow morning, remember? Just trust me. Everything's going to be fine. I promise. I'm going to make it right."

Hsiu Mei gave her a nod, and even a bit of a hesitant smile. Joy looked in her eyes and saw someone desperate to believe in someone and something. Maybe someone who wouldn't try to exploit her, or let her down, or vanish, for once in her life. No pressure, Joy.

"So, are you going to tell me what is going on?" said Mrs. Jakuba.

"I just told her that everything was going to be okay, and that I got a new idea to help her."

Mrs. Jakuba brows narrowed, and Joy was taken back to the few times she'd tried pulling one over on her mom. It had rarely worked. "That was long conversation for just that much." She said.

"Yes, but I'm summarizing because I'm in a hurry. Actually, I have to get some things from my room, and then I've got to go out."

"Go out? Go out and do what? What new idea is this?" asked Mrs. Jakuba. "You have thought of someone to help us, maybe."

"Yes, that's it," said Joy. "I remembered my instructor from my supplemental field training courses. You remember I told you about Officer Adachi, right?" Technically, nothing in that statement was a lie—she never said that Kodwo Adachi was here, only that she'd remembered him.

"Yes! That is right person to help," said Tishka. "See—I knew with a good meal you would start thinking clearly."

"There's not a lot your cooking won't improve," said Joy. "But if you'll excuse me, I've got to get some things from my room. I've got a lot to do tonight."

"I think it can wait maybe a few minutes," countered Mrs. Jakuba. "If one bowl improves your thinking a little, two will work wonders. I have seen you lately, and I do not think you are eating enough. I know you are in a hurry, but this will not take so long, I think."

Joy paused mid-turn. Ordinarily, she'd never turn down an offer of food from her neighbor. The aroma coming off the simmering stew-pot was pure heaven, and for a moment she considered it, but just for a moment. While she'd love nothing more than to gorge herself until she was too full to move, tonight was not the night for that. She'd already eaten enough to get her strength back. And Mom had always warned her never to eat a lot right before going swimming.

Chapter 39:

Typewriter Confessions

Joy made her excuses and hustled up to her room. First, she needed to retrieve her equipment. Most of it had been packed away with her lock picks, so she'd already cleared a path to the box where she'd stored all her impulse Army Surplus purchases. The only other thing she needed was a swimsuit, but the Army had her covered there. Standard issue for the physical fitness standards, which you could get out of if you were an analyst and would be sitting behind a desk, but Joy found that passing the physical took way less paperwork than applying for the exemption. One-piece, dark blue-grey, with about as utilitarian a cut as possible, and good thing, too. Because her only other suit was white with bright red hearts and ruffles. That would not do for stealth at all.

She stripped down, put the suit on, then put her regular clothes back on top of that. She gathered all her needed supplies: snorkel, mask, fins—those she could carry in her purse after she dumped out its current contents, though the heels of the fins ending up poking out of the top. And then there was her other treasure from the Surplus—a sleek little watertight pack, one that could be tightly secured to the small of her back. What would she put in that? Well, her lock-picks, obviously, and what else? She also had a heavy-duty waterproof flashlight. It was a bit bulky, but it fit in her satchel, and it could come in handy.

Was that it? Well, her pencil and notepad fit in there too, but she didn't see why she'd need them for this. But still—maybe she might run across some important info, something vital she needed to write down. It was a bit of a stretch, maybe just her reporter habits talking, but she didn't feel right leaving her apartment without her notepad and something to write with. And they didn't add much bulk or weight to the satchel, especially compared to the flashlight. Screw it, in they go.

Now, was there anything else she needed? Was she good to go?

Another stomach flip as the reality of what she was planning hit her. This was happening. She was seriously going to do this. What if she screwed up? What if something went wrong and she didn't come back? She had to plan for all possibilities. The memory of all those explosives stashed in Hsiu Mei's container crate flashed through her mind. She had no idea what these Sley-wie Anden were up to, but whatever it was couldn't be good. This was a threat to the entire city of Dodona—maybe even all of Kallistrate. The authorities needed to know, no matter what happened to her tonight.

Joy went to her typewriter and composed a quick report, addressed to the KIB. She even knew the correct format to present the information. She'd typed up hundreds of reports, just like this. But she'd never expected to have to do it again, and with herself as the subject. It was surreal, detailing the threats: the corruption of the City Guard, collusion with the Triad and the notorious war criminal Shiori Rosewing, arms dealing, human trafficking, assaults, threats, etc.

Joy double-checked her report briefly after she'd spooled it off the roller. Not bad, Analyst Fan. This would be sure to rocket up to the highest priority as soon as the agency got it. For a second, Joy felt a sense of reprieve. Surely the KIB could handle everything. Of course, they wouldn't be in time to prevent the Joanne Spaulding from leaving, but it was a big ship. It could be tracked down by the Navy. All the girls could be rescued by a team of well-equipped professionals. That was a way better option.

But Joy's sense of relief didn't last. Yes, the Kallistrate government could act, but would they? Certainly they'd investigate her claims about the smuggled weapons and Shiori. That would get top priority. But rescuing Lin Lin and the other girls....

Hunting down the Joanne Spaulding would take resources. The Kallistrate navy had few real warships—they were still transitioning out of the armored spikefruit cargo ships. And their true ironclads were stretched thin trying to patrol the entire Nokomis continent. Would they really divert one, just for the sake of rescuing a few girls, who weren't even Kallistrate citizens? How much priority would that get? Could she count on them to do the right thing here?

Joy remembered her trials with Quintus, the inaction of her boss, and the complete indifference, bordering on hostility, of the Guardman she'd reported it to. Well, that guy could've been Sleywie, but would it have been any different if he hadn't been? Could she count on the KIB to be any better?

Maybe they would be. Maybe they'd surprise her. But could she count on it? Could she stake Lin Lin's life on it? Joy knew the answer to that. No, this was still on her.

Fold up the letter, address it, stamp it. Once she put it in the mail, it should reach the KIB office the day after tomorrow, given the holiday, and then the Triad and the corrupt Dodona City Guard would be finished.

Or would they be? Despite typing a report in an official format, she wasn't KIB anymore. This was a bunch of wild claims coming in from an outside source, and it wasn't impossible that it might get buried due to bureaucratic incompetence. It might get dismissed as crackpot nonsense. They probably got dozens of letters each week from paranoid loons. She could easily be mistaken for one of them. And what then?

Well, if the authorities didn't act at first, exposure in the press could force them to. That was what a free press was for, after all. But all the legitimate newspapers had her blackballed. She couldn't count on them to pay attention to her either. She had to get her information to someone with credibility, someone who would listen—Professor Gelfland! That was it.

She sat back down in her battered writing chair and started to mentally compose her letter. She could say that her fiction research had taken her to the docks, and then list all of the relevant details about....

No. This was all wrong. She was tired of lying. And somehow, her shame about everything that had gone wrong with her career seemed trivial now. She would come clean, get it all off her chest while she still could. That felt right, but she found it impossible to begin typing. The blank page stared her down like a bouncer at a nightclub that was way too cool for her. She had so much to say—too much. She lacked the ability to explain herself without unleashing pages and pages in a torrent, and she didn't have time for that. She couldn't do it.

Wait, what's this "couldn't" nonsense now? She was a writer. She was a reporter. And dammit, she was good at her job, no matter what anyone else said. So, journalist, report the story!

She started typing, writing about herself as though she were a news subject—just the facts, as objective and impartial as she was capable of being. While working at the Journal, she'd faced constant sexual harassment from a male colleague, which she'd reported, and her complaints had been ignored. The harassment escalated to assault, and she'd been forced to defend herself. Editor-in-Chief Hartmann fired them both for fighting. Subsequent gossip by unknown persons lead to Joy getting a reputation for being unstable and/or violent, but apparently the same stigma did not follow her attacker. She'd accepted freelance work from the Gazette because it was it was the only newspaper that would hire her.

Joy gazed down at what she'd written in amazement. Simple, clear statements in neat black ink on clean white paper. That had been easy. She should have done that from the beginning. She felt an incredible lightness all through her body. The rest of the letter came out with even less effort, the relevant details about the Sleywie-Guard, the Triad, and the girls pouring out into a few brief paragraphs. She ended with a notice that she'd informed the KIB, that he should go public with this if they failed to act, and an apology for lying to him earlier. She signed the letter, stuffed it into a stamped envelope, and tossed it next to the KIB letter on her dresser.

Was that it? Was there anyone else she needed to inform—if she didn't make it back? She didn't have much in the way of contacts left anymore. Excepting Tishka, Joy could vanish off the face of the planet and nobody besides her family would notice.

Her family. That was what bothered her the most about this. Suppose she messed this up and disappeared forever. What would that do to her parents? Would they mount a search for her? Post a reward in all the papers and wait at home, night after night, hoping for some kind of news, some scrap of information that would tell them for sure to give up hope and begin grieving? She could see it happening. She could see them doing that. But was there anything she could do about it?

The problem was that the letter would take several days to get to Gortyn, and by that point it would all be over. Either she'd have made it back to the Temple, or she'd have gotten caught, and… well, best not to think about that. But the point was that she didn't want her parents to open a letter from her saying, "Hi, I might be dead by the time you read this," several days after she'd made it to safety. She couldn't do that to them. Sure, she could send a second letter after she got back, and they'd both likely arrive at the same time, but it still seemed like a cruel joke. What if they read the letters out of order? How could she phrase this? To say goodbye forever, but only maybe, but no, not really—just kidding, guys. False alarm, I'm actually okay.

This was impossible. She should get moving. Just get out there and get it over with. Hopefully she'd come back fine, and none of this would ever have been necessary. But a single, contrary thought kept Joy glued to her chair: what if it was necessary? What if she screwed up and never came back? What if this was her last chance to say goodbye? Was she fine with saying nothing? No, she wasn't fine with that, but she was stuck with the problem of what to write. Should she tell them about getting assaulted? About getting fired? About stumbling around freelancing for a lousy tabloid and blundering into the middle of a gang war? She'd be here all night. Joy pulled her knees up to her chin and curled in a ball, as her ragged office chair creaked backward on its spring, her stomach churning.

Enough. Whether she should or shouldn't write a letter was irrelevant. The truth of the matter was that she'd run out of time. She had to reach the docks and rescue Lin Lin before morning. That meant she had to leave now. And as for her parents...well, she'd just have to make extra sure that she didn't get caught, and then the whole issue would be moot. Yes, that was it.

Joy felt her anxiety abate as she stood up, reflexively patting her butt to make sure no stray bits of packing tape had stuck to her, went through one final inventory check of all her gear, and headed out on her daring rescue mission.

Part 6:

Rescue Mission

Chapter 40:

Night Swimming

Joy got out of the pedi-cab up by the ritzier end of the docks. It was amazing how much had been cleaned up from the cattle stampede just a few hours earlier. There were a few broken windows that were now boarded up with plywood, with apologetic signs taped to them, promising that these unacceptable eyesores would be properly replaced ASAP. A lot of the outdoor seating for the various restaurants was greatly reduced now, or completely absent, and in their place a throng of people milled about. There was an electric buzz in the air. Drifting past, Joy caught snatches of conversation, and realized they were mostly recounting the events of the stampede and the lunatics responsible.

Joy fought a sudden urge to duck her head and run. If someone recognized her from the stampede, they might call the Guard to detain her. She forced herself to relax and calmly walk by, like this conversation had nothing to do with her. Actually, the more she overheard, the less of a concern it was. The description of the "Mad Cow Girls" had warped in all the retelling. They were all to be on the lookout for two crazed street urchins in dirty, tattered clothes and wild, stringy hair, screaming and laughing like maniacs. Possibly high on Spike, and what was the world coming to now? Where were the parents? It was the collapse of society, that's what. Now, back when they were kids....

Fine. That was fine. She didn't need to be famous for cattle rustling. She just had to execute her mission. Joy left the boardwalk and headed down the wooden plank steps to the thin strip of sand that was Dodona's only beach.

Even in the late evening, there were a handful of people playing or swimming in the mild surf. It was summer, after all, and going out at night was a good way to beat the crowds. So there was nothing unusual about her being here—just out for a swim, like you do.

She ducked into one of the changing tents by the seaside, stripped out of her clothes—the same ones she'd worn for dinner—and into all the spy gear she'd stuffed in her purse. Since she'd bought them, she'd just used the snorkeling gear one time, and the watertight satchel only briefly, just to test that it worked. She'd had some idea that she might use the satchel for reporting a story going down in a flood, or a typhoon, or something, and needed to protect her notes. Of course nothing of the kind had ever happened, and all her gear did was take up storage space in the bottom of her trunk—until now.

She packed her clothes and shoes into her oversized purse and tucked it away over by one of the thick wooden posts of the boardwalk. Her satchel was stuffed to capacity as it was—she was having second thoughts about bringing the heavy flashlight, but it seemed too potentially useful to leave behind.

She took a deep breath, and waddled her way down to the surf, awkwardly high-stepping because of her swim fins. Putting them on in the water would have been better, but she still had bandages on her feet for her blisters and didn't want to get sand in them. She waddled past the other beachgoers, trying to avoid eye contact. Nothing to see here, just out for a little casual night-swimming—with an army-issue swimsuit, diving-mask, a snorkel, swim-fins, and a satchel belted around her waist. She looked ridiculous.

Well, no matter. If people noticed, nobody was impolite enough to say anything, or stop her as she grimly marched into the sea, dived beneath the waves, and started her long journey over to the docks.

The first thing she noticed was the sting in her feet as the salt water soaked through her bandages. And the water was a good deal colder than she'd expected. This was supposed to be summer—what gives? Or maybe the water was just generally this cold, but it was easy to ignore when the sun was out? Anyway, she just had to deal with it. And there were more pressing problems. After swimming around for more than a minute or two, she realized that what she was doing was even more dangerous than she'd accounted for. Forget being spotted, just trying to keep her bearings underwater in the middle of the night was proving to be a challenge. There was light coming from overhead, from the moon and from the dock lights, and the wide oval of her diving-mask helped bring clarity to the underwater world, but it was still really, really dark. It would be so easy to lose her bearings. Her flashlight was supposed to be waterproof, but it was stowed in her satchel, and she wouldn't have used it anyway, lest she risk giving away her position.

But now she had to recognize what that meant. She had to be careful, because it would be very easy to get disoriented, and if that happened, there was no one around to help her, and she would probably drown. And then no-one would be able to help poor Lin Lin, or any of the other girls.

She needed to stay as far away as she could from the docks, to maintain stealth, while keeping the long, black shapes of the boat hulls always in her peripheral vision on her left. At first she tried to make her dives as long and deep as she could, the better to avoid detection. Her black hair and blue-grey suit were nice and stealthy, but a proper frogman would have a black full-body drysuit. Every time she neared the surface to clear her snorkel, she felt a stab of fear, sure that the moonlight flashing off her pasty thighs would give her away. But, the longer she went on, the more the effort of holding her breath wore on her, and she had to surface more and more frequently. Exhaustion would be her greatest enemy.

And another thing she'd only just realized—the difficulty in identifying the correct ship from underwater. In theory it sounded easy—the Joanne Spaulding had a distinctive red hull, an ornate design on its paddle wheel, and was berthed near the huge crane golem. But colors weren't so easy to make out right

298

now, and she couldn't see the paddle wheel design or the crane golem without surfacing. Add to that the fact that there were actually several of those crane golems along the docks. She'd taken a long look down the docks from the boardwalk, right before heading down to the beach. She'd counted at least four of them, all lit up, rising to the sky. Which one was the right one? She wished she'd thought to count them earlier that day, but she'd been busy clinging to the back of an enraged cow.

She had to figure it out anyway, somehow. Several times she surfaced, letting the tip of her snorkel emerge first, then rose up just enough to bring the top half of her mask above the water line. She did this as slowly as possible, so as not to create any noisy splashes. Twice she saw the towering forms of crane golems and had to check the surrounding ships to see if they matched her memory. And of course that was impossible. She was looking at everything from a completely different angle. A crane, piles of cargo containers—that was the entire freaking dock.

No, it wasn't impossible. She couldn't let herself think that. She'd come this far. She wasn't going to give up now. Focus on the ship. She would have to identify the ship itself. She could remember what the Joanne Spaulding looked like. Colors were much harder to make out in the darkness, but that ornate design on the paddle wheel—that had to be unique. She just had to keep going until she found it.

It felt like it took forever, surfacing and diving and double-checking, passing ship after ship. Every time she surfaced, she worried that she'd be spotted. Every time she dived and swam, she worried she'd swim past the correct ship. Had she gone too far? No, she hadn't hit the Shackle yet. That was right—Pier 25 had the first crane golem before reaching the Ala-Muki. Worst case scenario, she'd turn back if she hit the mouth of the river. The realization should've come as a relief, but the mere thought of having to backtrack at all filled her with dismay.

She'd already done more swimming than she'd done in the past year, on top of a long day of hiking back and forth across the city, topped off with a few brief interludes of terror-induced sprints. The swim fins helped her speed, but they also added resistance, and her thighs were starting to burn uncomfortably, along with her lungs. Those sensations began to dominate her awareness, and she became even more concerned when she realized that she was losing sensation in her hands and feet.

She wasn't wearing a proper drysuit, and that had other disadvantages besides lack of stealth. The Dodona harbor wasn't freezing, but it sure wasn't a warm bath, either. People could get hypothermia from non-freezing water, if they were exposed to it long enough. How long had she been bumbling around in the dark? It felt like forever. She'd been told about this once, in one of those classes she'd taken? What were you supposed to do in this situation? She was having a hard time remembering, for some reason. Oh—that was right! The first thing you were supposed to do was get out of the water. She needed to find the ship, pronto!

Finally, she surfaced in view of a golem-crane, a large maze of stacked cargo-containers, and one of the ships nearby—a paddle wheel, with a cutout design on the side. She swam in, closer and closer, surfacing once midway there, as quickly as she dared. The possibility of being spotted terrified her. All she needed was for one Triad man to be looking in her direction at the wrong time, and the whole mission would be blown. That scenario got more likely every time she surfaced close to the docks.

A thought popped into her head: what if that ornate cutout pattern wasn't unique to the Joanne Spaulding? What if it was actually a common feature for paddle-steamships? Well, she didn't want to pop up next to the ship, close enough to read the ship's name in the darkness. That was guaranteed to get her spotted, and truthfully, she didn't think she had the energy for it. She was at her limit. If this was the wrong ship, then she was just flat screwed. She'd have to go for it and hope for the best.

She popped up in a pocket of air beneath the wheel, between two of the slatted paddle-spokes. She clung to the wood slats, and spat out her snorkel mouthpiece, taking long, deep gulps of air. Or at least, she tried to, but each breath came in with a shaky vibration. Her teeth were chattering. She needed to get her entire body out of the water, right now!

She pushed her diving mask up on her forehead and peered up at the wheel's structure. It was dark, but there was some moonlight filtering in through the decorative cutouts.

Now for the next stage of her plan—to use the paddle wheel spokes as a ladder to climb up to the deck, under complete visual cover. It was looking a lot harder now than she'd thought in her head, mainly because she was so tired, but it still looked doable.

The blades of the paddle wheel only had mass at their outer edge, and a series of levers kept the blades angled vertically when they were in the water. Aside from the hub itself, most of the wheel's center was empty space, though an outer framework of spokes, reinforced with two sets of concentric rings, provided plenty of handholds and footholds. It was practically a ladder, though this was a ladder that was constantly rocking up and down with the waves.

Joy hadn't accounted for this in her planning, but clinging to the bobbing paddle blade made her realize that she could use the motion to her advantage—wait until the paddle was submerged at its lowest point, get her feet on top of it then, and ride it up. She readied herself to perform the maneuver, when she remembered she was wearing swim fins. She wouldn't be able to climb in those. She pulled them off and let them sink into the black waters below.

She rested and observed the rocking of the boat to get a feel for the timing, then, on the next wave, popped up on top of the paddle blade, gripped high up the spoke to steady herself, and stood up.

Her triumph was cut short by excruciating pain in the back of her right calf. Her leg convulsed, her numbed fingers lost their grip on the spoke, and she couldn't suppress a yelp of agony and fear as she tumbled back into the black waters.

She fell crossways across the steel paddle on her way down, banging her ribs painfully, but somehow she managed to catch herself before going all the way under. She propped herself up by putting the paddle blade beneath her armpit, while she sputtered and coughed and tried to recover her wits. She managed to stop her leg from thrashing about by bracing her foot against the hull, forcing her calf to stretch out, and tried to ignore the searing ache spreading across her left side. Of all the times to get a charlie horse....

She stayed like that for a while, trying to will her calf to behave itself and return to normal. Suddenly, scaling the paddlewheel was looking a lot more dangerous than it had a minute ago. It was dark and slippery, it was rocking about, she was more exhausted than she'd thought, and her fingers were going numb. If she hadn't fallen the way she had, if she had hit her head instead of her ribs, if she'd gone all the way down, beneath the boat....

No. No time to think about that. No time to think about what almost happened. The important thing was that it hadn't happened, and she was still alive, and she had to take care of herself right now. Because at this rate, she was still going to die of hypothermia, trapped under the paddle wheel, out of sight where no one would find her, until the ship departed early next morning, leaving her bobbing corpse in its wake. If she was lucky, her body would get discovered by fishermen before the sharks did.

No! She couldn't think like that. She could do this. The pain in her side wasn't sharp or stabbing, so her ribs shouldn't be broken. Her calf was already starting to go back to normal. She just had to move slowly and deliberately, concentrate on each step as she went, and she would make it. She had to believe that. As soon as her calf went back to behaving like a normal body part, she began her climb again, being extra-careful. It was both easier and harder than she thought. Easy because of how nicely-spaced all the handholds and footholds were, but hard because of how unhelpful her own body was being. It felt like someone had replaced the top layers of her skin with rubber padding, so controlling where her limbs went was requiring a ridiculous level of concentration.

Joy made it to the top of the wheel. Her plan had been to climb out through the decorative cutouts on the paddle wheel cowl and onto the deck from there. It had seemed easy enough in her head, but now that she was actually here, with a body that wasn't working properly, her plan didn't seem quite so great. Still, she'd come too far to turn back now. She went to stick her head out the side to check her options, and winced as she banged her snorkel on the side of the cutout. Had to remember she still had that. For a second she considered ripping it off and tossing it into the sea, but decided against it. It wasn't that much of an encumbrance, and she might need it later.

But the banging around with the snorkel reminded her of something else—noise. She'd been making too much noise. This was supposed to be a stealth mission, but she'd been thumping around a lot. Had anybody heard her? She forced herself to be still, try and listen. It was hard. Her chill and discomfort dominated her awareness. There was a constant vibration in her lower jaw, that traced back to a point deep in her chest. It made her teeth clack together and her breath come out in a long wavering hum. She clenched her jaw and willed herself to be quiet. It took effort, but she was able to concentrate on the world outside her own body. Water splashed at the side of the boat as the paddles rocked up and down. The hull creaked. Seagulls cried out. She didn't hear footsteps, or snatches of conversation or anything like that.

She peered out along the outside cowl of the paddle wheel, which lay flush with the side of the ship above her. She wasn't seeing handholds within easy reach. That wasn't right. There should be a deck with a railing that ran right up next to it. Wait, she remembered now. The paddle wheels extended out from the side of the Joanne Spaulding's proper hull, so the deck at her level swelled out to meet it. That meant the railing would be angled away from her. Joy swallowed, made her way as far as she could to the edge of the wheel, and leaned out farther, so her head and shoulders were sticking out of the cutout. Now she could see it. The railing was right there. Just a few feet away. She looked along the side of the ship. It didn't seem like anyone was there. She looked away from the ship, out along the docks. Some people about. Quite a few of them. But they weren't close, and none seemed to be looking in her direction. She had to hope they stayed that way, and she had to move now.

The longer she waited, the more she increased her chances of being noticed. She repositioned herself in the cutout and reached for the railing, several times, but no matter what she did, she couldn't get any closer and keep her balance. Her arms were too short—by just a few inches. In a fit of inspiration, she detached her snorkel from her mask to see if she could use the hook of the breathing-end to catch the railing. Yes—it reached. But the tubing was too flexible. It wouldn't support her weight. She could tell by the way it bent when she tugged on it, like so—and then she fumbled and dropped it, saw it tumble down to plop into the water below.

Dammit! Joy stared back at the railing. She was not going to grab it while keeping her balance where she was. But she could jump for it. Not even a very long jump, more like a lunge—but if she missed...Joy looked back down. Even if she didn't bang her head on the side of the boat, or get sucked under the hull, a splash that big would certainly draw the attention of the dock guards, and that would be the end of it. There'd be no second chances this time. It would have to be all or nothing—get it right on the first go. Joy started to gather herself, prepare to spring, and felt a surge of doubt. The railing angled away from her, back towards the narrower section of the ship hull. No matter how well she tried to direct her lunge, it wouldn't be perfectly parallel with the hull. It would take her away from the ship, a least a little

304

bit. She would have to reach backwards with her arms as she was flying past her target. That made it so much harder. But not impossible. It wasn't that far. She'd jumped farther on the Caliburn courses.

She'd made far more dangerous jumps climbing trees or construction sites. Thinking back to it made her remember Hugh, lying in a heap, screaming with a spike in his calf, remember the lecture, the slap, and the burning shame. So foolish. So many times she could've died. But she hadn't died, had she? She'd made those jumps. She hadn't been afraid. No, that wasn't right—she *had* been afraid, but she hadn't cared about being afraid. She'd been having too much fun. This could be fun.

Joy looked at the railing, and told herself, "I can do that." But this time it was different, it wasn't a denial, an attempt to shout down the fear, the fear of falling, the fear of failing. This was her own voice from long ago, of a prideful little girl, the Caliburn champion, staring down the rest of the world and shooting her mouth off. "You think that's hard? Well, it isn't! I can do it. I can do it, no problem. Just you watch!" The declaration touched off a spark, deep in her chest, warmed her from within. She planned out her leap, visualized it in her mind. Once, twice, three times. And then—GO!

She felt her body arc out into empty space, saw the railing, within reach but drifting away. She saw her palms make contact with that railing, felt her numbed fingers fail to react in time, felt herself slip down... And catch herself on the lower, middle railing with one hand. Her upper body swung down like a pendulum to smack into the deck and lower railing, but she managed to slow the impact with her legs and her other arm, just enough to avoid making too much noise, she hoped. She managed to lever herself up though the gap in the railing, onto the deck, and froze, listening for any signs of alarm. Had anyone seen that? Or heard it?

But no voices cried out, and no one came running. Plenty of things go creak and thump on a ship, all the time. No cause for alarm. Still, she felt horribly exposed. And freezing. What did she do now? Why was it so hard to concentrate? She needed a towel or a blanket, and she needed to get under cover. Would they even have something like that? They must—they'd need it if a man went overboard. Emergency supplies—look for that. She found it within seconds—a metal cabinet, bolted to the wall, painted bright orange with bold white letters saying EMER-GENCY. Of course—you would keep them close on hand, make them easy to find. It had a nice, thick blanket and a small box of supplies. She grabbed all of it and ducked down a hall leading into the ship's interior.

Chapter 41:

Infiltration

Third door down was a storage closet, clearly marked on the door. Perfect. She slipped inside, shook the blanket open, and found it was actually a bundle of several blankets. She grabbed one of them and began frantically toweling herself off. She shed her mask, unhooked her satchel. Touching her own skin felt like touching a cold marble statue, and her suit felt worse. She glanced back at the door. Of course there'd be no lock on the inside of a storage closet. She hesitated a moment, then stripped off her suit. Scandalous!

Joy wrapped herself in the dry blankets head-to-toe and curled up in a little ball in the corner. Nothing to do now but lie and wait for her shivers to subside. Well, this rescue mission was off to a terrific start, wasn't it? Already there'd been more difficulties than she'd accounted for in her mental half-plans. What would the next screw-up do to her?

Joy felt another surge of dread, followed by a wave of guilt around her last, unwritten letter to her family. The cold and the fear did bring her one benefit: it had a clarifying effect, and she finally realized what she should have written, what she would've most wanted to tell them, if it was her final chance to tell them everything. She should have told them each one thing that she loved and admired about them.

Joy felt the list ordering itself in her mind, with barely any conscious effort on her part. Hugh had always followed her around, even to places he shouldn't have, determined to do anything that she did. He probably would've followed onto this ship, if he'd known about it. She knew he planned to enlist, even though the war was over, and it was so like him, to refuse to shirk the danger that others had faced. Hugh had courage; that was one thing Joy loved and admired about him.

Flora was very different, quiet and reserved, with her nose constantly buried in a book, or in her journal. But she wasn't ignoring people. Whenever someone in the family was really hurting, you could count on Flora to be there to pick them up. Flora had empathy; that was one thing Joy loved and admired about her.

Belle was the rebel of their family, prone to wild mood swings, and stubborn as a rock. She ditched school and got into fights—though usually, when the details came out about those fights, Belle was defending herself or someone else against a bully. And sometimes her stubbornness paid off in ways Joy would never had expected. Belle had a fierce, independent spirit; that was one thing Joy loved and admired about her.

June took a little more thought—the third-born child, smack dab in the middle, June tended to go along with what everyone else wanted. She was clear water, flowing along the path of least resistance. But there was more to it than that—every time there was a fight in the family, June was the one to bring the combatants back on speaking terms. More than anything, Joy realized, it was June's lack of ego was what allowed her to do this. June had humility, that was one thing Joy loved and admired about her.

Kane was easy. He was a builder. Joy remembered one summer project that turned out to be a steam-powered couch on wheels, that could carry all the Fan siblings down main street until it caught fire and went up in a blaze of glory. Joy always thought it was so cool how passionate he got with his projects. Kane had intelligence and creativity; that was one thing Joy loved and admired about him.

Dean came up clearest in her mind. He was the oldest after her, and she couldn't even remember a time when he hadn't been around. Likewise, when Kallistrate was in desperate need of men to crew the spikefruit ships, Dean was right there—someone needed to do it, so it might as well be him. Dean had a strong sense of ethics and responsibility: that was one thing she loved and admired about him.

308

And then her thoughts turned to Mom and Dad, and here her mind faltered. There was too much, and it was all so complicated. In so many ways it was easier to remember her resentments—all the ways she'd felt things growing up had been unfair, all the times when she'd felt the responsibilities of being the eldest weighing her down. She remembered that feeling of liberation she'd felt when she'd moved away to college, free and clear.

It turned out that freedom could be really lonely. There were so many things that she'd taken for granted—little details that came rushing to the surface of her mind: Mom's smiling face from when she tucked them in at night; Dad taking any excuse to torment them with lame jokes; Mom comforting her and dabbing ointment on a bee sting; Dad taking time to become the ferocious Cave Bear and chase them all around the yard; and a million other little things they'd done throughout the years—a million little ways of saying "I love you."

Joy wouldn't have called her parents the most passionate people in the world. She couldn't remember ever seeing them kiss each other on the lips. But she also couldn't think of two people who loved each other more than they did. It was something she'd never questioned, just like a fish never questioned being wet. That love had surrounded her growing up, permeated the house itself. It seeped in through all the floorboards, travelled through the plumbing, soaked in through the carpets and the upholstery, nourishing them all so they sprung up like weeds. It was the foundation for every other thing they'd do in their lives, and without it, they'd have all been lost.

Finally, Joy found the words to contain her feelings. The thing she loved and admired most about her parents was that they loved each other. That was the core, and everything else was just details.

Joy tried to wipe her eyes on the blanket, and winced at its scratchy texture. They made these things for emergencies, not comfort, after all. She found that she was able to uncurl from a fetal position without being overwhelmed by shivers. Little by little, a slow fire had built up inside the cocoon she'd made for herself. Feeling returned to her hands and feet—actually, it felt like they were on fire now, compared to the rest of her. The air felt warm again. It was still summer, after all.

Joy reached for her satchel and opened it up, which was a bit of a chore, as the waterproofing required unrolling the top and undoing triple layers of zippers, which would each need to be re-sealed with special grease before she could submerge it again. At least her hands were working properly now, with even the pins-and-needles sensation receding. She pulled out her notebook and paused, wondering at her actions. It was already too late to mail a letter. If she survived to make it to a mailbox, would she even need to write something like this? But—it couldn't hurt to write this down, either. Just in case. Just so she'd done it.

It didn't take long. The essence of it was simple: "To my family," as the heading, a neat, ordered list with seven sentences, signed at the bottom with her name in Kallish and Xiaish characters. Joy looked it over and it seemed completely bizarre, what she'd done. But part of her felt a small sense of relief, nonetheless.

She took the opportunity to scan the supply closet for anything useful, like ship blueprints or a set of keys, or a janitor's uniform—did they have janitors on a ship? Or were they called something else? Never mind—there was nothing in here except cleaning supplies, some simple tools, and the stuff she'd dragged in herself—her mask, her satchel, her reed sandals, her suit, the wet blanket, and the medkit from the emergency locker.

Or rather, the box she'd assumed to be a medkit—that actually held something else: three reddish-orange cylinders. Joy took a closer look at them. Signal flares? Ah, whatever. She pulled out her flashlight and sandals from her satchel, and, upon reflection, replaced them with the three flares. They could be useful. Might as well hang onto them.

She needed to get moving. She glanced at her swimsuit, lying in a sodden puddle on the floor. There wasn't any helping it—she had nothing else to wear. She wrung it out several times, patted at it with the blanket, and even tried snapping it once to air-dry it, which she instantly regretted. That wasn't quiet! Even with all that, putting the suit back on felt like donning a sheet of ice.

She hissed and wrapped one of the blankets around her shoulders again. But it wasn't that bad—no shivers. She put her sandals on, taking care with the portion that came up the back of her heel and tied around her ankle. She belted her satchel back on and strapped her diving mask around her forehead, for lack of a better place to put it. She decided to keep the blanket for now, wrapped around her shoulders like a cloak. Now for the really tricky part.

She had no good plan from here on out. A plan needed reliable information, and she'd had none. Ideally, she'd have done all sorts of reconnaissance and scouting beforehand, but if she'd had the time for that, she would've had time to contact someone qualified to deal with this instead of her. Everything about this was reckless and stupid—but the only alternative was doing nothing, so here she was.

Hsiu Mei had told her that the girls were somewhere in the ship's hold. But she didn't like the idea of blundering around lost, looking for a hatchway. It seemed too likely that she'd stumble across some crewmen if she wandered around like that. And, even if she found the girls, she still didn't know how she was going to get them off the ship and smuggle them to the Temple. What Joy needed to do was get as high as she could, all the way to the roof, get a visual layout of the ship and the docks, and then work out some kind of rough plan.

She cracked the door open, peered out into the hallway, and listened carefully. Thus began her daring stealth mission. The first leg was the worst. There was no place to hide in this corridor. She just had to move quickly, when no one was coming, and hope that things stayed that way. She went back the way she'd come. The top of the paddle wheel extended fairly high up the side of the ship. She knew she'd seen a stairway on the inner side of it.

The stair was narrow, metal, and so steeply angled that it was practically a ladder. No cover here either. She moved quickly, quietly, and prayed to any god that might be listening that no one else started climbing down from the other direction. She reached the top and poked her eyes just above the deck level. No one in sight. This was the bridge level. She looked about and saw one more stair/ladder nearby, leading up to the roof. There we go.

She reached the top deck and looked around. Behind her were two very large, angled smokestacks, and all around her was a forest of hooded pipes, their mouths covered by metal grates. Air vents? Anyway, they provided some cover, plus she was fairly confident that she wouldn't be seen from the ground if she stayed low on the deck, at crawling height. From here she was able to do some proper scouting. Most of the Joanne Spaulding was level with the main deck. The highest built-up section was in the middle, where she was. It was also the widest section by far. Joy hadn't realized how much bulk the paddle wheels added, but the deck at the paddle wheel section was easily three times as wide as it was towards both the prow and aft. It made Joy think of a matronly woman with huge hips. The ship had two masts, each located at the far ends of the ship, with cables strung between them, but neither had a crow's nest that she could see, or any sails, or places where you might attach a sail. She wondered why they bothered having masts, then? No matter—it wasn't important. Both the foredeck and aft decks were dominated by large hatches, with very simple manual block-and-tackle crane systems. Joy supposed they were used at ports that didn't have steam-powered crane golems. Hsiu Mei said the rest of the girls were in the hold, but she hadn't said if it was fore or aft. But that wasn't the main problem. The problem was the guards.

Joy had no problem viewing them. The docks were lit up all around, with gas lamps, and some of the new electric lights as well. It was even worse than she'd thought from her brief survey from the paddle wheel. Triad goons in suits were pacing the docks in pairs. Joy tried counting them and gave up after the first two dozen. The warehouse district was on high alert. Joy had to count herself fortunate that they'd all been directing their attention to the land approach, and not out to the sea, but this was a disaster.

She was somehow supposed to sneak a half-dozen girls out past all of this? How was that going to work? Maybe sneak them out by sea somehow? After her ordeal getting here, that seemed like a very bad idea. One lone snorkeler might be able to sneak through the harbor undetected, but seven? Trying to swim in a strange area in the middle of the night? What if one or more of them got lost or started panicking? She doubted she could keep track of them all. And what if one or more of them couldn't swim at all?

Okay, forget swimming. How about using a lifeboat? Make a break that way? Joy peered over at one of the dinghies, lashed to the deck and covered in a canvas tarp. Yes, just get that unmoored, quietly drop it over the side, and just row away at lightning speed. Totally inconspicuous. No downside there. No, she had to get them on the dock and past the guards somehow. Maybe try bluffing her way past? Pretend to be one of Benny's employees, relocating the girls to a safer spot? And why would they believe her? Especially since she was dressed in a military-issue swimsuit. Like that wouldn't raise any eyebrows.

This was all so frustrating. Joy peered out past the warehouse district into the city proper. She could see the spires of the Temple jutting out from the city skyline. Not so close, but not so far. Such an easy landmark. Anyone could find their way there, as long as they weren't stopped. But that was the problem.

The more Joy thought about it, the more her heart started to sink. She was not seeing a solution here. She had to face the possibility that, after coming so far, she might have to abort the mission and return with nothing. What then? Return empty-handed to Hsiu Mei? Oh, so sorry, but your new Big Sister is all talk after all. Just one more person to break their promises and let you down. The world just sucks like that.

Joy bit down a surge of rage and frustration. Stop it, Joy— that's not helping. She had to think. At the very least, she could try to figure out where the Joanne Spaulding was headed next. It would give them a way to possibly find Lin Lin later—steal her back from whoever bought her, if that's what it took. There would have to be documents with that information somewhere on board—logs, manifests, and the like. She peered down at the decks below her. At least the Joanne Spaulding wasn't swarming with people. She'd only seen two people on the ship so far, and only one had seemed to actually be patrolling.

She made her way down to the bridge, without running into anyone. She found a ship's log with their next several scheduled destinations. She started to tear that page out, but stopped herself before the tear was more than inch long. Missing pages would raise suspicion. She took out her notebook and copied the information by hand. On her way out, she passed a door that said "Chart Room."

That sounded promising.

There were tons of documents here, books full of receipts, shipping manifests. She flipped through them and saw page after page of very mundane information—long lists of numbers next to ordinary trade goods. Maybe if she spent a couple of hours studying it, she might find some discrepancies—but she didn't have hours. Besides, if you were engaged in illegal smuggling, would you leave records of that just lying around in the open? Wouldn't you hide it somewhere?

Well, there weren't any obvious hiding places in here—everything was clearly organized in cabinets lining the wall, secured with simple latches, she guessed mainly to keep the drawers from flying open during rough seas. But one of them did have a lock. Joy retrieved her lock-picks from her satchel and started in on it. About midway through she started to berate herself for wasting time. Probably secret documents would be stored in a completely different place, like in the captain's private quarters, or—

The lock clicked, followed by another metallic thunk. Joy tested the cabinet drawers. She could open them all now. That had been easy. Surprisingly so. In fact, she was sure she hadn't finished yet. Why had it opened early? She started back in with her picks again, and had her suspicions confirmed. There was another set of tumblers behind the first one. Joy got an image in her mind of a lock that could accept two keys—an ordinary, everyday use one with a short handle, and a second, special key with a long handle. She got back to work, feeling a surge of excitement. The second set of tumblers weren't nearly as cooperative as the first, but finally she got them to line up, and heard a second click. Nothing happened on the front of the cabinet, so she searched around the side, up and down, finding nothing until she lay flat on her belly and peered through the small gap between the floor and the legs of the cabinet.

She found a small drawer that hadn't been there before. Inside was a slim notebook, titled "Insurance." Joy flipped through it. It was a long list of names, titles, and numbers. Cash payments. And the names—a lot of them she didn't recognize, but a few she did—major politicians, magistrates, city officials. She wasn't sure what she had, but it felt big. Yeah, it had to be important, or else it wouldn't have been hidden away like that. Could she fit it in her satchel? Yes—just barely. At the back of her head a part of herself was dancing with glee. If she could get this evidence to the KIB, it could blow all the corruption in Dodona wide open. Maybe it would give her enough leverage to convince them to send warships and Jagdkommandos out to retrieve the girls later, if she couldn't rescue them tonight. She could only hope.

But first things first. Joy closed the secret drawer. Back to more pressing concerns. She needed to figure out where the girls were being kept. She knew they were in one of the holds, but which one? There was a cutaway diagram on the wall, a full layout of the Joanne Spaulding—just what she'd wanted. It showed the two main cargo compartments, fore and aft, which were further subdivided into several different decks. Now to just cross-check with the shipping manifest.... But, of course, the shipping manifest didn't have any listing for "slave girls." You wouldn't be that obvious, would you? Joy tried to contain her frustration, continued to scan through the long lists of very mundane goods, looking for something to jump out at her—some kind of euphemism. After a minute, Joy found something—an entry for "Wild Orchids." That had to be it. She just had to.... Wait a second. A few columns over, there was another entry: "Exotic Birds." And then, even further over: "Assorted Sweetmeats."

Joy grit her teeth. Any of those could be the girls, depending on how much of an asshole the captain was—and they were all in separate cargo compartments. Joy stared at the cutaway diagram, stuck by indecision. Was this even worth it? What was she going to do with the girls if she found them? She had no... Wait—now she was doing it, too. Thinking of the girls as things. They were people. Maybe they might have some ideas, something she hadn't thought of. At the very least, she could talk to them, tell them about Hsiu Mei. She could let Lin Lin know that her big sister was okay—that at least there were a few people who were thinking about them and cared enough to help. She could do that much.

Fine. She didn't know which hold they were in? So check them all. Hsiu Mei had told her they'd all been kept in a large cage. Shouldn't be too hard to find. Joy put all the logs back where she'd found them and snuck back out into the hallway.

She nearly made it out to the deck when she heard a rough, male voice call out. She spun around, sure she'd been spotted, but there was no one there. Wasn't calling her. But she heard the footsteps on the deck, and a metallic jingle in time with the steps. He was coming this way. She ducked back into the chart room. She'd already switched the lights off, but there

316

was nowhere to hide in here. What if he came in? Joy threw her back to the wall on the hinge side of the door, raised her flashlight up like a club, and waited, heart racing. The events of her fight with Yang and Chen played out again in her mind. She'd come out far better than she'd expected from that, but she wasn't eager to repeat the experience. Maybe she might get the better of any one crewman she ran into, if she managed to surprise him, but she had no confidence in her ability to knock a seasoned sailor out in one hit, to stop him from yelling and alerting the whole ship.

Out in the hall, the footsteps resounded on the deck floor, coming closer, along with the metal sound. A key-ring. A big one. The sound of doors opening. He was searching for something. She heard him come closer. Thump-thump/jingle. Thump-thump/jingle. He was right outside her door. She heard the creak of a door handle, the groan of the hinges... from across the hall. Some more sounds, some banging around, then quiet. Joy held very still, tried to breathe shallow, be small and unnoticeable.

The man's voice boomed out in the stillness, right outside, making her jump. "Jang! Sonam! Taku! Lee—where the hell are you bastards! Shirking duty? In the grog? I swear, when I find you jackasses, I'm gonna strip your rotten monkey hides and leave you out for the gulls."

No other voices rose up to answer. Joy heard her own shallow breath, the pounding of her own heart, the pulsing of her blood as it ran up through her neck and right beneath her ears. The hull of the ship let out the slightest of groans, more like a sigh, as the deck rocked gently beneath her feet.

"Worthless assholes," muttered the man outside. "Tonight, of all nights, to pull this nonsense." Joy could hear it now, the undercurrent of fear he was trying to mask with his bluster. "Where the hell... Better not be down in the hold... I warned 'em... They touch the merch...."

Joy heard a leathery rustle, followed by the sharper sounds of metal parts sliding against metal. She recognized those metal sounds from her supplemental courses, the ones that had taken her to the firing range. Safety off, bullet in the chamber, re-holster—but looser this time. The man outside wasn't happy at all.

"Gonna need a new crew." The low growl carried through the wall. "Pain in my ass."

The thump-jingle started up again, heading away from her. Joy let it recede, let it get a safe distance away, and then she opened the door, slipped out into the hallway, and started following it. It was the most terrifying thing she'd done so far, but in some ways, it was easier. Now she was the one doing the stalking. It was simpler like this—she knew where the danger was. She could hear every step. She also knew how dangerous it was—the man was armed and extremely agitated. But she didn't like any of that business about the hold, and missing crew, and "touching the merchandise." Something ugly was about to go down, and she needed to be there, to do.... well, to do something about it. Whatever she could.

The hardest part was going around corners. She had to be very careful to peer out without being seen herself—gauge the sight-lines, see what cover she had. The man she followed was on high alert. She had to be careful. Thank goodness for that key ring. Its jingling told her so much about where he was and what he was doing. She could tell when he descended the stair down to the main deck and stepped away from the ladder. She approached the top of the stair on her belly, peeked over the top, just barely. Her view stretched over the empty deck, but she couldn't see the man—the captain? She heard another jingle. He was at the bottom of the ladder. Right below her. She didn't make any effort to find him with her eyes. That would mean sticking her head out further, and that was a bad idea. If she couldn't see him from this angle, then he couldn't see her, either.

She did see his hands move out into her field of vision, to open a hatch on the floor, leading below decks. And then those hands were yanked away, and there was a brief, muffled sound of protest. Joy heard the key ring rattle about violently, and then that was cut short, too. Then silence. Joy froze where she was, trying to make sense of what she'd heard. What was going on? Joy heard the faintest of scraping sounds. It travelled across the deck to her right, followed by a sort of flapping noise, like a sail in the wind, followed by a thump like someone hurling sandbags. Then all was quiet, except for the cries of the gulls.

Joy stayed where she was, waiting for the sound of the jingling keys to start back up again, to give away the captain's position, but nothing happened. Cautiously, she leaned further over the edge, and still further, until she could see the entire deck. It was empty.

Not being able to see the captain made Joy nervous. Did that mean he was hiding, lying in wait now? Joy thought back to the last noises she'd heard, trying to parse out what had happened. It felt like they'd moved right. Joy scanned the deck in that direction. Weren't many places to hide—except one. One of the life boats rested in a sort of cradle on the deck, next to a pulley system that would hoist it over the side. It had been lashed down and covered with a canvas tarp. Except one of the corners of the tarp had been undone, leaving a flap hanging loose. It looked suspicious.

Joy took a deep breath, let it go, and climbed down the ladder to investigate, nerves on edge, flashlight at the ready if anyone jumped out at her. She approached the lifeboat like she was stalking a rabbit, wondering if she was being an idiot. This could be a trap. She scanned left and right, for any potential ambushers, and saw nothing. What if they were hiding in the lifeboat, ready to grab her when she looked in. But did that make sense? It was an awkward ambush position. Hard to get out quickly, and you wouldn't be able to see anything from in there. Something wasn't right. Something weird was going on here. And this was a scouting mission. She needed to know what was going on. She needed to know.

Joy climbed up to perch on the edge of the lifeboat hull. Balanced there, she noiselessly reached out and grasped the loose corner of the canvas tarp, preparing to spring away if something did try to strike out at her. She yanked the flap open and saw a pile of motionless bodies.

Joy successfully stifled the urge to scream and leap away, but her muscles got that message a millisecond later than they should've, and Joy wobbled and nearly fell off the lifeboat. She took the time she needed to collect herself. Breathe in, breathe out—slow breaths... Slow and steady. She pulled the corner flap open again and stuck her flashlight inside before switching it on again, so the light wouldn't attract attention from elsewhere. Now she could see these men had their hands bound behind their backs, with some type of heavy-gauge wire, and their ankles, too. Were they breathing? Well, they should be. Why would you tie up a corpse? Carefully, Joy reached a hand in to put in front of one of their faces, and felt hot air moving across her fingertips. Joy tried to count heads. Eight that she could see. That meant....

Joy felt her heart race. This had to be the entire active crew— the whole night shift. Right now, this ship was completely un-guarded. If she could find the girls they could just walk right off the boat, no problem. Until they got to the docks, and then there would be problems. Big problems. Joy glanced along their escape route, and didn't find it any more encouraging than before. It was so frustrating—this was the perfect opportunity. A chance like this wouldn't come again. She had to get them out now, while the Red Specter had taken out all the guards....

She stopped, realized what she was thinking. She wasn't even questioning it now. The Red Specter—or the copycat, what-ever—had done this. He was on board, somewhere. Maybe he could help her, if she could only talk to him. She scanned the main deck of the Joanne Spaulding again. It still looked empty, but now she knew it wasn't. The Red Specter was lurking about somewhere, and the thought of it sent a chill down her spine. For a second, she considered calling out to him, but thought better of it. She might attract the attention of the dockside guards, and besides, she had no way of knowing for sure that he'd actually be friendly. Just because the comic strip version was a hero, that didn't mean this guy was. She had no idea what his real agenda was. He could be a complete loon. No, it was best to proceed under the assumption that she was on her own here.

Joy found the captain's unconscious form, retrieved his key-ring, and headed down the hatch, into the hold of the Joanne Spaulding.

Chapter 42:

Exotic Birds

Getting down to the hold and searching it was a much easier task, now that she didn't have to bother with stealth. She spotted the girls right away, though the reason for that didn't make her happy. Their cage was suspended in the air, a good fifteen feet above the floor, dangling from a rope.

What the Abyss was this? Joy followed the path of the rope holding up the cage, down to a block and tackle that was secured to a hard point at the bottom of the hull. Joy stared at the pulley system at the anchor point, trying to see if there was some sort of winch or crank handle to lower the cage, but not finding one.

So much for this being easy. Hsiu Mei hadn't said anything about this! Kind of an important detail.

Joy sighed, took another calming breath. She couldn't let her frustration get the better of her. "Hello," she called out, in Wuyu Xiaish. "Hello, wake up! I'm here to rescue you, but I need your help. Wake up, please."

After a few seconds, the sleeping forms in the bottom of the cage began to stir, to turn to the sound of her voice. Six tired, confused, and suspicious faces peered down at her.

"What? What is going on?" said one of the girls. "Who are you?"

"My name is Fan Joy Song," she replied. "And I'm here to get you out."

"What? Get us out?" Some of the girls started to direct nervous glances around the hold. "Why would you do that? Where is the Captain?"

"The Captain has been knocked out and tied up, along with the rest of the crew. So you can escape now, if I can get you down. But I don't know how to use this pulley system. Can you tell me how it works?"

"You can't work it," said the girl, with narrow, wary eyes. "Not by yourself. It needs four people. It's to protect us."

Protect them? A likely story. But she could see already that the girls didn't trust her. Well, it was understandable. She was a stranger. Time to take a different tack.

"Is Lin Lin there? Wong Lin Lin?"

The smallest girl's eyes went wide. She looked at her fellow prisoners for a second, before raising her hand. "That's me."

Joy smiled back up. "Nice to meet you. You look just like Hsiu Mei. She's the one that sent me to get the rest of you. She didn't forget about you. She was really worried."

The girls looked confused. "The ones who bought Hsiu Mei want to steal the rest of us?" Said one of them.

"Nobody bought Hsiu Mei. She escaped. And found me."

"She escaped?" said Lin Lin, but the first girl shushed her, and then they all started whispering amongst themselves. Joy couldn't make out any of it. This was a ridiculous way to have a conversation.

"Okay, hang on," she said. "I'm going to come up to you."

Joy dropped her flashlight, put the key ring in her teeth, and began to climb the rope up to the cage. Climbing a taut rope at an angle was awkward, compared to going straight up and down, but she managed okay. This was like climbing a new Caliburn obstacle after they'd altered the course each season. About halfway up, she began to regret the decision to hold the keys in her teeth instead of her satchel, as her jaw started to ache and drool began to leak from the corners of her mouth. But it was too late to fix now.

She kept going until she got above the cage, then dropped down on top of it. She had a sudden moment of belly-lurching fear as her landing caused the whole cage to lurch and swing. Joy went to all fours to keep her balance, while the girls below clutched each other and stared back up at her. Her jaw clenched down on the key ring, and Joy realized she had a huge grin on her face. *Wheeee!*

She grabbed the key ring, tried to discreetly wipe it off on her suit, and dropped it through the bars on top of the cage. "Here you go," she called down. Six faces stared back up at her. Lin Lin picked up the keys and started trying them on their manacles. Joy crawled to the edge of the cage and stuck her entire torso over. Hanging upside-down, she reached down to brace one hand against a horizontal cross-bar and got a firm grip at the top of the cage with her other hand. Then she let her hips go over the side, using her wide grip and her core strength to keep control as she righted herself, sticking her feet through gaps in the bars to stand on the cage floor, while hanging off the side. She came face to face with the girls just in time to see their shocked expressions. Joy felt a little nonplussed. That move really wasn't all that hard. Did it look cool? Whatever, it wasn't important.

Lin Lin was going through key after key, and none of them were working on her manacles. They wouldn't even fit through the keyhole. Of course they wouldn't—only the Sleywie had the right key for those. Joy glanced at the chains leading up to their collars, each of which had a dangling egg-shaped symbol of Nibiru, possibly hiding a shimmering blue jewel inside. But they could deal with that later. Now they needed to open the cage door.

Joy aimed her most charming smile at the girls.

"May I come in?"

Lin Lin looked up, and started to come to her, but First Girl stopped her.

"Wait," said First Girl, turning back to Joy. "Who are you? Why should we trust you?"

"I'm Fan Joy Song, and I'm a friend of Hsiu Mei's," said Joy. "But she didn't mention anything about your cage being hung up like this. It's kind of extreme, don't you think?"

"It happened after she left," said Lin Lin. "The Captain did it. There's been all this talk—the buyers are acting strange. I've heard the crew say that maybe they wouldn't buy us after all, that maybe Hsiu Mei made them angry?"

"The captain heard the talk and decided he didn't trust his men any more. Around us," said First Girl.

As Joy looked at all the worried faces peering back at her, she couldn't help noticing that whatever agent the cultists had sent had been pretty selective. This cage would turn into a beauty pageant with a little scrubbing. For some reason, this pissed her off even further, but she fought it down, not wanting to frighten the girls.

"So he hoisted you all up like this, Miss.... I'm sorry, I didn't catch your name?"

"Ha Shao Yin," said First Girl, after some hesitation. Joy got the rest of them to introduce themselves as well. She tried to make mnemonic puns for each of their names, commit them to memory. It could help convince them that she cared. Two of them weren't from Xia provinces, but from farther off. The war had displaced so many people. But something about this crazy suspended cage wasn't making sense.

"Seems like a crazy plan to me, Shao Yin," said Joy. "How is a rope going to stop them from just lowering you down, if that's the problem?"

"That pulley is set so it needs four men to lower it," she replied. "Because four is too many to keep a secret. Or so the captain says."

On a ship? That made sense, but.... "It only takes one to climb the rope."

"The captain gave us orders. If anyone tries to open the door when he isn't here, all of us should kick them until they fall," said Shao Yin.

Okay, the captain knew what he was doing, kinda. "Wait, how are you getting food, and...."

Joy peered past the girls and spotted a sort of wastebin in the corner, thin enough on one side to pass through the bars, attached to a rope, and....

"It's that," said Joy, pointing. "That's what you use, right? That's perfect. You can climb down that rope and escape. I'll help you with that."

"Why?" demanded Shao Yin. "The captain isn't here. Why shouldn't we kick you off?"

"What?" said Joy. "But I'm not one of the crew. I'm here to help...."

Joy looked at the girls' faces, and saw a mix of suspicion, fear, and anxiety directed back at her. Gears clicked into place in her head. "You think this is a trick? You think one of the men hired me?"

Shao Yin just crossed her arms and glared. Lin Lin couldn't take it.

"If the sailors sent her, then why didn't she know about the pulley? It's because my sister didn't know—"

"She says she didn't know," countered Shao Yin. "Maybe she's just a good liar. And why would she help us? She doesn't know any of us."

"I know Hsiu Mei," said Joy.

"How?" said Shao Yin. She rounded back on Lin Lin.

"We've all travelled a long way. We're docked at a foreign city. Do-Do-Na." The strange word rolled oddly off her tongue. "Do you know anyone in Do-Do-Na? Do you have family here? I never heard you mention it."

Lin Lin averted her eyes and didn't say anything.

"I met her after she escaped," said Joy. "I found her while she was hiding."

"How did Hsiu Mei escape?" demanded Shao Yin. "That doesn't sound like her."

Joy took a deep breath and tried to organize her thoughts. These girls were already having a hard time accepting her story. The last thing she needed to do was start spouting nonsense about a "Red-Faced Ghost," or she'd be here all night.

"All these men—the sailors, the buyers, the Triads—they're all criminals. Selling people is against the law here. And these criminals have started fighting, each trying to double-cross the other. On the night they took Hsiu Mei out, a big fight broke out, and her guards ran. She saw no one was watching her, because of the fight, so she was able to run and hide...."

Joy was going to say more, but a firework went off in her head, and suddenly she knew exactly how she was going to get the girls past the dock guards. So simple! Now, if only she could get them to listen to her.

"Shao Yin, I know you don't believe I'd go this far just to help you, but I really am. I know you've had a hard time, but this," Joy waved her hand, a sweeping gesture to take in their manacles, the cage, the hold of illegal cargo, "this isn't the whole world. There are good people out there, and I want to prove it to you. So you just tell me: what do I need to do to convince you? Tell me that and I'll do it."

Shao Yin glared at her over crossed arms, eyes narrowed in concentration. Finally, she spoke.

"You say you're Hsiu Mei's friend," she said. "So then, tell us something about her. Something only she would know."

Six faces turned to Joy, expectantly. Joy kept her welcoming smile plastered to her face while she wracked her brain, thinking back over the past several hours, of the time she'd spent with Hsiu Mei. Joy had spent most of it giving her advice, or explaining things, or translating, or running for her life, or thinking of ways to solve her problems. Had she asked her any personal questions? At all? What a lousy reporter she was. There had to have been something....

"Hsiu Mei and Lin Lin both grew up on a farm," she said, stalling for time. Of course that wasn't going to cut it. "And they have an uncle, a Celestial Scholar. His name is Tan, he's married, and he lives in Genyen Province." Whew.

Five blank expressions turned to Lin Lin. Clearly, that was news to all of them.

"She's right!" said Lin Lin, face lighting up. "We do! Only Big Sister would know about Uncle Tan. She really did escape.

And now she's waiting for us."

"Great," said Joy. "Keys, please."

Lin Lin ran over. Shao Yin looked like she wanted to stop her but another girl stopped her. What was her name again? Waves in her hair, friendly-looking... Shu Bo! "She passed the test," said Shu Bo. "I think we should go for it. Whatever happens, it has to be better than being sold."

Shao Yin didn't look convinced of that, not by a long shot, but she didn't protest any further.

Joy had the door unlocked and was inside in a flash. She went straight for the bucket in the corner, though she had to deal with Lin Lin trying to hug her, which she could only do sort of halfway, because of the manacles, and had to deal with a bunch of questions about Hsiu Mei, how she was doing, where she was, and so on.

"She's at the Temple, the Prakasa Mandira—it's beautiful, and safe, and you'll be going to see her soon. Um... just hold on to the rest of that for now—we have to get going," said Joy.

She was starting to worry about the amount of time she had used up. Blundering around in the dark, shivering in a blanket, searching the chart room, and now, having to debate with her rescue-ees. Was that a word? Never mind—What time was it now? Would anybody be coming along to check on the ship crew? Would replacements come for a new shift? Better get out now, in case the answer to any of those questions turned out to be yes.

Joy got rid of the bucket, trying not to pay too close attention to its contents, though she couldn't avoid the smell. Barbaric, treating human beings like this. She chucked it a good distance away from the cage, idly hoping for it to land on something valuable and easily stained. She double-checked the knots anchoring the rope to the cage bars and gave it a couple sharp tugs, before she was satisfied. She tossed the rest of the rope out of the open cage door, and was pleased to note that it went all the way to the floor.

"Okay, time to get moving," she said, turning back to the girls and pointing out the door.

They looked at each other uncertainly. One of them shrank back, fell to her knees and clung to the side of the cage. "You want us to climb out? We can't do that! We'll fall!"

Joy did a double-take. This, she hadn't expected. "No, you won't," she said. "Trust me, that doesn't happen. Going down is easy. Anyone can do it."

"Even with these?" asked Lin Lin, holding up her manacled hands.

For a second, Joy considered breaking out her lock-picks and opening all the manacles, then decided against it. Too time-consuming. Besides which, those chains had plenty of slack between the wrists.

"Those are no problem," she insisted. She pulled up a body-length's worth of rope and held it up in front of her to demonstrate. "Going down is easy. You hold the rope close in, tight, see—and just walk down with your hands, like this."

Joy demonstrated the motion on the rope, then grabbed Lin Lin's wrists and moved them through that same motion. "See, no problem. And you don't even have to move your hands. If you want, you can just squeeze the rope—with your feet, too. Then you loosen up just a bit, and you'll slide down. You'll burn your hands a little, but it'll be fine. And we're not even that high up. It'll only be a second or two, and then you're down. So come on. I'll be right here to help."

Joy examined the exit and realized that the hardest part was getting past the cage floor. As it was, the girls would be scraping against the lower edge of the cage going over. Joy could easily see them getting their fingers caught between that edge and the rope, and then they might panic and fall. It would be a lot easier if there was some clearance there. After thinking it over, she pulled the rope back up and fed the end over the bar at the very top of the cage, by the door. Then she swung around to the outside of the cage, just by the door, hooked one knee around one of the horizontal crossbars, at around waist-height. She had her other foot braced against the bottom of the cage, and was able to lean out into space, with both her hands free, nice and stable. She grabbed the rope and held it so it no longer scraped the bottom edge of the cage.

She turned down to witness more shocked stares from the girls. What was the big deal? This was just like hanging upside down from your knees on a tree branch, like when you were a kid, only at a bit of an angle. Not many Caliburn climbers here? Well, whatever.

"So, who's first?" asked Joy.

Shu Bo started to step forward, but Shao Yin stopped her. "I'm first," she said.

Shao Yin marched forward, grim-faced, and grabbed the rope. She took a deep breath, and glared at Joy.

"Why are you looking at me like that?" she snapped.

"You're going first."

"So?"

"I know you still don't trust me," said Joy. "You think I'm lying. You think there's a man hiding down there to jump out and rape the first girl down. But you're going first?"

Shao Yin just tipped her chin up a bit and returned her gaze, saying nothing.

Joy smiled at her. "When I told you I was here to help, you didn't believe me. Because nobody would risk their life to help someone else, with nothing to gain in return. But the thing you think nobody does is exactly what you just did, without hesitation. With what you've been through, you've got every reason to be looking out for yourself and no one else, but you're not. Shao Yin, I think you're kind of awesome."

Shao Yin sort of flinched at that. For a second, her invisible wall of cynicism and hostility was shattered, and Joy got a brief glimpse of a very different person, someone achingly vulnerable and wounded. Then she turned away and jumped off the cage.

Joy stiffened herself in place, acting as a human strut. It worked. Shao Yin didn't hit the edge on her way down. The load wasn't too hard to bear, though she heard some fearful squeaks from the other girls as the shifting weight caused the cage to lean to one side. Joy had an unpleasant moment where she found her whole body start to pivot horizontally where she had weak support, but she held on until Shao Yin's weight left the rope. Joy looked down to see the girl crouched tensely on the floor, looking around frantically for hidden attackers. None came.

Joy shifted her position a bit to get better horizontal stability, and called for the next person. Shu Bo slid down without a hitch. The next three went pretty well. Joy thought she had done a pretty good job coaxing and guiding the scared ones. Plus, each girl who made it down was a successful role model for the next, calling up encouragement from the bottom of the hold. But then it came time for the last girl, and Joy's heart sank when she saw her seasick expression, which reminded her of seaweed—Noriko. Noriko was huddled in the far corner of the cage, clinging to the bars with a death-grip.

"Noriko?" said Joy, putting on her most inviting, encouraging expression. "Come on, now—it's your turn."

Noriko stared back at her, stricken, and curled up against the cage, forehead pressed against her wrists.

"Noriko's afraid of heights," called up a voice from below, helpfully.

"Lir's balls," Joy muttered, and took several long, deep breaths. She couldn't get impatient. She had to remember that everyone was different, and not everyone was a whiz on the Caliburn courses like she was. There were things she was scared of that didn't bother other people. Some people didn't mind spiders. Even had them as pets. Really big ones. Joy shuddered and decided to focus on the immediate problem.

She went to Noriko, put her arms around her, tried to calm her, reassure her, explain how easy it really was, but nothing worked.

But of course, you couldn't argue someone out of being afraid. Fear wasn't rational, and Noriko's terror was overwhelming. How in the world had she made it through the past several days like this? Not well, probably. But what could she do about it? They were losing time, and Joy couldn't even get Noriko to release her death-grip on the bars. How was she going to get her to climb the rope? If she panicked this much, she really would fall.

"I can't!" Noriko moaned. "Just... Just leave me. Take everyone else and go."

For a second, Joy seriously considered it. But only for a second. Everyone was coming. She would make it happen.

"Noriko, is that what you really want? To be left behind? To be separated from everyone else? Your friends don't want to leave you," said Joy.

From below, voices wafted upwards.

"Come on, Noriko."

"You can do it!"

"It's not hard. It's really easy."

"We're here. We'll catch you."

"Noriko!"

Noriko raised her head at the sound of the voices. She glanced over at the open cage door and the dangling rope, and her face twisted.

"I can't!" she sobbed.

Okay, different tack. Noriko really was incapable of climbing. So what then? Maybe lower the entire cage? There were five girls on the ground. But they weren't as heavy or strong as four sailors and Joy worried at their ability to safely unhitch the complicated knot-secured block-and-tackle that kept them aloft. Maybe they could do it, but a mistake would send the whole cage plummeting to the deck.

No, she couldn't take that chance. But it did give her a better idea.

"Hold on," said Joy. "We'll be down in a minute."

She grabbed the rope and pulled it all the way up. Then she took the end and started wrapping it around Noriko, around her chest and across her shoulders, to make a kind of harness.

"Wh... What are you doing?" She said.

"Okay, you're not going to climb," said Joy. "You won't have to do anything. I'm going to lower you down. I'll do all the work, okay?"

Noriko started moaning, but Joy stood over her and pulled on the rope, lifting with her legs.

"Feel that? It's solid," said Joy, tugging a few more times. "I've got you, and nothing's going to happen to you. You don't even have to look.

Joy got a burst of inspiration. "Yes, that's it—close your eyes. Close your eyes and pretend you're on solid... Pretend you're on a pier—one of those floating ones, mounted on a bunch of hollow barrels, just a few feet off the water. You know what I mean?"

Joy knew she had to pick something that floated for her image, given they were in a swaying cage in the middle of a ship.

"Floating pier," Noriko repeated. Joy saw that she'd closed her eyes. "Yes, I've seen those."

"Right, and they're nice and safe and wide and stable, just a few feet above the water. That's not scary, is it?"

"N-no. No, that's not scary."

"Okay, great," said Joy. "So, keep your eyes closed and just picture that. That's where we are right now. So, take my hand, and we can walk across the pier.... or crawl, crawling works fine. Now just... okay you can let go of the—of the rails by the mooring. With both hands. Both of them. Like... this, right?"

Noriko was turning her body to crawl with Joy, but leaving at least one arm behind, seemingly unable to force herself to sever her last connection to the cage bars. Joy had to pry her fingers off, and herd her away to prevent her from re-grabbing the bars.

The two of them crawled together, Joy with one arm around Noriko's back, gripping her makeshift rope harness and guiding her. It was like some whacko three-legged race. Good thing they didn't have far to go.

"Okay, that's great, Noriko. Now, what I want you to do is sit up for me. Don't worry, I've got you. I've got you, right here." Joy was hugging Noriko from behind now. The girl was vibrating, muscles locked in a rictus.

"So now, what you can do is stretch your legs out, and dangle them over the edge pier, just a few inches over the water—"

"Don't push me!" Noriko froze in place and leaned back, away from the edge. "Don't push me off!"

"What? I'm not going to push you. I would never do that."

"Y-you swear?" Noriko sounded desperate. It was practically a wail.

"I swear on my soul that I'm not going to push you off," Joy replied. "We're going to do this, but we're going to go at your pace. Nothing's going to happen until you're ready."

Noriko's tension relented, but only a little. "You're sure you're not going to push me?"

So suspicious. "Noriko, if I give you even a little push, then let me be cast from the Great Wheel into the freezing darkness of the Outer Abyss, my soul to be ripped to pieces by the hateful monsters who dwell there, 'til I am unmade, a shadow cursed to be exiled from the Cycle of Rebirth, wretched and pitiful, for all eternity."

Joy felt a tremor pass through the terrified girl's body, as she released a long breath. She let Joy coax her into dangling her feet over the edge, and was able to start scootching forward, inch by inch, while the other girls yelled up their own encouragement.

"That's it, that's good," cooed Joy. "We're almost there. It's such a hot day, doesn't a dip in the water sound great? Just picture that.

"Everybody else is out swimming, and they want you to join in. And the water's right there. Nice and cool and inviting—it's just below your toes. Just a few feet, see?"

334

That was the wrong choice of words, because it prompted Noriko to crack an eye open. Just a tiny amount, but enough to shatter the illusion.

"I can't!" She howled, and would've sprang back from the edge, except Joy pushed her off.

Noriko's shriek only lasted for a bare second, for the few feet she fell until Joy's hands clamped down on the rope. Those first few feet were crucial, to make sure Noriko's head had dropped well clear of the cage's edge.

Joy leaned back into the cage, feet braced against the bars on each side of the doorway, and let the rope slowly slide through her hands, listening to Noriko's sobbing from below, trying not to feel like a complete shitheel. And hey, maybe the Outer Abyss wasn't that bad. For all she knew, it could have a thriving theater scene. That would be something.

The rope went slack, and Joy peered down to confirm that the other girls had collected Noriko. Great. Joy took a moment to blow on her palms. Frickin' rope burn.

She wasted no more time climbing down after. Noriko was blocking the bottom, sobbing on Shao Yin's shoulder while the other girls tried to undo the knots on her harness. Joy had to do a little swing and drop to avoid landing on anyone's head. Shao Yin fixed her with a look of pure hate as she landed. Looks like that little breakthrough they'd had a minute ago was undone now. Oh well—sometimes doing the right thing meant being a heartless lying bitch. She thought about apologizing to Noriko, but decided against it. Noriko was not going to be ready to hear that right now. And Joy wasn't actually sorry about what she'd done. And they'd already lost too much time as it was.

Joy led them through the hold and up to the deck. On the way, she found another emergency cabinet with more blankets, one for each of the girls. She had the girls wrap the blankets around them like cloaks, to hide their chains. Then she led them up one more deck, keeping them under cover, so they'd have a good view for what she needed to show them.

"See that?" She said, pointing at the seven spires of the Pra-kasa Mandira, its ceremonial lanterns lit up with a warm glow, outlining it against the night sky. "That's where you need to go. Hsiu Mei is waiting there, along with Mrs. Jakuba. They'll be expecting you. The criminals won't be able to get to you there. They wouldn't dare to defile the Temple."

The girls all stared at the spire. "That's where you're taking us?" asked Shu Bo. "It seems far away."

"Not so far," said Joy. "Probably a twenty-minute walk from here. Just keep it in your sight and keep moving toward it. This city is mostly a square grid. If you find yourself going sideways from it, just turn a corner."

"What do you mean?" Said Lin-Lin. "Aren't you coming with us?"

Joy smiled at her. Hopefully it was reassuring. "I've got an-other job. See those men?"

Joy pointed at all the Triad men patrolling the docks. "Those men are a problem. So I'm going to create a distraction, and while they're dealing with that—you're going to slip past them."

"Slip past them?" Said Shu Bo. "How?"

Joy let out a long breath. Honestly, this was the diciest part of the plan. "I guess just try to walk out normally? Act like you're supposed to be there and nothing wrong is happening."

The girls just stared at her.

"If my plan works, they're going to be paying attention to other things. So try not to draw attention. I'm guessing most of these men don't know who you are, not like the men on the ship. Act like you know where you're going, like you're out for a stroll. That's my advice."

"What?" said Shao Yin, her voice dripping scorn. "That's your plan? What if your distraction doesn't work? What if not all the men leave their posts? What then?"

"I dunno. Try to bluff your way past? Say you're evacuating the fire, say you were told to go to one of the warehouses. Or just try to run for it? Split up, disappear into the streets and hide—then break for the temple when it's clear. I really can't predict everything that's gonna happen, so the rest is up to you—"

"I can't believe it," said Shao Yin. "You say you come to rescue us, but then you say it's up to us? This plan is awful. You're just going to get us captured again and punished. We were better off in the cage—"

"Is that what you think? Fine! Then you can walk right back down to the hold, climb up the rope, and lock yourself right back where I found you. Go ahead," Joy snapped, and was about to say more, but she saw the girls flinching back from her. She stopped, closed her eyes, and took several long, deep breaths.

"Sorry," she said. "I'm sorry for yelling... It's been a really long, stressful day. But I'm serious. This is your freedom and your lives, so it's your decision to escape. I can give you a choice, and I can...."

She glanced over at Noriko. "I can push you through irrational fear, but I can't make you do anything you don't want to do."

As Joy said the words, she felt a bit lighter. "And you're right. My plan isn't great, but I... It's just the best I could do, okay? If you can come up with a better one, go right ahead.

"That's not sarcasm—I mean it. Pick the best plan for you. And if that means not escaping at all, I'll understand. But just remember, not everybody is going to give you that option. This chance... If you don't take it now, if you get sold—I don't know when you'll get another. Might be a long time, and you'll have to look back, and wonder what could have been...."

Joy realized she was rambling now. "Look, all you have to do is make it to the Temple. Just get there, however you can, and you'll be fine. I'm going to go create your distraction now. You can think it over while I'm getting ready. Just... good luck, all of you. I believe in you."

Shao Yin just stared at her, taken aback. She looked back at the stairs leading down to the hold, but Shu Bo and Noriko both clutched at her shoulders and started whispering in her ears, pleading with her to stick together. It seemed to be working.

Joy turned to go, but Lin Lin grabbed her in another chain-restricted hug.

"Thank you," she said. "Thank you for helping us. Me and Hsiu Mei. And we don't even know you."

Joy smiled down. "Well, when I found her, I told Hsiu Mei to think of me like a big sister. So that means you can, too—alright. I guess... I felt I had to take responsibility. Live up to my words?"

"Thank you," Lin Lin repeated, anxiously looking up at her. "We'll see you again? After you start the fire?"

"How'd you know I was going to start a fire?" asked Joy. She hadn't recalled mentioning that bit.

"You said we could bluff by saying we're evacuating the fire."

"Oh, right. I did say that."

"You're going to be okay, right? You won't let the bad men catch you?" Lin Lin gazed up at her, eyes pleading.

"Nobody's catching me. I'm way too slippery. Same for you guys. I know you can do it," Joy ruffled her fingers through Lin Lin's hair. "I'll see you later, okay?"

Lin-Lin smiled up at her and nodded. Joy crossed to the other side of the ship, away from the dock, and started prepping the next part of her crazy-ass plan.

Chapter 43:

Light It Up

Joy retrieved the small tin of sealant grease from inside her satchel and made sure she still had everything important. Mainly the flares, her notebook, and the small "insurance" ledger. She'd lost her flashlight at some point. No matter. She swiped three of her fingers in the sealant, like she'd been taught, replaced the tin, and closed each of the three zippers in turn, sealing them with one fingerfull of grease each, before rolling up the top, and cinching the strap around her waist, as tight as it could go. She spent a long time surveying the docks, until she saw a ladder going down to the water level, one that didn't seem to be too tightly monitored. She fixed her diving mask in place, took a fast glance to make sure no-one was looking in her direction, and dived over the side.

Joy hadn't practiced diving nearly as much as she'd practiced climbing, but she knew the basics pretty well. A good dive, with proper form, should pierce the water with virtually no splash. And this was a very basic dive, with no flips or anything, so there wasn't any reason for her not to nail it. She felt good about her form as her palms hit the ocean, but one thing she hadn't considered is she'd never practiced diving with anything belted around her waist before.

The satchel slapped the water hard and rebounded to smack her in the ass. Ow. And the salt water was not loving her rope burn, or any of the other cuts and scrapes she'd gotten from climbing up the paddle wheel, but she ignored it and tried to dive as deep as she could. If anyone came to investigate the splash, they shouldn't see her. She aimed to surface beneath the docks, make that trip in one breath. It was harder going than before, without her swim fins. And she was still wearing her reed sandals. They weren't really impeding her, but she'd never tried swimming with them before. She completed the long arc to her destination, lungs burning and screaming at her. She forced herself to pierce the surface slowly and breathe through her nose when she did. She missed her snorkel.

Joy took a moment to orient herself, make sure she'd come up in the right place—the ladder wasn't too far away. She treaded water, listening for the sounds of people rushing over to investigate the splash from her dive.

After hearing nothing unusual, she climbed up the ladder, and, after some truly nerve-wracking moments of zipping between points of available cover, made her way to the cargo maze, the same one she'd gotten lost in earlier that day. She worked her way over to the maze's border, the one closest to the Joanne Spaulding.

There were two large rows of crates and sacks stacked high that weren't connected to the rest of the maze. Good. She didn't want the fire to drift over to the weapons container further in the maze. That would be bad. But what if these "safe" piles also contained explosives? That seemed unlikely. You'd want to conceal them better. And she didn't see any of the Nibiru markings that had been on all the other weapons crates. She couldn't be one hundred percent sure, but everything she was doing was already stupid and dangerous, so add one more crazy risk to the pile, right?

Joy pulled the signal flares out of her satchel. How did these things work again? She'd noted they had instructions printed on them when she'd grabbed them, but she hadn't paid any closer attention to them than that. Another mistake, not like her.

Well, she'd been up since morning. It was now ungodly late— who knew what time it actually was. Well past her bedtime. She didn't feel sleepy because she was so keyed-up, but her lack of sleep could easily be affecting her judgement. It probably was. So what? Was there anything she could do about it? Nope. So focus on the now. This should nearly be over anyway.

She managed to make out enough of the flare instruction to get the gist of it. The flare had a cap on the end, which she popped off, exposing the black core. It was like an oversized matchstick. There was even a layer of sandpaper on the end of the cap. Joy noted some of the flare's printed warnings with amusement—DANGER! HOT MOLTEN MATERIAL! Wear GLOVES and hold over WATER. Point AWAY from BOAT and BODY! She was breaking all the rules tonight. Hee hee hee!

Joy steeled herself and prepared to strike the flares. She took a minute to review her plan in her head. Was there anything she'd forgotten? Anything else left to do? No, there was nothing left but to go for it. She held the flare up to the strike paper. Or tried to. Her hands were shaking. Hoo boy. Deep breaths, breathe in. Breathe out. This is the last bit. The girls were waiting. They were counting on her. This was last thing she needed to do, and then she could run away and hide. She could rest then, and deal with whatever came next. She just had to get through this. Like Noriko going off the edge of the cage. Just do it and be done. Do it and be done.

She was all set to go, was scraping the flare against the strike paper, when she remembered she'd forgotten to re-seal her satchel. She was carrying paper goods in there. She fumbled with the cap and dropped it. It bounced off and rolled off in the darkness somewhere. Joy managed to stop herself from cursing. Just slow down and think. She had three flares total. Each had a cap. She stuck the flares under her armpit while she re-sealed her satchel, secured it, took another long breath, and lit the first flare.

The light from it seared her eyes, forced her to squint and look away as she ran to her first target and flung the blazing rod, end over end, to land at the base of the first cargo pile. Joy watched it do its thing. Oh wow. That was really effective. That blaze was really going up there. Joy's stomach flip-flopped as she readied the next flare and ran to the second target while shouts of alarm went up all around the docks. The second flare did its job even better than the first, and Joy retreated back to the main cargo maze while lighting the third flare. She reminded herself that for her plan to work, her distraction needed to be really big. She had to draw all of the guards, or as many as she possibly could, to give the girls their chance to run.

"DOWN WITH THE TRIADS!" She screamed, in Anyan Xiaish, waving the blazing flare overhead. "DOWN WITH CORRUPTION! DOWN WITH SLAVERY!"

The answering yells were an indistinguishable melange of tongues, as she repeated her tirade in Wuyu Xiaish, then Kallish. From the corner of her eye, she saw a swarm of figures rushing out of the darkness into the light of her bonfires. One of them spotted her, roared at her to stop.

"I'll NEVER STOP! JUSTICE FOR THE MASSES! JUS-TICE FOR—" a series of loud pops cut her off, just as she was ducking back towards cover, rounding the first corner of the maze. Something swatted her wet ponytail so it whipped about and slapped the side of her jaw, while shards of wood sliced across the back of her neck. Oh. They were shooting at her. Wonderful.

Joy gulped and kept running. "BENNY THE SHARK IS A BASTARD! HE SUCKS. HE... HE... SMELLS BAD! HE... Uhhh... Um..." Insults weren't Joy's strong suit. She was running out of material fast.

"HE'S REALLY NOT—Yeowch! Fuck!" A white-hot pain lanced through the back of her hand, and she dropped the flare. For a second she thought she'd been shot, but she realized it had actually been a hot ember from her signal flare. Waving it around wildly while running around like a maniac were defi-nitely violations of the safety warnings, to be sure.

Joy sucked at the burn, looked for the flare, and found it in the middle of a spreading blaze. It had hit a wall of cargo. Oh. She hadn't meant to do that. She'd intended to toss the third flare into the harbor. This... this was not planned. More shouts came from behind her, getting closer, and Joy sprinted away. That was probably enough of a distraction for the girls. More than enough. She should get out of here. Now, which way was out?

Joy remembered her plan. Up. Up was out. She spotted a stack of cargo that made a perfect climbing wall, and scurried right up, using all her Caliburn course mojo. She reached the top and spotted a clear, straight lane to the water. She also spotted a few Triad men who'd climbed up the stacks at other points in the maze. She scrambled her way over the uneven surface, getting maybe halfway before she was spotted in turn, more yells rang out over the docks, followed by gunshots.

Joy just gritted her teeth and kept going, hoping for the smoke and the shadows to help her as she ran as fast as she could, bent over at the waist to minimize her profile, until the last few yards, where she sprinted full out, leapt out into space in a long swan dive, aiming for the safety of the water. She had a moment of pure terror when she realized that the edge of the dock was further away from the cargo stack than she'd guessed, and she got to watch hard wood planks rush up to meet her, almost in slow motion, and then she'd cleared them by inches, into the cool, calm darkness of the harbor below.

She let the momentum of her dive take her deep. She needed to hide, to get away, get to safety. Officer Adachi had told her about how the ocean affected gunfire. A few feet of water would stop most regular bullets, or even cause them to ricochet or shatter at the surface. But she needed to dive to get that few feet of water for protection. Unfortunately, she also needed air.

Joy could never be sure how long she spent floundering in the harbor. If anything, it was even worse than the journey here. Her swim fins were gone, so she'd lost a ton of speed. Her snorkel was gone, so she had to stick her whole head above water to breathe, to hear a chorus of shouts from the men on the dock, and more gunshots. She made her way as best she could, blundering around beneath the huge black hulls of the boats above. She'd neglected to fix her diving-mask into place before her last dive, so it was gone, and now, she could barely see. She kept going, hoping that the next time she surfaced, the shouts of alarm would be gone, only to be disappointed each time. Of course, they could run along the docks faster than she could swim. She considered heading out to open water, but she was terrified of losing her bearings and drowning. She was so tired. Plus, they could get in a boat and chase her down.

She kept going until she reached a different section of the harbor, filled with smaller, privately-owned yachts and fishing boats. Here the piers were smaller, with multiple branches going out in different directions. Now she could surface directly beneath the pier, wait there, then double back, try to throw them off. She kept it up as long as she could, but each time she went under was harder than the last. Her lungs burned. Her arms and legs felt like lead. But the shouts were getting less frequent as well. It felt like her plan was working. She just had to keep it up a little longer. Just one more dive, she lied to herself, several times, before she'd finally had enough. She surfaced, and her desperate, frenzied gasping was the loudest thing around.

Had she finally lost them? Really, it didn't matter anymore. She was at her limit either way. She didn't bother diving again. She used a gentle breast-stroke to reach a ladder she'd spotted. Climbing it was way harder than it should've been. It took every ounce of her remaining strength to drag her sorry carcass up over the pier.

She lay on her back, sucking in long, ragged gulps of air, vaguely reminded that she should probably find someplace to hide. In a second. Just another second or two.

It didn't matter. A figure entered Joy's field of view from the top, looming over her. It was wearing armor.

"Look what I caught," said Shiori, leering down at her. The butt of her halberd twitched, and Joy's world plunged into darkness.

Part 8:

The Perils of Joy

Chapter 44:

Shark Bait

The next thing Joy became aware of was a cracking, crunching sound, followed by a dull ache across the right side of her skull, around the temple. It took a while for her vision to come into focus. She tried to rub her face but she couldn't.

Her hands were bound behind her back. She was sitting in a chair, her wrists were tied together around the back of the chair, and her ankles were tied to the chair legs. Wonderful. A big part of her wanted to just go back to sleep. She was still so tired. Another part of her called out alarm. She'd just hit her head, and sleep was very much the wrong thing for her right now. That part of her was weak, and she probably would've nodded off again, if not for that persistent cracking noise. What was that? It was so annoying.

Irritated, Joy shook off the fog in her brain and tried to get her bearings. She was in some kind of warehouse. Pretty big. Pretty modern, too. Electric lights. As her vision came into focus, she realized that she wasn't alone. Actually, there was quite a crowd. Big, tough-looking guys in suits, surrounding her in a wide semi-circle, standing around at attention. Not proper military attention—more like a Triad knockoff. As she scanned their faces, she found one she recognized. Yang leered at her, or tried to, but he had kind of a splint for his nose, secured in place with a white bandage going across his face and around the back of his head. So his grin turn into a grimace, and he seemed to have a hard time baring his teeth at her without hurting his face. He tried anyway.

Joy would've laughed, if she hadn't realized what an awful position she was in. Part of her did feel a surge of pride. She'd tagged him pretty good.

She looked for Chen to see if she'd bruised him up as well, but he was nowhere to be found. Instead she saw Shiori, leaning back against one of the looming industrial shelving units that stretched up to the ceiling. Next to her was another woman, one Joy hadn't seen before. She had a no-nonsense manner to her, peering over the tops of her wire-frame glasses as she scribbled away at something on her ornately-decorated clipboard. Must be far-sighted. Her hair was up in a bun, she wore a long, form-fitting, sleek green dress, in a distinctly Xia style, and she looked more composed and put-together than Joy had ever felt in her entire life.

But she was nothing compared to the man she stood behind.

He was sitting in an intricately-carved wooden chair. The seat, arms, and back were padded with plush red velvet with gold trim and tassels. She could barely see that much, because of the man's bulk. He wasn't fat, just broad, wearing a pristine, immaculately-tailored light grey suit, with a shiny satin finish. Joy spotted flashes of polished gold at his cuffs, buttons, pockets, earlobes, and collar. It stopped just shy of being gaudy. He had one of those heads that seemed to sprout directly from his shoulders. You knew the neck existed, but only by inference, because it vanished right into his jawline. And what a jawline it was. He had one of the biggest mouths Joy had ever seen on a person. It went out to the furthest corners of his skull, and opened wide, too. Growing up, Joy remembered one kid whose proudest achievement was his ability to fit his entire fist in his mouth. The man before her could probably triple that kid's record, but sticking a fist in this guy's mouth looked like a great way to lose a hand. He'd had some work done on his teeth.

When he opened his mouth, his lips pulled back to reveal two rows of polished gold triangles with razor-sharp steel edges. This was the source of the cracking sound that had woken her up. Joy watched in disbelief as the jaws closed around a large bone and bit down, breaking it in two. He then caught each end of the severed bone, and sucked on each broken end, before tossing them back onto a wide porcelain plate full of them, on a nearby wooden serving-table, in the same ornate style as his chair, looking completely out-of-place in this dingy warehouse.

He repeated the process with the two unbroken bones remaining on the plate, and then he was finished, carefully dabbing at the corners of his mouth with a cloth napkin. In retrospect, Joy had to be impressed that he'd done all that without spattering any juices on his expensive suit. He turned to her with a razor smile.

"Hey, you. Ever been to Narbonen?"

Joy felt ice water creeping along her spine. This was the most dangerous man in Dodona, the head of the local Triad group. Ben Li Fang, AKA "Benny the Shark."

She did not like having this man paying any type of attention to her. Even if she hadn't known who he was, even if he hadn't gotten those horrible teeth, he'd still be terrifying. There was something about his manner, his presence. It set off something at the base of her primal mind. It made her want to run, want to burrow in a hole and hide. Even speaking seemed dangerous, though she knew she had no choice but to answer. Cautiously, she shook her head.

"Well, I have," said the man. "Used to be a sailor. Seen the whole world. Well, in Narbonen, they have some real fancy restaurants—too fancy to let sea scum like me inside. Didn't meet their dress code, back then."

He tugged at one of his lapels and smiled even wider, in case she hadn't noticed that he was decked out in a suit that probably cost more than the Fan family's entire net worth. He had an oddly precise manner of speaking. It didn't match up well with any accent Joy was familiar with.

"Not a problem for me nowadays," he continued. "So, last time I was there... Hmm... How long ago was that again? Hey, Daphne."

The woman in the green dress paused in her note-taking, adjusted her glasses on the bridge of her nose, and let her eyes go unfocused for a second.

"Your last trip to Narbonen was the last three weeks of September, the year before last, so that's roughly one-and-three-quarter years ago, Mr. Fang."

"Hah! You hear that? 'Roughly one-and-three-quarters, she says. The head on this girl. I'd be lost without her," said Benny, before directing a scornful glance at the rest of his crew. "I swear, if even half of you idiots had a quarter of her brains, I'd be mayor of this city by now."

Daphne's expression didn't change. She inclined her head in gracious acknowledgment of the praise and went right back to her note-taking. Joy got the feeling this was a fairly common occurrence and tried not to be jealous. She never got that kind of positive reinforcement at her workplace.

"So, like I was saying," continued Benny, and paused, brow furrowed in concentration. "What was I on about, again?"

"Fancy Narbonen restaurants," said Daphne, without looking up from her clipboard.

"Goose liver!" said Benny. "That was my point. They had that at the restaurants in Narbonen, and, well—you just wouldn't believe it. It's the most buttery, fluffy, melt-in-your-mouth... Mmm!"

Benny smacked his lips, and the motion had an exaggerated quality to them. "I think I had that goose liver every night I was there, for the rest of the trip."

"You did, Mr. Fang," said Daphne.

"So I get back, and—I swear—first thing I do, is I summon my chef and tell him to fix up some Narbonen goose liver or find someone to teach him how. So he goes and comes back, and when he does, he's got this nervous expression on his face. And I know this type of face—when someone is going to tell me something that is going to make me unhappy. People don't like to make me unhappy."

He favored her with another serrated smile. Joy noticed a few small flecks of purplish crust on his lower lips—scabs. Benny had a head full of monster teeth. He could cut his own mouth

349

with them if he wasn't careful. But the Kallisian language had a few consonants, like 'f' and 'v', that required you to touch your lower lips with your teeth, and to make the 'th' sound, you had to bite your own tongue. Benny wasn't avoiding any of those sounds when he talked, he was just taking extra care when he did—though he must have the occasional slip up.

Was there some way she could use this information to her advantage? Well, it helped take her mind off of just how fucked she was now, just a bit. Though Benny hadn't gotten around to threatening her yet. He was still going on about food.

"So, I ask him what's up, and he says, all apologetic-like, 'I'm sorry, Mr. Fang—I can't make the Narbonen goose liver like you asked. It's illegal here.' It's because of all the Kovidhians. Apparently, they don't like it—because it's mean to the geese. Can you believe that shit?"

Silence followed that question, stretching until Joy realized it had been directed at her, and wasn't rhetorical.

"Oh! Um... No?" She sputtered. The official teachings of Kovidh spoke against cruelty to animals, but vegetarianism was only a requirement for the priesthood. Lay practitioners ate meat all the time.

"I mean... It is kind of weird," she continued. "Isn't eating any kind of meat mean to the animal?"

"Exactly!" Said Bennie. "But apparently, the Narbonens force-feed their geese to get their livers to come out right, and that's just beyond the pale. So I'm not very happy, but I'm not going to take it out on my chef. Illegal is illegal, and, hey—I certainly couldn't go *breaking the law*, right?"

Benny flashed his gold smile at his men, who all chuckled dutifully. Joy tried to manage a polite smile that she hoped didn't look too terrified. Daphne just went on taking notes, and Shiori continued to slouch off to the side and glower.

"But two weeks later, my chef came back with a special announcement, and this time, he's looking real pleased with himself," Bennie continued. "So I ask him what's up, and he says he's found a new recipe—something that can stand in for the goose liver. In fact, he says it's even better.

"I tell him that's hard to believe, but he serves it up, and, sure enough, he's right. If there's one thing I know, it's how to get good people. And do you know what it was, what he found to replace the goose liver?"

Joy shook her head.

"Bone marrow," said Benny. "It's great. I've had him serving it at all my business functions, my little get-togethers. Everybody loves it. In fact, it's touched off quite the culinary fad of late. There's a whole bunch of fancy restaurants serving it now. You heard of that?"

"No," said Joy. Why did he have to go on about food? Now she was terrified and hungry. "Sorry. As far as food trends go, if it isn't in a tin, I'm out of the loop."

"Too bad," said Benny. "You're missing out. This city is a great place to eat"

Yeah, it really was. When she'd first come here, she'd been able to spring for a night out with friends every so often. She'd been in loop, just a little bit. But now....

Joy stared at the pile of discarded bones on the fine porcelain plate, and she couldn't resist asking, "Um... do they normally... *cook* the marrow at the restaurants?"

Benny thought that was funny. He threw his head back and roared. "Hah! Yeah, that's right. If this was a proper sit-down meal, they'd be roasted up nice. But, you see, this isn't a proper sit-down meal. It's a late-night snack. You see, there've been a whole bunch of incidents. Requiring my personal attention. But that doesn't mean I've got to keep my poor chef up all hours, too. What kind of boss would that make me?"

Joy smiled nervously. She didn't like where this conversation was going. Saying as little as possible seemed to be the safest option.

"Oh, but listen to me. Where are my manners? I haven't introduced myself, have I? I tell you, lack of sleep does all sorts of things to a guy," said Benny, theatrically slapping his palm to his forehead.

"But, on the other hand, maybe it doesn't matter so much."

Benny favored her with another grin, stretching ear-to-ear across the span of his huge jaws, silver and gold reflecting the harsh glare of the electric lights, practically blinding her.

"You know who I am, girl?"

"You're Benny the Shark?" Joy replied, before it occurred to her that maybe saying 'Mr. Fang Ben Li' might be a lot more respectful and appropriate. But it was impossible to think of him any other way when he was baring his teeth at her like that. It just popped out.

But he didn't seem to mind at all. "Yeah, that's right," he said. "Tell me, you know why they call me that?"

Joy blinked. The answer seemed so obvious, she had to wonder if wasn't some kind of trick question. If there was, she couldn't figure it out.

"Because of your teeth?" she ventured.

The horrible teeth flashed at her. "That's what everybody thinks, Ms..." he said, trailing off a bit.

"Fan," she said, without thinking. Was there a point in trying to give a fake name? She could see that backfiring on her really easily. "Fan Joy Song."

"Pleased to make your acquaintance, Ms. Fan," he said, all exaggerated politeness. "Now, where was I? Teeth—that's right. People see these teeth, and, of course, they think that's where the name came from. But that's backwards, see? The name came first, and the teeth came later. And the story behind that—well, it's something else. At least, I think so."

Benny paused, lost in contemplation. "Well, you know what? Since we're all stuck here waiting for your friends to arrive, why don't I tell you about it? You see, it's my favorite story, but all these guys have already heard it a bunch of times. I don't often get to tell it to somebody new. You'll indulge me, won't you?"

352

Waiting for her friends to arrive? Joy had a sick sinking feeling in her stomach. Did he mean the girls? They hadn't made it? Had all of this been for nothing? But—it seemed an odd way to phrase the girls' recapture, if that was what he meant. Something felt off. And would the head of the Triads really come out personally at… whatever ungodly hour it was now, just for the girls? Maybe it was something else. Joy clung to the notion like a lifeline. But who could it be? Her 'friends?' She didn't have any friends. None left in Dodona, anyway. Maybe… the Kovidhian church? Would that be a good thing or a bad thing? She was dying to ask, but she didn't dare mention it. So far nobody had mentioned the girls. Until she was one hundred percent sure they were safe, she couldn't say or do anything that might draw attention to them. The smart thing was to play along.

"Sure thing," said Joy. "I'm not going anywhere."

It was a pretty lame joke, but Benny chuckled at it anyway. Then he started in on his story.

"So, way, way back—a bunch of years ago, before I got big, before the Great War, I was just a regular sailor. Roaming the seas, busting my back, drinking away my pay—traveling everywhere, but going nowhere, just like every other dumb scallywag on the sea. Well, one fine morning I wake up after a night that I mostly don't remember, and I find myself on a ship I don't recognize. Turns out it's a pirate ship what needed new crew, and I'm one of them. Now, I don't remember agreeing to that. Maybe I did, and maybe I didn't. But my new crew, they're serious that I'm staying, so that's that.

"And you know what? I really took to it. Sure, there can be some long, lean times when pickings are slim, but when you do get a fat kill? Split even. Everybody gets their fair share. Way better than the insult you get from the paymaster working regular crews.

"And we were doing well. Made a name for ourselves, got a reputation. We got too big. Got too much attention. Got a tip that led us to the fattest merchant vessel we ever heard of, running with no escort, loaded down with goods. Sounds too good to be true, right? We thought so too, but the prize was so juicy, we had to check it out. We tailed them for days.

"We're looking for concealed gunports, signs of extra hands, soldiers, catapults. But there's nothing. And the whole time we're watching them, we're also looking around ourselves. Maybe there are other ships lying in wait for us. But no, there's nothing like that. We spend a couple days chewing the fat, and then we decide to go for it. Open, clear water, with that big, fat junk just plodding along low in the water, slow and helpless.

"We make our move. We tack around on an intercept course, closer and closer. No problems catching them. We do things like normal. Fire a shot across their bow, make a signal for them to stand down. They do what they're told. Everything goes like normal, but the whole time we're moving in, my guts are roiling.

"Something's wrong. I know it, I can feel it, but I can't say what, so I don't say anything, chalk it up to nerves. Finally, we pull up alongsides, hooks ready, and by now I can see their crew, and then I know something is wrong. They don't have any weapons. They're not preparing to fight. They don't have their hands up. They're not trying to hide. They're just... watching.

"They're not angry, and maybe some of them look a little scared, but it's wrong. It's the wrong kind of fear. It's not us they're scared of. I should have said something then. Maybe it would've helped. Probably not. I wasn't the captain, back then, and it was too late anyway.

"Because right then, as soon as the first hook goes over, the doors to the cargo bay fly open—big, heavy doors on that hatch, and they damn near fly off their hinges—and something comes out, something we never expected to see, not in a million years. You know what it was? Can you even guess?"

Joy could only shake her head. Despite everything, she couldn't resist a good story.

"A dragon. A god-damned, true-to-life, actual dragon climbs out of the hold. We're all stunned, staring like idiots, blinded by the flashes of sunlight off its harness—they like shiny things, you know, so they get jewelry. Medals for winning battles, and they never take 'em off. And this one's got a whole bunch of them. Decked out like a pimp, and they're all polished up—even though it spent days in the hold, they're gleaming like something in a display case. We try to run. Drop all the hooks, try to push off. But it just rears up and cranes its neck until it's right over us, and then everyone on the dragon ship starts yelling, all panicked-like, and they start helping us push off. And I got a second to think, 'Why would they do that?' and I see that ugly green mouth start to open up overhead, and I do the smartest thing I've ever done: I jump overboard.

"I hit the water, go under, and the world above goes bright orange. I try to put some good distance between me and the boats before I come up for air, and when I do, my old ship has gone up like a candle. The men who aren't dead are leaping overboard, trying to put themselves out, only it isn't working.

"You get it? That dragon fire—calling it fire is... Well, it doesn't really give you the right idea. It's more like... blazing puke. Gobs and gobs of this blazing, white-hot vomit that sticks to everything and won't go out. Shove it underwater and the water starts boiling. Otherwise, it bobs on the surface, and now the ocean is on fire. And once it gets on you, even a little bit—that's it. All over except for the screaming. I heard a lot of screaming."

Joy shuddered. Working in Intelligence during the war, she'd been privy to a lot of the research recovered by Kallistrate biologists and chemists on the old Albion dragons. They had two separate venom sacs in their bodies, each with a different chemical, each of which led to a tube that terminated in opposite points in the dragon's forked tongue.

Each type of venom was poisonous by itself, but the true terror happened when they mixed together, which usually happened a few yards away from the dragon's snout, as the streams crossed and mixed with the air. The resulting chemical reaction produced the most terrifying and lethal substance known to mankind: Dragon-fire. Benny's old crew must have really been causing a big stir for the Empire to bother sending an actual dragon after them, hidden in a regular boat, instead of one of their specialized dragon carriers.

Benny continued with his story. "So I start swimming away from the fire—no plan, just get away—and the 'merchant' ship is doing the same. They've actually got oars out, getting as clear away from the fire as they can. And then the dragon climbs all the way out, dives overboard—damn near capsizes his own ship—I could see those poor bastards getting tossed around on deck, clinging to the rigging and the rails. And it swims out to the other ships. Now, they've got more time to make a break for it, and for a second, I think maybe they've got a chance, but I didn't count on how far that monster can spit. Turns out it's a long way, and once a ship's got that slimy tar on it, it's done for. Can't be put out, crew can't work—it's all over. But that wasn't enough for the dragon. It keeps on swimming until it finally catches the burning ships, and then it starts playing.

"That's what they do, you know? They're smart, so they like to play. Climb up the side of the boats and start breaking things. Rip at their guts, smash it all to splinters. And they don't eat people, but they'll play with them, as well. Chomp down, thrash around, see how far it can toss a man. Listen to all the amusing noises.

"It just went on like that, ship by ship, crew by crew, until that whole part of the sea is just a charnel house, mangled bodies and scraps of wood bobbing about on bloody waters, surrounded by sheets of flame. You know, I don't know if Hell exists, but if it does, I know exactly what it looks like.

"But anyway, after a good long time the dragon decides it's had enough fun and heads back to its ship. I've had a chance to get a way's away from everything else, and it's not exactly being methodical, so it either doesn't see me, or it can't be bothered to come after me. It climbs back on its ship, and they sail away, while I head back into that mess, looking for some flotsam that isn't on fire, something big enough to let me take a break from treading water, and see how many of us are left.

"Turns out it's not many, but there's a few tough bastards who aren't dead yet. I found a crate of soap to cling to. Lanke Mountain Snow Detergent. Stenciled on the side of the barrel. I'll never forget it. No idea why we had that in the hold. Must've been a weak haul to have bothered stealing that, But it's there, and it's floating, though it must've been leaking a little, 'cause there's suds everywhere. I was thinking to myself—at least I won't die without taking a bath first.

"We just floated there for hours, not saying much, except does anybody see a ship coming? At least the fire might attract attention, right? Except no ship comes along, and eventually, those weird, unnatural flames finally did go out. Too bad for us. Turns out they were the only things keeping the sharks away.

"We were floating in in a giant pool of meat and blood.

"Sharks will smell that for hundreds of miles, and so they did, coming in, circling closer, and then it started—the frenzy."

Benny paused and took a sip of his tea. "You ever seen a feeding frenzy? It's insane. The water churns up, looks like it's boiling, only in the middle of if all are these dark forms, grey fins slicing through the froth—a whole gang of maniacs with knives, going nuts. And they keep going, on and on, as long as there's meat.

"And there was plenty of meat in those waters.

"They went for the corpses first. Easier pickings, I guess. Gave us some hope that maybe they'd leave us alone. But the corpses were all around us, and the frenzy was relentless. You'd see the froth spread, surround some poor bastard, and then it'd happen—some random bite, tail slap, anything to draw blood, and that'd be it. A dozen of those beasties on him at once, ripping him to shreds in an instant. The others tried all sorts of things, huddling in groups, punching and kicking at any shark that got close. But Kovidh help you if you got the slightest cut, because then your mates would be shoving you away from them. You were shark bait now. But they only delayed the inevitable. Hour by hour, one by one, I saw my crew disappear. But I wasn't worried. Not anymore. And do you know why?"

Joy shook her head. Benny grinned again.

"Because, this whole time, I'd had sharks coming by me, one by one. I was on the edge of everything. None of those sharks were in their frenzy. They were just gliding along, nice and cool. They'd come up, so close I could see their eyes, these pools of black, and I'd stare deep into them. And each time, I got this weird jolt, deep inside me, but it wasn't fear. And each time the sharks would circle about, let me get a good look at 'em, sometimes even come up and bump me with those broad snouts of theirs. But I didn't panic, didn't punch or kick, and each time, they would turn around and swim away. This happened over and over, all throughout the day and into the evening, the sharks spared me even as they devoured everything else.

"And finally, after staring eye-to-eye with a dozen sharks, I realized what it was I was feeling, every time we made contact. I was thinking, 'I know this guy.' Recognition. That's what it was. None of them had come out to eat me. They were just saying hello."

Benny stared at her. "You believe in past lives, Ms. Fan?"

Joy was startled at the question. "Um, well... I'm a Kovidhian. And I know the church says that we all go through that cycle, on the Great Wheel. But you're supposed to forget your old lives when you're reborn, so nobody could ever really say for sure... I guess I haven't thought about it much?"

"Yeah, that's what most people say," said Benny. "That's how I was, too. Never thought about it. Until that day. That's when I learned the truth about myself."

Joy saw where this was going. "You think you were a shark in a past life?"

"Oh, I don't think I was a shark," said Benny. "I know I was. I knew it that day. The stars came out, the feeding went on.

But I'm not worried any more. I'm hanging on my crate in the middle of the wide ocean, gently rocking in time with the waves.

"I gaze out in the distance and it's a flat line in every direction. And then I get this feeling, like I'm expanding, until I'm so big that I'm the size of the whole sky, and then I come back down, but I'm not in my body any more. I'm in the water. I'm in with the sharks, swimming with them, and I am one of them. I cut through the water like it's not even there. All my senses are dialed up like you wouldn't believe. I can see for miles, and I can feel things through my skin, electric tingles that tell me where everything is. And the smells—that was the best. My nostrils filled up with all these spicy scents coming from everywhere, but one dominates—the scent of blood.

"The hunger takes me. My stomach is this empty pit driving me onward, commanding me to fill it, irresistible. So I do—I follow my nose along with all my brethren to the only source of food—ungainly flailing creatures. I take a bite and, let me tell you, no meal I've had before or since tasted so fine as that one—not even bone marrow. I eat and eat but my hunger never goes, and I know this has always been true, and always will be. It's my nature to always be hungry, to never be full, and that is what makes every meal the finest. I lose all sense of time or purpose. My only thought is to keep feeding until the meat is gone. And finally, that happens. I smell the change. All my kin sense it. Without the meat to bind us, our kinship is over.

"All my brothers drift away, no time wasted on goodbyes. We're not a sentimental folk, my people. They vanish off into the darkness of the sea, on their never-ending quest for more meat. And I find myself back in my old body, clinging to a crate of detergent, completely alone."

Benny paused and gazed off into the distance, savoring his favorite memory for a bit, before wrapping things up. "Anyway, I was marooned in a shipping lane, so I didn't have to wait long before I was able to bum a ride off another merchant ship. I was broke, all my old mates were gone, but I didn't care. I was different, from there on out. I knew who I was—who I really was, and there's a power in that. From then on, anytime I felt lost, confused, I knew to go back to being a shark. I even found people to help with that, get me to that state. And that's how I built my business and became the man I am today. And that's why people call me Benny the Shark."

Joy stared at him, not sure what to say. If his story had been meant to scare her, it had totally worked.

He flashed his teeth at her again. "You don't have to believe me. I don't mind. I wouldn't believe me either, except I was there, and it happened. Particularly the bit about the other sharks passing me up as food. If somebody else told me that, I'd call them the biggest liar on the planet."

"Oh, that part doesn't bug me," said Joy. "I just figured they didn't like the soap."

It popped out of her mouth before she had a chance to think it through. Or think at all. Every eye turned to her. Suddenly the warehouse was very, very quiet.

Benny's grin stayed plastered on his face. "What was that now? What did you mean by that?"

"Nothing," said Joy, "I didn't say anything. Nothing worth mentioning."

Unpleasant visions ran through Joy's mind, flashbacks to the Temple of Mithras, and the murderous levels of rage directed at her from the supposedly kindly priests there when she'd dared to point out the leaky pipe feeding into their miraculous weeping statue. She did not want to provoke that kind of reaction from someone who could literally murder her.

"Nooo, I definitely heard something," said Benny. "And I've got pretty good hearing. Don't think I imagined anything. You guys all heard it, right?"

All of the Triad goons murmured assent. Yang did so with distinct enthusiasm, eyes glittering. Benny turned back to her.

"I definitely heard something about soap, and I'd like to know what you meant by that," said Benny. "I insist."

Dammit, why did she always do this? Why couldn't she just keep her big mouth shut for once? Nobody ever wanted to hear it. Maybe she could minimize it somehow?

"Um... Well, it's not really important. Just a silly thought that popped up in my silly ol' head." She saw a twitch of irritation on Benny's eyebrow, and plowed ahead. "I just thought... it just occurred to me, that you said you were floating on a crate of detergent, and it was leaking into the water. And, you know, soap doesn't taste very good, right? So, maybe the sharks saw you, or smelled you, and thought, 'meat. But then, when they got close, were all like, 'Ew, soap,' and swam away. Just a thought. Probably totally wrong. I'm usually wrong. Wrong-way Joy. That's what they call me. That's..."

Joy realized she was babbling and decided to shut up before she made it any worse. She looked around. The Triad thugs radiated indignation and disgust. How dare she question their boss. Joy saw the slightest upward twitch at the corner of Shiori's mouth, but couldn't tell who she was laughing at, or what the joke was. And Daphne was examining her with some kind of clinical interest, enough to make her pause her endless note-taking, but with no other normal emotion Joy could detect. But they all kept quiet, waiting on a cue from Benny. Joy scanned his face, waiting for an angry denial, followed by rage.

Instead he threw his head back and laughed. "Soap! That's a new one. Can you believe this broad? All the times I've told this story, with the dragon and the sharks and the blood and guts—and what's her takeaway? Soap! And you know what—maybe that was the point. Getting soaked in all that detergent must've inspired me to clean up my act, huh?"

The thugs all laughed dutifully, Shiori kept smirking, and Daphne raised an eyebrow. Joy let out a long breath. She'd been worried over nothing again. Benny was actually much more secure in his beliefs than the Mithras priests were. He really didn't care if anybody else believed him or not. Or at least, his livelihood didn't depend on drawing worshippers to a shark-cult.

He'd gone through a profoundly transformative personal mystical event, and nothing would ever shake that out of him. Even if she were to mention that lack of food and sleep were known to induce hallucinations and out-of-body experiences, (Which is why mystics often went on fasts) it wouldn't make so much as a dent in his certainty. So bringing it up was totally pointless. Keeping her mouth shut about that, yes indeedy.

But did it make a difference? Benny the Shark hadn't clawed his way to the top of the Dodona Triad syndicate by being nice and letting things slide. Not the types of things she'd done. No matter what she did, he was still going to make her pay. The thought of it sent ice-cold panic shockwaves through her body. Her whole body tensed, strained against her bonds.

No—nothing good came of thinking like that. She just needed to survive. Somehow. How could she do that? She had to convince them she was more valuable to them alive. What did she have that they needed?

Information. She knew where the girls had gone. But she couldn't give them away—could she? Maybe she could. Once the girls had made it to the Temple, they'd be safe. It wouldn't matter if he knew about them or not.

And with all these delays, the girls must've all reached it by now. So she had no reason to keep it secret. But could she be sure of that? One hundred percent sure? Maybe some or all of the girls were still hiding in an alleyway, a few blocks from the temple, waiting for a clear path to emerge. Maybe they could still be intercepted if she talked. How likely was that? How much time had passed? How long had she been unconscious? She had no way of knowing; no way to make an educated decision.

Fine, what did she know? She thought back to her days as an analyst. What did she know about interrogation? About torture?

Not a lot. Her job had consisted almost entirely of sifting through reams of captured documents and intercepted communications, picking out the useful bits, and translating them. But she'd picked up little snippets from office chatter and from her Supplemental Courses instructors.

Bottom line: everyone broke under torture eventually. Some extraordinary individuals could hold out for a long time—weeks, or even months—but it only delayed the inevitable. And Joy wasn't feeling like an exceptional individual right now.

Fine. She'd try not to talk right away, but it would be better to fess up sooner rather than later. She'd just have to trust in the girls' sneaking abilities. That was the best she could do. But she didn't have to volunteer information, either.

What might they not think to ask about? Well, Mrs. Jakuba, for one. No need to mention her. And the letters she'd written to the KIB and Professor Gelfland. Just had to hope they didn't ask. Okay.

So, give up the girls' location, but only after delaying long enough so it wouldn't matter, hide Jakuba, Gelfland, and KIB. And then what? They get that info, get what they wanted from her, and then they had no reason not to kill her. She had to have something else. What could she offer? What did she have that they might want? She wracked her exhausted, sluggish brain for anything that might be useful.

What had she learned that day that Benny might... The jewels! The ones hidden in those amulets! Benny didn't know about the jewels. Were they significant? They must be, if the cultists had gone to such extreme lengths to hid them. So she could rat on the cultists to the Triads. And then they'd have what they wanted, and they'd go ahead and kill her anyway.

Joy fought down another wave of terror. It couldn't be information. That currency lost all value the instant she spent it. It had to be something she could do, that only she could do, something they needed. What could that possibly be?

This was the most vital problem she'd ever faced. Solving this puzzle held the key to her continued existence, and she attacked it with all her might, every last bit of concentration and mental energy, all her schooling, all training, all her life experiences.

She threw these troops into the breach, do or die, fight to the last man. She marshaled every last mental resource to bring her victory, and they came back... With absolutely nothing.

She had nothing to offer a man like Benny. There was no solution. She felt a yawning black pit of despair open up beneath her. This was the sum total of her entire life. They could carve onto her gravestone at the family plot. 'Fan Joy Song—Lacked Useful Skills."

A grating sound echoed through the cavernous warehouse, jolting her out of her reverie.

"Oh, good," said Benny. "Looks like your friends are here."

Chapter 45:

Who's That Girl?

Joy gazed off down the long aisle that stretched between the towering shelving, and heard the sounds of footsteps traveling down one of the rows. Seemed like a lot of people. She sent out a desperate plea to any god that might be listening—please don't let them be the girls, please don't let it be the girls, please don't let this all have been for nothing. As the steps came closer, Joy felt a surge of hope when she realized there was a noise that was missing: the rattling of chains. Hope turned to confusion when her 'friends' rounded the corner and she found herself staring at the Dodona City Guard.

Joy stared. How in the world were they her friends? What was...? But never mind. It wasn't the girls. That was the only important thing.

"Chief Gallach," said Benny. "So good of you to join us, finally."

"Have to forgive us, Mr. Fang," said the Chief, sounding strained. His throat was wrapped in bandages. "Some of us... haven't been feeling well."

The Chief was trying to talk while keeping the motion of his jaw to the barest minimum. To avoid pulling the skin on his neck. Ouch. None of the Guardsmen appeared to be in the best shape. Joy scanned their faces and saw numerous black eyes, cuts, bruises, missing teeth, and the like.

But Brannock had them all beat. He was shivering, even though he had a heavy cloak wrapped around him, and his pale skin was covered in a clammy sheen. His sunken eyes gazed straight ahead, focused on some point far beyond the back wall. MacInroy was hovering right behind him, making sure Brannock didn't fall over. He looked awful, but Joy didn't suppose she'd be in any better shape if someone had hacked off one of her arms a couple hours ago.

Benny noticed it, too. "Man, Chief. You need to treat your people better. When one of my boys gets worked like that, I give him the day off."

"Deep King calls us to serve," rasped Gallach, through pressed lips. "We all... bound to answer His call, regardless of... inconvenience."

"Sounds like a lousy boss," said Benny. "Not like me. I know how to appreciate my employees. Even when they let their enthusiasm get the better of them."

"Shiori," he said, gesturing to the battered Guardsmen. "Look at what you did. We've talked about this." Gently chiding her, like she'd left her dirty coffee mug in the sink too many times.

"Sorry," she said, shrugging, in a tone that was anything but. "They thought flinging a cow pie at me was cute. Had to teach them a lesson. Got a rep to uphold."

"Oh, you and your rep," sighed Benny, throwing up his hands. "I keep forgetting I'm dealing with a celebrity here."

"Should keep your woman on a tighter leash," muttered Gallach. "Get hysterical... when they leave home. Put her back in... kitchen. Or brothel."

All of the Triad men went very still and directed nervous glances over at Shiori. She bared her teeth at the Guardsmen, and very leisurely straightened up out of her slouch. Her left hand blurred, and Joy remembered their confrontation from earlier, and her deadly throwing knives. The Guardsmen remembered it, too, flinching and ducking behind their shields. MacInroy was the worst off — he had to hug Brannock to keep him upright, frantically hissing something in his ear.

But no knife appeared anywhere. Shiori's ended the feint with her hand up by her shoulder. She mimed flicking dirt off her pauldron, switched hands on her polearm, and repeated the gesture on her other shoulder. The Triad men laughed, and Joy let herself join in, remembering how nice and helpful Gallach had pretended to be when they'd first met. Now she was seeing the real man. Two-faced jackass.

The Chief turned to Benny, indignant, but the mob boss cut him off. "No, don't start with me. You had that coming. You were disrespectful. In fact, that seems to be the heart of the problems we're having here. Lack of respect."

Joy felt a jolt travel down her spine. For the first time, Benny's voice lost its genial, accommodating tone. Now it had an edge. Again she was reminded of why Benny the Shark was a name that inspired terror.

"Chief Gallach," he said. "I'm not an unreasonable man. I realize that I'm not the only game in town. I know that negotiations, even strained negotiations, are all part of doing business. You guys have been driving a hard bargain lately. We've got some merchandise in dispute. I can deal with that. But my patience has a limit. There's a line that you just don't cross. And sending in a little girl to steal my merchandise and torch half my dock while she's at it—that is very, very, disrespectful."

Benny put a slow, careful emphasis on the word 'disrespectful,' teeth flashing as he bit off each syllable.

"That. Is. Too god-damned far."

"What, her?" The Chief glanced over at Joy. "Not with us."

Joy was too stunned to reply. They thought she was working for the Guardsmen. Was that a good thing or a bad thing?

"Oh, she isn't?" said Benny. "So why, then, did she sneak into the cargo ship, knock out and tie up the entire crew, and make off with *only* the merchandise that we were in such heated negotiations over, while completely ignoring all the other goods in that ship—jewelry, concentrated Spike, art objects—goods that would've been much easier to re-sell? You expect me to think that's a coincidence? You really think I'm that stupid?"

Joy stifled a protest. They thought *she'd* knocked out the guards? Little ol' her? That was... kinda flattering, but really—

"No idea what you're talking about," said Gallach. "Never seen her before—"

"The hell you haven't," snarled Yang. "Boss, I saw them talking earlier, at the docks. They were helping her escape with one of the girls—the runaway—"

"Was saying," snapped Gallach, "Never seen this girl… before today, when—"

"Yeah, right," said Yang. "Boss, you gotta—"

Benny held up a hand. "That's enough, Yang," and this rebuke had steel behind it. Yang shut up.

"Ridiculous," said the Chief. "She look like one of us? We—"

"No, but she's just your type, isn't she?" said Shiori. "Fresh out of the cradle, just like you perverts like 'em."

"GOD DAMN IT, I AM TWENTY-SIX YEARS OLD!" Joy recovered from her outburst to see all eyes focused on her.

Oops. Now was not the best time for wounded pride. Even though it was totally justified.

"Enough," croaked the Chief. "Didn't come here for this. We paid you for property. You don't provide it. Give us accusations instead. That ends tonight. You give us our women, right now, or else."

The last word made Joy suck in a breath. Nobody made a move, nobody said anything, but the entire atmosphere changed. It was like everyone was vibrating. Joy felt her pulse racing, and she strained at her bonds. Her body was telling her she needed to get the hell out of here, just get up and back away slowly, but she couldn't. It was maddening.

"Or else?" said Benny, no amusement in his razor smile. "For-give me, Chief, but that sounded like a threat. You threatening me?"

Chief Gallach met his gaze, unflinching. "Yes."

"Well, that's interesting," said Benny. "You know, the heads at Cymru, they warned me against killing cops. Creates too much of a stir, draws attention, public outrage. And I listened. So I've been letting things slide with you people. You've been getting the kid glove treatment. But now—"

Benny gestured, and metallic clacking sounds echoed from all around them. On both sides of the aisle, more Triad men emerged from their hiding-places, wielding Manticore machine guns. That was the source of the clacking—safeties being switched off and rounds being chambered.

"Now I'm starting to think maybe a little public outrage isn't so bad. I'm starting to think the hassle might be worth it. After all, I didn't get where I am by playing it safe all the time, now did I? So tell me, what do you think about that?"

"I think," said Gallach. "You still don't understand at all."

He nodded at MacInroy, who yanked off Brannock's cloak, and Joy found herself reaching new levels of panic. Brannock wore a vest lined with row after row of dynamite. He fixed them all with a manic grimace and held out his one remaining hand, clutching a small handle with wires trailing back to his vest.

"Dead man's switch," said Gallach. "He lets go... we all go. He is prepared."

Everyone stared at the sweating, shaking Brannock, and they did not see a man overly concerned with future plans.

The Triad men held their positions, but Joy couldn't help but notice some of them shift back, just a bit, trying to get a little cover. Shiori kept her couldn't-give-a-shit sneer plastered on her face, but Joy had to wonder how much of that was bluster. And the threat of a massive bomb was enough to make Daphne actually look up from her clipboard.

Benny sighed and ran a hand over his slicked-back hair. "A bomb, Chief?" He sounded aggrieved. "You're going to blow yourself up, too? Isn't that a bit over-the-top?"

"We're not like you, Benny," said the Chief. "You only care for this world—material stuff. Transient. Our reward... greater, deeper. Dedicated to it, all of us. We.. give up everything. Prepared for it. You wouldn't understand."

The guardsmen stood shoulder-to-shoulder, grim faces showing no crack in their resolve. Joy felt her stomach bottoming out in horror as she realized they were not bluffing. They were serious. But there was something else, a flicker in the Chief's eyes, a deeper emotion driving everything else. She realized this wasn't stupid macho posturing or some overblown negotiation tactic. This was desperation. They needed to get the girls back, needed it in a way that went beyond life or death. What was going on here?

The staredown between Chief Gallach and Benny the Shark went on for what felt like far too long, every eye in the warehouse turned to them, everyone wondering if each moment would be their last. Benny spoke first.

"You're right," he said. "I don't understand you. But, at the very least, I can respect your conviction. Nobody would go this far if they were only trying to pull a fast one."

Benny twitched a finger and the gunmen relaxed a bit, pointing their Manticores toward the ceiling. MacInroy glanced over at Chief Gallach, and carefully laid his hand on top of Brannock's thumb. Joy saw some relieved exhales from a few of the Guardsmen. Despite their dedication, apparently some of them weren't eager to reach the next world right away.

"But, even so," Benny continued. "We still have a problem here. But maybe we can all be reasonable people, help each other sort things out. First things first: you say this girl don't work for you? You really don't know who she is?"

"That's right," said Gallach.

"So then, if I were to tell Shiori to give her an extra smile, going from ear to ear, right here and now, you'd have no problem with that, right?"

"Wait, what?" said Joy. "That's not fu—mmmph!"

A rough gloved hand clapped over Joy's mouth and yanked her head back until it pressed against something hard and unyielding. The pungent scent of sweat-infused leather swarmed up her nose as she stared down at the corded stitches binding the segments of steel plate on the back of Shiori's gauntlet. She felt a sharp prick beneath the far corner of her jawline, cold and merciless, but she couldn't see the knife.

She looked back to the City Guard, pleading, and saw a mixture of indifference, confusion, or annoyance. "If you want," said Chief Gallach. "Nothing to do with us."

MacInroy frowned and nudged the Chief. "But she might know something. Seems kind of a waste to—"

"I know how to get information," said Benny. "Setting your priorities is key. And what I want to know right now, most of all, is whether or not she works for you. You insist she don't? Never seen her before?"

"Not before today," said the Chief. "Saw her on patrol, talked a few minutes, found her later. Trying to steal the runaway. Then—"

"Well, let's test that out. Shiori?" Benny held up a finger, and Joy felt the point bite deeper into her neck, felt a hot wetness well up there, begin a slow trickle down her throat. She tried to break free, but it was like she'd been clamped in a vice. What was happening? Just like that? Without even asking her any questions? She tried to protest, but only managed a desperate whimper, smothered by Shiori's glove. Not like this! It couldn't end like this!

Benny took a leisurely sip of his tea, then fixed his gaze on Chief Gallach. "Carpenters and shipbuilders have a saying: 'Measure twice, cut once.' So I'll take one last measure of you, Chief."

He held up a finger, and Joy knew that finger held her life. "One last time. Does. This. Woman. Work. For. You?"

"For the last time, no," replied the Chief. "Wouldn't hire her. Women stay at home, not half-naked on docks in the middle of the night."

Benny inhaled, a long, loud sucking of air in through his nose. "Did you know that sharks have an amazing sense of smell? It comes in handy in time like these. Because when someone lies to me, I can smell it."

Benny sat up and took another exaggerated sniff. "And you, my friend, are absolutely reeking of..."

Joy felt her her heart race, utterly helpless in Shiori's grip. The letter in her notebook—the one to her family... it would never reach them. They wouldn't know—

"...the truth." Benny sat back and let his finger drift off harmlessly to the side. Joy felt the blade at her throat vanish, as Shiori released her vice grip.

"Aw, shucks," said Shiori, twirling her throwing-knife around in her fingers.

Joy collapsed, slumped down in her chair and took long, relieved gulps of air. She was alive. But still terrified. She was shaking uncontrollably, vibrating against her bonds. She knew she had to recover her wits, but she was so drained that it was impossible to do anything besides breathe, until Shiori's words registered in her brain.

'Aw, shucks?' You're disappointed? You didn't get to kill me, and you're disappointed? You bitch! You rotten fucking bitch!

Joy glared at her, but Shiori's attention was elsewhere.

"Great," said the Chief. "If we're done with this distraction, can get back to business. We—"

"Distraction?" said Benny, giving Chief Gallach a look that bordered on pity. "This is anything but. Think about it. If she doesn't work for you, and she doesn't work for me, then who does she work for?"

Chief Gallach shrugged. "Said she was a reporter. For the Gazette."

"Gazette?" said Benny. "What's a gazette?"

"One of the local newspapers, Mr. Fang," said Daphne.

"Eh? I thought we had our hooks in all the local papers. Now you tell me there's one I never even heard of? Why haven't you brought this up in any of your morning summaries?"

Daphne didn't even blink. "My apologies, Mr. Fang. The reason I haven't mentioned the Gazette before is because it isn't worth mentioning. Actually, calling it a 'newspaper' is being overly generous. It's a cheap tabloid stuffed with base speculation, gossip, exaggeration, and outright fantasies, lacking even the most basic journalistic standards, devoid of any useful information, whose readership is a pack of idiots. Which is why I don't bring it up, Mr. Fang."

Daphne ended her takedown with the barest flick of her eyes in Joy's direction. It lasted for a brief instant, but it was enough for Joy to read her cool contempt, and Joy felt her face burning. The worst thing was that she couldn't really disagree with Daphne's assessment, but did she have to sound so dismissive? You know, making up the right sort of entertaining bullshit was a lot harder than you'd think. She'd like to see Daphne try it for a day and see how easy it was. And who the hell was she to judge about nonsense? Her boss thought he was a shark. A freaking shark!

"Oh, I get it," said Benny. "Actually, that's brilliant. Perfect cover. But it's blown to the Abyss now."

Cover? What cover? Joy tried to gather her wits as Benny turned his attention back to her.

"Now, Ms. Fan, let's dispense with all the bullshit. Who do you really work for?"

"Me?" said Joy. "No-one, technically. I'm—"

The blow from Shiori's gauntlet caught her by surprise. Pain exploded across the side of her face, as her jaw clacked painfully against the rest of her skull and the whole world tipped and wobbled about.

"Ms. Fan," said Benny, sounding gravely disappointed. "Remember what I said about lying to me. That just won't work."

"But I'm not lying," she managed to get out. "I'm a freelance reporter, and right now I'm on assignment for—"

Joy saw another punch coming, but a word from Daphne stopped it.

"No more head shots, Shiori," she said, attention diverted back down to her notes.

"What?" said Shiori, whirling on Benny's assistant.

"We need her to stay coherent," Daphne replied, without looking up. "We're not going to get decent information if you knock her brains out through her ear, now are we?"

"Hah! Hear that? Always thinking, this broad," said Benny, turning to address his troops. "You guys should take note. This is how you get ahead."

"Really?" Said Shiori, fixing Daphne with a huge fake smile. "Maybe you'd care to take over for me, then, since you know how to do it better."

"Don't be childish," said Daphne. "It's a simple enough restriction. I'm sure you can work around it."

"Gosh, can I?" Shiori replied. "I dunno, it's pretty complicated..."

"I can do it," said Yang. "Just give me a—"

"Enough, Yang," said Benny. "This is professional, not personal. You're disqualified. And no sass from you, Shiori. Just do your job."

"Okay, boss."

She whirled and punched Joy in the stomach, gripping the back of the chair to keep it from tipping over, while Joy folded over as much as her bound hands would allow, croaking and wheezing.

"That was okay, right?" Shiori asked Daphne. "Not too violent or anything? Met all the right punching requirements, I hope?"

"It wasn't a blow to the head, so yes, that was fine," said Daphne, without deigning to look up from her clipboard.

Between gasps, Joy noticed the barely-suppressed tension between the two. Shiori did not like Daphne one little bit.

"We'll try this again," said Benny. "Who do you really work for?"

"But," said Joy. "It's the truth. I'm a freelance rep—oof!"

Joy was ready for the punch this time. She couldn't dodge, but she could use some of the tricks she'd learned in her Combatives courses. She tensed her stomach muscles while relaxing everything else, trying to intentionally fold over around the blow, absorb and disperse the energy. It didn't feel good, but it wasn't nearly as bad as before. She had a second to feel proud of herself before she remembered to act like it hurt much more than it did. They repeated this sequence a second time, and then a third, before the Chief interrupted.

"This is getting nowhere. What difference does it make? Maybe she is a reporter—"

"No, my nose tells me she's lying," said Benny.

"Your shark nose," said the Chief, not bothering to hide his disgust. "Expect me to believe that—"

"Yes I do!" snapped Benny, letting genuine irritation show through. "Because you know what this broad did? Snuck onto a ship—my ship, and she knew that—knocked out the entire crew, freed six girls from a cage—a cage that was suspended in the hold, fifteen feet over the orlop deck, and then torched half the dock. You ever heard of a reporter doing that? All on her lonesome? Does that sound like what a reporter would do?"

The Guardsmen all looked at each other, and then at her. Joy felt her mind racing. Hearing her exploits recounted like that, it did sound kind of insane. What the Abyss had she been thinking? But wait...

"I didn't knock out those guards," said Joy. "That wasn't me."

"Really," said Benny. "Then who was it?

"I... I don't know who did it. I just found them like that—" she managed to get out, before having to brace for another gut-shot. Each one hurt more than the last. Her abs were starting to tire under the abuse. But what else could she say? They'd never believe it was the Red Specter, and how could she prove it? She hadn't actually seen him.

"You just found 'em? Well, let's see what the crew has to say about that." Benny nodded to his assistant, who flipped through her notes.

"All of the crew of the Joanne Spaulding were recovered trussed up and stowed in one of the dinghies," said Daphne. "All of them appear to have been dosed with some unknown, yet powerful sedative. Whatever it is, it hasn't worn off yet. We can rouse them with smelling salts, but only briefly before they go back under. None of them have been able to give us a coherent description of their attacker. Most don't even remember being attacked. We have the captain here, if you want to see if he's recovered any."

"Bring him out," said Benny.

Two of the Triad men dashed off into one of the aisles and re-turned hauling the barely-conscious form of the captain between them. His feet dragged on the ground and his head lolled about from side to side. His porters struggled to keep their boneless cargo upright, gripping him by his belt and by a handful of his shirt, right beneath his armpit.

"Captain Ong," said Benny. "How good of you to join us."

The captain mumbled something incoherent as his chin flopped to his chest. Benny glanced over at Daphne, who nodded, tucked her clipboard under her arm, and knelt down to retrieve her purse. And that's when Joy realized that Daphne's dress was actually slit way up the sides. Like, up to her hips. Then she stood up, and the slits disappeared.

Completely. How on earth was she doing that? Joy stared at the cut of Daphne's dress, looking for extra pleats or folds, and could not figure out why it was no longer peeking open. Did she just have perfect posture or something? Joy realized she was staring, and she wasn't the only one, either, though most of the men were trying not to be obvious about it, waiting for Daphne to move again, so they could get another glimpse. Daphne didn't move, showing no recognition of any of the attention she was getting. Daphne was starting to piss her off.

Joy fought down a surge of irritation. She'd never be able to pull that look off in a million years. Didn't have the legs for it, obviously. No, she got people mistaking her for a kid. It was the damned swimsuit, that's what it was. Sure, millitary-issue, function first, whatever, but couldn't the designers have spared just a little thought to body line, and whatnot? Did it have to randomly squish everything together like a sausage? Not that she actually wanted to have a bunch of criminals leering at her, especially right now. So okay, fine—maybe that was best, after all. It was just—Arrrgh!

Daphne had pulled out and uncorked a small vial, took a pinch of its contents, and stuck them beneath Captain Ong's nostrils. His head jerked back and he opened his eyes.

"Wha... Where am..." Ong's head still wobbled a bit on his shoulders, as he blinked and looked around. "Not my ship... What you all doing... Here... Innah... Mmrrphl..."

His eyelids began to sink down as his speech became garbled, but he recovered a bit when Daphne slapped him across the face.

"Ow! Why'd you do—"

"Ong!" snapped Benny. "Straighten up. What's the last thing you remember? Who attacked you?"

"What? Attack? What attack? I don't..." He stared at them all in blank confusion. Daphne grabbed his chin and forced him to face her.

"Think carefully. Concentrate." She carefully enunciated each word, trying to pierce his mental fog. "What. Is. The. Last. Thing. You. Remember?"

Captain Ong furrowed his brows. He tried to shake his head like a dog—except Daphne was holding his chin. It was almost comical. "Was looking... For my crew..." he said. "They'd left their posts... Thought they were... And then... then I...."

His head started listing to the side. "Dunno... Everything all fuzzy...."

Daphne slapped him again. "Enough," said Benny. "Show him the other thing."

Daphne pulled a thin book out of her purse and held it in front of Ong's face, yanking on his hair to keep him focused on it.

"Care to explain this, Ong?" Said Benny. "Anything you'd like to say about it? Now would be the time."

Joy recognized the small ledger she'd found in the secret compartment. Ong's eyes focused on it. It was hard to read the reaction of such a badly drugged person.

"Whuh..." slurred Ong. "Where'd... get that?"

"Where'd I get it?" said Benny. "Why, we fished it out of the harbor. And how'd it get there, I wonder? Why don't we ask the fish?"

Joy found all eyes back on her. She saw no point in lying to protect Ong.

"I found it on the ship. It was hidden in the chart room. Secret drawer."

"Well, isn't that interesting," said Benny. Daphne kept the ledger up in front of Ong's face, flipped it open to the first page.

"Insurance, Ong?" said Benny, sounding genuinely hurt. "Insurance on me? After all these years? After everything I done for you, everything we've been through? This is how you repay me?"

Ong struggled to answer, weird half-expressions peeking out from behind the chemical fog that dulled his everything. "Jus' bizness..." was the best he could manage.

"Business, huh?" said Benny. "Well, now I gotta take care of business. If I was nicer I'd off you now, while you can't feel it. But I think we're going to have a detailed discussion about *insurance*, after you've slept it off. Get him out of here."

Benny's goons dragged the Captain off, even as he sunk back down into oblivion, even as Joy wondered exactly what kind of tranquilizer the Red Specter was using to get those results.

"Now that we've got that out of the way," said Benny, turning back to Joy. "Let's go back to the main issue of exactly where we found this little notebook. How did you find Ong's notebook? Who told you about it?"

"Nobody," said "Joy. I found it in the chartroom, in a secret drawer. I thought it might be news."

"Thought it might be news?" said Benny. "You're ducking my question. How did you *just happen* to find it, when it was hidden in a secret drawer? That you also *just happened* to find, without knowing anything about in advance?"

"I... I know how that sounds, but it's the truth," said Joy. "I was picking the lock, and I realized there was another set of tumblers, hidden behind—"

"Lock-picking, huh? They teach you that in journalism school?"

Joy blinked. "N-no, I took supplemental courses—"

Another gut punch cut her short. Each one hurt more than the last.

378

"Supplemental courses," snorted Benny. "In lock-picking. Just what every reporter needs. Hey, Yang, you talked to her, right? She seem like a reporter to you?"

"No way," said Yang, his grimace only slightly masked by the bandages on his nose. "It's definitely some kind of cover. Suckers you in with her act, and then—whammo! Definitely combat trained. She's got to be an agent for somebody."

"I'm not," said Joy. "That was—"

"Cut the bullshit," said Benny. "I been all over the world, and there's no way someone your size takes down someone like Yang without a ton of training. Years of it. Or are you saying that was more 'supplemental courses?' At Journalism School?"

Joy's mind raced, desperately seeking some way out of the trap she'd fallen in. How could she phrase the truth so it wouldn't sound so unbelievable? And what happened to Benny's lie-sniffing ability? It would've been really helpful if it actually worked.

"I... I didn't really beat him up," she said, "I took him by surprise. Sucker-punched him. And ran away before—"

"No way," said Yang. "Chen was there, too, and she tossed him into me. Definitely an agent. Knew exactly which ship to go for, knew exactly where the weapons crate was. That ain't no accident."

Joy cursed silently to herself. This was about Yang's ego. The only way he could save face was to build her up to pulp hero status.

"That's what I thought," said Benny. "So, let's talk about where you're getting your information. Who told you to target the Joanne Spaulding?"

"Some dock worker, I don't remember," said Joy, and realized she'd need to say more than that to forestall another beating. She needed to shift the thread of this interrogation. "Look, I stumbled into this whole thing. I came here on a story, related to a... a small riot at the docks, three days ago, involving an old woman, and the Red—"

"Old woman?" Said Benny, leaning forward, "What old woman?"

Joy was glad he'd interrupted her. She'd nearly mentioned the Red Specter and torpedoed whatever shreds of credibility she might have left. She started to answer, but got a vision of Triad thugs busting down Madame Zenovia's door. Sure, she hadn't liked the old fraud very much, but the idea of unleashing Benny the Shark on her was too awful.

"It... It doesn't matter who she is," said Joy. "She didn't tell me about you. It was something totally unrelated—"

Joy saw Shiori haul off for a punch, braced for it, and was surprised when it didn't come. She opened her eyes to see Shiori's gauntlet—motionless, about an inch from its target. Then she rapped her knuckles against Joy's taut abdominals.

"Agent, huh?" said Shiori. "Knows how to take a punch, at least. Time to switch this up."

Shiori stepped behind Joy and grabbed her left hand, isolating the pinky finger and bending it backwards.

Intense pain shot up her arm as the delicate joints were torqued in the wrong direction, small tendons stretched past the point they were meant to go.

Joy had no defense against this, no way to brace. She could only endure.

"You don't seem to get how this works," said Benny. "I ask for a name, you give me one. What you think is important don't matter, it's what I think. Now, who was the old woman? I want a name."

"Wait, but it's not—Aiiggh!" Slowly, inexorably, Joy felt her pinky forced backward towards her wrist. The pain ratcheted upward exponentially: for each fraction of a degree further it went, her agony doubled. And beyond that, the fear, the anticipation of how much worse it would hurt the more this continued, if her finger was ripped off, no she needed it, had to say something, but she couldn't think, it was going to break tobreak tobreakbreakingbreaking....

380

"Madame Zenovia! Madame Zenovia!" She screamed. "That's who it was, okay..." The pressure lessened to a point where the agony no longer overpowered her faculties, enough for her to feel ashamed. "But... she didn't say your name, or anything about you at all... you have to believe me, it was about something completely different—"

"Of course she wouldn't mention me," said Benny. "I wouldn't put any stock in a spiritual advisor if she didn't know how to keep her mouth shut."

"Yes, that's..." Joy blinked, surprise taking her mind off the pain for a bit. "Spiritual advisor? Madam Zenovia is your spiritual advisor? You?"

Joy though back to the woman she'd met, disheveled and confused, peddling pure nonsense—palmistry, astrology, aura readings, and...

"Past-life regression therapy!" she blurted out, staring at Benny. "She was helping you... remember how to be a shark?"

"That's right," said Benny. "Really helps with my focus. But you already knew that. It's why you went after her, isn't it? Acting surprised won't help you."

"Went after...?" Joy sputtered. "No, she contacted us—Ow!"

"Trying to shift blame on an old woman?" said Benny, favoring her with a look of contempt. "She wouldn't do that. You found her and tricked her, somehow. Wouldn't be hard, with the state she's in, lately."

"No, I... Wait a minute," said Joy, staring at Benny. "You know she's... err... not all there, but you're still getting her advice?"

Benny wasn't fazed. "Takes special people to do what she does. Spend enough time in the other world, messing with spirits and stuff—it's no wonder she gets lost in this one. But make no mistake—once she gets in the zone, there's nobody better."

Joy had nothing to say to that, trying to match that statement with the pathetic figure she'd met earlier that day. Well, at least she didn't have to feel guilty about giving her up. That relief vanished as Shiori started cranking her finger again.

"Now, back to the important point," said Benny. "Who tipped you off about Madam Zenovia? Who are you working for?"

"No, she contacted us, but not about you—Aighh! Ow! No, really—you have to—" Joy saw Benny shake his head, and Shiori increased the pressure. The agony overwhelmed her mind, and she began to panic. What was she going to do? She was telling the truth, and they weren't listening. What could she say to make them stop? She had to make them stop, stop the agony radiating out from her hand. Stop it stopstopstop—

"This is getting nowhere," said Chief Gallach. "We came here for one thing. Not this farce. You say she stole our women? Fine—make her tell what she did with them. Stop wasting time with—"

"Wasting time?" Benny snarled. "You call this wasting time? You're the ones who don't get it. Someone out there, someone we don't know, is messing with me. My men are being attacked, being disappeared. Wrecking my property, stealing my money, messing with me—messing with me! Benny the Shark! Nobody does that! Nobody!"

Benny had dropped the polite, mannered facade, showing the real man underneath—the crime boss, the pirate, the one everybody feared. Joy felt herself shrinking back in her chair as the tirade continued.

"Weeks of waiting for a lead, of waiting for these assholes to slip up, and finally they do. Finally we got one of 'em. And what do you idiots care about? Your women." Benny sneered at the Guardsmen. "You think I give a shit about half a dozen street-trash whores? You think I can't snap my fingers and get those replaced in five minutes? But the way you're fussing over 'em you'd think they were the Sidhe Crown Jewels or something. Walking in here with a fucking bomb. You guys need to get laid that bad? Fine, I'll comp you. Whatever."

Joy saw the Guardsmen step back, but more than that, saw a few of them flinch at the phrase "Sidhe crown jewels." And, finally, a burst of inspiration struck her—A way out of this mess, or at least, a way to buy time. Benny was right. It didn't make any sense for the Guardsmen to get so desperate over missing slave girls. It was what they carried, concealed in their manacles—those strange jewels.

They didn't care about the girls, and Benny didn't care about the girls, but the girls were all she cared about. And she knew where they were, and they trusted her, so she'd have no problem getting them to give her their manacles. Just get their manacles, and leave them alone. Solve everybody's problems. Something only she could do, that they'd need to keep her alive for.

"Benny, you're right, the girls aren't what they're after," she said. "They're hiding something, and it's—"

"Shut up!" roared Benny. "Quit trying to change the subject. I've been nice and patient and given you every chance, but that's over. Who do you work for? Spill it. Now!"

"No, wait—you have to listen—" Joy tried to protest, but the explosion of pain from her finger cut her short.

"Who do you work for?"

"Aighh—no! No!" Joy's brief moment of hope had been dashed to bits. She had real information, but they weren't even listening, didn't want the truth.

"Who do you work for?

Joy had to say something, anything to stop the awful pressure in her finger, stop the tendons from popping, tearing. Truth was no good. Think of something. Had to lie. But she sucked at fiction. But the pain, the pain, had to try, had to lie, had to think, oh her finger was going to tear off, come right off her hand, it hurt the pain thepain thepainpainpain...

"NO! Stop," she wailed. "I'll talk! I'll talk I'll talk just stop, please, please!"

Shiori released her grip and the agony went down to a dull throb.

"Spill it," said Benny.

"I work for..." said Joy, exaggerating her gasps of relief to buy time. "I work for The International Women's Liberation League."

Benny stared at her. "Never heard of it."

Not surprising, since she'd just made it up. "Well of course you wouldn't," she said, trying to project as much confidence as she could. "You're not a woman, are you? And we're new — but we're going big. We're sick and tired of seeing our sisters treated like chattel, like property, and we're putting an end to it. You hear that, Benny — we're putting you out of business."

Benny raised an eyebrow. "And this Women's League — they gave you all your training? Lock-picking, and—"

"No, the Kallistrate Intelligence Bureau did that," she said. "But the war's over, isn't it? I've got a new cause now, something that makes me feel better than killing people for the KIB ever did. I'm talking about freedom, real freedom, not like—"

About midway through Joy's rant, Benny leaned forward, took a huge snort of air, and made a sour face.

Shiori seized her pinky and cranked it hard. Joy felt tendons popping as her finger bent the wrong way, going past the point of no return, and searing agony tore through her, like nothing she'd ever felt before. She screamed and thrashed against her bonds.

The pain subsided a little from the first horrifying burst, but didn't go away. It left her with an awful feeling of wrongness coming from her left hand, like her pinky was twisting off at a weird angle, though at least it was still attached.

It felt grotesque. She wanted to check the damage, but she couldn't see anything with her hands behind her back.

"Women's Liberation? Bullshit," said Benny. "You think you can fool this nose? That lie stinks to high heaven. Who do you work for?"

"I... uhh..." Joy stammered, utterly stymied. The Women's Liberation League had been the best she could come up with. And screw your nose, Benny! Your nose couldn't smell shit.

"Looks like she doesn't much care for her fingers, Shiori."

"You're right, boss," came a voice from behind. "No point wasting any more time with those."

Joy's surge of relief was short-lived, as a rough hand seized her by the hair, and a cold steel edge pressed against her cheek, then slid back a bit.

"I say the next lie should cost an ear," Shiori's voice made her want to jump, coming inches away from her head, even as the blade came to rest right beneath her earlobe, preparing to slice through that connective tissue.

"That's assuming it's okay with Daphne here," said Shiori. "I wouldn't want to offend her delicate sensibilities or anything."

"It's not a blow to the head, so I don't see why you think it would," said Benny's assistant, ignoring Shiori's sarcasm, while scribbling away in her notes.

"No... No, wait," said Joy, terror rising, threatening to send her into a blind panic, ruining any shred of concentration she had.

"No more waiting, Ms. Fan," said Benny. "Who do you work for?"

Joy couldn't think, couldn't think, not with that knife there. They were going to mutilate her, had to stop them no she needed time, more time.

"I... I..." She stuttered, and the knife bit into her, started to slice upwards. No—not that, not that!

"Boss! Boss!" Came another voice, a man's voice, from far away.

The blade stopped moving, then pulled away from her. How much damage had it done? She couldn't exactly tell. The base of her ear itched like crazy, and hot liquid ran down her throat and jawline. Was her ear still on? She thought so, but it was hard to tell, not like you ever noticed your ears unless they touched something else—

"Big Sister Joy! No!"

Joy recognized that voice, and felt a new level of dread take her, as she also recognized another sound—the rattling of chains. She looked over, as best she could with Shiori yanking at her hair, and saw a dirty and scraped-up Lin-Lin being dragged closer by two big Triad men.

"Well, that's something gone right," said Benny. "One very small thing. This the only one you found?"

"Yeah, so far," said one of the men. "We're sweeping the area though. We think she was trying to run a distraction for the others or something."

"Found one. Good," said the Chief. "So, you can hand her over—"

"Patience, Chief," said Benny. "You'll get her when I'm done—"

"No! Let her go," said Joy. "You can! They don't really want her, they—"

Shiori's knife-point pressed down on the top of Joy's lips, forcing her to stop talking to avoid cutting herself.

"No interrupting the boss."

"No, don't hurt her," cried Lin Lin. "Punish me. It's my fault. I ran away. I'm sorry. I won't do it again. Please don't hurt Big Sister Joy."

Joy caught Lin Lin's expression and it tore out her guts. No. This was wrong. This was totally backwards. Lin Lin shouldn't be protecting her. That was Joy's responsibility. She was the eldest. Looking after everyone else was her job. And she'd failed. The one girl she needed to protect the most, the one she'd promised to rescue, was now trying to save her.

Joy had failed in every conceivable way. Just like she'd failed in every other aspect of her life. They should kill her now, before she spread even more misery.

"Oh, you care about your 'Big Sister,' do you?" said Benny. "Well, maybe we can make a deal, then. She's being real tight-lipped, and it hasn't been good for her health. Maybe you can be more reasonable?"

Lin Lin stared at Benny, and then looked over to Joy.

"Just do what he wants," said Joy. "Don't worry about me."

"Good, that's good," said Benny. "So let's get down to it. Who does your 'Big Sister' work for? Who's her boss?"

The question took Lin Lin aback. Confused, she kept glancing from Joy to Benny and back again. "I don't... I don't under-stand—" she said, and whimpered as one of the goons started twisting her arm behind her back.

"Stop that! She doesn't know anything," Joy cried. "Don't hurt her. If you're going to hurt someone, hurt me! Hurt me, not her!"

As soon as the words left her mouth, Joy realized it was the worst thing she could have said. Benny turned to her, and the corner of his mouth tugged up in a cruel steel smile.

"What's going on?" said Chief Gallach, unable to follow the Xiaish conversation prompted by Lin Lin's entry. "Speak Kallish. That's one of our women. Turn her over. That's why we're here."

"Hmmm... That's an idea, isn't it?" said Benny, switching to Kallish. "I could think that over, but there's just one problem. It's late at night, and I still haven't had a decent meal. Just snacks." Benny sighed and peered wistfully at his fine plate of cracked bones. "And now I'm all out. What else is there? Ah, I see something."

The Triad men dragged Lin Lin closer, forced her arm out, straight towards Benny, made her open her hand, fingers splayed out. Benny exaggerated his grin, clacked his teeth together. Was he serious? He couldn't be serious.

"Wait, what are you doing?" said Joy, as Benny opened his mouth wide and started closing in on the terrified runaway. "You can't do that. It's sick! That's disgusting! You can't—"

"You!" snapped Benny, thankfully turning away from Lin Lin. "You don't tell me what to do. You don't like this? You're the one putting me in this spot. This is all thanks to your obstinance."

"But I'm not—"

Benny wasn't having it. "Enough! You care about this girl? Don't want her hurt? Don't want her to become shark food? If that's what you want, then you need to stop lying to me."

Joy's frustration was surpassed only by her fear. She hadn't—well, she had lied, but only because they hadn't believed her when she'd told them the truth. And now they wouldn't believe her lies, either.

Just her expression alone was enough for Benny. He opened his mouth wide and turned towards Lin Lin, who reeled back in horror when she saw the monster-teeth—or she tried to, but couldn't break free from her captors. She started to scream, but one of the Triad men clapped a hand over her mouth. Slowly, Benny closed in on the girl, ignoring her muffled whimpers, her pitiful attempts to escape.

"No, wait!" said Joy, "Wait a minute—stop!"

Benny ignored her, inching nearer and nearer. Joy felt herself straining against her bonds, making her chair hop up and down, until Shiori leaned on her. She couldn't push back against that weight, couldn't do anything. She couldn't do anything.

Benny's wide jaws reached biting distance. Lin Lin's trembling fingers were held fast. She couldn't pull them away as they were forced into the insane pirate's open mouth.

This couldn't be happening. She had to stop it. She had to say something. Something, anything, anything, had to think, had to think.

Joy saw Benny's jaws tense, prepare to snap down, and Joy couldn't watch. She had to look away, but that was even worse, waiting to hear the sound, the crack and the meaty tearing, the thought of it triggered a final surge of panic racing through her body, and tore out one last, desperate scream.

"THE RED SPECTER! I'M WORKING FOR THE RED SPECTER, OKAY?" she sobbed, "Thats it! That's who you want, not her. She's got nothing to do with it! It's him you want. The Red Specter! He's the one behind it all! So don't hurt Lin Lin, please, please. PLEASE don't hurt her."

Joy was bawling like a baby now. She'd screwed everything up. The Red Specter? That was her worst lie yet. They'd never believe that. She couldn't look at them, couldn't bear to see what they'd done to poor Lin Lin, couldn't bear to see the blood, the look of betrayal in the eyes of an innocent girl, whose only

388

mistake was listening to an idiot failed reporter with delusions of being some kind of crime-fighting—

"What was that?" said Benny, and something in his voice was different. It made Joy look back up. He'd turned away from Lin Lin. His teeth were still shiny, unblemished gold. No red stains at all. Joy glanced over and saw Lin Lin's hand, still held out by her captors, with no signs of damage.

Benny peered at her, his gaze focused, intense. "What did you just say?"

Joy stared back, fought to control her breathing. "The... the Red...(hic)... The Red—"

"The Red Specter? The Red-Faced Ghost? The spirit of vengeance from the Great War? That's who's behind all this? You've met him?"

Joy felt the wheel of the world spinning beneath her. Had it worked? That story? But...

She looked around her, scanning the faces of everyone in the warehouse. Easy enough, because they were all staring at her. She saw incredulity, disgust, disbelief—from some of them. Daphne radiated disdain from over the top of her glasses, and Yang looked ready to explode, but quite a few of the Triad men shrank back, sending nervous glances at each other. But their opinions weren't what counted. Benny's did. And he wasn't looking dismissive. He was serious.

But of course he was. He believed in that stuff. He went to Madam Zenovia for advice. Joy realized she'd let Daphne's scathing contempt of the Gazette blind her. She should have pulled out the Red Specter from the beginning.

"Hey, I asked you a question," said Benny. "You trying to—"

"No!" said Joy. "I mean... you win, okay? I'll talk, I'll talk. Yes, it's the Red Specter. It's him. The one you're thinking of."

"Yeah?" said Benny. "So what's his game, then? What's he want?"

"As far as I can tell? He wants to put you out of business, Benny. And you guys, too," she added, glaring at the guardsmen.

"All the corruption, and drug-smuggling, and arms-running, and slavery, and—"

"Yeah, real noble of him. He thinks he can take us all down himself? How's he going to do that?"

"You think he sits down and explains his plans to me? I just do what he says."

Joy was on a roll. Spinning out each new bit of fiction came so easily that she almost believed it herself. "He keeps changing how he contacts me, never lets me get a good look at him. Every time we meet in person, it's always in some weird place with deep shadows.

"But I can guess some of it. He's been picking at your operations at key points, turning you against each other—"

"Nonsense," said the Chief. "Part of her reporter cover. Story on Red Specter sightings."

"Yeah, that's right," said Yang. "She was going on about that when we first saw her, too. And if Chen hadn't been dumb enough to listen—"

"What? What's that, Yang?" Benny sat up, a new, dangerous edge to his voice. "You didn't mention that, Yang. And I distinctly remember that I did say to tell me everything. But I don't remember hearing anything about the Red Specter until now. Tell me, Yang, is there something wrong with my memory? Is there?"

Yang flinched, withering under the simmering menace radiating from his boss. "Well... No, sir. There—"

"Then why, Yang, why did you withhold that little detail? Huh?"

"I'm... I'm sorry boss," Yang looked like a dog that been kicked. "I just... didn't think it was important, that's all—"

"YOU didn't think it was important? YOU didn't it was important?" And Benny the Shark was out of his chair, two steps and he had Yang by the collar, hoisting him up on his toes. "You tell me, Yang—do I pay you to think? Do I?"

"No... Boss," gasped Yang.

"Wait," said MacInroy. "This doesn't make sense. If she was secretly working for the Specter, why would she call attention to him in the first place? She—"

"It's called 'hiding in plain sight,' dumbass," Joy retorted. "And it worked, too, since none of you brought it up when you should've. And it's not even a giveaway, since the whole dock's been buzzing with Red Specter rumors, anyway."

"The whole dock has? And this is the first I've heard of it? Why is that? Daphne!" Benny whirled on his assistant. "Are you aware of this? Did you hear about any of these rumors?"

Daphne looked up from her notes. Her expression didn't really change, but she didn't answer right away. Joy noticed a slight whitening of her knuckles around her clipboard. "Well... yes, Sir. I do believe I heard something about that, but—"

"You heard about it? And you said nothing? All this time, we've had things going wrong, blown shipments, people going missing, and I'm wracking my brains, trying to figure out why, consulting with you about it, and you didn't say anything? I expect Yang to be stupid, but you? I get this from you, too?"

Daphne adjusted her glasses and swallowed. Oh, she was nervous, now! She could actually do that? Despite everything, Joy was starting to have fun.

"With... all due respect, sir," said Daphne. "I didn't think that sightings of a comic strip character were worthy of your—"

"DAMN IT, DAPHNE! The comic doesn't have anything to do with it," roared Benny. "The Red Specter has been around before they started with the funny-books. Look at Shiori—she's in that strip, too, and she's real enough."

"Hey! The Abyss I am!" Shiori's furious retort came from right behind Joy, making her jump. "That red-skinned skank has got nothing to do with me. Don't even joke about that shit."

Benny glared at her, but Shiori was the one person in the room he couldn't intimidate, and she was worked up. Joy was close enough to hear her muttering, "Asshole comic writers better hope I never find 'em, 'cause if I do I swear I'm going to tear them..."

The sudden intensity and vehemence of Shiori's reaction startled Joy. So, she really hated the pop-culture caricature of herself, did she? Under other circumstances, Joy might sympathize, but the real Shiori was too awful for that.

"So is that it? Is there anybody else who's spotted the Red Specter and hasn't bothered saying anything?" Benny leveled an angry glare at the entire room.

"Well, there's Madam Zenovia," said Joy. "She spotted him too. Happened when she wandered down to the docks about three nights ago. After one of your sessions, I'm guessing. Though her description was pretty wild, and she didn't use the words 'Red Specter.' She doesn't even read the comics."

"You're pretty chatty now," said Benny, advancing on her. "So let's keep talking. What's his next move? Why'd he have you sneak on the Joanne Spaulding? And torching my cargo, that the Specter's orders, too?"

"No, he just told me to create a distraction. Something big. Breaking the girls out was my idea. Because I hate slavery."

Benny loomed over her and bared his teeth. "Distraction for what? What's his plan? What's he doing right now?"

Joy felt her courage draining away as the gangster boss loomed over her, as he brought his monster teeth closer. Okay, he was scary. Nothing wrong with being scared of him—he was a pro. It was his job. But she had to keep it together—bluff with confidence. As well as she could.

"I-I told you," she said, forcing herself to meet his eyes. "He doesn't share his plans with me—but I can guess! And... and I don't know what he's done tonight, but I know it's big! Something real big. You're in... you're in serious trouble, Benny. You all are. By the time the Red Specter is done with you, you'll wish you'd—"

Joy's tirade was cut off as Benny seized her jaw and yanked her chin up, leaning in until they were nose-to-nose.

"Well, good thing for me I got something of his, don't I?" Said Benny, leering at her, then glancing over to Lin Lin. "In fact,

I got two of them. The question is, does this Specter actually give a crap about either of you? Because if the answer is no, the last day of your life is gonna be today, and it's gonna be bad enough to make you long for the Abyss by the end."

Joy felt herself shaking, fought to keep the tremor out of her voice as Benny loosened his grip enough to answer. It felt like she was digging herself in deeper with every new bluff, but what choice did she have? She had to keep them alive, keep buying time until... until something happened, some opportunity presented itself.

"That won't happen," she said. "He won't allow it. And if you hurt me—if you hurt either of us, the Red Specter will—"

"Oh, come on," said Yang. "Boss, listen to her. She's making this all up. Don't tell me you're actually buying into—"

"Don't recall asking your opinion, Yang," snapped Benny. "You're in enough shit as it is."

Yang blanched. "But Boss—"

"I said shut it!" Benny snarled. "Thanks to you I've been blindsided. This is a serious threat."

Yang shut it. Benny looked like he was about to say something more, but Daphne cleared her throat.

"Sir, forgive me, but I feel like I have to point out that we don't actually have any evidence to back up anything she says. Making assumptions based on that would—"

"Daphne. You think she could pull one over on me? Lie straight to my face and I wouldn't know?" Benny sounded almost wounded. "What's with you tonight. You know better than that."

"Of... course I don't think she'd get away with a blatant lie," said Daphne. "I'm just pointing out that—"

"I've no confidence in that," said Chief Gallach. "Sick of this farce. That Lin Lin girl is ours. Hand her over, or—"

"Or nothing," said Benny. "She's a hostage against the Red Specter, so—"

"Enough! Enough of all this nonsense," snarled the Chief, his anger overcoming the pain of his cut throat. "Wasting our time. Mocking us. Insulting our intelligence. Hostage against a comic character? Ridiculous. You'll hold her forever, and this is your excuse? War propaganda. A fairy tale for children. You expect us to take that seriously? Do you really? Let me spell it out for you: there is no such thing as a Red Specter!"

"FOOL. TRAITOR. FANATIC." A voice boomed out, echoing throughout the warehouse, coming from everywhere and nowhere. "WHEREVER TYRANNY REIGNS. WHENEVER EVIL STRIKES, THERE I AM—LURKING IN THE SHADOWS. SURRENDER NOW, VILLAINS! FOR NO INJUSTICE CAN ESCAPE THE WRATH... OF THE RED SPECTER."

For a second, Joy thought she'd hallucinated it. The voice was so strange, unearthly. Deep and resonant, but with a bizarre texture, like if gravel was a sound. But everyone else reacted as well, tensing and whirling around, trying to determine the source of the voice. Joy heard Shiori's armor rattling behind her as the Caliburn knight went on guard. She saw Benny jumping back and glaring up into the rafters, MacInroy clutching at Brannock, and Yang going pale with disbelief. Daphne actually dropped her clipboard.

"Nice of you to drop by, Specter," said Benny. "Now why don't you come out where I can see you? Unless you want your little girlfriend to—"

As he spoke, he signaled in Joy's direction, and she had a brief moment to anticipate yet another hostage standoff, before all the warehouse lights went out, plunging them into darkness.

Shouts of fear and confusion filled the black void. Joy realized that now was the time to escape. She thrashed against her bonds, making her chair hop up and down. She had to get free. Somebody crashed into her, and she and her chair tipped over. She landed on her side, painfully, as her bonds left her no good way to brace herself, though she managed to tense her neck enough to keep her head from cracking into the floor. She hissed as the back of her chair squeezed her arm against the concrete. Add another bruise to the collection.

394

There was a brief flicker of bright orange light from someone's cigarette lighter, followed by a meaty smack and a cry of pain, and the lighter clattered to the ground and went out. More yells and thuds followed, along with a new noise, a chorus of hisses coming from multiple directions, and Joy breathed in something dry and acrid. Smoke canisters?

More men pulled out their lighters, but their tiny flames only created brief, diffuse bright spots in the thick greenish smoke, and seemed to make them easy targets. Coughing and curses echoed out through the warehouse, followed by gunshots pounding at her ears, muzzle flashes illuminating the smoke like a lightning storm, even as smarter heads screamed at them to stop, to not shoot blind. Joy picked out MacInroy and Gallach yelling "Not yet, not yet, Brannock," and she remembered his bomb. Oh crap. She needed to get out of here.

She arched her back and shoved with her legs, over and over, inching the ropes on her ankles down until they slid off the ends of the chair legs. She managed to roll onto her knees, facedown, then got her feet beneath her, but her wrists remained bound behind her, tied to a crossbar on the back of the chair. She staggered about in the darkness, bent over with the chair smacking the backs of her thighs, wondering if she could try spinning around—maybe she could hit something hard enough to break the chair, when she felt a sudden, precise jolt, and her hands came free. Someone caught her with an iron grip around her waist, there was a loud hiss, and she felt both her captor and herself flying through the air.

Instinctively, she clutched at her captor for safety as they swung about. She struggled to figure out what was going on. She felt a few jolts, each accompanied by a vague sense that they'd changed direction, followed a final thump that seemed to indicate they'd stopped. She waited until her feet touched ground before she tried to struggle free.

She tried to put her hands in the stranger's face, reaching up—way up—to push him away, but instead of a face, she found a stiff, leathery cone, with some kind of hose trailing off it, curving around—

The figure caught her wrists. His grip was firm, but not painfully so.

"CALM DOWN. SAFE HERE." The voice lacked the booming quality from before, but it was still so deep and strange. Joy had to suppress a hysterical giggle. This was really happening. The Red Specter. She was going to be okay. Everything was—

"Lin Lin!" she hissed. "Where is she? Is she—"

"ON IT," said the Specter. "WAIT HERE."

The Red Specter made almost no noise as he moved away. Just the barest canvas rustle. Joy's eyes were starting to adjust to the darkness, enough to make out the vague shape of the Specter moving down the warehouse aisle. She found herself tiptoeing after him. Just as the Red Specter was rounding the corner, a voice cried out, "Cover your eyes!" There was a hiss and it was like a small red sun had been born in the warehouse. The tall shelves of cargo shielded Joy from most of the glare, but Red Specter was caught in the open. She got her first good look at him, a figure clad in a long canvas trench coat, forearms thrown up in an attempt to shield his face from the searing light.

Then she heard Benny call out, "There he is! Open fire!"

A continuous rolling thunderclap assaulted Joy's ears as the Triad men brought their Manticores to bear. The Red Specter staggered and twitched as he was struck by round after round. His knees buckled and he fell to the floor.

Chapter 46:

Breakout

Joy froze in shock from the suddenness of the violence, with no idea what to do. Then she heard a groan and saw the Specter try to roll to his side. He was still alive. Joy lunged out, just far enough to grab his wrists, and started hauling him back into cover. Oh, he was heavy. From the corner of her eye she watched out for the Triad gunmen, saw only rough silhouettes obscured by the smoky haze.

The poor visibility saved her, for she'd already made it behind cover before they noticed what was going on. She heard cries of 'He's moving,' followed by more gunfire, but they were shooting at the Specter's boots now.

She kept pulling until she'd dragged him a yard or so into cover, then dropped his wrists and tried to examine his wounds. Part of her knew it was futile—she had no medical supplies, and no idea how to treat multiple gunshot wounds anyway, but she had to do something, dammit! She rolled him on his back, trying to assess the damage, but the sight of his face distracted her.

His mouth and nose were covered by a flattened conical snout of an infantryman's gas mask, hose trailing around to a cylindrical air filter clipped to his shoulder, but the eyes were covered by an even stranger contraption, a bulky squarish funnel with its wide glass-covered mouth facing outward, tapering back towards the Red Specter's eyes, with a few textured knobs on the side. The strange thing was that Joy felt a stab of recognition, like she'd seen this type of thing before. But never mind that, she had to help him, put pressure on the wounds, or something. But where were the—

The Red Specter sat up, and Joy yelped, jumping back a foot. Slowly, he rolled up to a crouch, keeping his torso curled up protectively. Then, with obvious effort, he slowly straightened up to his full height, letting out a quiet groan. As he did, bits of detritus fell off him. They made little clinking noises as they scattered on the concrete by his feet—shiny mushroom-shaped bits of squashed metal, along with something else—odd black flakes. But no blood at all.

The Red Specter shook his arms, painfully flexed his hands, and more metal bits fell out of the hole-ridden sleeves of his trench-coat. He grabbed the metal funnel covering his eyes. Joy heard a click as the funnel detached, revealing a second set of circular lenses beneath them. Now the Specter looked just like he did in the comics, though his real outfit had a lot more detail to it than the print version. The Red Specter tucked his goggles inside his coat (That's what they were! Night-vision goggles!) and she noticed beneath the coat he had another form-fitting jacket, with a leathery sheen, as well as a harness, with all kinds of gear strapped to it.

"Don't just stand there, you idiots!" bellowed Benny. "Go get him."

Before Joy could react, the Red Specter had already grabbed her and pulled her close. From within his coat he produced a strange, bulky pistol with a small harpoon stuffed in the barrel, which he pointed at the ceiling. Instead of a bang, it made a hissing sound when it fired, then whirred as they both went airborne, soaring up to the rafters on the harpoon cable. They came to a stop above a catwalk and dropped down with barely a sound. The Red Specter released her, tugged his harpoon loose from its anchor, and re-loaded it into the pistol, each motion practiced and efficient.

"You could've warned—" she started to whisper, but he put two fingers up to her lips and shook his head. What, not even a whisper? Okay, fine—he was the expert, she supposed. He motioned for her to stay where she was, vaulted over the railing onto a cross-beam, and stalked across it, making no sound. She watched his retreating back as he headed towards the light, then examined the beam, and the long, long drop down to the concrete floor below.

No problem. And no way was she staying on the sidelines. He wasn't the boss of her. She stepped through the railing onto the beam—it was nice and steady, and at least a foot wide. Well, that was practically a sidewalk, wasn't it? Just needed to be mindful of her steps, and she'd be fine. She followed after the Red Specter, not as quickly, but just as quietly.

Frantic voices drifted up from below. "He's gone. Vanished. They both have."

"Impossible... Hit him. I know I hit him..."

"Blood trail... There's no blood..."

"But I saw it! I saw him get hit!"

"...Not human... Like the stories... He's not even alive!"

The Red Specter crouched on the beam a few yards ahead, studying the criminals scurrying below. The smoke had thinned out considerably, so she was able to see them all, either sweeping through the shelving aisles in increasingly frantic pairs, or clustered in a loose circle around their leaders, Benny and Chief Gallach, with Shiori standing off a bit to the side, holding a signal flare, nearly identical to one Joy had used earlier. Joy made the mistake of looking directly at the flare, and she had to turn her head away and stop walking until the spots cleared from her vision. She focused on the Red Specter instead.

Lit from below, he had a truly otherworldly appearance. And apparently he was immune to bullets? Or, they did hurt, but he could shrug off the wounds? That was in the comics, but how could that be happening in the real world? Could he really be some kind of ghost or spirit? The thought made her shiver, but she tamped it down. He hadn't felt like an apparition when he'd grabbed her. And why would a ghost need night-vision goggles? Or use a pneumatic harpoon-gun to fly around? There had to be another explanation. She remembered the little metal mushrooms hitting the ground when the Specter had stood up, and the odd leathery material hidden beneath his trench-coat.

Could he be wearing some type of bullet-proof armor? Joy had never heard of such a thing. Even full plate mail wouldn't stop a gunshot, and whatever the Specter wore seemed to be relatively light and flexible. Still, it was the only explanation that made any sense.

She got within a yard of the Specter when he whirled around, reaching over his shoulder for the hilt of some weapon strapped to his back. The motion startled her, but she managed to keep her balance okay. Fortunately, he stopped once he recognized her. Then he just stared. Joy smiled and waved. The Red Specter kept staring at her. It was so hard to read his expression with that full-face mask. She wasn't sure if that was admiration or incredulity she was getting from him. Angrily, he jabbed a finger at her, then back to the catwalk.

Well, while she was genuinely grateful for the whole 'swooping-to-the-rescue' thing, and she didn't want to minimize that in any sense, that fact alone didn't automatically give him the right to order her around either, just like she hadn't been able to order Shao Yin and Noriko around. And she would have told him that, but had no idea how to convey something that complex in Hand-Waving-ese. So instead she crossed her arms and stuck her tongue out.

This was met with another blank stare. Not her most mature moment, but it had been a really long, trying day, okay? The Specter shook his head and pointed down, then pantomimed pressing hard on top of something. What did he mean? Did he want her to lie flat? That would make her harder to spot from below. She went to all fours, then stretched out on her belly, leaning over the side furthest from the light source, putting one hand on the bottom of the 'I' to keep from falling over. This seemed to mollify the Red Specter, who turned his attention back to the criminals below. Joy peered as far over the beam's edge as she dared, suddenly aware of the danger of being spotted.

The Triads and Guardsmen had gone back to bickering. Joy heard Daphne insisting she had all the exits secured, that no-one

400

could've escaped, while the Chief was certain they'd swept the aisles, and nobody was there. Shiori seemed to be the only one with the idea to include "up" as a direction to look, but she did so only occasionally, and Joy made sure to pull her head way back when that happened, which meant she couldn't watch Shiori any more. Instead she looked at the Red Specter, who shrank back into the shadow of a triangular plate between the I-beam and a vertical support. When the Specter peered out from his cover, Joy knew it was safe for her to do so, too.

She heard Benny's voice drift up from below. "Still here? Let's test that. Forget finding them. We'll make them come to us. We've still got something they want."

Joy froze as she realized the implications. He was talking about Lin Lin. All he had to do was threaten to hurt her unless they turned themselves in. But if they did that, they'd surely be killed. But they couldn't let Lin Lin get tortured on their accounts, either. That was too awful to contemplate.

What could they do? Did the Red Specter have any ideas? He was the expert here... Maybe? She gazed over at him with pleading eyes, but he didn't acknowledge her at all, the impassive glass circles of his mask studying the scene below.

Joy turned back to the scene, to the two thugs holding Lin Lin, and Benny standing right next to her. The poor girl was utterly terrified.

"Listen up," Benny yelled. "Because—"

Bright light flooded in through the small windows located high up on the warehouse wall, and a new, somewhat tinny voice echoed out through the night.

"ATTENTION. ATTENTION. THIS IS THE SPECIAL OP-ERATIONS DIVISION OF THE KALLISTRATE INTELLI-GENCE BUREAU. ALL OCCUPANTS OF WAREHOUSE 23C, YOU ARE TO EXIT THE BUILDING AND SURREN-DER YOURSELVES FOR QUESTIONING. REPEAT: ALL OCCUPANTS OF WAREHOUSE 23C, YOU ARE TO EXIT THE BUILDING AND SURRENDER YOURSELVES FOR

QUESTIONING. THIS INCLUDES MR. BEN LI FANG, AS-SOCIATES SHIORI ROSEWING AND DAPHNE CHOW, CHIEF AEDAN GALLACH, SERGEANTS CIARAN MACIN-ROY AND DAVIN BRANNOCK, EVERYBODY. WE KNOW YOU'RE IN THERE. YOU WILL EXIT THE BUILDING WITH YOUR HANDS BEHIND YOUR HEAD. YOU HAVE ONE MINUTE TO COMPLY, OR WE WILL BE FORCED TO COME IN AFTER YOU. REPEAT: YOU HAVE ONE MINUTE..."

Joy tuned out the rest of the Special Operations agent's droning speech, reeling from the shock of it. KIB Special Operations? That was new. But they'd gotten her letter! Wait, no they hadn't. That was impossible. There was no way they could've even received her letter already, let alone mobilized a task force this quickly. Unless they had agents stationed inside each and every mailbox in Kallistrate monitoring everyone's correspondence for intel.

Joy suppressed a hysterical giggle at the thought, and glanced over at the Red Specter. If he was at all surprised at the sudden appearance of the KIB out of nowhere, he didn't show it. Instead he pulled something from his coat. At first glance, Joy mistook it for a small umbrella, but it opened the wrong way, in a cone of some stiff material, and what would've been the hook on an umbrella got held up to a port on the side of the Red Specter's head, around where his ear should be. A directional listening device? He had it trained on the Triads and Guardsmen, who'd clustered together in a fervent discussion. Were they actually going to work together now, united against a common enemy? At least they'd bought some time.

Suddenly, the two groups split up. It seemed a decision had been reached. Benny's group began to shift over to one side of the warehouse, while the Guardsmen clustered in a circle around Brannock, the Chief and the blazing signal flare. They bowed their heads as the Chief started talking, but Joy couldn't make any of it out.

She felt a tap on the crown of her head, looked up to see the Specter stow his listening device and gesture at her to follow him. He headed off in the same direction as the Triad group, darting across the grid of warehouse cross-beams like he'd been born up here. Joy couldn't go nearly that fast, though overall she thought she did a decent job keeping up with him. As she went, she couldn't help sneaking glances at the circle of renegade City Guard, who'd begun chanting, swaying back and forth, bobbing their heads in unison. She caught up to the Red Specter, who turned his back to her, went down on one knee, and motioned for her to get on.

A piggyback ride? Well, okay then. It took a second for Joy to even figure out how to manage this. The Red Specter had a weapon strapped crosswise across his back, his two-part spear weapon, just like in the comics. She still managed to get on, but she had a steel bar pressing painfully across her chest, and it took her a minute to find the right angle for her legs to wrap around his torso without banging into some hard lump of spy equipment. Well, the Red Specter had never claimed to be built for comfort, had he? Actually, once she was in position, the lumps of gadget whatevers seemed to be pretty secure on his hips, providing a shelf to keep her from slipping down.

The Specter glanced over his shoulder, gave her a thumbs-up, and began moving again, picking his way through the rafters, stalking the Triad group, who'd gathered at a point at the side of the building, about three-quarters of the way to the back. Most of the Triad men were standing in two rows, carrying a big fat section of what appeared to be a ship mast, pointing it perpendicular to the wall. Daphne had finally stowed her glasses and clipboard and stood on guard at Benny's side, brandishing a shiny silver derringer. Even at this distance, Joy noted by the way it gleamed that it had ornate engraved patterns with gold leaf accents. Dammit, even her gun was cute. Lin Lin still had one large thug holding onto her. She looked terrified and confused.

The Specter had his grapple-gun out. He'd led Joy on a path taking them around to get between the main front entrance and the cluster of Triad-men. Now he was edging them towards the wall, attention focused on the group of criminals. Was he preparing to swoop down and snatch up Lin-Lin? Joy sure hoped so. A noise from the center of the warehouse caught her attention. The chanting of the Guardsmen reached a crescendo, and they peeled away from Brannock, many of them giving him half-hugs or pats on the back as they did. They couldn't give him full hugs, because he had the signal flare taped to his stump. He staggered towards the main warehouse door, muttering and shaking, while one last Guardsman ran ahead of him. The rest of them ran to join the Triad cluster.

Outside, the KIB called out their final warning, telling the criminals to come out or else. The last Guardsman yanked one side of the warehouse door open and sprinted away, revealing Brannock, with his jacket of explosives and dead man's switch—a detail the KIB couldn't miss, thanks to the harsh illumination from his flare.

At the same time the door opened, Joy heard a hiss of air from the Specter's harpoon gun. She felt his muscles tense, preparing to push off. She looked down at their target, saw Shiori had scored a huge 'X' in the side of the wall with her polearm-blade, while the Triad-men began preparatory swings with the ship mast—a battering ram?

Why not use a door? Because the KIB would have all the doors covered, of course.

Joy heard the KIB loudspeaker switch to placating tones, trying to calm Brannock. But Brannock was beyond listening, chanting some type of litany, in a language Joy didn't recognize. There were plenty of languages she didn't speak, but normally she could at least identify what they were, or make a rough guess as to what linguistic family they belonged to, but the noises coming out of Brannock's mouth were wholly alien. They repeated in a sequence, growing louder, more fervent. This was

404

no bluff. Brannock was going to sacrifice himself so everyone else could escape in the chaos of the explosion.

Brannock's mantra hit a fever pitch, in defiance of the increasingly desperate cajoling over the loudspeaker, as the Triad men reared back, ready to charge. Joy couldn't stop herself from staring at the fanatic, as he finished his litany in an ecstatic shriek. She watched in horrified fascination as he released the switch...

...And nothing happened. Brannock stared at his trigger, dumbfounded, pressed it a couple times, shook it—still no boom. The men carrying the ram stumbled, bumped into each other and shouted, confused by their botched cue.

The Red Specter gave her a quick over-the-shoulder glance, and the angle was such that she was able to peer through his goggle-lens and see the real eyes beneath. They twinkled with mirth. He held up something in his free hand for a second. Joy got a brief look at it before he dropped it—two disconnected wires. He'd disarmed the bomb? When had he... It must have been when the lights went out. Well, it did make sense—of course that'd be the first thing you'd—

The Red Specter sprang into action. Time slowed down for Joy, as they leapt out into space and began their swing. She saw Lin Lin's captor turn, distracted, as Benny yelled at his men to ram the wall anyway. The Specter had it timed and targeted perfectly. But they hadn't swung more than a few feet before a hideous scream drew her attention back to Brannock, who charged out toward the lights of the KIB, and was met with a hail of bullets in response. The fanatic pitched forward, limbs twisting about. Joy would never know if what happened next was by accident or design, but the result was the same, as Branock brought the end of the white-hot signal flare around to touch his own chest, and he disappeared in a flash of light and an ear-splitting roar.

A concussive blast of air hit Joy from the side, and she clung tighter to the Red Specter's neck, even as she felt her legs come loose from his waist. Even worse, the shock knocked them sideways during their swing, and Joy saw them headed straight for one of the warehouse's upper windows for a brief second before the Specter's trench-coat whipped up and tangled around her.

Crashing through the window pane barely slowed their momentum. Far worse was the jolt when their tethering harpoon ripped free of its anchor point, leaving them spinning through space, out of control.

Joy resisted the impulse to cling to the Specter. Instead she pushed away, following her instinct to tuck and roll against the coming impact, free of obstructions. The Red Specter had other ideas, re-grabbing her and pulling her to his chest, spinning them mid-air to crash against a wall of corrugated tin. The impact collapsed it inward, sending them both through several layers of junk before they came to rest in a huge pile of detritus and refuse.

Joy groaned and tried to take stock of herself. She thought she was still in one piece. Still had feeling in all her fingers and toes. Which, in the case of her busted pinky finger, was a mixed blessing. Anything else? She had a couple nasty cuts, and a small piece of glass lodged in her right forearm. She'd have gotten way worse if the Specter's heavy canvas trench-coat hadn't flipped up like that—had he done that deliberately? She'd landed on top of him, and he wasn't moving. But she felt a rise and fall in his chest. Still breathing.

This was the first time she'd had a chance to get a really good look at his costume, at the body armor he had beneath the trench-coat. And it was armor, some kind of leathery substance—only it was scaly. The scales varied in size—wider body panels had larger scales, connected together with strips of the same material with finer scales. The connective material seemed to have been treated differently, was much more flexible, while the larger panels were stiff, almost like plates. As Joy looked closer, she saw some of the scales had cracked, were hanging off, or missing completely. Was that the damage from the gunshots? She was about to check when the Specter groaned, raised his head, and looked at her.

406

"Are you okay?" she said.

"YES. NO NEED TO YELL."

She was about to protest that she wasn't yelling, but noticed a weird ringing in her head, along with an odd muffled sensation. "I think the bomb hurt my ears a little. Hearing weird echoes of it."

"THOSE ARE GUNSHOTS. NEED TO MOVE NOW," said the Specter.

"Can't you move—oh! Oops!" Said Joy, as she realized that not only had she landed on top of the Red Specter, she was straddling him. In a swimsuit. She scrabbled to her feet and stood up, getting a better look at where they were. It was kind of like an apartment complex of shacks—some storage structure that had fallen into disrepair. The walls had been formed from tin strips nailed together, and their entry had punched one of those strips inward and peeled it overtop other junk piles.

The Specter climbed back up the pile and stood at its apex, looking into the alleyway separating them from the Triad warehouse. Joy followed, only to run into a group of men in strange uniforms pointing guns at them.

"Halt! Put your hands over..." said one of them, before a flash of recognition came over his features, and he relaxed, pointing his gun at the sky. "Oh, it's you. What's—"

"ESCAPE ATTEMPT. HEADING TO PIER 25. JOANNE SPAULDING. HEAVILY ARMED. DOZEN MANTICORES. ONE HOSTAGE: GIRL IN CHAINS."

"Shit! Okay, noted. We'll be... Wait, who's that?" said the man, noticing Joy for the first time.

"INTERNATIONAL WOMAN'S LIBERATION LEAGUE AGENT."

Confusion played across the man's face. "Woman's Liberation... What the Abyss is—"

"WASTING TIME NOW."

"Yes, right," said the man, who Joy supposed must be one of these new KIB Special Operations people, and turned to the rest of his team. "Okay, let's move it, people. Going to intercept, stay alert."

He trotted off, past the gaping hole in the wall where the Triads had broken through, the rest of his team in tow. Joy was watching them go, when she felt the Red Specter grab her by the shoulders, spin her around so she was facing him, his mask inches away from her face. In the dim light, his goggles were black mirrors, so she could see herself looking thoroughly intimidated.

"YOU," he growled, the harsh gravel sound echoing from his mask. "HAVE MADE A HUGE MESS."

"Uhhh..." She said, remembering her errant boat flare from earlier. What had Benny said? Torched half the docks? Was there any good way to try and explain that was an accident?

The Specter leaned in, and she leaned back, wondering what kind of trouble she was in, only to see him relent.

"GOALS ADMIRABLE," he said, and poked her hard in the sternum. "NEXT TIME, BE MORE CAREFUL."

"Uh, yeah," she said, putting on what she hoped was her best inoffensive smile. "Careful is good. Definitely need more of that."

"DEFINITELY," said the Specter, and hopped down to the street. Joy eyed the distance and prepared to follow, until she realized she didn't have to. Did she?

"You'll catch them, won't you?" she called out. "And Lin Lin! Promise me you'll rescue her."

The masked figure turned back to gaze up at her. "THE RED SPECTER ALWAYS PREVAILS."

And then he was off, heading in a different direction than the Special Operations agents. Was that an intercept course? Or maybe a flanking maneuver?

Whatever. It didn't matter. Wasn't her business. She was done for the night. The Red Specter and the KIB would rescue Lin Lin. She had to trust them. If she followed, she'd only end up getting in their way.

Joy sat down on the bent-over tin panel and took a moment to catch her breath. What now? She looked up to the sky, to the stars fading under the light of the encroaching dawn. Then she looked over to the spire of the Kovidhian temple, rearing up over the rest of the city skyline. Hsiu Mei and Mrs. Jakuba waited for her there. And Lin Lin would join them shortly. Man, she had a story for them. Though maybe she should edit out some of the really scary bits, for Mrs. Jakuba's sake. And then she'd be fussing for weeks about Joy's super-dangerous reporter job, not that being a reporter was normally this dangerous—it was just this whacko assignment...

Joy's whole train of thought came to a screeching halt as she realized something. Something important. The whole reason she'd gotten into this mess in the first place.

She'd met the Red Specter. She'd stared him in the eyes. She'd even talked to him.

And she'd forgotten to ask for an interview.

Joy leapt down to the alleyway and tore off in a dead sprint in the direction she'd last seen the Specter, determined to chase him down.

Chapter 47:

I'm Helping!

The Red Specter wasn't an easy man to spot. Joy turned the corner and caught a bare flicker of motion heading off into an alleyway. There was no way to be sure that was him, but she chased after it nonetheless. She could not let him get away.

Across the docks, Joy heard a chorus of yelling, punctuated with sporadic cracks. Must be the Triads and the KIB exchanging fire. Joy resolved to stay clear of them if possible, though the Specter seemed to be taking them closer. Already Joy felt her lungs burning from the effort of her sprint, but she resolved to dig deeper, for just a little longer. All she had to do was reach a point where she could keep him in her sights, while keeping out of sight herself. And then, once the whole fracas had ended, she could—

Joy turned another corner and ran right into the Red Specter's chest. She bounced off, and would've fallen if he hadn't grabbed her by the shoulders.

"WHAT'S WRONG?" He said. "YOU BEING CHASED?"

Beneath the odd gravelly rumble, the Specter's voice carried notes of genuine concern. Not really an impassive ghost—that was nice, but now she needed to catch her breath.

"Ih…" she gasped. "Inter… view…"

"WHAT?"

Joy bent over, took several long, deep breaths, forcing herself to calm down and compose her thoughts. This was her shot, and she had to make it count. Think calm, cool, and professional.

Joy straightened back up and stuck out her hand. "Forgive me, but I just realized that we've never been formally introduced. My name is Joy Song Fan, and I'm a freelance reporter working on assignment for the Dodona Gazette. And we'd really appreciate it if you'd agree to sit down for an interview for our paper, to let the public know a bit more about the man behind the mask—let them hear your side of the story. How does that sound?"

Joy gazed up hopefully into the blank glass circles of his goggles, awaiting his reply. It took longer than she'd have hoped for. He just stood and stared.

"YOU GOTTA BE FUCKING KIDDING ME."

The filter on the Red Specter's mask couldn't hide his exasperation. Joy found it interesting that his voice rose about an octave. She pressed on.

"Oh, I assure you, this is no joke, Mr. Specter. Is it okay if I call you that? I mean, calling you 'Red' sounds odd, but—"

"NO SUCH THING AS WOMEN'S LIBERATION LEAGUE, IS THERE?"

"Sure there is," she quipped. "As of several hours ago. I'm the President, Treasurer, Secretary, and founding member. Now, about that inter—"

"REALLY EX-KIB?"

"Yes, I really am," she said. "Though I wasn't an agent; I was an analyst. Translator. But I took a whole bunch of the Supplement Field Training Courses—"

"GO HOME!" The Specter snapped, pointing back to the city.

"Well, of course I'll be happy to go home," said Joy, keeping polite and professional. "Just as soon as I can get a firm commitment to an interview—"

"KIND OF BUSY NOW!"

"Well, of course you are," said Joy, letting some of her irritation through. "Or you should be, but instead you're standing around talking to me. We need to get moving and rescue Lin Lin!"

"BUT... YOU STOPPED ME!"

"No I didn't. I was chasing you and you stopped on your own," Joy pointed out. "I was just making sure I didn't lose sight of you before I got my interview, which is important, but we can save that for after you've finished doing your whole Red

Specter thing. Now hurry up and catch those crooks already. Don't worry about me, I'll be right behind you."

"BUT—"

"Less jawing, more stepping," said Joy, borrowing a phrase from one of her KIB instructors. "Before they can make it to their steamship and maybe get away or something. Rescue first, interview second. Where's your priorities, man?"

The Red Specter leaned in and glared at her, held up a finger like he was about to say something. Joy wasn't intimidated this time. This was her job. The Specter seemed to realize this, clenched his fist in frustration, and took off running, with Joy in pursuit.

"THAT SHIP WON'T ESCAPE," he growled over his shoulder. "AND THE RED SPECTER DOESN'T DO INTERVIEWS."

"Well, I think the Red Specter isn't considering the many benefits of a good interview," she yelled back, as he began to pull away from her. "Because if the Red Specter doesn't control his own public image, other people are going to seize on that opportunity to create their own media narrative, and..."

Joy had to cut her spiel short as the Red Specter clambered up a wall of cargo crates and disappeared over the top. She attacked the wall just like she was on a Caliburn course, and found it to be not so hard as all that, so long as she remembered not to use her injured pinky for anything. From her new vantage point she saw where the Specter was headed and ran along the top of the wall in pursuit.

They'd nearly reached the dock for the Joanne Spaulding. She saw the paddle steamship rocking in the water, next to the crane golem and the maze of cargo containers beyond that. Although that maze had been greatly altered, with the nearest section of it transformed into piles of blackened refuse—though it in no way could be described as "half the dock being burned down." It wasn't nearly that bad—way to exaggerate, Benny!

As if summoned, Benny and a cluster of his men came into view, staging a running retreat down the dock towards the Joanne

412

Spaulding. Shiori was with him, easy to spot with her black-and-pink flag draped over her armor, along with Daphne — and there was Lin Lin. One of the Triad goons had her tossed over his shoulder. The rear of their procession was a loose line of machine-gun-toting Triad men finding cover points and exchanging fire with the KIB agents, while a couple of them ran ahead and boarded the Joanne Spaulding.

The roar of the gunfire strung together in a continuous chorus. Some of the Triad gunmen didn't seem to know how to use their weapons properly, blasting out extended salvos of bullets, burning through ammo too quickly. The continuous kick of the automatic rifles was probably causing them to fire over their targets' heads. Even Joy knew you were supposed to use short bursts. She hoped that might tip things back in the KIB's favor, because otherwise they seemed badly outgunned.

Joy saw the Red Specter turn another corner, and she half-climbed, half-jumped her way down the cargo wall. The maneuver forced her to take her eyes off her quarry for a second, and she looked back up to find that he'd vanished. Panic sent a burst of energy to her legs, and she zipped off towards the location where she'd last seen him. She found him in the cleared area surrounding the crane golem, tried to close the gap, and had nearly made it to the base of the crane golem when she realized she was following farther than she'd originally intended — that she should've stayed under cover in the stacks of cargo.

Well, it was too late now, so when the Specter began to climb the ladder up to the control cab, Joy decided to follow, glancing back towards the firefight by the steamship. It wasn't going well. Men on the Joanne Spaulding had shoved cargo crates off the side of the deck onto the pier below. They'd cracked open upon impact, piles of heavy burlap sacks forming a barricade. The Triad gunners made the most of their new defense line. Just rearranging a few of those sacks gave them a terrific fortified position to hold until the Joanne Spaulding could be prepared to move out. Already there were small puffs of soot exiting the steamship's high smokestack. They were going to get away! And what was the Red Specter doing climbing up a crane while all this was going on?

Joy felt some of the heat from the crane golem's smokestack from the other side of the ladder. Large steam engines, for ships, trains, or golems would normally be left running on 'low steam' mode, rather than switched off—they could take hours to heat up from cold. But the crane's engine seemed to be more active than that. Joy realized that it had a container dangling from its right claw, a few yards off the ground. The crew must've heard gunfire and abandoned their posts mid-job, relying on the analytical engine to safely maintain the boiler pressure. It made sense—no job was worth getting shot over. The thought flicked across her mind just long enough to make her pause mid-climb. Maybe, after all this had ended, she should sit down and re-evaluate her priorities.

The Red Specter reached the top of the high ladder, something like thirty feet in the air, right below the control cab. He pulled out his grapple-gun, aimed it at one of the crane golem's outstretched claws, and fired. Joy watched in awe as the Red Specter leaped out into space and soared across the docks, swinging around to pounce upon the Triad barricade from behind.

One of the Triad men saw him coming and cowered back, pointed and screamed as the Specter released his cable and flew the rest of the distance, trench-coat billowing out behind him like wings. It was insane, charging into a tight group of armed gunmen, and Joy was sure the Specter would get shot to pieces, or gang-tackled when he landed. But half of the men didn't react properly. Instead of charging him, or lining up their shots, they shrank back. One of them even dropped his gun, and Joy, remembering Chen's reaction from earlier that day, began to realize the practical benefits to the Red Specter's ghostly persona. It was psychological warfare, meticulously carried out over the past few weeks, with carefully planned attacks and abductions, sapping the enemy's morale, terrorizing them

414

to point that in a direct confrontation, they'd freeze up instead of shooting.

But some of the gangsters were made of tougher stuff, recovering from their shock quickly, swinging their rifles around to get a bead on this new threat. But the Specter was already attacking, drawing his weapons from over his shoulder, that sword with the odd hilt and his combination buckler-baton; just like in the comics. They blurred as the Specter closed in on his prey with terrifying speed. At close range, the Triad men had a split-second to decide between trying to shoot or swinging their Manticores like clubs, and neither choice ended up being effective. Joy heard a scream and saw one of the gangsters drop his machine-gun and clutch at his hand. She saw a small piece of flesh flop away from the Manticore as it clattered across the dock. Was that a severed thumb?

Joy averted her gaze from the sight, just in time to catch another flurry of movement, from a tugboat moored at the end of the pier, on the opposite side of the Joanne Spaulding. Six Kallistrate frogmen lunged out from beneath a tarp on the deck, closing in on Benny's group trying to board the gangplank. The frogmen reached Daphne first, who calmly turned, kicked the lead man in the head, and managed to pistol-whip the second before getting tackled to the dock. But Benny booted that frogman off her, and then it was a full scrum between the two groups.

Joy's astonishment that Daphne was able to hold her own against real Kallistrate Army frogmen lasted only a second, before a thunderous peal of gunfire pulled Joy's attention back to the barricades. One of the gangsters had completely lost it, opening up full auto in a desperate attempt to stop the relentless demon tearing through their ranks. He drained his ammo drum in seconds, then watched in horror as his three buddies keeled over, while the Red Specter remained standing. The ghost stepped over the corpses, slowly stalked towards the gunman. The terrified gangster tried firing more shots from the empty gun, backed away, tripped over a sack of rice, scrabbled backwards on his butt, threw his useless Manticore at the advancing Specter, and missed.

Joy winced. She'd realized that the Red Specter's slow stalking routine was a performance to hide the pain of getting shot. She'd seen it at the warehouse. The Specter's armor might stop the bullets from piercing his flesh, but the energy from the impact must be like getting hit by a hammer. He was walking it off. It looked like he'd used one of the Triad-men as a meat shield, but Manticore bullets could penetrate all the way through a man's body. Some of them must've hit. The Red Specter closed in on his cowering target and lashed out with his sword, smiting the gangster in the head. Joy steeled herself for a fountain of blood and brains, but the Triad man just fell over, head intact. She noticed that the Specter had shifted his grip to strike with the blunt back edge of the sword. In fact, none of the fallen gangsters had any slices across their heads or torsos, just their extremities.

But there was no time to admire the Red Specter's restraint, for Shiori Rosewing had joined the fight, and she wasn't scared of his reputation one bit. She threw a dagger at him, which he barely deflected with his buckler, but she'd already closed the distance and drove him back with one powerful strike after another. His stiff, strained reactions told Joy that he was still hurt from the Manticore shots, and then two more Triad men with pistols swung up beside Shiori, getting clear lines of fire, and opened up on him.

The Specter barely reacted as the bullets slammed into him, and the gunmen shrank back, staring at each other in bafflement, but he staggered and swayed as Shiori pressed her attack, barely able to hold her off.

Joy saw Benny, a somewhat-mussed-up Daphne, and the rest of their entourage boarding the gangplank to the Joanne Spaulding. The frogmen all lay on the pier, either writhing in pain, or completely motionless. One of the thugs still had Lin Lin. Benny glanced back to the barricade, sent some more of his men to aid Shiori, and headed up the gangplank to board his steamship.

Everything had gone wrong. The good guys were losing. The bad guys were winning. She had to do something. Joy remembered where she was, looked up to the control cab above her. Well, it was worth a shot. She climbed the rest of the way up, hoping that the fleeing crane operator hadn't bothered to lock the door behind him. He hadn't! Joy slipped inside and gave herself a second or two to figure out the controls.

The crane golem was orders of magnitude simpler than the military steam golem, with its vast array of switches and dials. This had a meager handful of pressure and temperature gauges. Joy had no trouble finding the blinking display light that read STANDBY. She hit the big green ACTIVATE button below it, and she was in business.

Joy found that pressing each foot-pedal would rotate the crane in the corresponding direction; that was much simpler than the complex foot-tread drive system for a full steam golem. The arm controls were more intuitive as well—two control-sticks mounted on scale models of the crane arms, attached to the pilot's chair at around shoulder-level. Each control-stick had three ring-triggers, which corresponded to the operator's index finger, middle finger and thumb, allowing fine control of the crane golem's three-fingered claws. Her hands were a bit small for the rings, but found that she could manage them well enough, despite the pain from her left pinky every time she shifted her grip. That was practically background noise for her at this point. She had to stretch to push down on the pedals, which annoyed her, but she didn't have time to figure out how to adjust the seat.

Joy noted the golem still held a large container crate in its right hand, only it had been smashed into other piles of cargo. Testing the foot pedals had done that. Whoops. She flexed her fingers against the control rings, and the giant steel digits opened. The crate tumbled free, crashed to the docks, tipped over, and splashed into the harbor. Joy didn't pause to watch it sink. Hopefully there wasn't anything important in there. She swung the crane golem around to bring the duel between the Shiori and the Red Specter into view of the floor-to-ceiling glass front of the control cab, and reached out to grab Shiori with one of the huge claws.

The former Caliburn knight saw it coming and leapt back as the claw closed around empty air. Joy frowned. The military golem simulator had been much more responsive than this thing. She aimed another grab at Shiori, missed again. Already she felt the strain on her arms, pushing at the control-sticks to try and make them go faster, while the crane's hydraulics whined in protest. She supposed a machine designed for cargo loading, as opposed to dragon-fighting, wouldn't be engineered with fast reflexes as a priority. Fine—she could try this another way.

She kept her left claw interposed between Shiori and the Specter, put her right claw on the opposite side of her and the other Triad gangsters, and slowly brought her hands together. She'd force them to jump off the pier if they didn't want to get squished. Not that she was going to try to actually squish them, she just—

The staccato roar of one of the Manticores cut her train of thought short, as spiderwebs sprouted all over the glass in front of her face. Joy shrieked, instinctively throwing her hands up for protection. But the control sticks wouldn't move fast enough, and instead her whole body slid down in the seat, making her stomp down hard on the right foot-pedal. The cab spun around and around, until Joy calmed down enough to stop it, putting the back of the cab between her and the shooters.

That would be another big difference between a crane and a military golem. A real steam golem would have an armored cockpit, not a bunch of glass. Joy stared at the bullet holes in front of her and wondered why she wasn't dead. She looked behind her and saw more holes, most of them in a cluster where the roof and the back of the cab met. One of them had put a neat circle through the top of the headrest, still adjusted for someone much taller than Joy. Good thing too. The shooter had been firing low to high, with a gun that kicked up. It was Joy's lucky day, ha ha.

Whatever. She needed to see, and the glass in front of her was a mass of white fractures. Joy shifted back into position on the chair, and carefully brought one of the crane's claws around until its index finger pointed at the broken glass. It put Joy in a surreal position with the control-sticks, like she was going to poke herself in the face. She pulled her legs up and tried to shrink back in the seat as much as she could, as she brought the massive steel digit in, piercing the ruined windshield and raking up and down to clear the glass shards away. Joy felt a sting on her shin as one of the shards nicked her, but that was the worst of it. The cab floor was covered in broken glass now, but she was able to use the soles of her sandals to brush the foot-pedals clear without further injury.

Now she could see again, but what could she do without armor? The sight of the huge steel claw hovering a foot away from the cab gave her an idea. She rotated the claw so two of its fingers pointed skyward, palm facing her, then pressed it up close to the cab. Now she had armor. She spun back around to resume the attack. First, she spotted the KIB pressing the attack on the Triad's barricade, which she demolished with a swipe of her claw. The big drawback to her new armor was that it blocked her line of sight. She had to spread the fingers apart and lower her protective claw in order to pick a target, and then strike half-blind, as she hastily covered up to block retaliation shots. She saw Triads fleeing up the gangplank and swung at them. The sounds of screeching metal, banging, splashes, and screaming suggested that she'd hit. Joy searched for another target, and something pinged off the inside of the crane's fingers and lodged in the roof. Joy looked down to see Shiori, then looked up to see one of her throwing knives.

While part of her had to be impressed that the Caliburn had even been able to hurl a knife that distance, the other flailed out

419

in a rage, raking her attack claw down in an overhand smash as she was raising her shield claw up. Joy saw just enough to realize she'd overextended her swipe, as her claw pierced through a huge container of dirt lying on the deck of the Joanne Spaulding, and dragged it over the edge, to spill its contents onto the pier below. Or at least, that's what she thought. Joy lowered her claw enough to check, waggling the cab side-to-side as she did, to deny anybody a clear shot.

There was a huge pile of dirt on the pier, and more had spilled into the water. No sign of Shiori, and a sudden breeze from the harbor told Joy that what she'd spilled wasn't dirt. It was fertilizer.

But never mind what it was—it might interfere with KIB forces storming the ship. Joy reached over to clear the mess when she realized the ship was moving. It was pulling away from the pier. She had to stop it!

Joy lunged out with her right claw, shoving against the control-stick with all of her might, willing it to go faster, to make that grab before it was too late. Desperately, she grasped for the fleeing ship, saw her claw come down, barely catching it at the widest part of its hull, the back edge of the paddle wheel.

The steel digits ripped through the top of the cowl and snagged the steel paddle on the upward rotation, crumpling three of them together before the wheel screeched to a halt. The other paddle kept going, churning up a high spray of water on the opposite side of the ship. Joy tried to pull the steamship back in, but the metal of the crumpled paddles started to shriek and deform, and she realized she was in danger of ripping out her handhold.

She extended the crane arm to relieve the pressure and get a better grip on the ship. It worked: she saw the claw hook something a bit more solid, but Joanne Spaulding surged forward as she did, and now the golem arm was stretched out further, with weaker leverage. Now what?

Joy saw men scrambling across the deck of the captured ship, pointing at her. With guns.

She raised her shield hand to cover the cab. As bullets pinged off the heavy steel, Joy craned her neck to get a peek at the ship. She heard more metal shrieks and the sound of snapping wood. If she wasn't careful, the golem claw would rip through the hull again, and the Joanne Spaulding would get away.

A further issue was the shuddering and lurching of the cab itself. It occurred to Joy that this crane had been built to pick things up and set them down, so it was strong in the vertical direction—but this sideways shearing force was something else entirely. Joy was suddenly very aware of how high up she was, as the steel beneath her groaned, and the entire crane began to lean out towards the harbor. Joy felt her stomach lurch, and she let the gripping arm extend out, like a fisherman with a huge catch. Don't let the line snap. Keep it here until the KIB and the Specter can catch up. Then there was a huge reverberating bang, her gripping claw met resistance, and all the gunfire stopped. Joy lowered her shield claw enough to take a peek.

The Joanne Spaulding had skewed around diagonally, its asymmetric thrust combined with the crane grip causing it to grind against the pier on its right, while its butt had smacked into another cargo ship moored to the adjacent pier on the left. The gangsters on deck had been thrown off their feet by the impact. Joy saw a plume of spray shoot up from the far side of the ship, and it surged forward some more, at an angle to the docks, its front swinging around the end of the pier, its tail end jostling and grinding across the other ship.

But the Joanne Spaulding's bid for freedom was hampered by its wide hips, which flared out to accommodate the paddle wheels. The angled deck crashed into the corner of the pier, and the whole ship slewed around, rocking from side-to-side as it shoved against the ocean in a way that boats were never designed to do. It gave her an idea.

She ripped further into the steamship's hull until she caught a solid point— the mangled axle of the paddle-wheel, twisted, and shoved the claw arm against the side of the steamship, trying to amplify its momentum. The Joanne Spaulding fishtailed around the end of the pier, sending out waves that washed over the docks. Joy even tried lifting up on the axle as she pushed, hoping to reduce the resistance of the water against the hull, and the ship listed way over to the side, even as its nose swung around to point back at the docks.

The crane golem shuddered and shook, thrashing Joy around in her seat, while the entire display console flashed red. It was not engineered to get in wrestling matches with massive cargo steamships and was screaming against the abuse. Well, too bad. Joy kept up the pressure, even as she felt the whole cab list at an increasingly severe angle, the crane golem's steel spine bending under the stress. Instinctively, she tried throwing her shield-hand out for counterbalance, even as she hauled on the steamship, trying to drag it up onto the docks. The massive vessel crunched against the tugboat, shoved it under the pier as it flew by, engines steaming full.

By the time the captain thought to reverse engines, it was too late. The prow of the Joanne Spaulding crashed into the dock, sending up a cascade of exploding wood planks and splinters as the entire ship rose up, and Joy felt a violent shock as the crane golem's spine snapped, both of its arms seized up, and the whole cab tipped over with a horrifying screech. Joy felt her insides go all weird as she experienced a moment of weight-lessness, followed by a jarring impact that threw her sideways. She slammed against the cab door, knocking it open, and felt herself falling out into space.

Fortunately, she still had a death-grip on the control sticks, though she still might've fallen if not for the ring-triggers. It was a mixed blessing, as pain shot through her wrists and captured fingers, as they took the entirety of her weight at an awkward angle. None of this was doing her mangled pinky any favors, either. All the windshield fragments spilled out from the cab floor, rushing past to shatter on the ground below with a tinkling chorus, signaling an end to the symphony of destruction.

422

The remnants of the crane golem formed a lopsided tripod, with the control cab at the apex, and the two arms and spine as the legs. The spine hadn't been completely severed—it had been bent over midway, twisted at an extreme angle, still hanging by a thread, while the right claw lay tangled in the wreckage of the Joanne Spaulding's paddle wheel. The left arm was splayed out, bent at the elbow, all its weight resting on its wrist. Joy looked down, and found she wasn't too high up, though the ground seemed a bit farther than she'd care to drop, especially onto a concrete surface covered in broken glass.

She just hung there for a minute, trying to shift the grip on her right hand to something that wasn't too painful on her fingers. Then she began the tricky work of freeing her hands from the rings without losing her grip entirely. After a few nerve-wracking moments, she succeeded at climbing up through the empty hole of the broken windshield to rest on the upward-facing side of the cab. From here she got a good view of the devastation she'd wrought—the massive hole in the dock with a giant steamship lodged in the middle, bow tipped up, propped up on the wreckage of more cargo and equipment; the capsized tugboat; not to mention the destroyed crane golem she was sitting on.

Now that the immediate danger had passed, the sight of all this began to worry her. Maybe she'd gone a bit overboard? Just a tad? She started taking an inventory of the destruction: the busted thick wood planks, the mangled ruin of the paddlewheel, the scraped-up hull of the Joanne Spaulding, the twisted frame, bent-over smokestack, and busted drive-train of the crane-golem, and tried to estimate the cost of all this damage. Oh dear.

Well—maybe it would be okay? At least she was still alive. Compared to that, all other problems seemed trivial. She'd worry about the rest of it some other time. And she'd stopped the bad guys from fleeing with Lin Lin. That was what mattered most.

Joy saw motion on the canted deck of the beached steamship. All the remaining Triad gangsters were lining up on their knees, hands behind their heads, while the Red Specter stalked the deck, brandishing his sword and herding them along like a big, scary sheepdog. His charges seemed too dazed and shaken to bother resisting as they staggered out of the ship's interior. KIB agents scaled up ropes on the side of the ship. When they reached the top, they went down the line and started binding the criminals' hands behind their back. A sudden chorus of yelling rang out as one of thugs emerged escorting a hostage. Joy had an anxious few seconds, wondering if there'd be some kind of standoff, but the Triad man had no will for that, and surrendered peacefully. But Lin Lin cowered back from all the strange, shouting men, particularly the Red Specter.

In the morning light, Joy saw that he actually did have a red skull pattern on his mask. It wasn't painted on—it was a separate layer of material colored a deep, dark red—not nearly as bright as the comic version, but it was there. But it certainly didn't inspire trust. The Specter seemed to realize this and step back, but Lin Lin had no reason to trust a bunch of strange men in uniform, either. Joy stood up and began to wave and shout.

It took a minute to get their attention, but Lin Lin's face lit up when she saw her. Somehow Joy managed to convey that things were okay now, as best she could over the awkward distance, and Lin Lin allowed that nice KIB officer to take her into custody. The Specter looked her way, and gave her a brief nod, before returning to his business.

Joy let out a long sigh. She felt a lot better. At least she'd managed to do one thing right. And since the Red Specter didn't seem to be in any hurry to leave, maybe she could corner him and try to wrangle an interview. It was worth a shot.

Carefully, Joy picked her way down to the ground, being careful not to jostle her injured pinky too much. She picked the shortest route, via the left arm, since she didn't like the looks of the tangled mess at the end of the right. Wisps of smoke still trailed out of the ruined smokestack, and Joy had a short rush of anxiety when she considered what the state of the steam engine might be. But the whole thing was controlled by an analytical engine at the base, which should be smart enough to do an automatic emergency shutdown. After all, it was a spin-off of military hardware, where catastrophic failure was an expected event, right?

Even so, Joy decided to get the hell away from the destroyed crane golem just in case the worst happened and the boiler did go kablooie. So she picked a circuitous route through the ruins of the cargo maze on her way to the Joanne Spaulding. She made it to about twenty-five yards from the cluster of KIB agents gathered around the wrecked ship, when a soggy, smelly armored gauntlet clapped over her mouth and she found her arms pinned to her sides. She managed to tip her head enough to spot her attacker, then wished she hadn't.

For Joy found herself looking up into the eyes of Shiori Rosewing. She was sopping wet, she smelled like shit, and she did not look happy.

"Funny how we keep meeting like this," Shiori whispered, and Joy knew there was nothing about Shiori's sense of humor that she wanted any part of. Unfortunately, her opinions were moot, as the renegade Caliburn dragged her off through a narrow gap in the cargo containers, deeper into the maze, out of sight of anyone who could help her.

Chapter 48:

Showdown

They kept going until they reached another clearing, a wide aisle in the stacks of cargo, where fallen debris had cut off both ends. Joy didn't bother to struggle. She'd seen what Shiori could do, and what she was willing to do. Shiori wasn't Yang or Chen. She was in a completely different league. And Joy was just too exhausted to even consider fighting.

She had a tiny bit of hope left, based on the fact that she was still alive. Shiori could have killed her already, easily — and she hadn't. It was a faint hope, but it was something. She tried to cling to that as Shiori shoved her up against a pile of burlap sacks, hand still clenched around Joy's jaw, holding her mouth shut.

"I suppose you're wondering why I've brought you here — what I've got in store for you," Shiori said.

Joy felt just the barest loosening of Shiori's grip. It was enough to allow her to nod her head.

"Well, what we've got here is a bit of a lesson," said the former Caliburn. "This is where amateur do-gooders start to learn how the world really works. And what happens when they start to think they can get away with messing with the pros."

Shiori paused to let the weight of that sink in. Then she made a snapping motion with her free hand, and a knife appeared. Shiori brought it up to Joy's cheek and let it rest there, on the side that wasn't covered by her gauntlet.

"Did you think it would be fun?" She continued. "Did you think you could cross the Triads and get away with it? Did you think you could dirty my face like that? Try and hit me with a crane? Cover me in shit — twice — and just walk away? Who the fuck do you think you are?"

Joy tried to shake her head, deny it—the first time hadn't even been her fault, and the second time had been a semi-accident. She hadn't even seen the impact—she'd been hiding behind the claw-shield. But she saw the results, that Shiori stank and had been dunked in the harbor at some point; that despite her dunking, she still had gritty, gooey remnants of fertilizer lodged between the segments of her armor and smeared all over her precious Rosedeath cape. Her sword-on-a-pole weapon, on the other hand, appeared to be in fine shape, clipped to the back of her armor somehow.

"Nobody crosses me. Nobody crosses Shiori Rosewing. That's me. The Hemlock Witch. The Butcher of Brentonsville. That name used to mean something. Used to command respect. Before that insipid comic came out."

Shiori's face twisted at the thought. "Is that it, huh? You a comics fan? Think reality works like that? Foil the hapless witch's schemes every week, then skip off into the sunset? Is that what you thought? Huh?"

Joy still couldn't reply or shake her head in denial, though she hoped her efforts to do so conveyed that message to Shiori. And where had this rant about comics come from? All Joy had ever thought about was saving the girls and getting an interview. She hadn't been thinking about Benny or Shiori or their reputations at all. Why did Shiori have to make it all about her? And why wasn't Shiori letting her say anything, apologize? She'd be happy to—

Shiori leaned in, until the crest of her helmet pressed against Joy's forehead. "You scared now? You wondering what I'm gonna do now? Thinking maybe you're gonna die?"

Joy could only tremble in fear and gaze back at Shiori with wide, terrified eyes. That seemed to be the Caliburn's desired response.

"Well, guess what? I'm not gonna kill you," said Shiori, and Joy felt a brief wave of relief before she saw Shiori's vicious grin as she continued.

"I'm gonna do way worse than that."

Joy trembled under Shiori's grip, as she tried to avoid speculating about exactly what a wanted war criminal would consider to be 'worse than death,' and failed. Shiori snickered, apparently able to guess what she was thinking.

"You know what your deal is? I been watching you, and I can tell. You're vain."

Joy's confusion gave her a brief respite from her terror. *Vain*? Sure, she wouldn't claim to be free of faults, but of all the things to berate herself for, *vanity* wouldn't even be in the—

"Oh, you don't see it? You don't agree?" Shiori said, leering over her. "That's funny. It's funny how people are blind to their biggest flaws, when they're dead obvious to everyone else. Through that whole ordeal at the warehouse, I saw you get really mad one time, so mad you totally forgot where you were. You remember that?"

Getting constantly asked questions while being prevented from answering was frustrating, and Shiori knew that. But Joy had to try to think of the answer, or what Shiori thought was the answer. Joy was sure she'd been the most upset when Benny had been threatening to bite off Lin-Lin's fingers, but what that had to do with vanity was beyond—

"I'm twenty-six years old, dammit!" said Shiori, in a screechy falsetto, that sounded nothing like Joy's real voice, though she guessed it was supposed to.

"Of all the things to get mad about," said Shiori, snickering at her. "I wasn't even serious—I was just messing with those pedophile pigs, but you got soooo mad, didn't you?"

Oh, so she really hadn't looked like a little kid in her suit? She'd been kidding. That was…That was a relief? Even now? Joy felt a flush rise to her cheeks at the idea that a war criminal might be right about her.

"And when you were getting worked over—you took the punches okay. And you hated getting your finger cranked, but you didn't really start freaking out until I threatened to cut off your ear," said Shiori. "As soon as I threatened to ruin your pretty face—total panic time."

Well, of course I did. Amputation of anything would be scarier than a broken finger. A broken finger could heal up, but if something got cut off, that was it. That didn't have anything to do with vanity, it was just—

"So, that's how it's gonna go," said Shiori. "I'll leave you alive, but not until after I start cutting. We'll start with your ears. Then your nose. Then both eyes. Then maybe I'll carve out something on your cheeks. Haven't decided on what yet, whether it'll be a message, or a little doodle, or whatever. Maybe I'll get inspired. I'll save your tongue for last, so when you have to beg for help—which you'll be spending the rest of your life doing—whoever you cling to is gonna have a bitch of a time figuring out what the fuck you're asking for. I wonder who that's gonna be, if anybody? You got a boyfriend? Think he'll be willing to stick around nursing what's left of you when I'm done? I bet he won't. But we'll see, won't we?"

Joy gazed in horror as the knife twirled about in front of her face. This couldn't be happening. This wasn't fair. It wasn't right. And her terror had nothing to do with excessive vanity, either. Anyone would hate losing their speech and sight, and... and getting disfigured. Anyone would.

And so what if Joy cared about her appearance and wanted to look good? That was common. It wasn't her defining trait. It didn't drive her actions. A person driven by vanity would've never gotten herself into this situation to begin with. If anything, Shiori was the vain one—she was the one prepared to torture someone over an insult. Over a smear to her reputation. Talk about angry—Shiori got the maddest over how she was portrayed in a comic strip. This was projection! All projection! And stupid! If Shiori really cared about her reputation so much, the best thing to do was...

A bolt of inspiration hit Joy, and she struggled against her captor's grip, pleaded with her eyes. If she could just get her mouth free for a second, just a bare second, she had a chance. Just give her a chance! A chance to say one thing.

"Eh, what's this?" Shiori said, "You got something to say? Maybe you want to beg for mercy, huh?"

Joy made what muffled noises she could with the gauntlet over her mouth, and continued to beg with her eyes. Whatever answer gave her the opportunity to speak. That one. That was her answer.

"Or maybe you want to scream for help," said Shiori speculatively. "Maybe you think I'll just kill you then, instead of forcing you to live as a freak. Well, that won't work. I'll just have to work faster, is all. Sloppier. But maybe you'd prefer that, huh? Well, you know what? I'll be generous. You've got guts, if nothing else. But this better be good."

The vise grip on Joy's mouth relaxed. She would get her chance to speak. Joy couldn't waste this. She took a deep breath, looked Shiori square in the eyes, and said,

"How would you like an interview?"

Shiori stared back at her. "What?"

"Hello I don't think we've been formally introduced My name is Joy Song Fan freelance reporter working for the Dodona Gazette and I'd love to do an in-depth interview for the paper so the world can learn about the real Shiori Rosewing instead of some fake four-color tramp and—"

"Reporter?" Shiori narrowed her eyes at Joy. "We already went through this. That's your cover—"

"No, no—it's not!" Joy said. "That's the truth, it really is. But nobody believed it, and you started hurting me, saying 'tell the truth,' but I already *was* telling the truth, so then I had to start lying, to make it stop, and..."

"Bullshit," said Shiori. "No reporter does what you did."

"Well, I didn't plan on any of this!" Joy cried. "Not at the outset. I just got an assignment, rumors of Red Specter sightings at the docks, and I'm supposed to interview the witnesses, and so I talk to Madam Zenovia—just about the Specter, not

Benny—and she sends me to the Joanne Spaulding, and then Yang and Chen start harassing me, Chen freaks out when I mention the Red Specter, and then him and Yang started brawling, so of course I ran, and then they're chasing me, so I run and find a hiding place, except, hey, someone's already hiding there.

"So now I've found this slave girl in chains, so I go to the Guard, except they're crooked, and in on it, and you show up, cows fall—and I had nothing to do with that, I even tried to warn you—and then Hsiu Mei says her sister's being shipped out tomorrow, and I can't go to the cops, and I can't contact Central in time, so I've got no choice but to rescue them myself, even though I don't really know what I'm doing. So that's what I do, and of course I get caught, and that's really what happened."

Shiori stared at her, mulling things over. "Not a bad story," she said. "I'd almost buy that up until the rescue part. That doesn't make sense. Nobody does that."

Shiori bore down on Joy, bringing the knife up to her ear.

"Wait, why doesn't it make sense?" Joy said, fighting to keep her voice below screaming levels. "I told you, I didn't have any way to contact anyone else. I hadn't actually seen the Red Specter, and I had no idea the KIB was here already. The City Guard was corrupt, so I had no choice—"

"No choice?" Shiori snorted. "Sure you did. You could've skipped town, run to the capital, and ratted us out there. That's what anyone with any sense would've done."

"No, I would've lost Lin Lin—"

"So what?" Shiori countered. "People get lost all the time. Did you even know her?"

"No, but I couldn't..." Joy gasped. "I promised! I promised Hsiu Mei. What would I tell her—"

"Tell her to be grateful at least she got away. You don't owe her anything. It's not your responsibility."

"No, it is! It is! It's my responsibility. Mine!" Joy felt Shiori's blade reach the cut below her ear, still raw from before. It

431

was getting harder to think straight through all the terror and exhaustion. She was babbling.

"Really? And why is that?"

"Because... because I'm the big sister."

"What? You're not related," said Shiori. "Or are you changing your story again?"

"No! No—but I just told them. Call me Big Sister. Because—"

"What, that?" Shiori sneered. "That's just a custom. *You* know. The Triad boys are non-stop with that shit, 'Big Brother' this, 'Little Brother' that. They do that with me, too, in case you didn't notice."

"Huh?" Joy hadn't noticed that, unless... "Ah Nei Wei, is that—"

"Aneue," Shiori interrupted. "Ah. Nay. Ooh. Ay. It's a nice, *respectful* Zipangese word for 'Big Sister.' But it ain't the same as real family, and you know that. It ain't no reason to go on a fool suicide mission."

"Yes, it is! To me, it is. It's everything. It's who I am. I'm the eldest. I am. It's my job to look after everyone else. Always mine, for as long as I can remember. Always me, always my responsibility—mine! And every time... every time something went wrong, it was always my fault. I always had to set a good example. I always had to look out for everyone else. I had to order them around, even when they hated it. I had to be the nosy, bossy bitch up in everyone else's business, or I got yelled at, so that's what I did, even when they hated it and I hated it and it wasn't fair and I got so fucking sick of all that fucking bullshit that I moved away to a whole 'nother city where I don't know anyone and no one knows me and I'm free and all alone and poor and miserable and I miss them all so fucking bad...."

Joy began to sob, unable to stop the tears rolling down her face, barely even noticing when Shiori released her, letting her slump to the ground.

Well, she'd learned a new thing about herself, hadn't she? Though she wouldn't recommend exhaustion and threats of torture as a therapy substitute. As her tears began to subside, she noticed Shiori staring down at her.

"Man," said Shiori. "You are seriously fucked up, you know that?"

Joy flipped her off, too drained to care about the consequences. Shiori just laughed.

"You're really a reporter, huh?"

"Yeah, really."

"Well, then—suppose I believe you." Shiori grabbed Joy, hauled her back to her feet, and shoved her back against the wall of cargo. "That still doesn't give me a reason not to mutilate your sorry ass. I had a really sweet deal here, and now its all been blown to the Abyss. You know how hard it is to find an employer as good as Benny in this business?"

Joy stared at Shiori. "He thinks he's a damned shark."

The Caliburn knight stopped to consider that, but dismissed it with a shrug. "Eh, so he's eccentric, so what? It works for him, don't it? I mean, you seen his house? Even the toilets got gold on 'em. Dude's got so much money he literally craps on it. Can you imagine that?"

"I'd... rather not," said Joy, wincing. "But still... those teeth— you've got to admit, that's pretty extreme, right?"

"Extreme whatever," said Shiori. "He says he's got a shark soul. Well, maybe he does and maybe he don't. What do I care? Benny knows how to treat people. Doesn't matter who you are or where you're from—as long as you get results, Benny's got your back. Or he did."

Shiori narrowed her eyes, leaned back in. "Until you came along, and now it's all blown to the Abyss."

"Wait, me?" Joy protested. "I barely had anything to do with it. It was the Red Specter and the KIB. They were messing with you before I arrived."

Shiori's vicious expression didn't change, and Joy decided to try another tack. "Besides which, hurting me won't get your job back, will it? Benny succeeded by using people—letting them do what they're good at, right? You should be like him. You want the world to respect you—the real Shiori Rosewing. I can help with that."

"I dunno," growled Shiori. "It'd have to be a lot of help to make up for losing what I got. And for all the shit you've dumped on me. Literally."

"The first time wasn't me. And the second time... Well, I had no way of knowing what was in that crate, did I? But that's in the past, right? We should look to the future. Look to the bright side."

"Bright side?" Shiori snarled. "What bright side? Name me one good thing about what's happened."

"Uh... You won't have to put up with Daphne any more?"

"Huh," said Shiori, and Joy saw the corner of her mouth twitch upward, just ever so slightly. "Okay, I'll give you that one."

Joy saw the opening and pounced on it. "Well, it's not a small thing, is it?"

Joy adopted the haughtiest expression she could, and pitched her voice down an octave. "Oh, Mr. Fang, please—there's no need for you to remind me how perfect I am; I knew that already, you see. I didn't say stop, though."

She mimed adjusting her glasses, and glanced down at an imaginary clipboard. "Such a shame none of your other employees can meet my standards, though. Fortunately for you I was able to compile an extensive list of their shortcomings, which I'll be happy to go over with you later. It shouldn't take long; it's only thirty pages or so."

Shiori started laughing, and Joy started to relax, even as another part of her felt uneasy. Why was that? Why did this feel familiar?

Oh, right—this was exactly the type of thing that had been whispered behind Joy's back while she'd been going through hell at the Journal, and when she'd been job-hunting afterwards. Now she was acting just like those idiot gossips. But these were extreme circumstances. Psychopath with a knife here! She

434

needed to get out of here in one piece—the Sisterhood could take a flying leap.

"You're pretty funny," said Shiori.

"Ah, thanks. I—"

"Which makes me wonder what kind of *funny* stories you're gonna tell about me, as soon as I skip town." Shiori bared her teeth, and the knife came out again. "Maybe you'll decide to tell a really *funny* tale about how you put one over on me. Is that it, huh?"

Crap. She never should have abandoned the Sisterhood, not for an instant. Joy had to think fast. "No! I wouldn't do that—why would I? Because then... you'd come after me, right? And do all those horrible things you said you would. Why would I risk that? Spend my life looking over my shoulder, knowing you'd come after me? That's nuts. I don't want that! Who would?"

"But... that's if you don't mutilate me, right?" Joy continued. "Because if you did, I wouldn't be scared anymore, because I'd have nothing left to lose. I'd write the nastiest things about you that I could, so when you came to kill me, it'd be a relief—because I'm so vain. So, it's your smartest move to... to not hurt me, so I can concentrate on the interview. You can tell me your whole story, and I'll do a fantastic write-up—like my life depended on it, haha. You can even look it over before I turn it in."

"And you'll be getting what you really want—a chance to tell your real story, cement your legacy against all that comic nonsense. It'll make it easier to move forward—get in with another organization, or even start your own gang, or crew, or whatever. Be your own boss. Doesn't that sound nice? Much more useful than just hurting me, right?"

Joy watched Shiori's face, knowing that it held the key to her continued existence. Was she getting through?

"And you can make that happen, huh?" said the Caliburn. "Which paper did you say you worked for?"

"I'm freelance. That means I can sell the story to any of them." Joy saw a skeptical cast to Shiori's expression, and added, "I can definitely guarantee the Gazette will print it, if no one else will."

"Gazette," said Shiori. "Hey, is that the paper that prints all the weird stuff that no one believes?"

"Some people believe it," said Joy. "And you know what? It doesn't even matter. Nobody cares about the truth. Except me."

Joy swallowed her bitterness. She didn't have time for that now. "If a story is good, they'll repeat it—tell their friends about it. And they'll tell their friends, and so on, and after a while, nobody will even remember that it started in the Gazette. It'll just be something everybody knows—the story of the real Shiori Rosewing. Isn't that what you want?"

Shiori looked away, contemplative, and Joy held her breath, awaiting her fate.

"Yeah, okay—you make a decent case," said the Caliburn.. "We'll go with your idea. With one little exception. Hold still."

Shiori grabbed a handful of Joy's hair and shoved her head against a nearby crate, facing sideways.

"What? What are you—mmmph!" Joy felt something forced between her teeth. She looked down to see the cord-wrapped handle of one of Shiori's throwing knives.

"You can bite down on that," said Shiori. "And try to keep the noise to a minimum. You start screaming and the whole deal's off, you understand?"

Joy whined in protest, unable to form any coherent words. What was this? This wasn't the deal.

"What, you think I'd let you off scot-free?" Shiori said. "You convinced me to spare you from the full course, but you still crossed me, and an interview ain't enough to make up for that. There's still a price to be paid. We already started on that ear, now you're going to lose the rest of it."

Shiori snickered at Joy's panicked reaction. "Oh, don't be dramatic. It's just the one ear. It won't ruin your precious looks. You can get your hair styled so it covers that side of your head— maybe even start a new fashion trend. And it ain't gonna hurt you much with getting laid or anything. Trust me, I know guys. I know what they look at, I know what they talk about, and it

436

ain't ears. Bunch of pigs—you'll do fine. And you'll have plenty more left to be scared of losing, so this works out for both of us."

This doesn't work! This doesn't work at all! But even if she'd been able to speak, Joy had no idea what more she could say to stop this. She was all out of ideas. She'd already done more fast-talking than she'd ever done in her entire life, and she had nothing left to say. She was empty. All empty.

"Oh, c'mon. Think of how this benefits you. Look on the bright side," Shiori mock-consoled her. "You can make it part of your story—it'll make it so much more dramatic. How often do reporters lose an ear to get an interview? Not many, I bet. And this way, you'll be able to sell your story anywhere. You can walk right in, and be like, 'Hey, I interviewed Shiori Rosewing—psycho bitch cut off my fucking ear, see?' And you could, like, even throw your ear on their desk or something. I'll let you keep it. Be worth it for that. 'Cuz that's convincing. No way they wouldn't believe you after that. It's perfect. Now hold still if you want a clean cut."

There was nothing she could do. Joy felt hot tears roll down her cheeks and tried to put her mind elsewhere, somewhere far away. She wondered if it would all be worth it in the end. Maybe it wouldn't be so bad. She wasn't going to die. She just had to get through... to get through....

Joy bit down on the corded hilt as a piercing agony knifed its way high up into her jawbone, and then it was gone, as well as the pressure on her head, as steel rang against steel, and Joy turned to see Shiori backpedalling, drawing her sword-spear, as a tall figure in a trench-coat interposed itself between them.

Oh, sweet blessed Kovidh thank you thankyouthankyou! Joy clapped a hand to the side of her head to make sure her ear was still there, and it was, though her earlobe was free-hanging from the side of her head, sticky and warm. But still attached to the rest of her. For now.

The Red Specter had joined the two halves of his weapon together to make his own sword-spear, though his had a round buckler acting as a hand-guard midway along its length. He glanced back over his shoulder to check on her. As he did, Shiori's arm blurred.

Joy opened her mouth to shout a warning, before she could realize that it'd already be too late, as the sound of the impact of Shiori's dagger reached her ears. The knife ricocheted off the Specter's buckler and skittered across the concrete. Joy stared open-mouthed. He'd tracked the path of one of Shiori's supersonic daggers with his peripheral vision (while wearing goggles?) and blocked it with the barest of motions.

For the first time, Joy thought she saw Shiori look unnerved, though she recovered quickly, and sneered back over at Joy.

"Ooh, looks like you're gonna get an even better story," she said. "You can watch as the real Shiori Rosewing kills the real Red Specter, and then you can tell the whole world about it."

The Red Specter made a sound, echoing from within his mask. Something like a cough or a snort.

Shiori narrowed her eyes. "Hey, you got something to say, Spooky?"

The Red Specter just stood still, implacable glass lenses staring back at her.

"Hey, I asked you a question," Shiori yelled. "You got something you want to say to me? Better do it now, while you're still breathin'. You won't be doing that for much longer."

The Specter tilted his head. "NICE COSTUME. ROSE-DEATH FLAG IS MY FAVORITE PART. VERY CREATIVE."

Joy thought she'd seen Shiori get angry before. She hadn't. It was as if the Specter had reached out and slapped her. The shock got replaced by a cold, murderous fury that made Joy shrink back against the crates.

"Looks to me like you're the one in a stupid costume, ass-hole," she said, readying her polearm and advancing on the Specter. "And it's Rose-WING, not Rose-DEATH. Get it right."

Joy blinked, completely thrown by the non-sequitur. But that *was* a Rosedeath flag draped across her shoulders—the

438

symbol painted on the ceramic pots that contained the lethal gas. Granted, that name wasn't common knowledge—Rosedeath had been an ancient secret weapon of the Albion empire, so secret most of their own military had no knowledge of it, even as it was being deployed. Most people on both sides of the conflict had called it 'Hemlock Gas.' Joy only knew the real name from her stint as a KIB analyst, translating intercepted high-level enemy communications. But Shiori was infamous for using the gas—and she didn't know what its real name was?

The Red Specter made another sound. This one definitely sounded like a snicker.

"Oh, you think something's funny? This a game to you?" Shiori spit the words out like she was chewing nails.

"GOT LAZY WITH THE ARMOR, THOUGH. REAL CAL-IBURN ARMOR IS—"

"I KNOW what real Caliburn armor is…" Shiori's face flushed as she bit off the rest of her sentence. "It got shot to pieces, moron. So I had to make—"

"DIDN'T HEAL?"

"Heal? What… I said my armor got shot, you idiot—I healed up fine. You…"

But the Red Specter was just shaking his head, dismissive. Like you do when listening to someone who hasn't got a clue, who doesn't know up from down. Like when you're listening to a great big phony.

"TIME TO DROP THE ACT…'SHIORI'" Joy could practically hear the quotations around her name when he said it. "TIME TO—"

"I'll SHOW you who the FAKE one is, ASSHOLE!" Shiori shrieked, charging at the Specter.

What followed was the most amazing exhibition of spear combat that Joy had ever seen, unmatched by anything she'd witnessed in a fencing match, or on a theater stage, or martial arts school, or anywhere. Shiori's blade was a blur at the end of the pole, and it was in constant, frenzied motion. It was both

439

wild and controlled—each strike was precise, powerful. Joy heard the hiss of the blade as it cut the air, and would swear she felt the gusts of wind from each swing of the blade, yards away from her. The strikes came relentlessly, one after the other.

All the Specter could do was block—just hang on and survive. Shiori constantly pressed him back, forcing him to keep circling, around and around. As the fight went on she grew bolder, pressing him harder, rushing him so the hafts of their polearms clacked together crosswise, shoving him up against a wall of cargo and hacking at him for a finishing move.

And each time the Red Specter was only barely fast enough to avoid disaster, managing to twist or spin at the last second, as Shiori's blade tore through the space he'd occupied just a second before, shredding wooden crates and burlap sacks, sending splinters flying, as their contents bled out onto the concrete, as the Specter backpedalled to the center of the alleyway, barely able to bring his own spear up again to block Shiori's next series of blows.

Always a block, for Shiori's constant onslaught gave him no space for offense, and Joy's dismay rose as she realized how badly overmatched the Specter was. His awkward multipurpose weapon was outclassed by Shiori's elegant sword-spear. The small buckler bolted midway along its length helped with parrying, but it must throw off the weapon's balance. And the Specter's blade looked heavier as well, especially with the steel prong running parallel to it by nearly a foot.

That weight grew more and more apparent as the fight went on, as the Specter's parries grew shorter and weaker, each motion just barely enough to deflect the blow, to hold off death for just a few more steps. This happened over and over, until it was all the Red Specter could do to hold his spear out in front of him, shaft perfectly vertical, twitching just a few inches to either side to fend off her attacks. Joy cringed at the sight, awaited the final exchange, the finishing blow, as Shiori battered at the Specter's weapon, again and again, until finally, she let out a bestial howl and… staggered back, sucking her breath through her teeth, glaring at the Red Specter in frustration.

And then Joy realized something: the Red Specter was just holding his weapon out, barely moving it—*and Shiori couldn't get past his guard.* She was stymied, frustrated. And, more than that, she was blowing air like a forge bellows. Joy could hear it from yards away, could see the sweat streaming down her face and soaking through the padding beneath her armor. Shiori screamed again and bull-rushed the Specter, who batted her spear-tip away and neatly side-stepped, letting her charge meet empty air. Shiori managed not to stumble and fall, but it was a near thing, and her legs wobbled as she spun around to guard position again.

Joy had completely misread the fight. The Red Specter had never been overwhelmed; he'd just been efficient. Instead of trying to match Shiori blow for blow at her frenetic pace, he'd played defense until she'd exhausted herself and he'd learned all her moves. Now she was in big trouble, and she knew it, staring in dismay at his basic guard, which had suddenly become too much for her.

"STRONG. FAST. TOUGH. ACCURATE." The Red Specter spoke, and there was no strain in his voice, no sign of fatigue at all. "AND THAT'S ALL YOU ARE. NO DEPTH. NO STRAT-EGY. NO IMAGINATION."

He shook his head. "NOT SHIORI. NOT EVEN CLOSE."

"Shut up, SHUT UP!" Not-Shiori howled, lunging at him, but the Specter parried, and, for the first time, lashed out with a counterattack. The blow smashed into the the side of Shiori's helmet, and she staggered back, woozy from the impact, des-perately trying to ready herself to block the next strike—a strike that didn't come.

Instead the Red Specter just stood there and watched, impas-sive. Letting her recover? That didn't seem like a good idea to Joy, but then again, this battle was so far over her head that she felt unqualified to critique anybody's tactics.

"Going easy, you bastard?" Not-Shiori snarled. "Looking down on me, huh? I'll make you regret that, fucker. C'mon, let's dance."

The Specter didn't move, didn't speak, didn't shift his guard. Not-Shiori let out another scream, launched another attack—or started to, but saw the Red Specter shift in response, ever so slightly, and she aborted, scrabbled back in anticipation of the counterstrike. She bared her teeth in frustration. The Specter was beating her attacks before they even started.

The Red Specter watched her circle about. She couldn't attack. She wouldn't run. Her pride wouldn't allow it. Finally, he spoke. "I DON'T UNDERSTAND YOU."

Not-Shiori sneered in response, but the Specter wasn't done. "SHIORI ROSEWING. MASS MURDERER. POISONER. BETRAYER. YOU FIND THAT ADMIRABLE? ENOUGH TO TAKE THE NAME?"

"Shut up."

"SO PRIDEFUL. OF SOMEONE ELSE'S REPUTATION? WHY NOT BUILD YOUR OWN REP? WITH YOUR OWN NAME—"

"NO, It's MINE," screamed Shiori. "It was MY name, MINE! I'm Rosewing. I earned that name. I did. She stole it! Fucking stole it from me."

Shiori drew herself up, gaining energy from her rage. Joy had no idea what she was talking about, but, whatever it was, it was a deep pain, the kind of grudge that needed years of aging, a knockout whiskey that would sear your throat and eat holes in your stomach.

"I worked my ass off! For years! All I wanted... All I wanted..." Shiori choked on the words, fighting herself for control. "...And I did it! My third attempt. The last one. Do or die. And I did it! I finished in the top. Made the cut. I earned that, you hear me? I EARNED IT!"

"And then... they took it. They didn't care, didn't care," Shiori's voice took on a sing-song quality, sounding much younger.

442

"Awww.... Awww... Look at the poor widdle injured girl. Poor widdle injured girl, isn't she brave? Isn't she brave? Well, FUCK THAT! Fuck it all! It's MY name. I took it back. Took back what she cheated me out of. You hear me? I was CHEATED! I was CHEATED!"

The Red Specter had lowered his guard completely, a silent witness to Shiori's rant. Joy had such a hard time reading him, with his mask and his goggles and his great big coat, but something about him right then... she saw a deep, profound sadness.

"NO," he said. "YOU WERE LUCKY."

Joy had no idea if that was meant to console or enrage Shiori, or something else, but her eyes flashed white-hot fury, and she lashed out with her spear. The Specter parried, and their weapons locked together, Shiori's blade trapped by the heavy forked prong of the Specter's odd polearm. The Specter cranked down with a twisting chop, and Shiori's blade snapped in two. The severed steel edge skittered across the concrete, and Shiori was left gawking at the jagged metal stump where her blade used to be. Then the Specter did something too fast for Joy to follow, and the remnants of Shiori's spear went flying out of her hands in several pieces. The Red Specter brought the tip of his spear up inches from her throat, and she had no defense.

"SHIORI ROSEWING," said the Specter, almost placatingly. "YOU WILL KNEEL, PLACE YOUR HANDS BEHIND YOUR HEAD, AND SURRENDER. FAILURE TO COMPLY WILL—"

And then Shiori turned and looked straight at Joy, eyes filled with such levels of hate, it made her shrink back, want to protest, *What did I do? Why me, all of a—*

Shiori's hand blurred. So did the Specter's blade, and Shiori's hate was replaced by a look of profound surprise. A throwing-knife tumbled loose from her fingers and went sailing way over Joy's head, flipping end over end. Shiori clutched at her throat, tried to speak, but only managed to make a sick bubbling noise. Bright red liquid soaked through her gauntlets, and she stared at the two of them in shock, looking so lost and alone. She seemed to collapse in slow motion, first going to her knees, then curling into a ball, facedown on the pavement, before a final sideways lurch left her in a fetal position, as her blood continued to spill out, forming a red halo on the ground.

Joy suddenly had a very hard time standing. The whole world seemed unsteady, wheeling and dipping around her. Oh, she was going to puke.

"EASY," said the Red Specter, who had appeared next to her, blocking her view of the woman dying on the ground. "SIT DOWN. DEEP BREATHS. PUT YOUR HEAD BETWEEN YOUR KNEES."

Joy complied, and it helped. Eventually, the nausea passed, without Joy having to lose any of her stomach contents. She wiped her tears away and nudged the Specter aside so she could look again. Curled up in her armor, Shiori... or, whoever she'd really been... resembled nothing so much as a dead beetle, but she'd...

Joy stared up at the Red Specter. "Why...why me? I mean, with the knife... she aimed at me..."

"DISTRACTION. REVENGE. AN EASY TARGET." The Specter shrugged, though his tone wasn't unkind. "WASN'T GOING TO TAKE CHANCES. PATIENCE EXHAUSTED."

"Um... Thank you," said Joy, for lack of anything better to say. Was there a proper etiquette for this kind of situation? Did she want to find out?

"YOU FEEL SORRY FOR HER?"

Joy gazed up at the Red Specter. Backlit by the sun, she couldn't see anything behind the flat round circles of his goggles.

"SHE HURT YOU. WAS GOING TO HURT YOU MORE. WOULD'VE KILLED YOU WITHOUT A SECOND THOUGHT. HAS DONE WORSE BEFORE. STILL FEEL SORRY FOR HER?"

She puzzled at the question. Part of her wondered why he was even asking. She decided to answer anyway. It felt important.

444

She turned it over in her head, but her head was a mess. But this wasn't a head question anyway. What did she feel, deep in her chest?

"I... guess so?" She said. "I mean, I know she was a... a bad person, and I guess she deserved it, but... still..."

The Red Specter nodded. "I UNDERSTAND. MORE THAN YOU KNOW. BUT IT'S A MISTAKE. BIGGEST MISTAKE I EVER—"

It happened before Joy had a chance to call out, but she saw it clearly—a massive bullet-shaped head, barely recognizable as human; a mouth filled with shiny gold-plated razor-teeth, opened up wider than any person should be able to. Benny the Shark reared up behind the Red Specter, taking him unawares, savagely chomping down into his neck and shoulder.

Joy shrieked, horrified—not only by what she'd just seen, but what she was about to see, the mauling that would happen as Benny bit down with those awful teeth, tearing away hunks of flesh, of the man who'd saved her. And it was already too late, too late to stop it....

Only it didn't happen. The Red Specter just stood there, utterly indifferent to the leech that had clamped onto his shoulder. No gouts of blood or gore appeared, and Joy remembered that the Specter was wearing some pretty impressive armor, strong enough to stop bullets. And, that despite the strength of Benny's beliefs, no matter what type of surgeries he got, or how many bones he ate, or how many times he pretended to regress to past lives, at the end of the day he was just a man with a big mouth. And his bite was just a man's bite, with nothing like the force and power of a real shark.

Benny shifted, wiggled his head a bit, and Joy realized he was stuck. His teeth were stuck in the thick scale-leather of the Specter's armor, and he couldn't get them out. He'd literally bitten off more than he could chew. Benny directed a sidelong glare at the Specter. Under other circumstances, Joy supposed it would've been intimidating.

"Marrgll!" he said.

The Red Specter turned to look at Benny. Or, he tried to, but there wasn't much space to move his head before the cone of his mask bonked into the Triad boss' forehead.

"YOU," said the Specter. "ARE *WAY* TOO INTO YOUR FUCKING GIMMICK."

With a click, the Red Specter separated his spear weapon into two separate halves, and proceeded to use the pommel of his sword to hammer Benny the Shark between the eyes, again and again, until those eyes rolled up, the gangster went limp, and he slid free to collapse in a boneless pile at the Specter's feet.

Part 9:

Joy Does What Joy Wants

Chapter 49:

Cleanup

"WOULD YOU LOOK AT THIS? UNBELIEVABLE." The Red Specter tugged at the collar of his trench-coat, pulling it out to reveal a large circular hole ripped in the canvas at the shoulder.

The Specter returned the two halves of his weapon to the custom sheath on his back, then flipped Benny onto his stomach, securing the unconscious man's hands behind his back with steel cable ties. Then he repeated the process with Benny's ankles, and linked the two sets of ties together, forcing the gangster into an awkward arched-back pose. He kept muttering the whole time.

"A BITE? A FRIGGIN' BITE? WHAT THE ABYSS IS WRONG WITH... OH, LOOK AT THIS!"

The Specter yanked something out from beneath Benny's jacket and showed it to Joy.

"A gun! Genius WAS carrying AND INSTEAD OF using it LIKE ANY sane PERSON, JACKASS TRIES TO bite ME! Moron!" The Specter yelled at Benny's slumbering form, and Joy noted his voice was slipping in and out of the deep rumble he normally used. Was it an affectation?

"Well, maybe he got way too into *your* gimmick," said Joy. "He thought you were really a ghost, so he thought he needed to beat you with his... er, shark powers? I guess?"

The Red Specter stared at her, his posture indicating just how stupid he thought that idea was.

Joy shrugged, noting that the Specter hadn't denied that he was using a gimmick. No insistence that he really was a ghost. "Well, I don't know, but maybe it made sense to him. Plus, everyone knows that guns don't work on the Red Specter."

"THE ABYSS THEY DON'T," said the Specter. "DAMNED THINGS HURT LIKE A BASTARD."

448

"But Benny didn't know that, right?" Joy said, noting the Specter's voice had gone back to 'normal' as he'd calmed down. "And isn't that the point of your outfit? To intimidate your enemies into making mistakes? Or was it something else? Why did you decide to become the Red Specter?"

"I DIDN'T..." The Red Specter stopped and stared at her, then started to walk away. "SHOULD BE FINE FROM HERE. GO HOME. NO INTERVIEWS."

"Hey, wait!" Joy said, and started to follow, but after two steps, a searing pain in her foot brought her up short. She cursed, staggered, sat down, leaning up against more cargo crates.

"WHAT IS IT NOW?" The Red Specter had stopped a few yards away, back facing her.

"I stepped on a nail," said Joy.

The Red Specter stalked back, grabbed her ankle and held her foot up to the light. Indeed, the sole of one of her reed sandals had been pierced by a fat bent nail, attached to a scrap of wood, likely part of the debris from the duel with Shiori. The Specter glared at her.

"What are you getting mad at me for?" she said. "It's not like I did it on purpose."

The Specter kept glaring, and cocked his head at her.

"What? Really?" Joy said, her indignation boiling over. "Really? You honestly think I would deliberately injure myself just to get an interview? Is that really what you think of me?"

The Red Specter leaned in. "I HAVE NO IDEA WHAT TO MAKE OF YOU. NOT SURE IF YOU'RE SOME KIND OF GENIUS, OR A COMPLETE IDIOT."

Joy just glared at him. He let out a long sigh, then grabbed the scrap of wood with both hands and snapped it in half along the grain, freeing it from the nail. Joy hissed at the vibration in her foot and yelped as the Specter scooped her up and started carrying her.

Oh, hello there. Joy knew she didn't weigh much, but the ease at which he'd picked her up was... Well, obviously he was strong, of course he'd have to be, considering all the things she'd seen him do, but to experience it directly was... well, it was just impressive, that was all.

From this angle she could get a close look as his mask, at the subtle scaled texture on the hardened leather plates, and what was more, the sunlight shone through his goggles so she could see his eyes inside. She couldn't really discern their color with the glass in the way, but their shape was perfectly clear. She thought they were rather pretty.

Joy was about to ask where they were going, but they'd already arrived. The KIB had set up an impromptu field headquarters next to the wreck of the Joanne Spaulding, agents milling about, herding the captured Triad gangsters into large self-propelled armored troop carriers, sorting through the wreckage, cordoning off the area, sifting through the rubble, and so on.

Someone flagged them down, and Joy recognized the head agent from before. "There you are. We've got a..." He paused as he noticed Joy. "Oh, hello again. You're that Woman's Lib agent? What is..."

The Red Specter snorted, and the agent peered at him questioningly.

"Ah... that's a teensy little misunderstanding," said Joy. "I'm actually a reporter."

Confusion played over the agent's face. "DON'T ASK," said the Specter. "NEED TO DROP HER OFF AT FIRST AID."

"I stepped on a nail," said Joy. "And I've got some other things too. Deep cut on my ear. Oh, and I think there's something really wrong with my pinky finger. And also—"

"SAVE IT FOR THE MEDIC," said the Specter.

"We're set up in one of the warehouses, but..." The agent hesitated for second, then shrugged. "Follow me."

"WAIT. SEND AGENTS THAT WAY," the Specter managed to point with the hand that supported her knees. "FIVE ROWS, THEN LEFT. BENNY AND FAKE SHIORI. NEUTRALIZED. BODY BAG FOR THE FAKE."

450

The agent frowned, but did as the Specter asked. "Well, that's everybody accounted for, then," he said, as he led them towards the warehouse. "Pretty sure we got all the cultists in the..."

The agent trailed off as he remembered Joy was there. "All the corrupt Nibiru cultists working in the City Guard, you mean," said Joy, enjoying his startled reaction.

"Ah... I'm afraid I can't comment on that, ma'am," he said.

"Call me Joy," she said, with a smile. "Joy Song Fan, free-lance reporter, working on assignment for the Dodona Gazette. I'm here to interview the Red Specter."

"SHE IS NOT," said the Specter, as the agent did a dou-ble-take. "SHE IS GETTING DROPPED OFF AT THE MEDIC. PERIOD."

Joy smiled indulgently. "Don't mind him, Agent..."

"Funaki. Special Agent Sam Funaki. And, um—"

"Oh, that's a nice name. Very strong. It suits you," said Joy.

The Specter just snorted in response. Agent Funaki cleared his throat.

"Thank you, Ms. Fan—"

"I told you, call me Joy."

"Ah, well...I'm afraid, Joy, it might be a while before we can have someone take a look at you. Our field medics are really busy right now, you see—"

"IS IT BAD?"

"All things considered, we got off light. The main squad stuck to the plan, and fortunately most of those Triad goons weren't trained on Manticores—burnt through their ammo and didn't hit much. The hostage rescue squad, on the other hand..."

The Red Specter shook his head. "THAT WAS A MESS."

"Well, it was a short-notice rush of plan, but I ran it past the boys, and they said they wanted to go for it. It was just..." Agent Funaki shook his head. "It was that crazy secretary of his— nobody expected that, and it totally tipped the scales against them."

"THEY GONNA BE OKAY?"

"Hopefully," said Agent Funaki. "Gunter and Harris have major stab wounds to the chest and abdomen, Gyasi has been shot five times and hasn't woken up yet, and Rafiki has a really nasty...er, *bite* wound."

The Red Specter made a disgusted sound and muttered under his breath, while Joy shivered and tried to avoid visualizing that. They entered the KIB's warehouse, and Joy noted the buzz of activity in one corner, cordoned off by freestanding curtains. She got a glimpse through them and saw two people in scrubs rushing about to aid others lying on cots. Joy noted that, despite the activity and equipment, there weren't nearly as many people running around as she'd have expected. They seemed under-staffed. Curious. The Specter kept walking, heading to another section of the warehouse.

"Civilians need to be separate," said Agent Funaki. "Not that we have many. Right now it's you, and—"

Joy heard yelling, and spotted a familiar face. Lin Lin was struggling with a KIB agent—a woman wearing an elaborate head-wrap over her uniform. The sight alarmed Joy for a minute until she realized the agent was actually being gentle, concerned with keeping her charge from bolting off.

"Can we—" Joy started to ask, but the Red Specter was already walking her over. Joy called out to reassure Lin Lin, who managed to calm down and wait until they made it over, before falling all over Joy, bawling and apologizing and offering thanks.

The Red Specter lowered her down so she could hug and be hugged while balancing on one foot, though he still supported most of her weight. They stayed like that for a long time before Lin Lin came up for air. She had been cleaned up, her shackles had been removed, and she didn't seem to be injured anywhere Joy could see.

Joy tried to deflect further thanks, insisting that she was okay, though Lin Lin freaked out a bit when she saw the nail in Joy's foot.

"Lin Lin, I think your brave big sister needs to go get that looked at," said the female agent, not unkindly, and in Xiaish, too. "Plus, we've got a treat for you. Our radio team just reported in from the Kovidhian temple, and there's someone who wants to say hello."

Lin Lin stared blankly at the odd heavy box on the table next to the agent. It must've looked bizarre to her, with all the weird dials and lights, and the strands of wire protruding out of the top, bent around in arcane geometric patterns. She jumped when the box started talking to her, with Hsiu Mei's voice, but recovered enough to reply, as the agent showed her the microphone and told her to push a button to talk.

"You have voice transmission over radio?" said Joy, marveling at the contraption. "I thought that was only theoretical. What's the range on that? How long has it existed?"

"Specific details about the radio are classified for now, Ms... er, I mean, Joy," said Agent Funaki.

Was it, now? Joy was about to ask some follow-up questions, but Lin Lin pushed the microphone in front of her, to talk to Hsiu Mei and all the girls, who'd made it to the temple. She had a round of them all thanking her, and Shao Yin and Noriko were especially effusive, apologizing for giving her such a hard time earlier. Really, it was no big deal—they'd had no good reason to trust her, and all the praise and thanks was getting embarrassing. The female agent came to her rescue, reminding Lin Lin that Joy needed to see a medic.

Joy said her goodbyes and the Red Specter scooped her back up again. As they walked away, Joy overhead bits of their conversation.

"Big Sister Joy was amazing," said Lin Lin. "The bad guys had her tied up, and their leader was a monster with sharp metal teeth, and he even tried to bite me! But she yelled at him and made him stop. She wasn't scared at all."

"He's lucky she was tied up," came Hsiu Mei's tinny reply. "Or else she would've beaten him up, like she did to the other one...."

Agent Funaki stared at her, and Joy felt her face grow hot, amazed at Lin Lin's skewed perception of what had gone on.

They'd mostly been speaking Kallish in those exchanges, so Lin Lin had used her imagination to guess at what all that gibberish meant. At some point she'd have to have a talk with the girls, maybe correct some of their misconceptions about her...

"You're tougher than you look, if you can really go toe to toe with Benny the Shark," said Agent Funaki.

"Ah, I think the girls got a bit of a mistaken impression about me," she said.

"TRY FULL-ON DELUSIONAL."

Joy scowled at the Red Specter. He wasn't... wrong, exactly— but did he have to sound that dismissive?

"I could take Benny," she said. "As long I got to use that crane golem again. I mean, I was pretty effective with that, right?"

"Wait, that was you?" Agent Funaki went wide-eyed. "*You* were the maniac running the..."

He stopped and looked away while noisily clearing his throat. "Ah... Ahem. Yes, um... I guess your... efforts with the crane golem did disrupt their defenses. And umm... Oh, look—you can wait here for the medic."

Agent Funaki directed them into an abandoned office containing four empty collapsable cots. The Red Specter began to lower her onto the nearest one.

"Ah, thank you," she said. "Well, since we're waiting here, why don't we do the interview?"

"NO INTERVIEWS," said the Specter, who deposited her on the cot and turned to leave—or tried to, except Joy wasn't letting go of his neck, so he remained bent-over as he tried to peel her off him.

"What? But you have to—at least a little one, right?" Joy said. "You need to think image control. And this is a major event. The people of Dodona have a right to know."

"DON'T CARE. NOT MY PROBLEM," he said, prying her fingers off him, one by one.

454

"But it *is* my problem. It's my job," said Joy. "And I really, really need this interview. You wouldn't turn me down now, after all I've been through? If it hadn't been for me, the bad guys would've gotten away."

"NO THEY WOULDN'T HAVE."

"What?" Joy yelped. "Now, you see here—if I hadn't grabbed the Joanne Spaulding with that crane, it would've—"

"IT WOULD HAVE SUFFERED AN IRREPARABLE ENGINE MALFUNCTION IN ROUGHLY ONE HOUR'S TIME. ADRIFT UNTIL THE NAVY COMES TO RESCUE."

"What? How could you possibly know..." Joy paused as she remembered all the drugged crewmen and Captain Ong, from when she'd found them all stuffed in the dinghy. So that was what he'd been up to. But wait, did that mean everything she'd done had been....

The Red Specter broke free and ducked out of reach before she could react.

"AND IT WOULD'VE BEEN LESS DESTRUCTION," he added.

Joy felt her stomach sink, but Agent Funaki jumped to her defense. "Well, that's true, but there could've been a nasty stand-off with the hostage, too, which we avoided this way. That was a huge concern."

She thought back to the events of the night—of all the gunfire, but only the "Hostage Rescue Team" had suffered casualties. The KIB hadn't been trying to cut the Triads off from their ship—they'd been herding them onto it. Gather them on a boat, one guaranteed to go adrift, but take away their hostage first, then send the navy to force a surrender. But... wait a minute... how would they have known in advance...?

"STILL GOING TO BE A BIG BILL," said the Red Specter.

"We'll see," said Agent Funaki. "Though I'm guessing most of the damaged goods are going to be declared contraband, or seized by the State anyway. And it turns out, we found some interesting, ah... *insurance* in that secretary's purse. Bunch of names there, including the Harbormaster. He's going to have some *explaining* to do as to... well, let's just say he's going to have other things on his mind than—"

"Wait—you found something in Daphne's purse?" Joy blurted out. "Captain Ong's 'Insurance' ledger? A huge ledger of names and payments to people who are on the Triad's take?"

"What? How did you—" Agent Funaki stopped himself from saying more, but it was too late.

"That's mine," she said. "I mean, I found that. In the chart room of the Joanne Spaulding. And it was hidden real well, too. In a secret compartment. You'd have never found it without me. That's worth an interview, right?"

The Specter stared back, unimpressed, while Agent Funaki replied. "Ahem... I'm afraid I can't comment on evidence pertaining to an ongoing investigation."

"But you brought it up in the first place," Joy pointed out.

"THIS IS WHY YOU'RE NOT CLEARED TO TALK TO PRESS," said the Red Specter. Agent Funaki shrugged and gave him an an apologetic smile, earning a dismissive noise from behind the Specter's mask.

"WHATEVER. I'M OUT," said the Specter. "GOODBYE, MS. FAN."

"Wait, wait," she said. "You can't—"

"Sorry," said Agent Funaki. "We'll have a medic come see to you, as soon as one is available. It was nice meeting you."

"No, no—" Joy watched the Specter reach for the door, open it as Agent Funaki trailed him, and knew that if he left, she'd have lost. But she was so close. There had to be something she could do. Something she could offer in exchange for an interview. Something they needed. Something she knew and they didn't. Of all the crazy things that had happened to her over the past twenty-four hours, she had to have seen something... something....

"Shining blue jewels!" Joy blurted out, and saw both men pause, midway through the doorway. "Big blue jewels, about the size of a walnut, smooth on the outside, polished like stones in a river. But they don't quite look it, because on the inside, there are all these weird lines that reflect light, makes you think of facets, but they're not."

The two men looked at each other, then at her. Agent Funaki started to speak, but the Specter stopped him.

"ARE YOU SAYING THAT YOU'VE SEEN JEWELS LIKE THESE?"

"Am I saying that?" Joy said, making a big show of thinking it over. "Hmm... Yeah, I think I can definitely go that far. I can say that I'm seen them."

"HOW MANY HAVE YOU SEEN, AND WHERE ARE THEY?"

"Weeell, there's one that I've actually seen, and a bunch more where I'm pretty sure where they are...."

"YOU CAN QUIT BEING VAGUE NOW." The Red Specter had a commanding, no-nonsense tone, but he was hardly the scariest thing she'd dealt with tonight.

"Mmm... I'm sorry, you're asking me a bunch of questions, but you're not answering mine. That doesn't seem very fair, does it? How about a trade?"

The Red Specter loomed over her. She could see his narrowed eyes through his goggles.

"THIS COULD BE CONSIDERED OBSTRUCTION."

"Obstruction? You mean, like, obstruction of an official investigation?" said Joy brightly. "So, would you like to confirm your status as a KIB agent? At this point, you might as well. What is your official title and authority? Although, may I remind you, if there's any authority that *requires* me to answer questions—especially in the absence of legal counsel—I'm not aware of it. Furthermore—"

"Joy, listen," said Agent Funaki. "You don't understand. Those crystals are very dangerous. It's of vital importance that we secure them as soon as possible."

"Oh, so they're *very important*?" Joy replied. "How interesting.

Would you care to elaborate on that, Agent Funaki? What are these crystals called, and how are they dangerous, exactly?"

Agent Funaki winced as the Specter glared at him some more. "I'm... er, not cleared to talk to press—"

"ENOUGH. I'LL HANDLE THIS," the Red Specter shooed Agent Funaki out of the room, turning to her before he left. "BE RIGHT BACK."

Yeah, you will, thought Joy, proud that she managed to refrain from a triumphant fist-pump-slash-victory-dance until after the door had closed. But still, she couldn't get too complacent yet—not until she cleared the final challenge: the interview itself.

Chapter 50:

Interview with a Red Specter

Joy lay back on her cot and waited, and the wait turned excruciating almost immediately. Literally so—without any other stimulus to distract her, it was very hard to ignore the fact that she had a nail stuck through her foot. And a messed-up pinky, which had swollen up to twice its normal size, and was poking off at a weird angle. And a whole series of bruises and cuts from being banged around. Hard to get comfortable like this, with all her injuries nagging at her.

The Red Specter returned bearing a case of medical supplies, plus her waterproof satchel, which he tossed to her. They'd recovered it! Joy retrieved her notebook and pencils, and watched in surprise as the Specter stripped off his gloves and started rifling through the med kit.

"What, are you going to be my doctor now?"

"FASTER THIS WAY," he said. "AND I'M NOT GONNA SUBJECT ANY OF THE MEDICS TO YOU. THEY'VE HAD A ROUGH DAY ALREADY."

Joy glared at him, though she thought he was kidding. "Or maybe you don't want me asking them any questions. Is that it? And speaking of which—"

"HERE'S THE DEAL," said the Specter. "I DO YOUR INTERVIEW. YOU TELL ME THE NUMBER AND LOCATION OF ALL THE BLUE JEWELS YOU KNOW OF—AND THEN YOU FORGET YOU EVER SAW THEM. THEY STAY OUT OF YOUR STORY. NO MENTION OF THEM AT ALL. NOT TO YOUR READERS, NOT TO ANYONE."

Joy's rush of victory faded at the second half of the deal. "Wait, you want me to withhold information from a news story?"

"THOSE JEWELS ARE DANGEROUS."

"Well, you say that, but..." Joy tried to think it through. She'd worked in intelligence. She knew that some secrets had to be kept, for the good of all, but still... "How is it dangerous just to know that they exist? That doesn't... I don't know that...."

The Red Specter loomed over her.

"YOU KNOW THAT ARSON IS A FELONY, RIGHT? COMBINE THAT WITH RAMPANT DESTRUCTION OF PROPERTY. INCLUDING, BUT NOT LIMITED TO, A CRANE GOLEM AND AN ENTIRE STEAMSHIP."

"What?" Joy yelped. "I thought we were over that. It was in the service of a greater good—the emancipation of exploited young girls. I was helping you. I was, err...."

The Red Specter crossed his arms and waited, while Joy ran all the events of that night over in her head and tried to stay calm. She really had caused a lot of destruction. Noble motives might be a mitigating factor if she was charged, but still—

"INTERVIEW," repeated the Specter. "IN EXCHANGE, YOU REVEAL THE CRYSTALS TO ME, AND NO ONE ELSE. DEAL?"

Joy knew she should take that deal. That was the smart thing to do. But this whole business of keeping secrets from the public—it didn't feel right. It made the words catch in her throat.

The Red Specter watched her hesitate, and let out a long sigh, seeming to deflate. It came as something of a shock as Joy realized that he was nearly as tired as she was.

"YOU KNOW, I DID SAVE YOUR LIFE THREE TIMES," he said, sounding more than a little peeved.

"Oh, right! Okay, fine—it's a deal," said Joy. "You should have brought that up first, instead of making threats. Aiyah!"

The Specter just stared at her, and Joy decided to let it slide.

"Okay," said Joy. "You know all those chains the girls had on them? There's a link right below the collar that's actually more like an amulet or a brooch, with an image of Nibiru embossed on it. There's a jewel inside each of them."

"YOU'RE SURE OF THAT?"

460

"Sure I... well, actually—no," Joy admitted. "I only know for sure about the one I found in Hsiu Mei's collar, but it seems likely—especially given how desperate Chief Gallach and company were acting. They were prepared to blow themselves up, remember? Seems a bit over-the-top if it's just about getting an extra wife, don't you think?"

The Specter nodded. "THE ONE YOU FOUND. WHERE IS IT NOW?"

"Hidden in my apartment."

The Red Specter opened the door and issued orders to someone waiting outside, then returned to prepping his medical supplies.

"AFTER WE'RE DONE, AN AGENT WILL ACCOMPANY YOU TO YOUR APARTMENT. TO RETRIEVE THE CRYSTAL."

Now Joy really wanted to know what was up with those crystals. This smelled like a huge story, and part of her already regretted the deal she'd made to shut up about them. Joy told that part of her to quit being greedy. She already had a huge story on her hands, and she should focus on that.

The Red Specter tossed her a damp cloth to wipe the dirt off all her minor cuts, and some that weren't so minor, where she'd been gouged by shards of broken glass. The Specter cut off her sandals, and started swabbing her feet with alcohol. It stung a lot, made her hiss through her teeth.

"NEED SOMETHING FOR THE PAIN?" Said the Specter, producing a hypodermic needle.

"Painkillers? Oh, sweet blessed Kovidh, yes please—No, wait!" An image of the barely-coherent Captain Ong flashed through Joy's mind. "Are there going to be any side effects? Like, it's not gonna make me all loopy, will it?"

The Red Specter just stared at her. "HOW WOULD YOU NOTICE THE DIFFERENCE?"

"Oh, you're hilarious," said Joy. "But you owe me an interview, and I need to be—"

"TOPICAL ANESTHETIC, NOT GENERAL."

"Well, fine then," said Joy.

Joy felt a sharp jab in the sole of her foot. The Red Specter tossed the empty syringe away, and repeated the process on a large gash on her thigh.

"NEED STITCHES HERE," he muttered, and peered at the side of her head. Joy felt him poking at her raw, bloody ear-lobe, where Shiori had been slicing at her. "HERE, TOO. BEST DONE SOONER THAN LATER."

"Um, okay," said Joy. "It's...not too bad, is it? I'm not going to always have to style my hair to one side, or..."

"BE FINE," he said, swabbing the area clean. "SMALL SUTURES, SMALL SCAR."

"You sure you know what you're doing?" Joy asked, although it did feel like he did from the way he worked—very practiced and efficient. He had strong, callused hands, but his fingers were more slender than she would've expected.

"And um... maybe you could see better without that mask on?" She added. It was worth a shot.

"CAN SEE FINE," he said, returning to her foot and poking at it.

Joy decided she was too tired to do anything but shut up and let him work. She kept especially quiet while he stitched up her thigh and ear. She wanted his full concentration for that. But when he switched to just wrapping bandages over everything, she decided to probe a bit.

"So, how long has the Red Specter been working with the KIB?"

"WHO SAYS I AM?"

Joy snorted. "Oh—come on. It's obvious that you're working together. I've seen you give orders to the lead agent here."

"THOSE ARE SUGGESTIONS. WE HAVE MUTUAL GOALS."

"So, can I take that to mean that you are *not* working for the KIB in an official capacity?"

"DIDN'T SAY THAT, EITHER."

"Oh, really?" Joy said. "Then, would you care to comment on—Ow!"

The Specter had moved on to her left hand, was probing the bottom edge of her crooked pinky. "THAT HURT?"

"Yes!"

"HOW ABOUT HERE?"

"Owowowow!"

"DISLOCATED. NEED TO POP IT BACK IN PLACE."

"Um, that sounds really painful."

"IT IS."

Joy scowled at him. "You know, Doc, your bedside manner is—"

"COUNT TO THREE."

"What? Oh, um..." Joy took deep breaths. "Okay... One... TwooOOYeeeouch!"

Searing agony shot up her forearm as the Specter yanked on her pinky. She felt the small bones click into place.

"What the Abyss! I wasn't ready!" Joy yelped, using the back of her good hand to wipe away tears.

"WORKS BETTER THAT WAY," said the Specter, then glared at her response. "STOP WIGGLING AROUND. NEED TO IMMOBILIZE IT NOW."

"*You* hold still," she retorted, cocking her arm back for a punch, except the door opened and Agent Funaki came in, carrying a stack of papers.

"Hey, Agent Funaki," she said. "I'd like to register a complaint about the quality of my medical care," she said.

He glanced over at the Specter. "Let me guess—beside manner? I can log it, but it won't do any good. It's gonna get buried under the rest of this list."

Agent Funaki pulled out a heavy stack of paper. "Harbormaster just presented me with an itemized list of all the damages. He works fast. Though he 'reserves the right for further amendments.'"

The Specter skimmed through the manifest. A low whistle emanated from the depths of his mask, and Joy winced. That didn't sound good.

"I LIKE HOW HE ORGANIZED IT ACCORDING TO WAVES OF DESTRUCTION," said the Specter. "FIRE, BULLET DAMAGE, STEAMSHIP CRASH, CARGO RUINED WHEN TOSSED INTO HARBOR BY BERSERK CRANE GOLEM..."

"Well, that wasn't very much, was it?" Joy said, reaching for a bright side. "The last one, I mean. Just the fertilizer and that one container at the beginning—I mean, was that one extra-valuable or something?"

"ARNSEN'S PET SUPPLY COMPANY," said the Specter. "WHOLE CONTAINER WAS FULL OF PUPPIES AND KITTENS. ALL DROWNED NOW."

Joy felt a shock, like she'd just been dunked in ice water. "What? No..." She said, and her voice sounded very far away, to even her own ears. "Puppies... and... and...."

"Huh? That doesn't..." Agent Funaki said, leaning in to take a second look at the manifest. "Wait, that says 'Arnsen's Textiles, Inc.' It's a bulk fabric shipment."

"OOPS. MY MISTAKE. MUST HAVE MISREAD IT."

Joy stared at him in disbelief. "You... you asshole! I can't believe... Jerk! Jackass!" She looked around for something to throw at him, but came up with nothing. She had to settle for glaring at Agent Funaki.

"It's not funny!" she snapped.

"Not at all, ma'am," he said, trying to keep a straight face, and failing.

"NO. IT'S A LESSON," said the Specter. "ABOUT CARELESSNESS AND DESTRUCTION. YOU COULD HAVE GOTTEN PEOPLE KILLED."

"I... okay," Joy didn't have the energy to fight anymore, and she had a sinking feeling that he was right. "You're right. I just... I just wanted..."

"You know, you don't need to be so hard on her," said Agent Funaki. "And, quite frankly, that speech is a little ironic, coming from you. Didn't we have this discussion earlier? About setting off a cattle stampede, as I recall?"

The Red Specter stiffened. "THAT WAS DIFFERENT," he mumbled.

Joy felt some of her energy return. "That's right! That was you—you dropped cows on everyone! An entire herd of cattle. Do you feel... Oh, wait—"

She retrieved her notebook and pencil from the bedside table, flipped it open to a fresh page, and managed to prop it up in her lap without putting a strain on her injured pinky.

"Mr. Specter, would you care to comment on your actions from earlier today? I'm specifically referring to dropping a very large container full of cows from roughly five or six feet in the air into an area full of people?"

The Specter looked from her to Agent Funaki and didn't see much support. "THAT WAS... THAT WAS A RAPIDLY ESCALATING SITUATION. WAS ABOUT TO TURN INTO A BLOODBATH."

"So you decided to defuse the situation by adding a hundred tons of angry beef?" Joy asked. "Was that really the best solution available? Do you have any messages for the restaurant owners who had their property destroyed by the resulting chaos? Or the pedestrians who may have been injured or traumatized by encountering a cattle stampede in a busy tourist district?"

"BEST SOLUTION..." the Red Specter said. "LOOK, IT HAPPENED REALLY FAST. HAD TO ACT FAST. GRAB FIRST SOLUTION AVAILABLE...."

"Oh, really?" Joy made a point of noting that down. "So would you say that you did the best you could with limited information and resources, even though it was still really dangerous and caused a lot of chaos and destruction? Can I quote you on that?"

The Red Specter glared at her, even though she thought she had framed the question pretty sympathetically. She was being very sweet and not gloating at all.

The Specter let out a long sigh. "SURE. FINE," he growled. "WE'LL GO WITH THAT."

"Excellent," said Joy. "Oh, but you didn't answer the bit about the shopkeepers and pedestrians—"

"NO COMMENT," he said. "AND, BEFORE YOU ASK, NO ONE WAS SERIOUSLY INJURED, EITHER. WE CHECKED. AND I DON'T CARE ABOUT MENTAL COW TRAUMA."

"Red Specter indifferent to bovine suffering..." Joy muttered, scribbling away in her notebook. She noticed him glaring at her and grinned.

"Kidding! That's a joke. We like those, right?" Joy said, but the Specter continued glaring.

"You know, you're not nearly this cranky in the comics," she said.

"WHAT COMICS?"

"The ones that run in every newspaper in Kallistrate, for free," she said. "Are you claiming not to have any knowledge of them? None at all?"

"THAT'S RIGHT."

Joy cocked her head at him. "Then why did you quote from the comics? You did that thing—the catchphrase."

"He did what?" said Agent Funaki, perking up and grinning at the Specter. "You did a line from the comics? Really?"

The Red Specter stiffened up and looked off into the corner of the room.

"NO, I DIDN'T."

"You most certainly did," said Joy. "It was that long one he always does. How did it go? Um... let me think..."

She pitched her voice as low as she could, though it wasn't anywhere near Specter-level. "Beware, Villains! Wherever There Is Tyranny, Whenever There Is Evil, I Am There, Ready To Strike From The Shadows. Surrender, Evildoers! For

No One Can Escape The Wrath... Of The Red Specter—he said that."

"R-really?" said Agent Funaki, covering his mouth with his hand, while his eyes danced. "How dramatic. What a showman."

"Actually, it really was," said Joy. "I mean, everyone was talking about him, all scared, and then someone was like, 'There's no such thing as the Red Specter,' and then this spooky booming voice comes out of nowhere, with that whole spiel. You should've seen their faces. All these big, tough criminals, and they were ready to poop themselves, they were so startled."

"NO IDEA WHAT SHE'S TALKING ABOUT," said the Specter. "SUFFERING FROM TRAUMATIC STRESS. TOO MANY BLOWS TO THE HEAD."

"Oh, that must be it," lied Agent Funaki, before turning back to Joy. "So, were there any other... dramatic lines that you heard him—"

"DON'T YOU HAVE SOMEWHERE TO BE?" The Red Specter loomed over Sam. "PAPERS TO FILL OUT? REPORTS TO LOG? THAT TYPE OF THING?"

"Eh, nothing urgent, no. I thought I..."

Something switched over in the Specter's demeanor, and Agent Funaki backed up a step. "Well, unless maybe Joy needs me to get something..."

"Some water, or maybe some tea," said Joy, noticing that she was parched. "I mean, if that's not too much trouble, Agent Funaki. I don't want to be a bother...."

"Oh, it's no bother," he said. "And call me Sam."

"Sure thing, Sam," said Joy.

"Actually, you're in for a treat," he said. "We managed to recover this really nice tea set from the Triad warehouse. Miracle that it survived the blast, but it did. I think they've got it set up already."

"That sounds heavenly. And that's so sweet of you to offer. Isn't he sweet?" Joy asked the Specter.

"IT'S LIKE HE'S MADE OF SUGAR," the Specter growled. "HOPE HE DOESN'T DISSOLVE IN THE TEA. BEFORE HE FINISHES ALL THAT WORK HE SHOULD BE DOING."

"Oh, don't worry about me," said Agent Funaki, as earnest and sincere as a person could possibly be. "I wouldn't shirk my duties. Because I know the Red Specter will be watching—ready to *strike* from the *shadows*. And I sure wouldn't want that!"

He escaped from the room, leaving the Specter to glare at the door as it swung shut, then back at Joy as she succumbed to fit of giggles.

"SAID YOU WANTED AN INTERVIEW," said the Specter. "WE GOING TO DO THAT, OR NOT?"

With some effort, Joy got herself back under control. She shifted on the cot, got her notepad and pencil ready, and gathered her thoughts.

"Well, all right then," said Joy. "Would you care to elaborate on your relationship with the KIB?"

"NO."

Joy scowled at the impassive figure next to her cot. Was she going to have to treat this as a hostile interview? She'd rather not, but...

"But you do work together. I've observed you tonight. You worked together to take down the Triads and the Guardsmen."

"CONVERGENT GOALS."

"Oh, come on—it's more than that," said Joy. "Agent Funaki knew that you sabotaged the Joanne Spaulding. And I saw you two meet up just after the warehouse exploded. He recognized you immediately and took your... 'suggestions' without questioning them. Surely you can't deny that you've been working collaboratively."

The Red Specter stood in silence for a minute, looking her over before answering. "I GUESS I CAN'T DENY THAT. FOR THIS OPERATION."

"For how many other operations have you worked together?" Joy asked. "You and Agent Funaki seem pretty friendly."

"NO COMMENT."

As the interview went on, Joy discovered that "No Comment" was the Red Specter's favorite phrase, using it to stymy all her questions about the Dodona investigation: what had tipped it off, which faction he'd been going after, why he'd chosen to intervene here, everything. The most she got him to say was that he sought to protect the lives and peace of the citizens of Kallistrate and defeat all who would oppose or undermine that. Attempts to clarify that vague answer led to another series of "No Comments."

Joy decided to switch to broader questions. "When did you decide to become the Red Specter?"

"I DIDN'T."

Joy gritted her teeth, forced herself to try and parse the evasion. "You know, when I bargained for an interview, I expected you'd actually answer questions."

"THERE ARE QUESTIONS I CAN ANSWER AND QUESTIONS I CAN'T."

"Well, which questions can you answer?"

"FIGURING THAT OUT IS YOUR JOB," said the Specter, and Joy couldn't help but notice the smugness in his tone.

"Okay, fine—be that way," she said, rolling her eyes.

Nothing about this job had been easy, why should she expect it to change now? But as she thought about it, she realized that Specter's recalcitrance might be a boon. It was so easy to forget who she was working for. Garai and the Gazette readership didn't actually want to know everything about the Red Specter, after all; they wanted him to remain a mysterious figure. So she had to get enough details to be intriguing, but not enough to make him mundane. Now, how should she go about that?

"As far as I know," she said, "the first reported sightings of the Red Specter are from the Great War. Have you been... dressing up like this from before, during, or after the Great War?"

The Specter didn't answer right away, which gave Joy hope. "DURING THE WAR," he finally answered.

"So you became The Red Specter during the war?"

The Specter turned away from her, gazing off into the middle distance. "YES. YOU COULD SAY THAT."

"Who came up with the name, 'The Red Specter?'"

"NOBODY KNOWS."

Well that sounded mysterious, but it probably just meant some anonymous soldiers caught a glimpse of him and came up with the name, which caught on and became legend.

"Did the Red Specter rumors start before or after you started wearing this costume?"

"DON'T KNOW EXACTLY WHEN THEY STARTED."

Joy narrowed her eyes. Blessed Kovidh, could he be any more pedantic? "When you first put on this costume, had you personally, at that point in time, heard any rumors or tales about the Red Specter?"

"NO."

"Who were you fighting for during the war?" Joy asked. "What was your overall goal?"

She got another long pause for that question, but she'd learned to view that as positive. It meant an answer of some sort.

"TO OVERTHROW AND DESTROY THE HYPOCRISY OF THE ALBION EMPIRE," said the Red Specter, with a fervor that Joy hadn't heard from him before. She made a note of it.

She asked more questions about wartime, but ran into another "No Comment" wall, and she began to wonder if she should just wrap things up. She was on the verge of calling it a day, when one final detail popped into her head.

"Oh! How did you know that Shiori was a fake?"

A sharp tension ran through the Red Specter as he turned to stare at her. He recovered quickly, but not fast enough to fool Joy. What was this? That was the biggest reaction she'd got from him for the entire night. She smelled a story.

"ARMOR WAS ALL WRONG," said the Specter, but it wasn't convincing.

"Well, I'm sure that's true, but was that the only thing that tipped you off? I don't think so."

"SHIORI IS A WANTED WOMAN. HUGE BOUNTY ON HER. HASN'T BEEN CAUGHT. YOU KNOW WHY?"

The Red Specter was asking her questions now? This was a change.

"No, why?" Joy asked.

"BECAUSE THE REAL SHIORI ROSEWING KNOWS HOW TO AVOID CAPTURE. KEEP A LOW PROFILE. USE ALIASES," said the Specter. "SHE DOESN'T RUN AROUND IN BROAD daylight DRAPED IN A stupid-ass Rosedeath flag, ANNOUNCING HER PRESENCE TO THE whole god-damned world, AND shooting HER mouth off LIKE A complete fucking idiot!"

Joy gaped as the Specter's voice wavered drastically for the second time since they'd met. This was definitely a thing—his voice going up an octave when he got upset. It suggested that the normal, booming voice was an affectation, requiring conscious control.

"Have you met Shiori Rosewing? Seen her face to face?" Joy asked. "From the way you're talking, it sounds like you know her."

This earned her another long pause. "WE'VE MET."

"So that's how you knew," said Joy. "What's she like? The real one, I mean."

"TALLER. ABOUT MY HEIGHT. DARKER SKIN. PRET-TIER."

The real Shiori was as tall as the Red Specter? That was pretty tall. Joy tried to picture it in her head.

"So she is pretty? Like the comics version?" Joy blurted out, to her own annoyance. "Haha, sorry. That's a silly question, but you made me think of a fashion model or something."

"DON'T KNOW IF I'D GO THAT FAR," said the Red Specter. "IT'S NOT SO MUCH LOOKS WITH HER. SHE'S NOT IN YOUR LEAGUE. IT'S MORE LIKE... SHE'S GOT THIS ENERGY TO HER, AND—"

"You think I'm pretty?" Joy said, and immediately bit her tongue. Wow, stress and lack of sleep had mentally regressed her to thirteen years old or something. "Whoops, never mind, scratch that, I'm... listen to me babble, haha, asking about the comics, like she'd have red skin and run around in lingerie or something."

"WELL, HER SKIN IS LIGHT BROWN," said the Specter. "AND OF COURSE SHE'D WEAR ARMOR IN BATTLE. BUT OTHERWISE... IF I SAW HER IN THAT OUTFIT, I WOULDN'T BE SURPRISED."

"What?" Joy said, thinking back to her comics marathon. "But... that costume is... I mean, it's a drawing. If you tried to wear it for real you'd be, like... popping out of it, and—"

"LIKE SHE'D CARE," said the Specter. "SHE'S ALWAYS GOING ON ABOUT IT, TOO. 'OH, YOU GUYS ARE soooo uptight. NO ONE ON ONO-IKI cares ABOUT THAT STUFF. IT'S just THE HUMAN BODY.' BUT I SAY SHE JUST uses THAT AS AN excuse, so she can...."

The Red Specter stopped and turned away, started pacing around the room. Something about Shiori Rosewing really got under his skin. She needed a follow-up question, quick.

"Ono-Iki?" said Joy. "That's one of the Kotu Islands, right? But isn't she from Zipang? I mean, with that name—"

"HER GRANDMOTHER WAS ZIPANGESE," said the Specter. "NAMED AFTER HER."

"Wow, I never knew that," Joy scratched away at her notepad, determined to get as much down as she could. "Those are some personal details. What is your relationship with the real Shiori Rosewing? How well do you know her?"

The Red Specter went very still. Joy could practically feel the tension radiating off him.

"HOW WELL DO I KNOW HER?" He spat the words out like they were full of needles. "BETTER THAN MOST PEOPLE, BUT NOT AS WELL AS I ONCE THOUGHT I DID."

"Would you care to elaborate on—"

"NO," said the Specter. "NO, I WOULD NOT."

472

It was like a door slammed shut. Joy could already tell that her follow-up questions on this topic would not be answered, even though she really, really wanted to ask them.

But she didn't want the Specter to end the interview, either, and he was looking agitated enough to do just that. What else could she ask?

"Um... the fake—she said something about her name being stolen." Joy thought back to Not-Shiori's tirade. "Something about... 'poor little injured girl.' Do you know anything about that?"

She got another long pause from the Specter, longer than any of the previous ones, and Joy started to worry that this time he really wasn't going to answer, but then he spoke.

"YOU KNOW HOW THE CALIBURN RECRUITED NEW MEMBERS?"

"Of course," said Joy. "The annual trials at Cistonia stadium. A big race through an obstacle course."

"MORE THAN THAT. ALL-AROUND ATHLETIC COMPETITION. PLUS WRITTEN TESTS AND INTERVIEWS. OBSTACLE COURSE IS THE FINALE. GROUP WITH HIGHEST OVERALL SCORES GO OFF TO CALIBURN TRAINING. USUALLY."

"Usually?" said Joy. "Meaning sometimes they pick kids who didn't finish highest?"

"THE REAL SHIORI... HAD AN ACCIDENT IN THE OBSTACLE COURSE. INJURED HERSELF. FINISHED LOW. CALIBURN SELECTED HER ANYWAY."

"So that means—are you saying the fake Shiori was one of those kids in that same trial group?" Joy said. "And she got bumped out of the finalists by the real one?"

The Specter shrugged. "SEEMS LIKELY."

"Well, that's..."

Joy stopped and thought that over. "You know, it's funny, but that actually makes me feel a little sorry for her. That fake Shiori, I mean."

The Red Specter cocked his head at her, and she could tell he was looking at her stitches and bruises; her bandages and her left hand propped up on a bag of ice.

"I mean, don't get me wrong. She was vicious and horrible and all," said Joy. "I just... I know how that feels—to work so hard, to bust your ass to get something and just... have it all taken away from you, by some stupid, obtuse, close-minded, head-up-his-ass... um...."

Whoops. Now she was the one getting all worked up. She tried to re-organize her thoughts, but the Specter spoke first.

"SHIORI HAD BEEN LEADING IN THE SCORING BE-FORE THE FINAL TRIAL. SHE GOT INJURED... IT WAS FROM HELPING ANOTHER CANDIDATE. CATCHING THEM WHEN THEY FELL. STILL COMPLETED THE COURSE, LIMPING TO THE FINISH WITH A TWIST-ED KNEE. GOOD INSTINCTS FOR A SOLDIER. THAT'S WHY."

"Really?" Joy said. "Well, I guess I can see that. Sounds kind of noble, actually. It's funny, but that story doesn't fit the real Shiori's reputation, either. Doesn't sound like the type of thing a monster would do."

"GOOD AT FOOLING PEOPLE. VERY CHARISMATIC.." Again the Specter's voice took a hard, bitter edge. "IT'S AN ACT. ALL OF IT. SHE'S RUTHLESS. VICIOUS. PLAYS THE LONG GAME. PLAYS TO WIN."

"Could you tell me more about—"

"NO."

"Um, okay, but how do you feel about—"

"NO COMMENT."

Joy felt the door slam down between them again. The Red Specter was done with this topic. As if on cue, Sam entered the room with a steaming cup of tea.

"How's it going?" He said.

"WE JUST FINISHED."

"What?" said Joy. "No, wait—"

474

"WE'RE FINISHED," said the Red Specter, walking to the door. "AFTER YOUR TEA, SHOW SPECIAL AGENT FUNAKI WHERE YOU HID YOUR CRYSTAL."

"But you..." Joy sighed and threw her hands up. She didn't have any idea how to proceed from here, anyway. "Okay, fine. We're done... for now."

"FOR NOW?" The Specter turned back to her.

"For now, I'm out of questions, but I'm sure I'll have more next time."

The mask tilted at her. "WHAT NEXT TIME?"

"The next time I see you, of course. Next mission or whatever." Joy smiled as the two men stared at her.

"What, you don't think you'll get rid of me that easy, do you? I'm a reporter, and whatever you guys are up to is going to be news."

"Ma'am—I mean, Joy," said Sam. "We're not going to be staying in contact—"

"You won't, but I will," said Joy. "Don't you worry about the details. That's my job."

The Specter snorted and shook his head. "GOOD LUCK WITH THAT. SEE YOU LATER... MAYBE."

Was it her imagination, or did that not come out as sarcastic as he'd probably intended? She waved and favored him with her sweetest smile.

"See you later... definitely!"

The door closed behind him and he was gone.

Chapter 51:

Freelance

The tea was the best she'd ever had, warm and soothing with a nice delicate hint of peaches, mixed with honey. Sam gave her a bathrobe and some fuzzy slippers (later on she'd wonder where he'd gotten them) and escorted her to a pedi-cab waiting outside.

He nudged her awake when they reached her apartment. She'd been mortified to discover that she'd nodded off and drooled all over his jacket, or she would've been, but he didn't seem mad at all, and she was finding it very hard to worry about those sorts of things right now. She led Sam right to the potato sack with the hidden jewel, watched while he retrieved it with gloved hands, (he'd insisted, didn't want her touching it at all) and placed it in a metal lockbox with thick padding on the inside.

He'd said his goodbyes and left before she could remember to be ashamed of the squalid, hovel-like conditions of her apartment. Whatever. She staggered over to her mattress and flopped onto it, ready for sleep to take her. Except it didn't. Instead she lay there, her head racing with all the events of the past twenty-four hours. Madame Zenovia. Yang and Chen. Gallach, MacInroy, and Brannock. Brannock was dead now. Blown up. Hsiu Mei and Lin Lin. She could see them, if she went to the Temple. But maybe they were sleeping by now. Or not.

The bright morning sun was leaking in past the window blinds. That wasn't helping, but it wasn't really the problem either. It was the figures in her head. Daphne the Ice-Queen. Benny the Shark, but he'd really only been a man after all. Scary Shiori. No, it was Not-Shiori. Not-Shiori had held a knife to her throat, threatened to torture her, to kill her. And she'd believed it. Joy had really thought she was going to die. That had happened, just a few hours ago. But scary Not-Shiori was dead now. What was her real name, anyway? Who had she really been? Would they ever know?

And then there was the Red Specter. Spooky, faceless, mysterious, heroic—but not a ghost. He was definitely a man. There was a human being inside that costume. She'd seen his eyes and felt his hands on her. He had pretty eyes behind the goggles. He'd said she was pretty. Like a fashion model. Or implied that, anyway. Maybe. She was too short to be a model. She knew that. Ugh, those were all silly thoughts and she should stop thinking them.

But her head wouldn't stop. Too much had happened, and her catnap in the pedi-cab had taken the edge off her exhaustion. Her thoughts kept swarming and churning through her mind. They refused to give her any peace.

She rolled on her side and found herself staring right at her tiny writing-desk with her typewriter and her busted office chair. Her worn-out, beat up cheap office chair, bound up with tape to keep the stuffing from leaking out. It was just like her. They matched each other. It was challenging her. Screw it. There was only one way she was going to free herself from her thoughts.

But first things first—Joy stripped off her swimsuit and got in the shower. It wasn't as relaxing as it could've been. She couldn't allow herself to stand directly under the shower-head, or else she'd soak her bandages. She managed to sort of splash and soap her non-bandaged bits without causing too much of a mess. A nice bath sponge would've worked wonders here, but she didn't have one of those.

She had to do the whole operation on stitched, blistered feet, which didn't allow her to stand normally. She had to balance herself in odd ways to keep at least some of those bandages dry. At least she had no problems shampooing her hair. And boy, did her hair need it. She finished up, replaced the bandages she hadn't managed to protect, threw on her old dark grey Kallistrate army sweats and a ratty pair of black canvas work shoes with flat rubber soles. The shoes held her bandages in place, so she could walk normally again.

Then she sat on her tattered chair, fed a fresh sheet of paper into her typewriter, and let the words pour out of her. She started off simple, with a sentence or two about the rumored sightings of the Red Specter by the docks, followed by her meeting with Madame Zenovia, and just let everything that had happened to her spill out on the page.

Her useless splinted left pinky was a major annoyance at first, but she found that re-training her ring finger for double-duty on the typewriter keys wasn't as hard as she'd feared. And once she got going, it felt amazing. It didn't feel like she was even there at all. She was just a conduit for the story. She took a break when she noticed she was having difficulty seeing the words on the page. Her room had grown dark.

She got up, opened her blinds, and the room was light again. The sun had gone overhead, so it no longer shone directly in through her window. It was noon, or maybe past noon. By how much? Her sense of time was screwy. She took a minute to stretch, felt a series of pops in her spine, shoulders, and hips, felt her stiff, exhausted muscles pull at all her bruises—a lot of which she hadn't noticed until now, and she felt a hollow sensation in her stomach, a void that begged to be filled. She really should have asked Agent Sam if they had any snacks to go with the tea. And what was she going to do for food now? She was flat broke. Well, she could heat up tinned stuff....

No. Screw that. She was sick of that shit. She was not capping off a day like today with some pathetic pauper meal. An idea formed in her head, and she went back to her desk. She typed a bit more, until she'd finished describing the cattle stampede. That seemed like a decent point for a cliffhanger ending. She did a quick review of what she wrote, mainly for clarity. She was seeing a lot more typos than normal, but she could blame her busted pinky for that. Whatever. She picked a few major points to hit with correction ink and her fountain pen, blew on them to dry them out faster, and organized it all into a neat stack, which she tucked under her arm as she headed out the door.

The street was a bright festival of light, color, and noise. Liberation Day was in full swing. People were decked out in red and gold, or wearing their old army uniforms, smiling and laughing. She got plenty of waves and high-fives, just for wearing her military sweats. Though some folks did double-takes when they noticed her injuries. She kept her smiles polite and kept moving until she reached the Gazette offices, grateful that she didn't have to cross the Victory Parade route to get there. She had no doubt that Garai would be working on a holiday. The news never took a break—and neither would he.

As Joy entered the mostly empty office she noticed today's issue, lying around in stacks, as always. The headline caught her eye, and she picked one up to get a better look at it.

"DERANGED COWS STAMPEDE THROUGH
SWANKY DOCKSIDE RESTAURANTS.
Are Malevolent Pixies to Blame?
One Citizen Says Yes!"

Joy laughed all the way to Garai's office, but managed to compose herself before entering.

She didn't bother knocking, so she got a good look at the surprise on Garai's face as he glanced up from his desk.

"Eh? What is..." Garai did a horrified double-take when he recognized her. "Good gracious! Ms. Fan, what happened to you? Are you all right? You look like—"

Joy slammed her stack of paper down on his desk. "I've got your lead story for tomorrow," she said, though a part of her found his reaction unnerving. Did she really look that bad? Whatever. It wasn't important.

"You do? That piece on the Red Specter? You have that—"

"Yep, I got that interview you wanted, and a lot more besides. This is the first installment."

Garai stared at her. "Is this..." he said, gesturing at her injuries, "...somehow related to the—"

"Read it," said Joy, grinning at him. "All will be made clear. I'll be waiting right here."

Garai gaped at her some more, but he did as she asked. She supposed something about her expression, or her wild appearance, made him not want to argue with her. He started out slowly and carefully, but with each successive page, he went faster, and his eyes grew wider with every new detail, till she started to worry they'd pop right out of his head. He reached the last page, dropped it on his desk, and stared at her in amazement.

"It was you?" He said. "You were the crazed pixie who stampeded those cows?"

"No," said Joy. "I am not a pixie, and that stampede was not my fault. It was the Red Specter who actually dropped the—"

"Red Specter?" Garai started flipping back through the papers again. "Where? I didn't catch—"

"Well, I didn't either, not completely," she said. "I caught a half-glimpse of him. I mention it here, see? At the time I wasn't sure who it was—"

"Then how do you know it was him?"

"Because I confirmed it later. In the interview—"

"Interview? What—"

"Next installment." Joy grinned. "I can have that ready tomorrow. Or—hmm... maybe the day after. But my interview with the Red Specter might not be in that installment either. There's a lot to cover in the meantime, what with me sneaking onto the Joanne Spaulding and liberating all those captives—"

"You what? You did what? You are not seriously—"

"Oh, I'm serious," said Joy. "Look at me, Garai. Look at this. This is my serious face."

"But that sounds extremely dangerous," he said. "What if you got had gotten caught? If the Triads caught you—"

"They'd work me over, threaten to kill me, and start breaking my fingers," said Joy, waving her splinted hand around for

480

emphasis. "That'll also be in the second installment. I'm pretty sure that'll fit in the second installment. The rest might need a third section. That's when the Red Specter shows up, rescues me, and I get to interview him."

Joy waited patiently as Garai gaped at her, struggling to regain his powers of speech. Finally, a broad, gleaming white grin split his dark features.

"Ms. Fan, you amaze me. You have finally done it. I always knew you could. Although," he added, holding up a finger. "I did not want you going to such dangerous lengths, and I do not want you risking yourself like this in the future; still I cannot fault your results."

He neatened up the pages of her story, laid the stack on his desk, and gestured to it. "Do you know what this is here?" he asked.

"It's thirty cents a word, is what it is," Joy replied.

"What?" Garai said, clearly having something else in mind. "Thirty cents a... Ms. Fan, that is three times what I normally pay."

"Yeah," said Joy. "I'm aware."

"Well... ah, then you should know, that I can hardly—"

"Oh, you don't want it?" Joy snatched the stack of paper off his desk before he could react. She'd been ready for this. "Well, that's okay, I guess. I'm freelance, after all. If you're not interested, I could always shop this around to the Journal. Maybe they'd like it. Or I could try the Chronicle, see if they'd go to thirty cents—"

"You can't do that!"

"Sure, I can," said Joy. "I can sell this story to any paper. And you know why? Because it's real journalism. All of it. I didn't make any of it up. I didn't write fiction."

Joy was enjoying herself so much she was almost giddy. This was a triumph. It felt so good.

"No, I mean you can't go to other newspapers because they all have you blackballed!"

Joy didn't allow her expression to change. She'd expected him to bring up the fact that he was the one who'd given her the first lead on the story. She hadn't expected that. Well, she'd always suspected a blacklist, but there was something about getting it confirmed that hit her. It was a mix of anger and relief. Mostly relief—her struggles really had nothing to do with her abilities. It never had. But there was something else.

Despite her problems with Garai, she'd always been grateful that he alone had been willing to give her a chance. But there was another way of looking at that, too. You could also say that he'd been exploiting the situation to snare a quality employee, one that he'd never have been able to get otherwise. Or maybe both things were equally true. Who knew?

So that's how the game was played, was it? Well, fine—Garai had a business to run. But she was in business, too—and it was time she acted like it. Time for her to play her own game. Any guilt she had about haggling evaporated. She favored Garai with her sweetest smile.

"Oh, I'm blackballed? How interesting," she said. "Well, you know, I have to wonder just how committed these editors are to their little blacklist. Especially considering their top news story for tomorrow is going to be all about a series of disasters at the docks: a raging fire, a huge bomb detonating, a massive shootout between Benny the Shark's Triads and a secret KIB task-force, and a wreck involving a golem-crane and the Joanne Spaulding, which ended up destroying the crane and beaching the steamship halfway up the docks. Are they really so committed to screwing me over that they'll turn down my eyewitness account of all of that? Gosh, won't it be fun to find out?"

Joy thought Garai did a really great job of keeping his expression neutral at that bit of news. But she saw the effort it took.

"Well, hmm..." he said. "Given the nature of the story, for this particular instance, I think I could make an exception, and raise the rate, for this one time, to as much as twelve cents per word—"

482

"Oh, that's too bad, then," said Joy. "Looks like it'll be the Journal who gets the exclusive bits that only I know about—like how the Red Specter was working with the KIB, and all the special equipment and tactics he uses—do you know he has armor that can stop bullets? Stops teeth, too. I know this because I saw Benny the Shark actually bite him, and what happened next... well, it was something else."

"Fifteen cents, Ms. Fan, so long as you keep that rate a secret," said Garai. "For if all my writers demanded that rate, I would surely go bankrupt—"

"You really can't afford to go to thirty?" Joy replied. "Then I guess you'll miss out on my account of a spear duel, to the death, between the Red Specter and Shiori Rosewing."

"Shiori Rosewing?" Said Garai. "She was here, in town? And she fought the Red Specter? The real Shiori Rosewing?"

"Was it the real Shiori? Or was it an imposter?" Joy said. "An interesting question, and I've got the answer, but I guess you'll be reading about it in the Journal."

"Twenty cents, and that is my final offer!" Said Garai. "And you certainly will not get any higher from the Journal, either. They are not nearly so generous as I, nor do they—"

"Really? They really wouldn't pay thirty?" said Joy. "Well, maybe you're right. Maybe a newspaper isn't the appropriate venue for this story. Maybe this is more of a book—a bit short, but I bet the book publishers don't have any vendettas against me. And I bet there's at least one of them willing to offer a nice advance to get this story."

"Ah, Ms. Fan—let us not be hasty here..."

"Now that I think of it, I'm sure that with a decent amount of research, this could expand to book-length easily," Joy continued. "I could go into the history of the Specter myth and why it resonates with the public—I've already got a contact who can help me with that. Plus biographical research on a bunch of the other major figures, like Benny the Shark. Oh—and I barely even mentioned it, but there's this fringe cult of some weird god called Nibiru, and they'd managed to seize control of the City Guard. I could do more research there, and on top of that—"

"Ms. Fan! You have crossed the line into blatant extortion, and I do not appreciate it one bit," fumed Garai. "But if you are so determined, and though it pains me greatly, I may just be able to slash my budget elsewhere, just barely enough to squeeze out twenty-five—"

"Thirty cents, Garai, or—"

"Ms. Fan!" Garai sputtered. "You may not know this, but there's a certain etiquette to haggling. You are supposed to set your first offer at a much higher level than what you are willing to accept, so you can come down when I make a counter-offer, and then we meet in the middle. You don't start with—"

"NO, GARAI!" Joy said, slamming her fist on his desk. "*You* don't get how this works. Because you know what? You know what I had to go through to get this story?

"Over the past twenty-four hours I have been yelled at, threatened, chased, insulted, had my best business outfit ruined, been assaulted by gangsters, chased some more, had knives thrown at me, been caught in a frickin' cattle stampede, nearly drowned, barely staved off hypothermia, was captured, tied up, punched multiple times in the head and stomach, had my finger dislocated, got terrorized by a shark lunatic, got insulted some more, then caught in a bomb blast, got shot at again, had another lunatic threaten me with disfigurement and actually try to cut my ear off—I've stepped on a nail, and... and... been falsely accused of mass puppy murder, and I am tired and I am starving and I am *getting* THIRTY MOTHERFUCKING CENTS A WORD!"

Joy stood there, glaring at Garai and trying to catch her breath after her tirade, while he leaned back and stared at her. They stayed like that for a while, letting the silence stretch through the empty office.

Finally, Garai spoke. "Very well, Ms. Fan. You will get thirty cents a word on this story, but—"

"On each installment of this story."

"Yes, fine," said Garai, scowling. "But I am not going to be haggling with you over a story again. From now on, you will be on salary."

"Salary? What sal..." Joy paused as the implication hit her. "Wait, you're offering me a job?"

"Certainly. It will be worth it if you can bring in more stories like this."

"Oh. Well... hold on, let me think," Joy said. A salary! That meant stability. Regular income—reliable money coming in every week. She could afford to do research. She could really turn her story into a book. But she'd be an employee of the Gazette. Professionally, she'd be tied to it. And she hated the Gazette. She wanted to work for a real newspaper....

Or did she? The Journal had been a massive disappointment. Suppose she did try to relocate. She could swallow her pride, translate propaganda, spend a few months scrimping and saving, and relocate to a new city with a clean slate and a new reporter job. She'd have to start from the bottom again, and what if there was another Quintus at the new paper? It wasn't improbable. It wasn't like there was a shortage of assholes in the world. And it would only take one to completely undo months of her hard work.

Fuck that. And fuck moving. Why should she move? Dodona was *her* city. The thought startled Joy, but it was true. She lived here and they weren't going to chase her out. But if staying meant working for the Gazette, was that any better?

Was it even a good choice for her? The only Gazette-appropriate story she'd ever turned in was this one, and only because it had been about the Red Specter. But what a story that was! Joy replayed all the events of the last twenty-four hours back in her head. Looking back, it was unbelievable. Most journalists could go their whole lives without getting a scoop like... no, not just one scoop. This had been like, five or six scoops, any one of which could make a career. But could she repeat that?

Well, maybe she could and maybe she couldn't. And if she couldn't, she'd quit or be fired and be no worse off than she was now. But if she could really do it again, if she kept landing stories like this one...

"All right, Garai—but I've got a couple conditions," she said. "I want to be the exclusive reporter covering Red Specter stories. And I want an expense account so I can track him down. Travel costs, mostly. Train tickets and hotels and the like."

"Track him down?" Garai said. "How are you going to—"

"I'll make it happen," she said.

Garai looked her in the eyes, and she didn't flinch. Apparently he saw something he liked, because he favored her with a wide, toothy grin.

"Very well," he said. "I will hold you to that."

A small part of Joy tried to talk herself down, tried to tell her she was making promises she couldn't back up, that she wouldn't be able to do it. She stomped it down, reminding herself that at worst, she'd be in the same spot she'd been at when she'd started this crazy story.

"Hey, if I'm an employee now, does that mean I get worker's comp?"

Garai paused, taking a long look at her bruises and bandages. "Yes," he said, somewhat reluctantly. "For injuries sustained *after* your hire date."

Well, shoot. She couldn't say that was unfair, though.

"Oh—and I keep the book rights to my stories," she added.

Joy saw Garai's face twitch at that, but he recovered quickly. "You know, arranging a book deal is a complicated thing," he said. "Finding the right contacts, editors, and such. And you'll be busy with writing and research. But I do have contacts with publishers, and could easily handle those details for you—in exchange for twenty percent of the royalties."

"Ten percent," Joy countered.

"Fifteen."

"Deal."

486

Joy negotiated her salary in the same way, taking Garai's advice and asking for way more than she wanted, countering to the middle, and ending up with more than she'd expected to get.

"And I want an advance on my story," she said, calculating how much she'd need to get some decent new clothes, plus general expenses for the next few days. And maybe a new desk chair. "Five hundred dollars."

"Eh?" Garai looked a bit startled. "Well, fine. I can write you a check—"

"No, cash. I insist."

"What? I can't do that." Garai noticed her expression and threw up his hands. "That's not some sort of tactic, Ms. Fan. You know I simply don't carry that type of money in the office."

"Well, a check won't do me any good," said Joy. "It's a holiday and the bank's going to be closed."

"You can't wait until tomorrow—"

"No, I can't wait, Garai," she said. "I'm starving, I need money to buy food, and I am completely fucking broke right now."

Garai looked at her like she'd grown another head. Joy wondered what his problem was, then groaned inwardly when she realized it. Admitting to being broke wasn't the best move after playing hardball financial negotiations, when neither of them had actually signed anything.

She watched Garai, waiting for some type of indignant outburst, or a sudden interest in re-negotiating their deal, but instead he tipped his head back and roared with laughter, slapping his desktop.

"Ah, that is amazing," he said. "I knew there was a reason I liked you. Flat broke!" Garai succumbed to another wave of laughter. He managed to fight it down after a minute or two.

"Yes, keep that attitude and you'll go far in this business," he said, wiping tears from his eyes. "Well, I do have a hundred in cash I can give you. Will that suffice? Or did you intend to stuff five hundred dollars' worth of food in that tiny stomach of yours?"

Joy breathed a sigh of relief and grinned back. "I was going to give it my best shot. But I'll go with a hundred for today."

He counted out her cash, wrote up a check, and reminded her to come in tomorrow with her next installment, and he'd have her employment contract ready. She thanked him and headed to the door, trying not to let her knees wobble. Her hand was on the doorway when he called out to her again. "Ms. Fan!"

Something about the way he said it touched her. It was an ordinary enough thing, just calling her name, but there was a new quality to it—something in the intonation, that marked a new stage in their relationship. She wasn't some screw-up trainee, she was an equal, someone who could stand up for herself, a partner in the business of reporting the news. It was a new feeling, and it was kind of awesome.

"Yes, Garai," she said, turning back to him. "Something else you need?"

"Ah, no," he said. "It's just that you have a large piece of packing tape stuck to your rear end."

"Thank you," said Joy, with as much dignity as she could muster, while removing the offending tape, which also had chunks of cotton stuffing stuck to it as well. She'd been walking around with a lamb's tail. Maybe she'd replace her desk chair before her clothes. That damned thing needed to be put out of its misery.

"See you tomorrow," she said, and fled the offices of the Dodona Gazette.

Chapter 52:

Victory Lap

Joy stepped back out into the street, and took a long, deep breath. She'd done it. She had money in her hand and more would be coming in the future, guaranteed. She had more to do—more story to write, but it wasn't urgent. Today she was free. The sun warmed her face and hair, and the breeze funneled its way through the bright city streets, carrying all her worries away with it. She felt so light without them.

Well, that wasn't the only reason she felt light. Her stomach was an empty void, and that needed fixing. But she could do that now. She stuffed the wad of cash she'd gotten from Garai into the front pouch on her sweatshirt. Her purse was still stashed beneath the boardwalk, down by the harbor, assuming nobody had swiped it. She could look for it later. She kept both her hands in her sweatshirt, protecting her little stash, as she strolled to her destination, with her copy of today's Gazette rolled up and tucked under her arm. Sure, her money wasn't likely to fall out of her pocket or anything, but why take the risk?

She smelled the Golden Banquet before she saw it, sweet and savory and warm. The golden koi sculptures flanking the entrance greeted her like old friends. The hostess wasn't nearly so warm. She took in the wreckage of Joy's general appearance, her bruises, her bandages, her sweats and tatty work shoes, and adopted one of those careful, cool customer-service expressions of "We're so very sorry to be unable to assist you today, ma'am."

Joy didn't let things get that far. "Hello, there," she said brightly. "I'd like a table for one, please—anywhere is fine. Oh, and I'm sorry about... all this," she said, making a gesture to encompass her entire appearance. "But the other day I was having an early dinner at this delightful little cafe out by the harbor, and, well... I know this is going to sound crazy, but I got caught in a cattle stampede. And I just got out of the hospital and I could really really really use some comfort food right now. That's okay with you, right? Please tell me that's okay."

Joy got a table in the far back corner, which was fine by her. They weren't that crowded anyway, since she'd managed to hit the late-afternoon lull between lunch and dinner, holiday traffic notwithstanding. The restaurant's red-and-gold decor matched really well with the Liberation Day decorations too. Naturally patriotic. But the important thing was being able to hail down all the wandering food carts, and she'd managed to surround herself with a series of steaming baskets in no time flat.

She started off with the barbecue pork buns, her favorite, and had to remind herself to be careful not to burn her tongue, to break them open first, blow on them to cool them, and just take little nibbles while they were so hot. She ended up burning her tongue a little anyway. It was so hard to wait when they were so good. But aside from that she could mix things up — get the steamed pork meatballs wrapped in noodles, and the steamed shrimp dumplings, too. Plus she had remembered to get the savory string beans, because you needed veggies in there, too. Oh, and they had that pressed turnip cake with the bacon bits — turnips were vegetables, right? And then there was —

Joy found she had to slow down. She had a sudden tight feeling in her chest. Her poor shrunken stomach was reeling under the onslaught of all this delicious food. It felt like it was piling up to where it was reaching the bottom of her throat. She didn't stop eating, though, just took her time chewing, giving her insides a chance to shift things around and process them through. She thumped on her own chest in what she hoped was an encouraging manner and directed positive thoughts that way. *Don't worry, little guy. You can do it. I believe in you.*

And her insides did indeed rise to the challenge, which was a good thing, because one of the sweets trays caught her eye, and they had the phoenix egg buns with the sugary egg custard inside, which she hadn't had for ages, plus those red bean jelly cakes floating on a layer of condensed coconut milk, along with a few more custard buns. And then there was another cart with more pork dumplings, only these were wrapped up in balls: gooey, sugary rice dough rolled in sesame seeds. She couldn't let those go by. And they also had the marinated shredded jellyfish salad—though really it wasn't so much the jellyfish she was after, as the pickled carrots that came with it. Those were to die for, though of course she ate the jellyfish too. And then there was....

Joy kept on like that until she was well and truly stuffed—her belly straining against the waistband of her sweats—fat and happy. She'd not quite managed to blow her entire cash advance on this one meal, but she'd made a decent run at it. She paid up, thanked the staff on her way out, and shuffled out to the street again. One of them stopped her for a second to hand her the copy of the Gazette, which she'd nearly forgotten. Why did she have this again? It was getting harder to think. The huge meal had turned her sluggish and lazy. She hailed a pedi-cab to take her back to her apartment. Pay for a cab? Instead of walking? How deliciously decadent!

When she reached her apartment, she had just enough energy to close the blinds and peel off her sweats before collapsing on her mattress. She was about to drift off when she noticed the Gazette lying on the floor, and remembered something.

The Gazette had a comics page. They had the Red Specter comic, the one that had left her on a cliffhanger yesterday. She fumbled out with one lazy arm and managed to snag it.

A box of text brought her back up to speed. "Poisoned by the notorious witch Shiori Rosewing, poor innocent Lilla is being transformed... into a GAS MAN! Is there nothing our heroes can do to stop it?"

Lilla lay on her back, with Kolton cradling her head and shoulders.

"She's starting to dissolve," he cried. "She's turning into GAS! We have to stop it. We need to do SOMETHING!"

"My boy..." said Professor Zhang, "It's too late... all my learning... all my science... It's worthless now."

Feebly, Lilla reached out to the Red Specter, streams of vapor trailing off the blurred edges of her arm.

"Please..." She whispered.

There was a single panel of the Specter's expressionless mask. Then, in the next panel, he spoke.

"STEP BACK AND TURN AWAY. ALL OF YOU. NOW."

"WHAT?" said Kolton, enraged. "Are you telling us to give up? After all she's—"

"No, my boy," said Professor Zhang. "Do as he says, right now. HURRY!"

The next panel showed all the men facing away from the Specter as he knelt over Lilla. He began to unzip a section of his mask; the cone that covered his nose and mouth. Had there been a zipper like that on the real one? Joy thought back as best she could. That... could be accurate. Interesting.

The Red Specter leaned further over Lilla, but it was shown from an angle where she couldn't see what was going on. Was he giving her mouth-to-mouth? All she saw was his back.

Whatever he'd done, it worked, because Lilla sat bolt upright and gasped, all traces of the gas-infection gone. All the men rushed over to check on her.

"Lilla" said Kolton. "You're okay!"

"Oh, thank the heavens," said Professor Zhang. "I'd shame my ancestors if I let anything happen to you."

"That's some convenient magic there, Specter," said Baz. "But just what the heck did you do to..."

He trailed off as he looked about to realize the Red Specter had disappeared, and chuckled as he did. "Well, isn't that typical?"

"SPECTER! Come back," cried Lilla. "You saved me! You saved us ALL! You need to let us thank you!"

From somewhere off-panel, somewhere in the darkness, came the Specter's spooky voice. "NO NEED FOR THAT. THIS IS MY PURPOSE. WHENEVER TYRANNY REIGNS,

WHEREVER EVIL STRIKES—LOOK TO THE SHADOWS, AND I'LL BE THERE. FOR NO INJUSTICE ESCAPES THE WRATH... OF THE RED SPECTER."

And that was the end of the comic, of this adventure. But of course there'd be a new one tomorrow.

Joy smiled to herself as she let the paper fall back to the floor. What a cheesy line. What a cheesy comic. The real thing was way more interesting. And she was going to prove it. Joy savored that thought as she let her eyelids fall. That would be an adventure for another day. And she was looking forward to it.